THE WEIGHT OF IT ALL

ALSO BY DAVID SLOCUM

GENESIS DAY: AN APOCALYPSE ROAD TRIP

THE WEIGHT OF IT ALL

a novel

DAVID
SLOCUM

PROTOTYPE PRESS

for the ones who made it out,
and especially for the ones who didn't

TABLE OF CONTENTS

SEVEN

EIGHT

NINE

EPILOGUE

THE WEIGHT OF IT ALL

PROLOGUE

TO BE GABRIEL MOORE

GABRIEL MOORE WAS a nearly perfect Christian.

His family attended church every week, and he'd been baptized twice. Once as a baby and again of his own volition at six years old. By the time he was ten, he'd memorized dozens of verses about sin and salvation and the nature of God, and he was the only one in Sunday school who could recite Psalm 91 without prompting from Mrs. Hollis. She beamed when he completed the passage. His classmates glared.

Each week, he learned about the dangers of the world.

Tattoos led to drugs and Satanism. Secular music and movies turned hearts against Jesus. Impure thoughts were like spitting in the face of God. And when worldly values didn't *seem* so bad, you needed to be especially wary of deception.

When he was thirteen, Gabriel began attending adult services. He did his best to pay attention, but most sermons were dry and dull, and he couldn't keep his mind from wandering. By eighteen, he had mastered the skill of staring intently at Pastor Evans while his eyes glazed over and he planned out the rest of his Sunday.

And then Pastor Evans took the stage one blazing August morning. He adjusted his notes, bald head reflecting the spotlights like a beacon. His oversized brown suit fought to contain his protruding stomach, and his neck fat spilled over his shirt collar. Gabriel wondered if Mrs. Evans found him attractive or if she was only with him for the status of being a pastor's wife—not that she had any real power. Women weren't allowed to preach at Redemption Fellowship.

"This won't be an easy message, but it's time for a gut check," Pastor Evans said, gripping the podium with both hands. The auditorium quieted under his piercing gaze. "We've been so focused on getting people to like us that we've lost sight of the truth. We don't recognize sin anymore. It's *appalling*."

Gabriel tensed. He knew this message. He'd heard it once or twice a year since he left Sunday school. Gabriel closed his eyes, bracing for what came next.

"We're letting these...*homosexuals* prance around and invade our schools and government, and we're *praising them!* With men dressing up like women, no wonder our kids are confused." Pastor Evans shook his head, neck quivering with holy anger. "It's time we stand up for the truth. *Can I get an amen!*"

The church exploded with vigorous clapping. Gabriel's dad nodded to himself, and his mom waved her Bible in the air. Gabriel focused on his hands, a bit nauseous. Adrenaline weakened his body, and it was like a knife had pierced his chest. Lightheaded, breath coming short, it was all he could do to keep himself from collapsing in the pew.

Pastor Evans quieted the room with an upraised hand. "If we stick to the truth, the *unquestionable* word of God, we will help heal this deceived and broken world."

Cheers and whistles drew attention to eager faces and ferrel eyes. There was blood in the water now. They could taste it, and they were ravenous for more.

The message continued, but Gabriel only heard muffled sounds as his mind left his body and floated through the sanctuary. Through the parking lot. Over the hills and neighborhoods and past downtown Boston, finally settling at Massachusetts Bay on a fishing trawler called *Queen's Dream*.

And there, on the gentle water, the world was quiet.

You see, Gabriel Moore was a *nearly* perfect Christian.

He did all the things that were expected of him. He memorized verses, sang passionately, and always felt guilty when the sermon demanded it. He went on mission trips and family retreats. He attended youth group and church camp. And he was determined to read the entire Bible one day, but he could never make it through *Leviticus* and *Numbers*.

He did it all.

Sometimes, everything is not enough.

Gabriel has never said this aloud:

No matter what he did for the Kingdom or how much he learned about God, he's never felt all that close to his creator. He's never heard a booming voice from heaven, not even a whisper. He's never experienced spontaneous laughter or speaking in tongues like the elders of his church. And despite all his mission trips and the stories from guest speakers, he's never witnessed someone be raised from the dead or get out of a wheelchair.

It didn't make sense. He did everything right, and it was like God had forgotten him. All he felt during worship was an ache in his soul. All he knew during the sermon was a hollowness that never seemed to fill.

He understood the problem wasn't his church or the people in it.

On the outskirts of Boston, most everyone was Catholic or atheist, making Redemption Fellowship one of the few Spirit-led gatherings in the city. It was a chosen group of believers. No truth was quite so powerful as theirs.

"This country needs revival, and it starts with us," his mom once said when her friends gathered in the Moore's living room. "We're nearing the End Times. We need revival to show God we're ready to be with Him."

At statements like this, the other moms would nod and moan and beg for God to cleanse the world.

Gabriel hated these meetings. Thinking about the end of all things made him queasy. He refused to open texts like *Daniel* and *Revelation*, and he simply didn't know why everyone was so excited to be dead.

But these people seemed to hear from God when he couldn't. This left the most likely scenario: *He* was the problem. And if he were brutally honest with himself, he could tell you exactly why.

But Gabriel can't be honest.

Not with his friends or parents. Not with his pastor. Not even with himself.

Because—sometimes—it's easier to lock things away than face a reality you can't escape. Sometimes, it's easier to pretend the problem doesn't exist than acknowledge all the ways you will never be enough.

No one chooses where they are born, or when, or why, or to *whom*.

In this way, Gabriel didn't choose to be a Christian. He didn't choose Christian parents or friends or where he went to church. From the moment he entered this world, his fate was set. So, when he prayed the 'sinner's prayer' and agreed to be baptized, it wasn't his choice so much as the inevitable outcome for his current situation.

And even if there was doubt, he *had* to believe. He had to try, at least.

If he didn't, he was destined for hell, and hell was a place of eternal torment. It was a place of fire and sulfur, of the flaying of skin and the gouging of eyes. It was a place where minds and souls were torn apart over and over until the end of time. And so, his devotion to God was also an act of self-preservation.

In the same way he didn't choose the faith or family he was born into, Gabriel had no control over the people he was drawn to.

For years, he didn't notice how his attention focused on certain men, or why his gaze sometimes lingered on lips and eyes and open shirts. It didn't happen often—him noticing someone. Hundreds of men could pass him on the street without so much as a pang in his heart. And then he'd see a picture of Hugh Jackman, and everything would ache for no reason at all.

Maybe he *was* truly oblivious.

Or, maybe, deep inside, he had a vague idea of the truth. Maybe that's why he shut it down so completely, even before he could possibly understand what any of it meant.

Maybe all he knew was this:

Those feelings meant death.

Hell.

Endless torture at the hands of an angry God.

THESE ARE THE threads that make up a life.

And *this* is what it means to be Gabriel Moore.

ONE

HOW TO SHAPE A HEART

As the youngest of five kids in a four-bedroom house, Gabriel was twelve when he got his own room. Currently, it was stripped bare, save for a queen bed, a wooden dresser, and two empty bookshelves. Gabriel stood in the center of the floor, clutching a tattered paperback with both hands.

Just this morning, the room and book had been Isaac's. Now, Gabriel's brother was off to New York to work on set as an assistant editor for a nature documentary. He was only twenty-two.

For that matter, all his siblings seemed to have their lives on track. Heidi was twenty, but she was already engaged. Rachel was eighteen and was about to start college. Jacob was entering his last year of high school, but he already knew he wanted to be a pastor.

Gabriel couldn't help but wonder when he would discover his purpose.

He sat on the edge of his new bed, turning over Isaac's farewell gift with reverent hands and a weighed-down heart.

The Perks of Being a Wallflower.

This version had a light yellow cover that was almost green and a two-inch picture of a boy in slacks and dress shoes, shown only from the knees down. The bottom right corner had been folded over so many times Isaac had strengthened it with Scotch tape. The pages themselves were yellowing, and the book had the distinct, inspiring musk of an abandoned attic in the heat of summer.

When Gabriel was seven or eight, he browsed Isaac's floor-to-ceiling bookshelf as his brother sat cross-legged on his bed, computer in his lap. Each shelf was crammed to the last inch. Books stood vertically and on their sides and leaned in front of others. It was like the forgotten stacks in a vintage bookstore: Much too full, but brimming with promise.

His fingers traced the uneven spines, pausing here and there. He pulled *The Perks of Being a Wallflower* from a stack near the floor. The pages *whirred* as he flipped to the back, taking in the scent of aging paper—

"Don't tell mom and dad if you read that," Isaac said.

Gabriel's attention broke away from the mysteries inside. He closed the book. "Why?"

"It's…controversial," Isaac said.

Gabriel examined it again, knowing it held ideas he longed to discover. Sometimes you knew that about a book, or a person. It was a quiet *this might change your life* kind of feeling that couldn't be ignored.

Gabriel nodded once and returned the book to the shelf.

He understood.

Isaac often read books their parents condemned. Gabriel only knew some titles and virtually nothing about their content beyond the agenda to push worldly values. Gabriel was happy enough to avoid those stories, but his curiosity never faded. He wanted to find out if they were as dangerous as everyone made them out to be.

Isaac knew, though, and he explained why he crammed his

shelves so full. "With so many books, you start to lose track of what's there. Mom and Dad won't recognize a book like this because they have no reason to look for it when it's in the open." He paused, heaviness building behind his eyes. "But sometimes you do have to hide things."

"Like what?"

Isaac shrugged. "Harry Potter."

Gabriel's eyebrows shot up. *That* one he knew. His parents said it was a celebration of witchcraft and death, and Sunday school taught that reading Harry Potter made you vulnerable to demonic possession.

Cold and empty fear squirmed to life in Gabriel's being.

"Where do you keep the books?" Gabriel asked.

Isaac looked him over, grimacing. He opened his mouth. Closed it. Shook his head.

Gabriel dropped his eyes, knowing what Isaac meant without being told. Trust only goes so far, and secrets only stay hidden if you never let them out.

Yet, sometimes, even silence isn't enough.

A FEW MONTHS later, Jacob discovered a box under Isaac's bed.

"I was looking for my Airsoft gun," Jacob explained as he dragged Gabriel into the room. "And then I found this."

Gabriel warily eyed the cardboard box. It was roughly six inches tall, two feet wide, and three feet long. Isaac could have hidden anything in there.

Quite sure he *didn't* want to know what was inside, Gabriel glanced at Jacob. His brother bounced on his toes in anticipation. He was slightly pudgy around the middle and had full, pink cheeks. Gabriel sat down and peeled it open. The top layer was old T-shirts.

Gabriel pushed these aside, revealing the cover of a thick paperback book.

Harry Potter and the Goblet of Fire.

Gabriel's stomach lurched.

"There's more," Jacob said.

Gabriel kept digging until the entire series was scattered on the carpet.

This was bad. This was really, *really* bad.

"Did you know about this?" Jacob asked.

Technically, he hadn't *seen* the hiding place. Gabriel shook his head.

"We have to tell Mom and Dad," Jacob said.

"We'll just put it back," Gabriel said, returning the books to the box.

Jacob grabbed Gabriel's arm and yanked him away. "They have to know."

Gabriel wrenched out of Jacob's grasp and pushed him. Jacob stumbled. He shoved Gabriel in return, and Gabriel smacked the floor with a grunt and a *whoosh* of air leaving his lungs.

"I have to tell them," Jacob said.

Gabriel didn't respond. He didn't cry. He just rolled over to his stomach, struggling to breathe. He wouldn't win this argument or the fight. Anger boiled in his veins, but he didn't let it escape. He just picked himself up and left the room without a word.

JACOB TOLD THEIR parents that afternoon.

That night, yelling shook the foundations of the house.

Gabriel's siblings huddled in Heidi and Rachel's room to read the Bible and pray. Still burning inside, Gabriel sat at the top of the stairs to listen to the intercession below.

When the shouting died down, a significant hush fell over the house. Gabriel crept to the bottom step and peered around the corner to the front room. He saw three silhouettes illuminated by the wood-burning stove. Gabriel's dad knelt on the left, fervently praying for God to cleanse Isaac of his sins. Their mom rocked back and forth on the right, only speaking in tongues. Isaac remained between them, silent and trembling as he tossed the offending books into the fire.

Isaac wasn't quite the same after that night.

Gabriel noticed it in the way Isaac avoided the rest of the family and said very little when they were together. When he did talk, it was often in reaction to something their parents said over dinner.

Whatever the cause—the collapse of marriage or big companies embracing abortion—it followed the same pattern:

A defensive comment from Isaac and a sharp response from Jacob or Heidi. Another back and forth, raised voices this time. Then the yelling would start, and no one would listen to anyone but themselves.

Gabriel always dropped his head and pretended to be invisible. He never spoke up, and no one asked for his opinion. He didn't know what he would have said if he were dragged into the conversation.

But he *did* know Isaac was falling away from the faith, and there was nothing they could do to make him see the truth. During every fight, Gabriel couldn't stop thinking about the scriptures that predicted Christians abandoning God.

Pastor Evans promised that in the earth's final days, families would turn on each other like they did in the Civil War. Parents and kids alike would be deceived by the Devil and led into eternal destruction.

Gabriel just didn't think it would happen to his family. He never imagined it would be Isaac who fell. But the end of the world *was* coming. Probably in his lifetime, according to his mom. That terror kept him awake at night, and it never really went away. It just hovered, building like an ink-black cloud on the horizon of his mind.

ISAAC BECAME A ghost when he left for college. He only came home for a few days during Thanksgiving and Christmas, and spent the rest of his time off visiting friends across the country. During the summers, he always had an out-of-state internship.

The morning he left for New York, he told Gabriel to keep in touch.

"This is for you," Isaac said, handing over *The Perks of Being a Wallflower.* "Don't let them burn it."

Gabriel swallowed the lump in his throat. "I won't."

Then Isaac was gone, and Gabriel couldn't help but wonder if his brother would ever return.

Sitting on the bed, Gabriel traced his index finger over the cracked spine of the book. There were answers inside. He could feel it.

He just didn't know if he was ready.

THE FAMILY UNIT

GABRIEL'S DAD WAS the definition of practical. Six feet tall and cut from stone, he started his career as a software engineer and became the CEO of a small firm within a decade. He expected the same excellence from each of his kids. Business was the preferred path, but Isaac proved the arts could be successful, too. Only, this route was seductive and corrupting. Isaac proved that as well.

"Strong foundations build strong men," Gabriel's dad repeated ad nauseam. "Rock holds, sand crumbles."

Although his work kept him away for long hours, he always had time on weekends to mentor young minds in the ways of God and business. He set up shop in the garage and tinkered with his newest motorcycle while teenagers from church dropped by to pepper him with questions.

Gabriel wasn't particularly impressed by business talk or motorcycles, so he found other ways to pass his time. Besides, the motorcycles never lasted, so there was no point in getting attached. Every six or seven months, Gabriel's dad sold his current ride for something faster, sleeker, *better*.

The church kids loved it.

"Your dad's a badass," Josiah Miller told Gabriel one day.

Gabriel just nodded. Everyone said that.

If only they saw the way his mom paled every time her husband showed up with a new bike that she hadn't agreed to. Or heard her voice breaking as she yelled about trust and money. Or witnessed his dad's explosions over how he deserved something nice after all he'd sacrificed for the family.

Gabriel learned early on how to curl up in his room and read through the noise.

At dinner—after fights like that—Gabriel's mom would refuse to look at her husband until he crumbled and apologized. Then she would start crying, and his dad would promise to return the motorcycle the next day.

Sometimes he did.

WHILE GABRIEL'S DAD was all about work, his mom liked to play, and that's how she homeschooled her kids.

To her, bookwork was necessary, but the real point of education was to teach someone how to think and enjoy the process of life. She didn't mind if Gabriel spent the whole day reading or playing math games with his siblings instead of working from his textbook. And every chance they got, they went on field trips to creation museums, zoos, and observatories—anything to get them out of their living room classroom.

It wasn't all that challenging, but Gabriel was *free*.

THE SAME SUMMER Isaac left, Heidi married Thomas Keller. She was twenty. He was twenty-six.

Some people said it was too fast, or that Thomas was too old for her, but to Gabriel's parents and their friends in the church, it couldn't happen soon enough. Heidi was happy and in love, and that's what mattered. Besides, in ancient times, women were as young as thirteen when they married.

Pastor Evans performed the ceremony, and Gabriel's parents cried as they watched their daughter start her new life. They smiled especially wide when Pastor Evans shared that Thomas and Heidi's first kiss as husband and wife would be their first kiss ever.

"How incredible is that?" Pastor Evans asked the crowd before focusing on the couple at the altar. "Your commitment to purity is inspiring. I hope to see the young people here follow your example."

Gabriel's ears grew hot as dozens of eyes found the back of his head. He stared straight ahead and tried not to fidget. During the reception, the men kept mentioning *tonight* and *the honeymoon*, and then they would wink and laugh, and Gabriel would laugh, too, because he didn't want to be left out. He just didn't know why it was funny.

Less than a year later, Heidi had her first kid.

While some outsiders talked about her age, others worried she would never have a career or go to college.

The world didn't understand. It never would.

Heidi had no intention of getting a degree. All she wanted was to have a family like her mom. And the family unit was clearly defined. The husband made the decisions and provided a comfortable life. The wife raised Godly children and kept the house in order. The kids obeyed their parents and made them proud.

It was simple, and that's what made it beautiful.

Of course, there were always exceptions.

Rachel studied accounting and economics in college and secured a job at Charles Schwab upon graduation. She and her boyfriend moved in together in the following months, and he was still working as a bartender in Boston.

This arrangement was almost too progressive for Gabriel's parents, but they took it all with a smile.

"As long as you're happy, we are too," they always told her.

She was the one who seemed to get away with things, but Gabriel didn't mind. Out of all of his siblings, she was the easiest to be around. She was smart and kind, and when Gabriel needed a moment of quiet, her door was always open.

AND THEN THERE was Jacob.

Five years apart, he and Gabriel spent the most time together growing up—shooting each other with Airsoft guns, building forts, *fighting*. Because of their age gap, one of Jacob's favorite jokes was that Gabriel had been a 'happy accident.'

Gabriel laughed nearly as hard as Jacob, but he still didn't know what this meant. So far, all he knew about babies was that kissing had something to do with it. The confusing part was that his parents still kissed on occasion, but they'd never had another kid. Maybe it was a specific *type* of kiss. That had to be it.

Regardless of how it happened, Gabriel wasn't going to take any chances. He vowed never to kiss a girl until his wedding day, just like Thomas and Heidi had done. The last thing he wanted was an accident to take care of before he was ready.

When Heidi announced her second pregnancy, Gabriel remarked to Jacob over breakfast, "They should stop kissing so much, or they'll have a third next year."

Jacob raised his eyebrows, staring at Gabriel, then burst into the kind of laughter that shook his entire body.

Gabriel tried to play it off with a shrug. "Just a joke."

Jacob laughed harder. "You're an idiot."

"It was a joke!"

"That's not how it works."

"I *know*."

"Alright," Jacob said, and Gabriel knew he'd fallen into a trap. "How does it work?"

"How does what work?"

"Sex."

"Sex?" Gabriel swallowed. He'd only heard that word a few times. It felt wrong thinking it, and worse saying it aloud. He gave another shrug and stirred his cereal. "I don't feel like explaining it."

Jacob rolled his eyes. "Let me summarize," he said, adopting his teaching voice. "Alright, so…every guy has a…*thing*, right?"

Gabriel looked at him blankly. "A thing?"

"A penis."

Right. Gabriel blushed. He'd forgotten what it was called. His mom had never covered this subject in school. And even though there were a few educational books throughout the house, Gabriel always felt sick to his stomach when he opened them.

"And sex is when the guy puts his thing into the girl's…*place*, and then there's a moment where you," Jacob waved his hands in the air, "*arrive*, let's say—where you feel really good. And then you'll have a kid in nine months."

Gabriel nodded, cheeks burning. Even Jacob's face was pink. For a minute, they scraped their spoons on the bottom of their cereal bowls.

Gabriel didn't think he could do those things to his wife. He didn't know how *anyone* did that. But maybe everyone else was ashamed, too, and that's why no one talked about it.

Jacob abruptly stood up, dumped his bowl in the sink, and said,

"If you have any questions, ask Mom and Dad."

Gabriel *did* have questions. Dozens of them. But the thought of asking his parents mortified him. He knew that sex was sacred and should not be casually discussed. Anyone who did was courting sin.

No, he'd have to figure it out himself. He just hoped he knew what he was doing by the time he found a wife.

A SECOND HOME

GABRIEL'S PARENTS KNEW virtually everyone in their church, but they were only close to a handful of other families. They met the Millers and their three kids—now ten—before Gabriel was born, so it was primarily obligation that kept them in the same circles. The O'Mara's owned a farm far outside the city where they hosted 'summer camps' every year. It was just manual labor for the boys and household chores for the girls. For years, Gabriel begged his parents not to send him anymore. They finally listened when he turned twelve.

Every Friday, Gabriel's family attended the Miller's worship night, where spirit-led, spontaneous praise went long into the night. Everyone would sway and sing and pour over their Bibles. There were visions and times of prophecy. Each meeting, tears flowed and destinies changed.

Sometimes, claustrophobia forced the air from Gabriel's lungs, and he had to pace the kitchen slowly. In those moments, it felt like something was trying to claw its way out of the depths of his being. When the pacing failed to bring calm, Gabriel would leave the room and lay on the ground, eyes shut, until the feeling passed.

No one thought this was odd. They just said he was soaking in the Spirit.

Gabriel never corrected them. It was a better excuse than he would have come up with, anyway.

INDIVIDUALLY, GABRIEL'S DAD met for Bible study at Mr. Rhode's house every Wednesday, and his mom had frequent lunches with Mrs. Evanston and Mrs. Robbins. They spent their time lamenting the crumbling nation and sharing sorrows over prodigal children.

It made Gabriel sad when they talked about Isaac with such regret. He tried not to listen.

By association, Gabriel had to be friends with all their kids. Most were alright. Some were hard to trust in public settings.

Josiah Miller wore an eyepatch to help his lazy eye and almost always talked in a pirate accent. He brought wooden swords to church every week to stage fights with kids many years younger. They adored him. Gabriel kept his distance.

Daniel Robbins quoted Gandalf like he was Jesus, continually shouting, "YOU SHALL NOT PASS," on the playground.

Peter Evanston ate worms for a dollar each. Gabriel once paid him $10 to see what would happen. Peter threw up after seven, but Gabriel let him keep the extra money.

"You earned it," Gabriel said, smothering a grin.

ONLY AROUND THE Alis did Gabriel feel most like himself.

He met them when he was six, and they'd crossed paths in the potluck line after church. The parents talked for the next two hours while Gabriel and Jacob dominated the playground with the two Ali children.

The Moores and Alis became nearly inseparable in the following years. They sat together in church, had regular barbecues, and vacationed in Cape Cod one summer. Fifteen months after meeting, the Alis moved three houses down and across the street so they didn't have to commute so much for the kids to spend time together.

Adrian was two years older than Gabriel but three grades ahead. He was lanky, fair-skinned, and found it particularly satisfying to be the one in charge. He almost always chose the games and what characters each person would play. Gabriel hardly minded. He just liked being around Adrian because he was bold and *older.*

Chloe had a sharp tongue and an innocent expression. Her nose wrinkled when adults annoyed her, and she would huff slightly and twirl one of her brown French braids. When Adrian wasn't around, Gabriel and Chloe spent the summers chasing grasshoppers in the backyard and cataloging their sizes in a spiral notebook. Sometimes they would throw rocks at squirrels, and—once or twice—at each other. This stopped when Chloe went to the ER with a half-inch gash on her forehead and blood streaming down the right side of her face.

Gabriel felt so guilty he refused to talk to the Alis until his parents forced him to make a formal apology when he saw them at church the next week. Chloe seemed to accept this, and they went off to Sunday school. Twenty minutes later, Gabriel had a chunk of hair missing from the back of his head. Chloe didn't even try to hide the scissors in her hand.

"I guess we're even," she said with a smirk.

Of all the moms Gabriel had met, Mrs. Ali was the most imposing. She had straight blonde hair parted down the middle, high cheekbones with quite a bit of makeup, and she was a few inches taller than Mr. Ali. She often wore high heels, and the other moms at the church flocked around her, just happy to be in her presence. She eventually started a small group, and within two months, she was leading married women and teenage girls and was even working on a book about Biblical marriage.

Mr. Ali wasn't a particularly large man, but he was solidly built with broad shoulders and muscular arms. He had curly black hair, perpetual stubble, and light brown skin. Generally quiet, he came alive when talking about his work, questions about whiskey, or any news about the Boston Bruins.

Years ago, he'd purchased a deep-sea fishing trawler and named it *Queen's Dream*. He was gone every year from May to November as his crew scoured the Massachusetts Bay. Every return, he came back with new stories of the breathtaking ocean and massive hauls of fish.

Each spring, he planned a weekend trip for the men who wanted to get away from home. The first time Gabriel's dad let him go was when he was thirteen.

Gabriel loved every moment.

He listened intently as Mr. Ali explained the process of casting the nets and how they trailed on the ocean floor, catching thousands of tons of cod, then how to reel them in and use a crane to dump the catch into the processing vats.

They never used heavy equipment on these trips, but Gabriel still learned to gut fish, cook in the galley, and use the emergency comms. And in the twilight hours, everyone would stand on the deck, bundled under sweatshirts and raincoats, drinking hot chocolate, coffee, and whiskey for the dads. The men would talk about running a business and advise the kids about love and relationships.

In those moments, life was exactly how it needed to be.

On the last night of his first trip, Gabriel, Adrian, and their dads watched the sunset from the forward deck. Adrian brought up the subject of a girl from his youth group, Savanah. Soon enough, the conversation turned to Gabriel and whether any girls had caught his attention.

He shirked the question, embarrassed by the prospect of dating. "I don't like anyone right now."

"Well," Mr. Ali said playfully, "I know Chloe's been talking about you recently."

Gabriel paused, hot chocolate halfway to his lips. "Really?"

"God, it's so annoying," Adrian said.

Gabriel fought a smile. She'd noticed *him?* What did that mean? Did they have to date now?

"We're just friends, I think," Gabriel said.

Mr. Ali gave a shrug that said *maybe, maybe not.* "Of all the young men she knows, I wouldn't be opposed if you two went out."

Gabriel had trouble processing the significance of that blessing. He was *in.* Approved of. As simple as that.

"Maybe in a few years," Gabriel's dad cut in.

"Of course. High school, at least," Mr. Ali said.

"We'll see. Not too soon," Gabriel's dad said.

In his bunk that night—Adrian breathing lightly in the bed above him—Gabriel smiled to himself. In the last seven years, the Ali's home had become an extension of his own. Their family was his.

In the back of his mind, he imagined, someday, that might become a permanent thing.

LOVE

ENTERING HIGH SCHOOL—despite the knowledge Chloe *might* like him—girls and romance were still the furthest things from Gabriel's mind. And even if he did like her back, he wasn't allowed to date until he was sixteen. Gabriel hardly cared. He just wanted to start school strong and not worry about a relationship too soon.

After being taught at home through eighth grade, high school would be the first time stepping into an *actual* classroom. And yet, it felt somewhat unofficial. Maybe because it was so hard to explain to anyone on the outside.

St. Michael Christian High School only had fifty-three students—fourteen in Gabriel's class—and since the school was too small for its own building, it had to rent space from a local church. There was chapel every Monday, and they only met three times a week. This meant they had extra homework to supplement the days off.

Gabriel had all the usual classes. Algebra. Biology. English, etc. He even signed up for Drama. Adrian forced him into it so they could mess around all year. Gabriel didn't picture himself as an actor growing up, but after the first week, visions of red carpets and movie deals flooded his mind. If that happened, he vowed to stay humble and use his platform to spread the gospel.

Upon auditioning, he was cast as a glorified extra. He only had three lines.

Maybe that wasn't his destiny after all.

Adrian, though, secured one of the lead roles, and Gabriel helped him practice lines during study hall and at home after school. Adrian was a natural. He nailed the jokes and sometimes improvised when it was just the two of them. By October, he'd memorized all his lines and was working on the rest of the play.

"You never know when you have to jump in," Adrian said, turning the page of his script. The entire thing was covered in yellow highlights with notes scribbled in the margins.

Gabriel looked at him. Adrian's face was furrowed in concentration. He mouthed a line, then closed his eyes and repeated it. He paced the room, arms waving at his sides.

Gabriel fought a smile and focused on his own script.

In all his other classes, he and Chloe sat together and whispered jokes when their teacher's backs were turned. It didn't take long for Gabriel to get used to the eye rolls thrown in his direction every time he and Chloe ducked their heads together.

Gabriel relished the disapproval. He was proud to be such good friends with a girl. Most people he knew thought that wasn't possible. He was happy to prove them wrong.

Peyton Miller and Sean West liked to point out that even though he didn't *have* to date Chloe, they would make the perfect couple.

"It's like you're already together," Peyton said after school as they walked to the coffee shop a block away.

"We're just friends," Gabriel said. "And we've known each other forever. It would feel weird to date."

"It's your loss," Sean said. "Someone else will ask her out if you don't."

Gabriel shrugged, then frowned. "Who?"

"Evan, as far as I know," Sean said.

"Williams? The sophomore?" Gabriel said, getting vigorous nods from Sean and Peyton.

Gabriel fell silent, thinking this over. It's not that he particularly *wanted* to go out with Chloe, but the idea of someone else dating her tightened his chest. That would virtually end their friendship. Sure, they'd be able to see each other at events, but never one-on-one. They'd never be able to watch movies together or do homework while listening to music in her room.

He couldn't lose that.

Mind spinning, Gabriel hardly said a word on the drive home. He immediately went to his room and sat at his desk.

The truth was, he liked her. A lot. She was funny and relaxed, and she *was* pretty. He'd just never felt that vague and undeniable *spark* of romance. He didn't feel butterflies or ever imagine what it would be like to kiss her.

Maybe he was overthinking it.

Maybe all couples were just friends, and that's why the relationship worked. Maybe passionate romance was all made up, and it wasn't about attraction at all. Could it just be about respect and devotion and wanting to be around the other person?

If that were the case, wasn't he already in love?

That thought struck him like a bolt of lightning. He rocked back in his chair.

He *could* see himself with Chloe. He could see them having romantic dinners and talking late at night, but the thought of anything physical made him slightly nauseous. As much as he liked her, he didn't *want* to kiss her, and it felt wrong to imagine. Maybe the attraction would develop in time. That had to be it.

Gabriel broke into a smile. He put his hands on his head. *I like Chloe.* He paced the room, unable to keep still at the revelation. *I like Chloe.* He laughed. It seemed so obvious now.

Wait, no…

I love her.

Gabriel flopped on his bed, grinning from ear to ear.

Now that he knew, what was the next step? He couldn't tell her yet, right? Of course not. He needed to give it time to make sure he was really in love. Besides, he still couldn't date for thirteen months. Maybe that was a good thing. It would certainly give him time to work on himself. She would appreciate that.

Gabriel was proud of how considerate he was being.

He stayed up late that night imagining how he would eventually tell her and what they would do on their first date. He made a mental list of everything he wanted to improve about himself.

Getting up early was big, and he had to start working out. Even more important was being completely reliant on God. That meant going to church and the Porter's worship nights every week. Reading the Bible every morning. Praying for Chloe's well-being and that she was also preparing herself for marriage. And if he had time, he would listen to extra sermons and podcasts. You could never have too much time with God.

Gabriel rubbed his forehead in the dark. It was a long list, but he had to do this to become the man he wanted to be. His wife deserved the best.

The next day, Gabriel slept through his alarm for school. His mom pounded on the door, waking him with a start. "Ten minutes, Gabriel!"

"I'm getting ready!" Gabriel shouted back.

He jumped out of bed, threw on a shirt, and brushed his teeth. Downstairs, he chugged orange juice and crammed buttered toast in his mouth, full of guilt for failing already.

FOR THE NEXT two months, Gabriel planned how he would share his feelings with Chloe. He eventually decided to confess at the Ali's annual Christmas party. It was a big affair with six or seven families, and the festivities would make the moment even more special.

Gabriel dressed up in an ugly sweater with a reindeer on the front and detachable ornaments hanging from the antlers. He found some of Jacob's old body spray and applied a liberal amount to his chest and armpits. Not that he smelled bad. He'd showered specifically for this event and greased his hair until it was set in stone.

Once dressed, he practiced greeting people in the mirror. He practiced his smile and casual shrug for when people complimented him on how much older he was looking. He practiced for when people asked him if he had a girlfriend, and how he'd tell them he had someone in mind before giving a telling glance towards Chloe.

And when dinner was over, he would find time to talk to Chloe alone. He'd offer to get them refills of hot chocolate before the big reveal. Maybe they'd hold hands for a minute before returning to the party.

It was perfect, just like in the movies.

A sharp knock on his bedroom door shattered his thoughts.

"Gabriel! We have to go!" his mom said.

"One second!" Gabriel returned.

He adjusted his sweater the entire walk across the street. When did it get so itchy? He berated himself for not wearing a shirt underneath.

The Ali's house was ablaze with activity.

Gabriel weaved through the maze of bodies to the kitchen and found Chloe leaning against the counter, cookie in hand. She was wearing a red sweater, her hair in two braids. Gabriel smiled at her, stood stiffly at her side, then reached for a cookie because he'd waited too long to hug her. He was already sweating.

The entire dinner, he couldn't help but steal glances at Chloe. The thought of confessing felt more impossible by the minute. He still hadn't found the right opportunity by the time the kids filtered into the basement. Gabriel and Adrian stood together as they watched Peyton and Sean play ping pong. Chloe was with a group of girls setting up a board game across the room.

Adrian sniffed the air and glanced at Gabriel. "Maybe take it easy with the body spray next time."

Gabriel swallowed. "Really?"

"It's a bit strong."

Gabriel's face burned. He tucked his nose into his sweater. How was he supposed to know it was too much? The point was to smell it, right?

To make things worse, he hadn't stopped itching himself the entire evening, and the sweater was so warm he was close to suffocation. It took another hour before he mustered the courage to ask Adrian if he could borrow a shirt.

"It's too hot down here," Gabriel explained casually.

"No problem," Adrian said.

Gabriel bounded up the two flights of stairs to Adrian's room. He rifled through the drawers until he found a navy shirt. It was a few sizes too big, but Gabriel would have taken anything at this point. He smelled the sweater again with a grimace, then dropped it on the floor.

He surveyed the room.

It was an intimate thing, being here alone.

The bed was roughly put together. Shirts lay on the floor in front of the closet. On Adrian's desk was a picture of him and Savanah at homecoming. She didn't go to their school, so Adrian had been allowed to attend an actual public school for the event.

They both seemed so happy in the photo.

Gabriel found it hard to swallow.

All too soon, Adrian would move on. Everything would become about his girlfriend and college, and there would be no room for Gabriel. Returning the picture to the desk, Gabriel sat on Adrian's bed, heavy with their inevitable parting of ways.

BACK IN THE basement, Gabriel joined Chloe's game of Dutch Blitz. He settled next to Peyton as they organized their cards. Chloe's phone buzzed. She leaned back and covered the screen, smiling to herself.

"Who's that?" Peyton's sister, Joni, asked.

"No one," Chloe said, turning off her phone.

"Oooo, it's him, isn't it!" Joni burst out.

"Who?" Gabriel asked.

"No one!" Chloe said. "It's nothing."

"People only say that when they're hiding things," Gabriel said to annoy her.

Chloe gave him a withering glare. "Fine! It was Evan saying Merry Christmas."

Gabriel frowned. "Williams?"

Joni nodded vigorously. "She's in love."

Chloe's face went red. "*I'm not in love.* We like each other."

"Oh," Gabriel sounded, feeling like he'd been punched in the gut.

Peyton gave him a sympathetic shrug and a *told you so* look.

"It's not a big deal, shut up," Chloe said.

Gabriel gave a casual shrug, but his mind was spinning. He felt betrayed, somehow. Did she not like him anymore? How could everything fall apart so quickly?

The night became a haze. Gabriel returned upstairs and drifted in and out of conversations with adults who wanted to talk about his first semester of high school. He couldn't focus and left the party early after giving Chloe a tentative hug.

Gabriel trudged across the Ali's snow-packed grass. He stopped in the middle of the street and did a slow circle, taking in the Christmas lights of the neighborhood. Some had blinking icicles over the garage or an inflatable snowman in the yard. Hands in his pockets, Gabriel stood in front of the Jensen's, looking up at the sleigh mounted on their roof.

There was a gaping pit deep down, and it wouldn't go away. Finding out Chloe liked someone else was a blow to the gut. And for some reason, his thoughts kept returning to the picture of Adrian and Savanah.

For a split second, Adrian's eyes flashed in his mind. His smile. His lips—

No.

Gabriel clutched his chest and started walking. He kept his eyes on the pavement to avoid the cracks, breathing deep against the squeeze of fear. He walked until he was shivering so badly that he had no choice but to return home.

"Where'd you go?" his mom asked as she filled the fridge with leftovers from the party.

"I went for a walk to see the lights," Gabriel said.

"Oh, that's nice. In just that? What happened to your sweater?"

Gabriel looked down at his shirt. "It was too hot, so I borrowed this from Adrian. I'm going to bed."

"Alright, good night. I love you!" She called after him.

"Love you too," he said, shuffling upstairs.

Gabriel changed silently, then sat on his bed, lips a tight line. He closed his eyes and prayed for God to purify his thoughts and cleanse his soul. There were things he hardly knew were there, but he needed them gone. He hoped God understood what he meant.

Turning out his light, he curled up under his covers.

He wondered if God could see him crying in the dark.

THE HOMOSEXUAL AGENDA

CHLOE AND EVAN talked throughout the rest of the school year. At first, Gabriel thought their romance would fade after a month or two, and likely over summer. And he certainly didn't think it would last until they were halfway through their Sophomore year. Soon after Chloe's sixteenth birthday, she and Evan went on their first official date.

That night, Gabriel was a mess of jealousy, relief, and sadness that things were bound to change between him and Chloe. In need of a distraction, he suggested to his parents that they watch a movie. They selected *The Perks of Being a Wallflower.*

Gabriel hadn't pushed for it, and since he still hadn't read the book, all he knew about the story was what the trailer showed. It seemed fun and heartfelt, even though it was PG-13.

From the opening credits, Gabriel had that strange, elusive feeling that this film might change his life. From the first lines, it was clear that Charlie *knew* him. He knew what it was like to observe and be quiet, keeping everything in.

Gabriel melted into the story. It wrapped him tight, like a thick blanket on a cold night. He cherished every scene, and a few in particular.

The montage to *Asleep* by The Smiths.

Charlie—alone and deeply anxious—watching everyone dance at Homecoming, then inching toward Patrick and Sam.

The party, where Charlie confesses that his best friend killed himself, and how he wished he'd gotten a note.

But when Charlie walked in on Patrick and Brad kissing at that same party, Gabriel's mom scrambled to turn off the TV.

"That's a shame," his mom said.

"I didn't like it anyway. It was too vulgar," his dad said.

"We should have read reviews," his mom added. "Let's play a game instead."

Gabriel offered no protest. That would have invited trouble. He just sat on the couch, staring at the blank TV. It stared back, taunting.

His parents usually allowed kissing in movies, but if clothes started coming off, they would skip the scene. If it happened more than once, or if there was nudity at any point, they would turn the movie off.

Years of enforcement made Gabriel instinctively cringe every time he saw a kiss. It was a sacred thing, and yet it was inherently lustful. It was beautiful in marriage but could be so easily perverted.

It felt wrong to think about. It felt shameful to want.

Even though there was some leniency for romance, anything that related to homosexuality was immediately shut down. Gabriel's family staunchly opposed movies, people, and businesses that pushed the homosexual agenda.

There was no room for debate.

So, this is what Gabriel did:

He played cards with his parents, and when everyone went upstairs, he read until his parents turned out their lights. He waited another hour before he felt safe creeping downstairs with a pair of corded headphones.

He used the office computer because the TV would be too loud, and his phone was still restricted from downloading streaming apps. No matter. He'd memorized all the computer passwords last year, so it only took a moment to bring up the movie. He cautiously plugged in the headphones, turned down the brightness, and started from the beginning.

By the end, he was a storm of rediscovered emotion. It thrummed in his veins. It pounded against the walls he'd built.

He shoved it down as best he could, an aching lump in his throat.

With a profound sense of loss because it was *over*, he re-wound the movie to the original stopping point and deleted the computer history showing his activity. Clutching his headphones, he crept back upstairs, filled with the twin stones of unquenchable guilt and long-buried memories.

Two summers ago, shortly after Gabriel's first trip on the *Queen's Dream*, his family took a vacation to Hawaii.

Between walks from their hotel to the ocean, they often stopped in convenience stores for snacks and water. One day, Gabriel discovered a certain calendar amid the shelves of souvenirs. It had a beautiful, scantily clothed Hawaiian woman on the front.

On the back, each woman was completely naked.

He'd never seen that before.

Gabriel started shaking, but he couldn't look away. His mouth became dry and metallic as adrenaline flooded his body.

He knew it was a disgusting thing to do, but every time they went back, he sought out that calendar. As far as he knew, no one found out. By the time the trip ended, Gabriel was so sick with guilt that his mom thought he had sun poisoning.

Weeks later, he went on the office computer late at night and tried to find those pictures again. He did, and more.

The following morning, his parents barged into his room. Apparently, the computer had monitoring software. For more than an hour, Gabriel sobbed on his bed while his dad yelled about the dangers of lust and the perversions of the internet. His mom shared how violated she felt that he'd seen those pictures.

Then they prayed and read the Bible, and Gabriel vowed never to do it again.

He really *did* intend to keep that promise.

GABRIEL COULDN'T SLEEP after watching the movie.

He couldn't stop remembering getting caught after Hawaii. He couldn't stop the terror that he might be caught again.

Nothing happened the next day, but Gabriel couldn't relax.

For the rest of the week, he processed the movie and what it meant for him. When he felt ready, he pulled the book off his shelf and started to read. It was done in two days. Then he lay on the floor of his room, staring at the ceiling fan.

Anger blazed in his lungs. Bottled fear, like poison, seeped from his bones.

He wished he'd read the book sooner. He wished he wasn't so afraid. He wished he was someone else.

Failures plagued his mind. They weren't staying down so easy anymore. They wanted out.

Breath gasped and halted as he fought for control.

WHAT HUGH JACKMAN THING?

PEYTON WAS THE first person who told Gabriel about masturbation, and he was fourteen the first time he tried it. He didn't even have to look at anything. He just closed his eyes and pictured that Hawaiian calendar. The sudden euphoria was so intense he thought he would pass out.

Then guilt flooded him. Shame cut off his air.

He immediately threw himself on his bed and clawed at the covers, begging for God's forgiveness. He knew he didn't deserve it. He was defiled now.

He did it again a week later, then three days after that.

Every subsequent time, Gabriel was utterly convinced it would be the last, that God would be fed up with his groveling and failures and strike him down with a bolt of lightning. It hadn't happened yet, but that didn't erase the belief that it would.

It *would*.

He got his first phone at fifteen, and it only took a few months before he learned how to navigate around the monitoring software installed by his parents. Specific sites were restricted, but some Google photos weren't blurred out. It was just a matter of clicking around and finding the right thread. If he was careful, no one would know.

Besides God.

Around this time, he discovered a love for the X-Men movies. Maybe, unconsciously, it was for the story: A hated group fighting for survival. Maybe it was the action and superpowers.

Or, maybe it was shirtless Hugh Jackman.

The first time Gabriel looked up his Wolverine photos, he trembled so badly he thought he might collapse.

But he had to see. He had to know.

He had to find out if that's what he really wanted.

So he did.

And for just a few minutes, there was incredible peace.

AFTER, HE KNEW something else.

He was a vile, disgusting sinner, and he was glad Chloe didn't like him anymore. He didn't deserve a girl like her.

At each church service, it felt like he was tempting God to smite him where he sat. Every time Pastor Evans talked about the dangers of lust, Gabriel shrank even more in his seat. Panic made it impossible to breathe, but he dug his fingers into his thighs to keep himself from moving. He wondered if anyone knew what he was hiding. He couldn't meet people's eyes when they talked about sin.

When it was just Gabriel and his dad, and the silence between them grew too wide, his dad would sometimes ask if Gabriel had looked at porn again. Gabriel always gave a casual, "No, I'm good. Honestly." His dad seemed to buy it, but maybe that was a front, too. They never really *talked* to each other, and this was a topic both could do without exploring.

Even with his friends, Gabriel never once admitted to looking at explicit photos, which made it feel like it never happened. He was getting better at blocking things out.

And the Hugh Jackman thing?

What Hugh Jackman thing?

Christians didn't have to deal with that sin.

Every time a *homosexual* was mentioned, Gabriel coiled up. Somewhere deep in his being, he hated them. After all, they were perverting what it meant to be an honorable family. How could they live with themselves, parading like they did?

He was scared of them, too.

They were the worst of society, the murderers and rapists. That's what Pastor Evans said, at least.

Despite all his efforts, there were moments when his walls cracked and some of the truth leaked out.

It was here that he sobbed into his pillow late at night, begging for God's forgiveness. He vowed to become a monk or a pastor or lead missions in hostile countries. He fantasized about being martyred for his faith—of being skinned alive or fed to wild dogs or dropped in boiling oil—and never denying God. He would give it all away if God cleansed his sin so he could be with Him forever.

And in *this* life, all Gabriel wanted was to marry a woman and have kids. He didn't even have to like her. He could choose to make it work. Love was a choice, right? He could choose to like girls, however impossible that seemed.

And then horrible realization would flood his body, worse every time. He could have dated Chloe, maybe even married her. God had probably sent her into his life for that very reason.

Gabriel repented endlessly for messing it up. He prayed even harder for a second chance.

THOSE FLEETING HOURS

RIGHT BEFORE SENIOR year, Chloe broke up with Evan.

When he heard the news—for a moment—Gabriel thought this was his opportunity to make a move.

Sometimes, second chances come too late.

He'd slipped closer to sin in the last two years. Maybe he'd let himself fall. And though Chloe was now available, Gabriel didn't think she was who he really wanted.

"All he talks about is the car he's building," Chloe said in the aftermath. She and Gabriel were sitting on the floor of her room, eating ice cream and listening to music. "He hates reading and thinks frozen pizza is a perfect date. I couldn't do it anymore."

Gabriel nodded along. He knew his job right now was to listen and agree, and he couldn't have agreed more.

"And he didn't like you," Chloe said offhandedly.

Gabriel lowered his bowl. "Really?"

"He didn't like how close we were."

"God forbid platonic friendships."

Chloe stirred her ice cream. It used to be mint chocolate chip. Now, it looked like green soup with irregular chunks.

Gabriel listened to the music and ignored the things they hadn't talked about. He'd never told her how he felt for her, or how he *thought* he felt. And he did love her, but not in the way he wished to love his partner.

He wished to feel a spark. A *pull*. Something like quiet, tender desire.

He'd been able to admit that in the last two years, and he set his sights on finding someone at college. There would be plenty more options once he went away to school—

"Oh!" Chloe burst out. "He wanted *so many* kids. Eight or nine. He told me two months into dating."

Gabriel grinned. "Better get started now."

Chloe groaned and rubbed her face. "That's too much. I don't even know if I want kids."

"Really?" Gabriel asked, instantly focused on her reply.

Chloe must have realized what she'd let slip, for she backtracked quickly. "I mean, *of course* I want kids." She picked out some chocolate chips and crunched them thoughtfully. She turned her attention to the ceiling. "But I also want my own life. Just me, maybe."

Gabriel dropped his eyes to his empty bowl and nodded. "I know what you mean."

An hour later, Chloe had unloaded what she needed, and they settled down to watch *Logan*. It was the last film of their X-Men marathon. She hadn't seen it yet, but it was one of Gabriel's favorites.

Now, he watched and read whatever he wanted, and there was a *burning* under his ribs the more he consumed. It was the anger of discovering *good* in the things his parents condemned as evil. It was strangled frustration for being kept in the dark for so long.

Was this how Isaac felt?

Gabriel settled deeper into the couch and dug into the bowl of popcorn between him and Chloe. He bathed in the relief of escape.

You see, not only did he watch what he wanted now, he watched *whom* he wanted—Hugh Jackman included—and he refused to feel guilty. He wouldn't let it in. It couldn't even find him. For in those fleeting hours, he wasn't Gabriel Moore. He was someone else entirely with a life not his own.

It was *then*—when he was no longer himself—he could finally let go and dream.

SENIOR YEAR

SENIOR YEAR SLIPPED away like a perfect moment gripped too tightly.

The days blurred with classes and piles of homework. The weekends flew by with school events and graduation plans. Occasionally, Gabriel squeezed in a movie night with Chloe, Peyton, and Sean, or an afternoon at the coast. Before he knew it, the whole family was back for Thanksgiving. Then, it was frantic studying before the end of the semester.

At the Ali's Christmas party, Gabriel circled the liquor table for the third time. There were a dozen bottles of opened wine, spirits, mixers, and glasses. He eyed a Pino Noir but made up a story in his head about studying the typography of the label.

"Do you think they'll notice if we take a bottle?" Chloe asked, coming up behind him.

"Absolutely," Gabriel said.

"We should do it anyway."

"I think so."

At that moment, Mr. Ali approached from the kitchen. Empty glass in his hand, he reached for a Cabernet Sauvignon and poured himself four *glugs* of wine.

"You know," he said, "if you're trying to figure out how to get your hands on a drink, you should be less suspicious."

Gabriel forced a laugh as if the very thought was absurd.

Chloe took the opposite approach. "Can we try some?"

Mr. Ali examined the glass in his hand, then looked over his shoulder. "I mean…"

"Just a sip," Chloe prodded.

Gabriel knew how delicate this negotiation was, so he remained silent and still, trying all the while to seem mature and disinterested.

Mr. Ali looked them over, scratching his short beard. "Don't tell your mom," he said, handing his glass to Chloe. He rested his hands on his hips. "Actually, I don't care. You can have your own."

Chloe had already taken a sip, and her eyes lit up at the allowance. She handed the glass to Gabriel, and he set it on the table. Mr. Ali poured two new glasses, each the size of his own. He considered the remainder, shrugged, and divided the final inch between the kids.

"This is why you're my favorite," Chloe said.

"Same," Gabriel said.

Mr. Ali's eyes sparkled as they clinked their glasses. Gabriel swirled his wine like they did in movies, breathed it in, and took his first sip of alcohol. He frowned, mulling it over. Another sip. He liked this one less than the first.

"What do you think?" Mr. Ali asked.

Gabriel scrunched his nose. "Tastes like dirt."

Chloe snorted.

"*Good* dirt, I mean. Lots of minerals," Gabriel said.

Chloe nodded with a sophisticated air. Mr. Ali sighed and squeezed Gabriel's shoulder. "Can't wait to hear what you think about whiskey."

"You offering?"

"Not my good stuff, no," Mr. Ali said. "You'd probably say it tastes like burnt rubber."

"It does," Chloe said, grimacing.

Mr. Ali cocked his head at his daughter.

"Uh…so I've heard," Chloe said with a tense grin.

Mr. Ali *tsked* as he wandered off again.

Gabriel wheeled on Chloe. "You tried whiskey without me?"

"I was bored!"

"Unbelievable."

"You would have hated it, anyway," Chloe said.

Gabriel rolled his eyes and sipped his wine.

On New Year's Eve, Peyton smuggled a bottle of Jamison into the Ali's party. He, Gabriel, Chloe, and Sean drank the entire thing in her room, chasing it down with soda and juice. For so long, Gabriel had avoided drinking, but for all of Pastor Evans' preaching, these moments didn't feel wrong. They laughed too loud and played music and cards. At midnight, they joined everyone downstairs, and Chloe and Peyton kissed. Adrian and Savanah did, too, and Gabriel tried not to stare, a pang in his heart.

Spring semester, Gabriel pushed himself to audition for the school play, *Barbecuing Hamlet*. He secured one of the most significant roles—Sarge, the sarcastic handyman.

He loved every moment.

The manic excitement as the curtains opened. His first lines and relaxing into the performance. Playing to the audience and the well-timed jokes. The laughter. The costumes. The eyeliner and makeup.

And then congratulating the other cast members. Talking to strangers he'd never see again. Celebrating at Red Robin.

But most of all, it was the feeling. It was the euphoria of being the most important person in just a few people's lives, even if it was just for the night.

Never before had Gabriel felt so whole.

NEARING GRADUATION, THE fear of moving on loomed in his mind.

Out there was his future. It was college, a career, a wife and a family. It was all he thought he wanted, and it was a terrifying thing to imagine all at once.

Everyone had a plan.

Chloe was going to an Industrial Design school in California. Peyton was heading to Denver for Mechanical Engineering. Sean was taking a year off to drive across the country in a van.

There was no question or debate about where Gabriel would go. His destination was the family college, Morrison Christian University.

His parents had met there. Isaac fought not to attend, but he lost that battle. Rachel and Jacob gladly went, saying it was a wonderful experience. Most of *their* kids would probably go there, too.

Morrison accepted him within a month of his application, and he was to study Business Management with a minor in Marketing. The school was located in a small town three hours west of Boston, and there were just over four thousand students when Gabriel enrolled.

The student handbook outlined a wealth of expectations.

Midnight curfew. Mandatory, daily chapel. Weekly participation in a local church.

No consumption of alcohol, tobacco, or drugs while enrolled as a student—regardless of legal age.

No one from the opposite sex was allowed into your hall or room except during Open Dorms. Biblical marriage was the standard, and anything outside those bounds was a violation of sexual purity. Students facing sexual temptations were encouraged to seek out

Biblical instruction from the University's counseling services.

Any violations of these guidelines could result in fines, academic probation, or dismissal from the school.

Gabriel rubbed his jaw, uneasy. There were so many ways he could mess up.

He navigated the online student portal and signed the agreement that bound him to the University's guidelines. Next, he signed the Confession of Faith, which affirmed Morrison's beliefs were his, too.

"It's not hard to follow the rules," Jacob said over the phone, calming his fears. *"Just find a good group, and you'll do fine. There's so many good things about the school."*

Jacob went on about the wealth of campus events, clubs, and intramural sports, and Gabriel's qualms faded. Weeks later, he couldn't remember why he'd been so worked up. *Of course* he'd have a wonderful experience. He'd study, meet incredible people, and join clubs in his free time. He might even find his future wife.

At the Senior banquet, he paraded the venue in his tailored grey suit and shared his plans for the future. He talked with people he never usually looked at and promised to keep in touch when they were all off at college.

At graduation, he basked in the thunderous applause and endless compliments. He was important again. They knew who he was, and he knew he deserved to be recognized.

And then it was just him, Chloe, and a handful of others cleaning up the discarded plates of cake and half-drunk punch.

Just like that, high school was over.

IN THE MIDDLE of June, Gabriel found himself at a coffee shop downtown, writing about the things he hoped to do in his first year of college. He would wake up early, read the Bible in the morning, work out three times a week, and read at least one book a month. Once he settled in, he would look for a job and maybe start dating.

Reviewing his list of attributes he wanted in a wife, Gabriel's attention drifted through the coffee shop. Once again, he found himself watching the two men at a table by the entrance. One had silver hair, a trimmed beard, and a kindness to his eyes that Gabriel longed to see up close. When the man got up to refill his mug, Gabriel watched his every move. The barista handed the cup back and complimented the man's blazer. They talked for a minute. Gabriel heard the word *husband*. The barista nodded with a smile, and Gabriel saw a ring flash on the older man's finger. He soon returned to his table, squeezed his partner's hand, and focused again on his computer.

It is just a moment.

But a moment is enough to turn a kernel of jealousy into a sea of burning rage. It consumed every fiber of Gabriel's being, searing him from the inside out.

He hated them, *hated* them, and he took comfort in the fact these men were going to hell. And yet…they seemed happy. They probably didn't care they were going to hell. They probably didn't even *believe* in hell.

For the first time, Gabriel wished he didn't believe in God.

He wished he didn't believe in the eternal torture of sinful people. He wished he didn't believe it because even if it were true, he would be happy and free and maybe be like the men on the other side of the coffee shop.

But he could never have that.

He wondered once again why God made him this way. Why he still didn't hear His voice. Why he was so terrified over his fate despite following God's commands to the best of his ability.

He wondered if he would ever find peace. If he would ever find the happiness others seemed to have so easily.

And again—for the first time—he wondered if any of it even mattered.

SUMMER WEDDING

JACOB AND NANCY'S wedding was the last big event of the summer.

The entire family was there, even Isaac. Gabriel hadn't seen him in nearly two years, but he was a groomsman nonetheless. As siblings, there was an obligation to be in the wedding party, no matter the previous conflict. Even so, out of the six selected to stand next to Jacob, Isaac was second to last, and Gabriel brought up the rear.

Adrian had flown in the previous night from his internship in Nashville. Gabriel gave him a tight hug, and his eyes lingered over Adrian's tailored burgundy blazer and the open buttons of his white dress shirt. Adrian had gotten a tight fade haircut and sported suspenders.

Then Savanah was at Adrian's side and Gabriel hugged her too, and he immediately wished to be elsewhere. But when he retreated to prepare for the ceremony, he longed to return to Adrian's side.

It was a battle he could never win.

After the first dance, Gabriel watched from the sidelines as people flooded the dance floor. He sipped a sparkling cider. Adrian came up to his side and threw an arm around his shoulders. For a moment, all they did was stand. Gabriel bit his lip, restless.

"I think she's the one," Adrian said.

"What?" Gabriel asked.

Adrian dropped his arm and nodded to the dance floor. Gabriel picked out Savanah amongst the bridesmaids. "I think I'm going to marry her."

Gabriel did his best not to squeeze his plastic cup to pieces. "That's great."

There was a minute of silence.

"How do you know? You're so young," Gabriel said. "How do you know it's right?"

"I think you just *do*."

"Something you feel…"

"And it makes sense in here," Adrian tapped his chest. "Can't deny what's in your heart."

What about me? Does that count for me?

"I think I'm going to propose this year," Adrian said.

"That's incredible."

"Getting married young is special. When do you think you want to get married?"

Gabriel finished his drink and stared straight ahead. "No idea."

"You're going to have such an amazing wife. I can't wait to raise our kids together."

"That sounds amazing," Gabriel said. He loosened his tie, but it didn't relieve the claustrophobia coming from inside. He clenched his jaw, steeling himself. "I'm really happy for you."

Gabriel hugged Adrian, cherishing the moment because this was all he would ever get.

"Congratulations," Gabriel said.

"Thanks," Adrian said.

Adrian pulled away and stormed the dance floor. Gabriel refilled his cider and sat at the wedding party table with a second piece of cake. Isaac sat next to him a few minutes later. He had shaggy hair, a trimmed mustache, and Tom Ford glasses.

"I heard you're going to Morrison," Isaac said to break the ice.

Gabriel nodded. "I'm leaving in a month."

"Don't go."

Gabriel laughed.

"I'm serious."

"What?"

"That place will fuck you up."

Gabriel picked at his cake, then took a small bite. "I'm not you."

"*Wow.*"

Gabriel ducked his head and finished his cake in silence.

"Wasn't this supposed to be a dry wedding?" Isaac asked after a while.

Gabriel glanced at his brother. "Mom and Dad wanted that, but Nancy said it would be good for people to have a few drinks."

"Thank God for her. If this were all I had tonight, I wouldn't be able to make it," Isaac said, pulling a silver flask from his breast pocket.

"Mom and Dad will be pissed if they see that."

"Let 'em."

"Just get a drink at the bar like a normal person."

"And then spike it with *this*, brilliant!" Isaac's eyes lit up.

"That's not what I said."

"And humble."

"Why are you like this?"

Isaac regarded the flask, a distant look on his face. He took a drink and screwed the lid back on, then reached for an abandoned cider that wasn't his and took a chasing sip. "I'm a product of my environment."

"No, *Jacob* is a product of his environment."

"We all are. We just react in different ways," Isaac said plainly. "The question is, who are *you?*"

"I'm just me."

"Gabriel the wallflower…" Isaac mused, and Gabriel's eyes darted to his brother.

They were silent again. They didn't have to say anything because both of them knew what it meant to stay quiet.

"You're not as innocent as they think you are," Isaac said after a while.

"You have no idea," Gabriel said.

"Yeah? Say something that would surprise me."

Obvious sins bubbled to the surface of Gabriel's mind. He rubbed his neck as his pulse shot upward.

The masturbation. The porn. His attractions.

The wish that God wasn't real.

But he could never say those things aloud, so he just said, "I don't know," with a dismissive shrug and a tight smile.

Isaac took a swig from his flask. "You know exactly what. Here," he said, quickly pouring a splash of clear alcohol into Gabriel's apple cider.

"What the hell!"

"It's just a bit of courage," Isaac said, unconcerned at ruining Gabriel's drink. "You know you can say fuck around me, right? 'What the fuck, Isaac?' Now you try."

"No."

"They've got you locked up tight, don't they?"

"I don't know what that's supposed to mean," Gabriel grumbled.

Isaac's aura quieted. "You can tell me anything. I'm not a talker."

He poured some of his flask into the cider before him until it reached the brim. "But I get it if you don't want to talk to me, or even be *around* me. Just find someone you can do that with."

With that, Isaac rose from the table, drink in hand. The flask had disappeared into his pocket, and he had a smile on his face once more. "I'll let you be."

Gabriel watched him go, a lump in his throat.

Find someone you can do that with.

The words echoed in Gabriel's head. He scanned the venue. His eyes flashed over his dad talking with Pastor Evans, his head bobbing with the music. His mom doting over Heidi's youngest daughter. Adrian tearing up the dance floor without a single care in the world.

And Gabriel couldn't imagine talking to any of those people.

He looked back at the spiked cider and took an experimental taste. It smelled faintly of cleaning products and apples and settled uncomfortably on his tongue.

Then his eyes found Chloe slicing herself another piece of cake.

Maybe.

And Mr. Ali chatting to the bartender, a glass of amber liquid in his hand.

Maybe…

But *maybe* was all Gabriel's subconscious would allow. Soon, all thought had shut down, and Gabriel became a simple vessel to *watch* —through a tunnel that was slowly closing.

THAT BLAZING AUGUST MORNING

TWO WEEKS LATER, on that blazing August morning, Pastor Evans took the stage. He condemned the sinners—the homosexuals. His followers clapped and whistled.

Gabriel did the only thing he could. His mind shrank away. Escaped. Found refuge on a fishing boat in the open ocean.

For a little while, everything was quiet.

Gabriel found peace next to Adrian in those happy years before he understood how he really felt. Back then, it was just the solidarity of fishing and laughing and talking about their futures as if they had any clue what they might bring.

"These people are broken and desperate for God. We all are. *They* just don't know it yet," Pastor Evans said.

Adrian's lips floated in Gabriel's mind. His laugh rang in his ears. His wedding outfit shimmered with desire.

"It's our job to help them see the truth. *Can I get an amen?*" Pastor Evans shouted.

The crowd erupted in agreement.

Gabriel snapped back to the sanctuary. Back to the unquenchable fear.

That's when it happened.

That's when he realized his wayward thoughts weren't a passing fancy.

And that's when he *understood*—for the first time—if something didn't change, his eternal fate was to burn in the fires of hell.

TWO

AFTER ALL THIS TIME

ON THE LAST Friday of August, Gabriel drove to Morrison University alone, his rickety Honda Accord packed to the brim. He didn't let his parents help him move in. He wanted to do this on his own. They'd be visiting him soon enough, anyway.

For a while, he sat in silence, brightly aware of the changing of things.

He'd never been on his own before. He could reinvent himself if he wanted. Leave behind all that came before. Become someone else, someone more true.

A whole new life was just ahead.

He merged onto the highway, and something released between his shoulder blades. Something lightened in the back of his mind.

He was free.

After all this time.

It was hard to believe.

ROOM 116

ROLLING GREEN HILLS passed on both sides of the two-lane highway. Oak and maple trees dotted open fields. The road dipped and weaved and carried Gabriel over occasional rivers.

The town of Morrison appeared out of nothing.

At first, it was a dilapidated barn. Then a house at the end of a long gravel driveway. Then many houses. In minutes, he'd driven by the post office, ice cream shop, and the only hotel in town. The first school buildings came into view.

Red brick dorms rose on the right side of the road, and Gabriel slowed to a crawl as cars clogged the street leading up to the main campus entrance. Volunteers beckoned them on, waving signs and running back and forth, directing people like sheepdogs. New students, parents, and siblings crossed the street at random, consulting maps, their belongings in tow.

An hour later, Gabriel stopped in front of his dorm. It was made of red brick, three stories tall, and had metal letters reading MILTON HALL above the glass entrance.

Gabriel got out and did a quick spin, hands on his hips. Volunteers swarmed his car. He gave them his room number—116—and they charged into the building, arms full of his things. Gabriel grabbed a laundry basket of shoes and jogged to catch up. Entering the building, they passed stairs on the left and marched down a hallway to the right. He followed them to the last room along the right wall.

"This is you!" The last volunteer said. He was squat and round with a scraggly beard, and he huffed from the effort. Grant, was it?

Gabriel surveyed the room, his mound of possessions in the center of the floor. It had white cinderblock walls and a fluorescent light on the ceiling. A small walk-in closet on the right. Wooden dressers. There was a window straight ahead with a desk underneath. Textbooks and a backpack covered the surface. On the left, the bottom bunk bed sported a navy comforter.

Gabriel excavated a lamp from the pile and set it on the remaining desk at the feet of the bunk beds. The volunteers streamed back into the room, dropping off the rest of his things.

After moving his car, he sat on his desk, feet propped on the chair. For a while, he just listened to the sounds of his dorm coming to life.

He took a deep breath. Held it. Let it out.

Gabriel peeled himself from his desk and set to work. Slowly, the cinderblock room transformed into a temporary home.

He stretched bedding on the top bunk. Hung his jackets and collared shirts in the closet. His shoes went on the floor, belts on a hanger, and bathroom supplies took up the top shelf. He loaded his desk drawers with pencils and notebooks and heaved his black bookshelf onto his cherry wood dresser. His books filled in the bottom cubbies. There was the hardcover study Bible Morrison had mailed to him as a welcome gift. His own cracking leather Bible with years of notes and highlights. A few writings by C.S. Lewis and other theologians. Then, a small personal collection. *The Perks of Being a Wall-flower* found a sliver of space in the bottom right cubby, opposite the Bibles.

And then there was nothing else to arrange.

Gabriel stepped back, nodding to himself. The room wasn't exactly cozy, but it would have to do. Laughter in the hallway drew his attention. He followed it out.

A WHOLE NEW WORLD

GABRIEL WANDERED THE hall, poking his head into rooms as people unpacked and bustled in and out of the dorm like a colony of ants. There was a mixture of grades, and not everyone had moved in yet. Only a few of the names stuck.

In 106 was Mason, a junior Chemical Engineering major. Red-haired, tall, and broad-shouldered, he talked excitedly to another junior about the new school year. His roommate Grant—a senior RA —scratched his thin beard as he watched his dominion come together.

Across the hall from Gabriel was Andy and Micah—freshmen—in room 115. They talked about retro video games while they settled in. Micah was tall, had long brown hair, and wore a Legend of Zelda T-shirt. He adjusted the angle of a 60-inch TV on his dresser while Andy stood on his desk and taped Anime posters all the way to the ceiling. Andy had a buzz cut, rosy cheeks, and a silver chain with a cross around his neck.

Gabriel soon left to get his ID in the Student Union. It was a ten-minute walk from his dorm, and he skirted the lake in the center of campus. It held murky, green water, so no one was allowed to swim in it, but it was a pleasant feature nonetheless. Trees and academic buildings rose in every direction.

Having visited the campus many times over the years, Gabriel had a good idea of how to navigate the school. He couldn't help but smile to himself at the packs of bewildered, wide-eyed freshmen. Outside the Union, Gabriel skirted a mom and her daughter as they consulted a paper map, faces scrunched in confusion.

He could have stopped to help, but they'd figure it out. He had other things to do, anyway.

GABRIEL LURCHED AWAKE as someone burst into his room. After lunch, he'd laid on his bed to read. It had only taken a few minutes for him to fall asleep.

"Oh, shit! Sorry," the intruder said. He had shaggy brown hair and sharp cheekbones. Gabriel waved him off. "You're Gabriel, yeah? I'm Jason," The intruder said, ducking into the walk-in closet. He returned to sight and pulled on a white sweatshirt. He wore short shorts, Adidas shoes, and white calf socks. "I'm getting dinner with some others, so I'll be out of your way in a minute."

Gabriel rubbed his face. "It's fine, I needed to get up anyway."

Jason examined himself in the mirror he'd stuck to the back of their door. He teased his hair, lips pursed. Gabriel climbed to the edge of the bunk and dropped to the floor.

"Alright, see you later," Jason said, ducking out of the room.

Gabriel huffed at the quick introduction and disappearance of his roommate. At least he *seemed* normal, and he cared how he looked. It could have been worse. He could have been stuck with someone who hadn't showered all week. There were plenty of those students around at a school like this, and they rarely knew how to dress.

No, Jason was probably the best he could have hoped for.

GABRIEL MET MOST of his hallmates over dinner in the cafeteria in the Student Union. Jason didn't show up, and a few others were missing, according to Grant. After eating, they marched to the Ministry Center for the school's first official gathering.

Gabriel scanned his ID at the auditorium entrance before following Grant and Mason down the center aisle. They found a stretch of seats to the left, about twenty rows from the stage. A group of girls occupied the seats in front of them. One of them turned around to scan the auditorium, and Andy waved at her. They struck up a conversation.

Despite this being his first time meeting girls at the school, Gabriel didn't bother joining in. There would be plenty of time for that later, and he didn't want to come off as desperate. Then again, if he were going to meet a girl, he'd have to actually *meet* her. He tuned into Andy's conversation just as a man in a red blazer and kaki pants bounded onto the stage. The screen behind him projected his upper body to the auditorium. He had brown hair cropped short on the sides and combed over with gel.

"Welcome back, Morrison!" He shouted, voice booming. An excited roar greeted him. "For the new faces, I'm the university President, Doctor Stone—"

"We love you, Doctor Stone!" A guy yelled from the balcony above Gabriel's seat.

"I love you too," Dr. Stone said with a smile, shielding his eyes from the spotlights as he looked over the crowd. "It's been a lonely few months without you, but it's good to see all these wonderful faces again. And so many new people! This year, we have over twelve hundred incoming students, our largest class to date. Freshmen and transfer students, make some noise!"

Gabriel bellowed with the crowd.

"Sophomores, where are you at?"

Another roar.

"Let's hear it for the Juniors!"

Mason jumped to his feet and yelled, high-fiving a girl in the row in front of him. The cheers faded, and Dr. Stone returned to the podium.

"I think that about covers it," he said.

Shouts of protest rose throughout the room. Dr. Stone played dumb until someone in the front row caught his attention.

"You forgot us!"

"Forgot who?"

"You know!"

Dr. Stone nodded to himself a few times. He paused, another smile poised above the microphone. Two seconds. Three.

"DO WE HAVE ANY SENIORS IN THE BUILDING?" He shouted.

The auditorium thundered and Gabriel's ears rang. Dr. Stone smiled wide. It took him a few minutes to quiet the room again.

"I don't know about you, but I'm excited to be back," he said, surveying the crowd. "Let's pray."

Heads bowed in waves, and just like that, the school year was officially underway.

GIRLS

GABRIEL WOKE EARLY the next morning, groggy and anxious. He'd hardly slept all night as he and Jason shifted in their beds, trying to get used to the presence of an unfamiliar person.

Crawling to the edge of his bed, Gabriel dropped to the floor. He picked himself up and checked his phone. It wasn't even 7 a.m. He gathered his bathroom caddy and towel and trekked down the long hall to the communal bathroom.

On the right were four sinks and a wall of mirrors. The side left was a row of stalls and urinals, split down the center by a short hallway to the showers. One was running, and someone's toiletry bag was on the counter by the far sink.

Gabriel relieved himself, brushed his teeth, and showered in under ten minutes. Pulling on new underwear in the shower stall, he headed for the sinks. Mason was shaving at the far left sink in his tight black briefs. He greeted Gabriel with a smile as he washed his razor.

"You're up early," Mason said.

"Couldn't sleep."

"Yeah, it takes a while to get used to a new place."

Gabriel fluffed his hair with his towel and rubbed in a pinch of matte pomade. Mason glanced at him in the mirror a few times as he worked.

"I'm about to get breakfast if you want to join," Mason offered.

Gabriel didn't have a reason to say no, so he agreed to join Mason in twenty minutes. Jason was still sleeping when he returned. As quietly as he could, Gabriel sorted through his clothes. He was acutely aware of presenting his best self in the first days of school.

A collared shirt was too formal, and a graphic tee sent the wrong message. He settled for a white T-shirt and a pair of slim, dark jeans. For a minute, he toyed with rolling up the sleeves, tucking in the shirt, and completing the look with a black belt.

Then the fear took over. He'd never worn something like this. He couldn't start now and risk social ridicule. Jason shifted in his bed, and Gabriel hastily untucked his shirt, then removed the belt because his jeans were more than snug enough to hold themselves up.

"You should go for it," Jason's sleepy voice said.

Gabriel twisted around. "What?"

"It looks good, the outfit."

"Really?" Gabriel asked, turning back to the mirror.

"It looks good. Don't overthink it," Jason mumbled, flopped around, and didn't make another noise.

Gabriel looked himself over again. He didn't tuck the shirt back in, but he kept the rolled sleeves, and he cuffed his pants, too, then slipped on his cream Toms.

Better.

He smiled to himself and sat at his desk to read the Bible.

"ARE YOU DATING anyone right now?" Gabriel asked as he and Mason settled at an open table near the windows overlooking the lake.

They'd used the self-service griddles to make scrambled eggs. Gabriel had added mushrooms, green peppers, and onions to his. Mason kept his simple with cheese on top, and he snagged a plain bagel to supplement the meal.

Mason nodded excitedly and held up a finger as he chewed his bagel. He gulped down water. "I am. Her name is Kayla. She graduated last year, so we're waiting until I graduate before we get married."

"That's awesome," Gabriel said.

"She's living back home in Indianapolis right now, so we're doing long distance, but we're doing great."

"Can I see a picture?"

Mason fished out his phone and presented a selfie of them on a hike. Mason had his characteristic big grin, and Kayla was…a girl.

Not particularly striking. Wide eyes and flushed cheeks. Brown hair, frizzy from the exercise.

Gabriel soon became aware that he still hadn't given a response, so he put on an enthusiastic smile. "That's great!"

Mason smiled at his phone, and Gabriel wondered what he was missing.

"She's great," Mason continued. "She's really funny, smart, all the stuff you could want."

"I bet," Gabriel offered in a non-committal way.

"Has anyone caught your eye yet?" Mason asked conspiratorially.

"I haven't been looking."

"There's so many great girls here. I can introduce you to some if you want."

"Yeah, maybe."

"What kind of girls do you like?"

Gabriel shifted in his seat as he took another bite. "I don't know, good smiles, funny, relaxed…"

"What about the curvaceous features?"

"What?"

"Do you like the front or back more?"

Gabriel narrowed his eyes. "Front or…oh! You mean ass or tits?"

Mason balked. "I wouldn't have put it like that, but essentially."

"Probably, uh…" Gabriel cupped his hands in front of his chest, "*breasts*, you know? But I'm not really sure."

"I'm a front man myself," Mason said with a nervous smile.

Gabriel hesitated as he brought his fork to his mouth. He had the sudden urge to curse to see what Mason would do, or ask if he wanted to watch *Deadpool*.

He probably already knew the answer.

THE DAY WAS a whirlwind of activities.

Dozens of booths had been set up in the fields surrounding the lake, each representing a different club or intramural sport. Gabriel navigated the fair with Andy, picking up brochures and snacks from groups he had no intention of joining but didn't know how to reject.

There were inflatable slides, dunk tanks, and carts for cotton candy and snow cones. After lunch with his dorm, Mason started a game of ultimate frisbee behind the Biblical Studies building. For two hours, Gabriel sprinted back and forth until his legs were Jello and his shirt was soaked with sweat.

After a shower and dinner, Gabriel followed a stream of students to the field in front of the Student Union. A thirty-foot movie screen had been set up to show *Indiana Jones and the Last Crusade*. A timer counted down from ten minutes. Gabriel stood in the center of the field, trying not to look lost as he waited for Andy to show up.

Andy texted him a few minutes later: *I'm going to be late. I had to go to the store.*

All good, Gabriel sent back. He sighed and tucked his phone into his pocket. He did a quick survey for anyone he knew. A girl on his left kept looking at him, so he pulled out his phone and pretended to be texting.

"Hey!"

Gabriel looked up. The girl waved at him, smiling.

"Want to sit with us?" She asked.

"Uh…"

"Are you waiting for someone?"

Gabriel looked at his phone again and shook his head.

"Come on," she said, patting the slim patch of blanket on her right.

Gabriel shuffled over and sat down in the grass.

"I'm Jenna," she said, scooting over to give Gabriel room on the blanket. Their knees and shoulders touched, but Jenna didn't seem to notice. She had short brown hair that brushed her ears and glasses with clear frames. She seemed completely at ease in a grey sweatshirt that was three sizes too big, and there was a playfulness in her smile that made Gabriel impulsively smile back.

On Jenna's left were Darcey and Addy, but they were too involved in observing nearby guys to pay much attention to Gabriel.

"Ooo, check him out," Darcey said, pointing somewhere ahead and to the right. "Blue sweater, glasses."

Gabriel spied the guy traversing the crowd. He was alone, but he did it in a way that wasn't nervous. He paused to run his hand through his hair and survey the crowd.

"We should talk to him," Darcey said.

"Absolutely," Addy said.

They jumped up without saying goodbye.

"Sorry about them," Jenna said, watching them trail in the wake of the mystery guy.

"They seem nice," Gabriel said. He casually leaned back, acutely aware it was just him and Jenna and barely an inch between them. "How long before one of them starts dating him?"

Jenna scrunched her nose. "A few days?"

"And until they break up?"

"A few weeks, probably."

Gabriel nodded, smiling.

"Can't blame them, though," Jenna said, looking over. "Everyone knows all the good people are taken in the first week."

"*Everyone* knows that," Gabriel agreed.

"What about you?"

"Me?"

"Do you have a girlfriend?"

Gabriel shook his head, keeping his smile on. "Do you?"

Jenna laughed. "Noooo."

"Ah, just checking. You never know."

Jenna grimaced. They lapsed into silence as they watched Darcey and the mystery guy talk in front of the projector screen. The timer had less than a minute remaining. Addy was nowhere in sight.

The movie started, and Gabriel sat up to wrap his arms around his knees. He focused intently on the screen, but his mind spun, unable to focus. Jenna leaned in every few minutes to comment on the film, and he laughed and made his own jokes.

And in the strobing light of the screen, their arms touching every few minutes, Gabriel felt something akin to affection. It might have been the excitement of being at college. It could have been all the new people. Or maybe it was Jenna and all the prospects of what this chance encounter could mean for his future.

SIGNS FROM GOD

GABRIEL'S EYES SNAPPED open as a door slammed in the hallway. He burrowed under his covers. Last night, he'd stayed up until 1 a.m. with Andy and Micah, playing Mario Kart and talking about girls.

But that didn't mean he could skip church the first week. He had to show God he was devoted and thankful.

Groaning, Gabriel rolled out of bed. Once showered and dressed, he walked ten minutes with a group of upperclassmen—Grant, Stephen, and Ricky—to their local church. It was a brick building with a white steeple piercing the sky, and it had the stuffy feel of a small town church. Wooden pews. Stained glass. Middle-aged congregants. Gabriel fiddled with his Bible, only opening it twice when the pastor highlighted important verses.

After the service, they got lunch at the diner in town. It was a red and white building that bustled with activity. Gabriel ordered hash browns, poached eggs, and biscuits and gravy. For a while, all they did was attack their food.

Grant sat back, sipping his coffee. "What are your thoughts on the sermon?"

"I'm trying to think. It was really good..." Gabriel offered, brow furrowed in pretend concentration. He'd perfected this art years ago: Talking about the sermon without saying anything of note. It was the art of someone who rarely paid attention.

The others grunted in agreement.

"The topic of being a good neighbor is especially relevant for us right now," Stephen said. "We're all in the same dorm, so it's about ensuring we're respectful, cleaning up after ourselves…"

"Building each other up," Gabriel supplied.

Perfect. Now, he could sit back and tune out.

Ricky nodded. "Making sure we're pointing towards God, keeping each other accountable."

"That's exactly what I wrote down," Grant said, holding back a satisfied smile. "How do we do that? What should our response be if we see a brother going into sin?"

"We have to confront it," Stephen said with conviction. "First, we go to the person and share the truth. If that doesn't work, we find someone else to help. Finally, we bring it to a higher authority. That would be the RD or the President, someone who can remove the person from school."

Gabriel navigated his plate, scraping up his remaining hash browns.

Grant nodded. "What kinds of sins do we need to look out for?"

"We want to be uplifting, so staying away from music about drugs or…sex," Stephen said, dropping his eyes. "The same goes with movies. Most R-rated films today are just drugs and porn."

Gabriel breathed in a piece of egg. He coughed violently and pounded his chest. He gulped down water.

"You good?" Grant asked, patting his back.

Gabriel waved off the looks of concern. He wiped his watering eyes. "I don't know if that's true," he squeaked. He coughed again.

"There's plenty of good R-rated movies. *Gladiator, Saving Private Ryan*—"

"But the violence is excessive, right?" Stephen said, looking around the table. Grant nodded along.

Rickey pursed his lips uncertainly. "They *are* war movies."

"But it's not glorifying to God. That's what I'm saying," Stephen said.

"*The Passion of the Christ?*" Gabriel asked, and he knew he had them.

It was the one R-rated movie Christian parents *encouraged* their kids to watch, often at twelve or thirteen. The kids Gabriel grew up with bragged about who had seen it at the youngest age. Some were as young as seven or eight.

"I just think we should be careful about what we're watching and listening to," Stephen said.

"And what should you do if someone admits a sin to you?" Grant asked, directing the conversation again.

"Depends on what it is, but I'd keep pointing them to God. If someone's struggling with a porn addiction, you should be keeping them accountable. You should check in every day. Get internet monitoring software. Study verses on purity," Stephen said.

Grant nodded along. "That's excellent. And I'm not saying any-one here struggles with that, but come on," he raised his hands and gave them a knowing look, "we're all guys here. There's so many beautiful women around. We can't help but have thoughts."

This drew a tense laugh from the table, and there were uncom-fortable nods and faint smiles. Tension lined every movement, and eyes wouldn't meet for more than a split second.

"But if anyone *does* struggle with that, there are support groups that help break the addiction. Even if it's a few times a week, it has to be dealt with. God doesn't have any tolerance for these sorts of things. Sexual sin struggles are the worst kind," Grant said, receiving a hearty round of grunting from the table, Gabriel offering his voice so as not to be singled out. "I want everyone here to know we're all brothers. You can share anything, and we'll help you through it."

Somber looks overtook Ricky and Steven's faces. Gabriel focused on his plate. The vice on his lungs tightened, and the sharp pain between his ribs twisted. He fought to keep his mind blank, as if they could read his thoughts or see the vague images of half-naked men behind his eyes.

GABRIEL SPENT THE rest of the afternoon walking the campus to find his classes. It would be a zig-zag path every day, but he'd have to make it work. Next semester, he'd make sure to plan a better schedule. That evening, almost everyone in Gabriel's hall gathered in front of Grant's room. Gabriel skirted the group.

Andy waved him down. "Coming to dinner?"

"I'm meeting Jenna," Gabriel said, hands raised apologetically.

"Have fun with your girlfriend!" Andy called after him.

"We're just friends," Gabriel shouted over his shoulder, nearly crashing into Jason, who was coming out of the bathroom. They exchanged *sorrys*.

"Gabriel has a girlfriend?" Mason asked down the hall.

"Pretty much," Andy said.

The rest of the conversation was lost as Gabriel pushed through the doors into the lobby. As much as he didn't want people talking about his potential love life, Gabriel couldn't help but relish the feeling of importance.

He met Jenna outside the cafeteria, where they exchanged a tentative hug and got in line to scan their IDs.

She *tsked*. "You're late."

"Only because you were early, so *technically* it's your fault."

"Ah, classic gaslighting. Nice."

"I do my best."

They entered the cafeteria.

"What did you do today?" Jenna asked.

And they were off, talking about what classes they were taking and plans for decorating their rooms. Every few minutes, Gabriel glanced at her and asked himself that impossible question: *Could she be the one?*

Maybe God hadn't forgotten him after all.

Maybe she was the answer to his prayers.

ON THE TOPIC OF HERESY

GABRIEL'S FIRST CLASS in the morning was Spiritual Formation. He took absentminded bites from an energy bar and merged into the flow of students, raw excitement gnawing at his bones. The classroom was in the Biblical Studies building on the west side of the lake. It had five rows of desks that curved toward the front of the room. Not wanting to impose himself on anyone, he chose a seat in the third row on the right. He removed his spiral notebook and a pen and relaxed in his chair.

A man in his late thirties stood at the front of the classroom, locked into his computer on the podium. He wore a fitted, powder blue dress shirt, the sleeves rolled up and the top buttons undone. His dirty blond hair had been parted to the side, and he sported a trimmed beard.

"Mind if I sit here?" someone asked on Gabriel's right.

"Go for it," Gabriel said, looking over.

The boy had messy black hair, but not unruly. He wore a loose-fitting long-sleeve and round tortoiseshell glasses. He retrieved his notebook and pencil case and extended a hand to Gabriel.

"I'm Luca," he said.

Gabriel introduced himself, and they shook hands. Luca had piercing blue eyes, but there was a softness to them that drew Gabriel in.

And for a fraction of a second, there was nothing but quiet.

Just…stillness. Somehow. And it was the kind of quiet that came from inside. The kind that contained the entire world in this single, perfect second.

Luca's eyes drifted from Gabriel, shattering the calm. The noise of the classroom flooded Gabriel's ears. He inhaled sharply and gripped the edge of the table.

"You alright?" Luca asked.

Gabriel released the table. "Just nervous."

It took Luca a moment to respond. "I get nervous, too."

It was a simple statement, but those words usually didn't carry the weight of how they sounded coming from Luca's mouth. He caught Gabriel's eye and he gave an imperceptible smile.

It was here Gabriel's spirit whispered, *this one's important.*

Luca flipped through his notebook. Gabriel searched his mind for something to say, but all his clever thoughts were nowhere to be found.

"What are you studying?" Gabriel asked, going with the only question in his brain.

"Graphic design, and I'm minoring in film studies," Luca said.

"Wow, that's…really cool actually."

"What about you?"

"Business Management."

"Ah, that's good! You can do a lot with that."

"Everyone says that," Gabriel said. "I don't know what that's supposed to mean."

They were quiet, and Gabriel feared he'd killed the moment. He scrambled for something to say. "Can I see some of your designs?"

Luca smiled, and Gabriel felt a shimmer of warmth. Luca retrieved his phone, found a photo album he'd named POSTERS, and handed it over. Gabriel did a quick scroll while Luca hovered over his shoulder.

Gabriel stopped and selected one in the middle of the roll. It was a grainy, black-and-white photograph of Collin Firth. It only showed his upper half and had a blurry background. On the left was the title in thin white font: *A Single Man*.

"Everyone, find your seats, please," the professor said above the din of conversation.

Gabriel rubbed his forehead. "Wow."

Luca's body tensed. "Yeah, it's…one of my favorite movies."

"What's it about?"

Luca hesitated as a girl took the open seat on Gabriel's left. Gabriel glanced at her, then at the guy to Luca's right, and the people in front and behind them. He settled back into his chair and let the subject drop.

"Alright, it's time to get started," the professor said, walking around the podium to face the room. "I'm Charlie O'Brien. I'm one of the *many* professors of theology here." He paused as the room rippled with chuckles. "Technically, I have a doctorate in New Testament Literature, but I'm not particular with titles. You can call me Doctor, Professor, Mr. O'Brien—whatever works for you. I want this class to be about thoughtful discussion and understanding things from other perspectives. If you have any questions about the Bible or other teachings, I'd love to unpack that as a class. I'm expecting you all to participate…yes, blue shirt."

A boy in the second row on the left put his hand down. "Is that graded?"

"As long as you sign in and do your best to participate, you'll get full participation credit," Professor O'Brien said. He took the next thirty minutes to review the syllabus and class expectations.

"Your last assignment is a paper. Everyone write this down," Professor O'Brien said, turning to the whiteboard. "I want you to answer the question, *what do I believe?*" He scrawled it on the board in neat green letters. Then he wrote *why?* below and underlined it. "I want you to explore the reason you believe that. Although this is a Baptist school, people come from all different religious backgrounds, so I want to know what it is you believe, *if* you even believe anything."

If?

Gabriel leaned forward. He'd never had the option *not* to believe.

"You can take this in any direction you want. You can talk about your family, whether you grew up in the church or not. I want to hear your ideas on big topics like heaven and hell, what things don't make sense to you, the nature of sin, old earth and new earth, evolution… whatever you want. This is a personal essay, so make it personal. *Don't* write what you think I want to hear."

The classroom rippled with whispers. Professor O'Brien focused on his computer. He looked up after a minute. "I won't be sharing these with anyone else. And to be clear, I don't want to know all your secrets. This is just an opportunity to bring light to things few people discuss."

The class buzzed with conversation as they were let out a few minutes early. Gabriel packed his things, simultaneously excited and nervous. This whole assignment seemed borderline heretical.

Luca said goodbye, and Gabriel watched him leave. He wished to keep talking—to find out the movie's subject, but he'd already forgotten the title.

No matter. He could ask next time.

GABRIEL HAD FUNDAMENTALS of Speech next, which was sure to promise an anxiety attack at some point this semester. The class ended late, and Gabriel rushed to chapel where he sat with Jenna. At lunch, he navigated the cafeteria alone, searching for familiar faces. At the end of his lap, he spotted Jason sitting with two other guys. Gabriel thought he recognized them from his hall, but he hadn't talked to them yet.

"Mind if I join you?" Gabriel asked, coming up to the group.

"Yeah, sure," Jason said, and Gabriel settled on his left.

The boys across the table introduced themselves as Arlo and Hunter. Arlo had dark skin, short bleached hair, and a blue hoodie. Hunter was pale, red-haired, and wore a car mechanic's T-shirt with the name Tom on it.

"They're in room one-ten in our dorm," Jason said. Gabriel nodded.

"She was a bitch, though," Hunter said, diving back into the conversation Gabriel interrupted.

"Right?" Arlo exclaimed.

"Who was?" Gabriel asked through a bite of his burrito.

"Some RA in chapel saw my nose ring and wrote me up," Arlo said.

"Why?"

"Apparently guys can't wear facial jewelry," Arlo said.

"But you *can* be a bitch," Hunter offered.

"So…" Jason said with a leading voice, glancing at Gabriel. "You have a girlfriend already?"

Gabriel sighed as Arlo and Hunter's attention turned fully to him. "She's just a friend."

"That you got *dinner* with," Jason pointed out.

"So?"

"It's not nothing," Hunter said with a shrug.

"I guess."

"And he doesn't even care," Hunter said approvingly. "Some people are so desperate. Grant cornered me yesterday to talk about how he's trying to get married before he graduates. He's not even *dating* anyone."

"Yeah, no shit. He's got the personality of a *ferret*," Jason said.

"Kind of looks like one, too," Gabriel said. "Just really overweight."

Jason barked out a laugh and covered his mouth with a hand. Arlo and Hunter grinned. They spent the rest of lunch comparing their hall mates to animals. When Gabriel checked the time, he realized he had two minutes to get to his next class. He scrambled to his feet, said goodbye, and set off at a brisk pace. He refused to run. He'd seen one guy sprinting to the cafeteria earlier today and heard everyone snickering in his wake.

He slowed down as he neared his classroom, taking deep breaths to not seem winded. The professor had already begun talking. Gabriel slipped through the doorway and found a spot on the end of the third row.

"The last one has arrived!" He exclaimed, consulting a sheet of paper on his desk. "Gabriel, is it?"

"Yes."

"Get lost trying to find us?"

"Lost track of time."

"Ah, well, try not to be late in the future," the professor said, jovial. He might have been in his fifties, but he had a youthful presence and was moderately fit. He had a brown goatee and wavy hair that brushed his ears.

"I'm Professor Davis," he said, handing Gabriel an extra syllabus before returning to the front of the classroom. "As I was saying, this is Freshman Composition, but don't let that fool you. It's one of the hardest classes in the English major—second only to Advanced Composition, which I also happen to teach. How many of you are English majors?"

Half the classroom raised their hands.

"Awesome, you guys will be stuck with me for the next few years. Everyone else, tough luck on the professor assignment," Professor Davis said with a smile. Despite the proclamation of doom, he drew a handle of chuckles from the group. "I'll say it now: I'm one of the toughest graders in the department, but I want to bring out the best in you. Whether you're studying English or Business or Nursing, I want you all to be excellent writers."

"Is it too late to transfer classes?" A guy asked on Gabriel's left.

"Oh, you're doomed," Professor Davis said with a gravelly voice, then broke into another smile. "You'll be fine. Who likes movies?" Hands immediately went up around the room. "Brilliant. I have a list of foreign films picked out, and most of your assignments this se-mester will be based on the film you choose to study."

Professor Davis explained they would be writing four papers based on a single movie. There would be a theme essay, compare and contrast, a critique, and then a research paper about how the culture behind the film influenced the story.

"If you're late turning in a paper and don't go to the writing center to review it, you'll be lucky to get a C in the class. You English majors need that to pass," Professor David said.

Gabriel swallowed uncertainly. He looked around the classroom. Grim expressions lined every face. Professor Davis didn't seem to notice, and he began playing movie trailers. Only one caught Gabriel's eye: *Calvary*. It was an Irish film about a priest who receives a death threat from someone in his church. Out of fourteen students, Gabriel was the only one who volunteered to watch it.

"It's not an easy watch," Professor Davis warned. "Gabriel, I'll let you pick another movie if you don't like it. But I'm excited to hear what you think."

"Me too, thanks," Gabriel said.

"If you have a DVD player, all of these films are available at the library," Professor Davis said to the class at large.

Gabriel didn't have a DVD player, but he went to the library anyway to study. Mottled grey carpeting covered the floor. Tables formed a grid, shelves beyond. Study rooms lined the walls.

Curious to see what he was getting into, Gabriel located the movies on the basement floor and pulled *Calvary* off the shelf. He checked the back of the DVD and zeroed in on the R rating.

Sexual references, language, violence, and drug use.

He smiled.

Perfect.

VERSES

GABRIEL'S SECOND DAY of classes was less interesting than the first, but he and Andy had Principles of Biology together. They sat next to each other in the massive lecture hall. Andy amused himself by doodling in his textbook.

"Notes for the next person," he explained in a whisper.

"You're going to get in trouble when you turn it back in," Gabriel whispered back.

Andy shrugged and continued drawing a rather long penis on a Giraffe in the middle of the Sahara Desert.

Wednesday morning, Gabriel and Mason got scrambled eggs and bagels again.

"How have the first few days been?" Mason asked, digging into his plate.

"Not bad. I'm looking forward to the year."

"That's good. How do you feel like you're fitting in?"

Gabriel tilted his head from side to side. "Jason's nice. Andy's fun. I've met a few others here and there."

"That's great, community is important. I'm starting an ultimate frisbee team if you want to join."

"Yeah?"

"I think Andy, Grant, and a few others will play. Maybe you can invite your *friend*," Mason said, wiggling his eyebrows.

"Uh…sure. Sounds fun."

Mason examined his bagel. His expression grew serious. "Not to get too deep, but…how's your relationship with God?"

Gabriel chewed slowly. He reached for his chocolate milk. "It's good, I think," he said, adopting a thoughtful expression. "I try to read the Bible when I can, and go to church, pray—"

"And chapel."

"Can't forget chapel."

"I love that it's five days a week."

"Yeah," Gabriel said, then grimaced. "I mean, five days does seem like a lot."

"Nah, you get used to it. You're going to need it to keep you out of trouble."

Gabriel gave a strained chuckle. "I guess."

"I know *I* need it," Mason said. "My mind is a *swamp*. It's just girls *all the time*—fighting temptation. But I'm glad I have my girlfriend. Otherwise, who knows what I'd be doing."

"Sure," Gabriel said in a non-committal way.

"It's hard in a relationship, like how far do you go? I'm kind of glad it's long distance. I'm just so…*charged* all the time, you know? I don't know if I'd be able to control myself if she was around all the time," Mason said, shaking his head. Gabriel nodded along, tension filling his body. "But protecting our minds is the best defense against sin."

"Hmm," Gabriel offered.

"Would you want to memorize verses with me?"

Gabriel's insides twisted.

"I haven't done that in years," Gabriel said, flashing back to reciting verses in Sunday school. He wondered if he still remembered Psalm 91.

"All the more reason to start."

"I don't know."

"Come on, it'll be fun! We can make it a competition."

Gabriel didn't know how to get out of this. "Yeah, I guess."

"Brilliant!" Mason reached over the table and shook Gabriel's arms with excitement. Gabriel gave a tight smile, looking at Mason's hands. Mason pulled back and composed himself, focusing on his food. "Try to come up with some verses or passages today, and we can go from there."

"Today?"

"We can meet before the Grant's testimony."

"Sorry, what?"

"Grant is giving his testimony in the hall tonight. Just sharing about his life, his walk with God, his struggles…it's really powerful. He started it last year, and everyone in the hall shared their testimony throughout the semester. Grant should be sending an email about it today."

"Oh," Gabriel said.

"You're going to be there, right?"

"I think so," Gabriel said, suddenly wishing he had an excuse to avoid the dorm tonight.

"Awesome. You don't want to miss it."

Gabriel nodded, quite sure that he *did*.

THAT EVENING, GABRIEL crawled on his bed to watch the movie for English Composition when he heard a knock on his door.

"What's up?" Gabriel said.

Mason opened the door. "I'm ready if you are."

"For what?"

"We were going to choose what passage we wanted to memorize."

What the hell.

Gabriel rubbed his forehead and looked at his computer. "Sorry, I forgot."

"That's fine. I picked out a few sections already."

Gabriel swallowed his sudden, blinding anger. Being interrupted was one thing, but to memorize verses? He couldn't think of anything he wanted to do less. He shut his eyes and took a moment to compose himself. He closed his computer.

"Alright," Gabriel said, crawling to the edge of the bed.

Mason smiled and fully entered the room. He plopped on the floor. Gabriel retrieved his Bible from the shelf.

"I have everything marked in here," Mason said, waving his Bible. "If you want to share."

"I'll just use my own," Gabriel said, sitting across from Mason.

Mason opened his Bible and flipped to the first passage marked with a sticky note. "I thought James One was really good. Verses two through eighteen."

Gabriel started to open his Bible, but Mason handed his over. Gabriel reluctantly took it and began reading to himself.

Consider it pure joy, my brothers and sisters, whenever you face trials of many kinds...

Gabriel grimaced, a sick feeling settling in his gut. He was familiar with the passage, but the more he read, the more agitated he became. And when he got to verse twelve, he could hardly keep still.

...Blessed is the one who perseveres under trial because, having stood the test, that person will receive the crown of life that the Lord has promised to those who love him...

Gabriel felt no comfort from the verse, just a trapped feeling in his chest. He finished the passage and looked up.

"Good, right?" Mason asked, taking the Bible and flipping to the next selection.

Gabriel read this one. And the one after that. They were all about facing trials and turning away from temptations. Mason watched him closely as he read, which made it hard to focus. When he finished, they talked about which one was their favorite. Gabriel just reflected what Mason said. He no longer cared what they picked because he didn't want to do it anymore. Mason chose James 1 and set a goal to have the first three verses memorized by this time next week.

"I'm glad we're doing this," Mason said, standing up. "Everyone should be meeting in my room soon."

"I'll be there in a minute," Gabriel said.

Mason squeezed Gabriel's arm and left. Gabriel shut the door. He felt like a stretched rubber band, ready to snap. The room was too small. He paced back and forth, shaking his hands at his sides.

He should want to do this. He should *want* to memorize verses to be closer to God. But none of it felt right. Gabriel kept pacing. He could only take six strides before he had to turn on a heel and go the other way. He did this a couple of times, then looked at the window. He drew the blinds and went back to circling the room.

Another lap, and he bent down, getting into a push-up position. He did seventeen before he couldn't do any more. After a minute's rest, he did another set. He barely got to thirteen. His arms trembled.

Things weren't so cluttered when he stood up. The room expanded. Gabriel rubbed his biceps.

Was this how it felt to work out?

Maybe he should start.

Gabriel drank water and steeled himself before marching down the hall for Grant's testimony.

THE REST OF the week went by quickly. He continued talking with Luca before classes, and they exchanged numbers so they could ask questions about homework. Gabriel soon found out that Luca was also living in Milton, but he was on the third floor, so they didn't have much chance to run into each other.

Professor Davis checked in with the class to see if anyone had started their papers. Only two people had.

"Come on, this isn't something you want to put off," he said.

Gabriel shrank in his seat, consulting his planner again. Maybe he'd watch *Calvary* tonight. After English, he found an empty study booth on the bottom floor of the library. It was a tiny room, maybe four feet on each side, and a small desk was on the wall opposite the door.

Gabriel set up the movie and leaned back, headphones in.

The first shot opened on the priest—Brenden Gleeson—in a confession booth. He had a full beard, streaked with white and red. Out of frame, someone settled into the other side of the booth. The priest opened the partition, but the camera stayed focused on him.

He waited.

"I first tasted semen when I was seven years old," a man said in an Irish accent.

Shit.

Gabriel paused the movie. He rubbed his face and looked around the tiny study booth. Bracing himself, he pressed Play.

The camera never wavered from the priest, and the characters exchanged a few lines. The other man said, *"I was raped by a priest when I was seven years old."*

Gabriel's stomach turned as the man explained what had happened to him for the following five years. Gabriel bit a knuckle, fist clenched in front of his face.

"*There's no point in killing a bad priest, but killing a good one? That'll be a shock. They wouldn't know what to make of that,*" the man said. The priest's brow furrowed in confusion. "*I'm going to kill you, Father. I'm going to kill you because you've done nothing wrong…*"

THE FIRST STRAND

THIS IS THE kind of story you know will not have a happy ending, but you *have* to watch on the off chance it does.

Gabriel is paralyzed at the crescendo. He can't breathe. He hopes for what cannot be as two men and a gun meet on a windswept beach in an attempt to reconcile the impossible.

No. You can hope all you want, but some people just don't get a happy ending.

KNOW THIS:

The right story at the right time has the power to change the course of a life. But this might be the wrong story for Gabriel. It might be the wrong time.

Because there has been a years-long numbness in his mind, his soul—a kind of floating resignation and a penchant for separating the difficult parts of life into neat little boxes. This keeps the worst at bay. It is the only way to live in contradiction.

He prefers this kind of numbness to facing what cannot be faced.

But, like all things, it will not last forever.

At the end, Gabriel sat, overcome with shock and rage and *hurt*.

And truth.

On the slow walk back to his dorm, his ears rang with the pleading of a man who had experienced such terrible pain, such suffering from the one thing that was supposed to bring comfort and peace.

Didn't he know something about that?

A frayed strand in his chest gave way. It parted from itself, and the barrier between him and everything he couldn't look at trembled.

This is how a heart begins to break.

I WANT TO KNOW WHO YOU ARE

THE MILTON HALL barbecue occurred two weeks into the semester.

Gabriel arrived at the first-floor common area where RAs pre-pared foil containers of hotdogs and hamburgers and set out lettuce, tomatoes, cheese, and condiments. Gabriel headed for the courtyard behind the dorm. There were already dozens of students milling about. The two picnic tables were filled, and a handful of people watched the RD as he talked about grilling the perfect burger.

Gabriel spied Jason with Arlo and Hunter in the distance. Andy and Micah played corn hole with two others. Mason and other upperclassmen threw a frisbee in the empty street behind the dorm. Gabriel selected a Sprite from one of the coolers and headed for Andy's group. They were in the middle of a game, so Gabriel contin-ued to search the crowd.

Luca soon emerged from the dorm entrance and everything brightened. Gabriel waved and Luca shuffled over, hands in his pockets. He wore a cream long sleeve with a green pocket and blue pants with rolled cuffs. Gabriel introduced Andy and Micah.

"What's with the long sleeves?" Gabriel asked. "It's like eighty degrees out."

"I just don't want to embarrass anyone with my oversized biceps," Luca said smoothly, a smile playing on his lips. Then a flicker of something buried.

"Ah, is that it?" Gabriel asked, playfully squeezing Luca's arm between two fingers. He felt strong. Luca flinched.

"If you're ripped under there, the rest of us don't stand a chance," Andy said, jumping in. He had his hands on his hips, intently watching Micah throw his first bag.

"Doubt it," Luca said.

"Are you serious? You look great, you…" Gabriel cut himself off. He sipped his soda. Luca scratched his nose, but there was a twinkle in his eyes.

They watched the game. Luca looked down at himself, tugging the cuff of a sleeve.

"I don't like T-shirts," Luca said.

"What?" Gabriel asked.

Luca gave Gabriel a furtive glance. "I don't like the feel of T-shirts."

"That's fair," Gabriel said, and he had the distinct impression there was more to it than that. He didn't press the matter.

A piercing whistle silenced the crowd, and all eyes turned to the RD—a burly man with a black beard and wavy hair. "Let's pray before we serve the food."

Heads bowed as the RD blessed the meal. Gabriel stole glances around. Luca had his eyes fixed on the sky. The prayer ended and the crowd surged forward. Gabriel selected a hot dog and burger, smothering them both in ketchup and mustard, adding cheese and a reluctant piece of lettuce to the burger. He, Luca, and Andy found an open patch of grass and sat down.

"Gabriel, how's your girlfriend doing?" Andy asked.

Luca looked up, mouth full. Gabriel waved him off. "She's just a friend."

"That's what they all say."

"Believe it or don't," Gabriel said.

"Do you have a girlfriend?" Andy asked Luca.

"I'm not looking right now," Luca said.

"Last to get one is the gay one," Andy said.

Gabriel stopped chewing. He reached for his soda. An unconscious part of him knew he had to say something. "Sucks to be you then."

Andy laughed it off.

"Why is that so important though?" Gabriel asked. "Why does everyone keep asking if we have girlfriends?"

"I don't know, some people just love love, I guess," Andy said. He abruptly stood up. "Hold on, Micah got me a seat at the table."

They watched him leave. Gabriel opened his bag of Doritos.

"I get it," Luca said. "Everyone's obsessed about dating."

"Especially here," Gabriel said.

"Ring by spring."

"And maybe a kid, too, if you're lucky."

Luca snorted. "I wish I could just *be*, you know? Why does that have to be defined by someone else?"

"Exactly."

"Have you ever dated anyone?"

Gabriel grimaced, embarrassed. "No."

"Same."

"Really?"

"I've never been that interested."

"Yeah…" Gabriel said, pouring the rest of his chip crumbs into his hand. "I just don't know what that's supposed to feel like. There are girls I like, but I don't know if I *like* them."

"That probably means you don't. And I think you know it when you feel it," Luca said, meeting Gabriel's gaze. "Something about the person. How they make you feel. And it just *makes sense.*"

Gabriel had forgotten his half-eaten burger because he was sinking with things he didn't want to understand.

Luca looked away with a shrug. "But what do I know?"

"More than Andy, no doubt."

"Well, *that's* obvious," Luca said, wiping his hands on a napkin and leaning back. He looked at Gabriel again. He had a way of doing that, of making it feel like you weren't being watched so much as *seen.* "I think you notice more than people realize."

"I think it's just about looking closely."

"But you have to know what to look for."

"And what's that?"

Luca scrunched his nose. "Nothing I can describe."

They lapsed into silence.

"Do you know what you're going to write for your paper?" Luca asked.

"No idea."

"Neither do I." Luca leaned forward, putting his forearms on his crossed legs. "What do you believe?"

Gabriel considered this. "All of it, I guess. The Bible. Everything in it. Heaven, hell…sin…but…" Luca looked at him patiently. "I don't know. It's just what I grew up with."

"What kind of church did you go to?"

"Not like this. Charismatic. Pretty out there."

"Those are the wild people, yeah?"

"You could say that."

"Like healings and stuff?"

"And speaking in tongues, resurrections, prophesy, demonic possession…"

"Wow."

"And I think I believe it. I *do*. It's just…"

"Up here," Luca supplied, pointing to his temple, then to his chest. "But not really here."

Gabriel nodded, face twisted. "I've just never seen anyone be healed, and everyone says God talks to them, like *really* talks, and I don't know what that's like. Is it a feeling? Words?"

"I couldn't tell you," Luca said, looking back to the sky. "My family is full of strict Baptists, so it's pretty different."

"What's that like?"

"A lot of rules, really. Not as much heart."

"Ah."

"Does it ever bother you that there are so many denominations? I wouldn't say I believe in healings, and speaking in tongues makes me uncomfortable," Luca said, and Gabriel just nodded. "But that's *gospel* to your church. And baptism for my church is *the* thing, but a lot of churches couldn't care less about it."

"So…who's right in the end?"

"Exactly, and maybe none of them are."

Gabriel watched the people playing corn hole. This was a dangerous line of conversation. He ripped at the grass, jaw clenching.

"I'm sorry," Luca said. "Sometimes I should stop talking."

"No, don't. I just haven't really questioned things before."

Luca watched him for a moment. "Because you're scared of what you'll find out?"

Gabriel couldn't even nod. He just pursed his lips, looking away.

"We don't have to talk about this anymore," Luca said. "We hardly know each other."

"But I feel like I've known you for a while," Gabriel said quietly.

Luca tilted his head. "You keep a lot inside, don't you?"

"And you thought I was the observant one?"

"I never said I wasn't."

"That's true."

"But I like you. I want to get to know you. I want to know who you are."

Gabriel smothered a smile by biting the inside of his lip. "You too."

They returned to watching, and Gabriel's mind raced with their conversation. He'd never allowed himself to voice his uncertainty. And now that he had, it felt all too real.

SO MUCH, NOT ENOUGH

ON A SATURDAY evening at the end of September, they had their first Open Dorms. These nights were rare and short, and it was the only time someone from the opposite sex was allowed into your room.

Jason was out for the night, so Gabriel and Jenna got burgers from the Union and headed to his room to watch a movie. They had to follow strict rules—doors open, lights on, no laying on beds—but Gabriel felt he had to take advantage of the opportunity.

Jenna gave her ID to the RAs operating the desk at the dorm entrance and wrote down who she was visiting. Walking his hall, Gabriel and Jenna received second looks from everyone they passed. Gabriel set his food on his desk in his room and plugged in the white Christmas lights that lined the ceiling. Jenna made herself at home by sitting on the floor.

"Nice place," she said appreciatively.

"Hey!" Andy shouted from across the hall. Jenna's head jerked toward the disturbance. "You bring someone over and you don't say hi?"

Andy appeared in the doorway. Two girls stood behind him, and Micah was in front of their TV, setting it up. The girls introduced themselves as Julie and Tara.

"Hi?" Gabriel offered.

"Too late," Andy said, shaking his head. "Want to watch a movie with us?"

Gabriel and Jenna exchanged a look. They'd made plans for just the two of them, but Gabriel didn't know if he wanted the pressure of an evening alone.

"Sounds good to me," Gabriel said.

Jenna shrugged. "Yeah, sure."

Andy's room was now thoroughly crowded with six people inside, and it instantly smelled like French fries from Gabriel and Jenna's food. He and Jenna sat on the floor, with Julie on Jenna's left. Micah lounged on the top bunk. Andy and Tara sat on the lower bunk.

Gabriel picked up his phone to see a text from Luca.

What are you doing tonight?

Watching a movie with some people in 115. You should come down

Nice, I'll be there in a few minutes

"I think Luca's going to join if that's alright," Gabriel said to the room at large.

"Sounds good, man," Andy said, distracted by the TV.

Jenna picked at her fries. "Who's Luca?"

"A friend from class. He's on the third floor," Gabriel pointed to the ceiling.

"Oh," Jenna said.

She leaned away from Gabriel and began scrolling through

Instagram. Wait, was he messing things up?

Luca floated through the doorway, and Gabriel's reservations faded. He sat on Gabriel's right, their arms almost touching. Jenna leaned forward, examining him with a neutral expression. She introduced herself, but she didn't ask him any questions. Her phone stole her attention again.

For a long while, everyone suggested movies, but no one could agree on what to watch. Gabriel's food was long gone when they settled on *Back to the Future*.

"I made a poster for this, too," Luca said.

"Yeah?" Gabriel glanced at him. "Can I see it?"

Luca brought up the image on his phone. It was like a scrapbook page, with cut-out images of the DeLorean, Marty McFly, and Marty's skateboard pasted to the canvas.

Gabriel grinned. "This is amazing."

He showed Jenna and she nodded, only saying, "Cool."

Gabriel frowned, and he felt the tug of guilt. He shouldn't have agreed to join Andy's group. He should have just sat with Jenna and no one else and left Luca out of it.

He was supposed to be thinking about his future.

He was supposed to be looking for a wife.

Why was that so difficult?

By the end of the first month, Gabriel had settled into a routine.

Sundays, he joined Grant's group for church, and they always ate at the diner afterward to discuss the message. Gabriel didn't particularly enjoy it, but he knew how to turn his thoughts inward when he needed to. Every chapel, he sat with Jenna, Darcey, and Addy—plus Luca, now—and he got lunch with them on Tuesdays and Thursdays.

Monday, Wednesday, and Friday, he had lunch with Andy, Jason, and Arlo. Reluctantly, Gabriel ate breakfast with Mason most days, and Mason eventually convinced him to attend an off-campus prayer night called The Gathering.

Every Thursday night, roughly twenty-five students crammed into Ben Salazar's living room. The house was a ten-minute walk from Gabriel's dorm. Ben—a Biblical Studies major—led the meetings by sharing a short message. Three other students guided everyone in worship before and after the message. And then everyone mingled and talked about how good God was.

From his first meeting, Gabriel's guard was raised.

He knew exactly who these people were. They were the ones with broad smiles and searching questions, but no real interest in *you*. These were the kind of people who rushed from one conversation to the next, with constant shouts across the room of, "Love you, man! Let's get coffee soon."

Only a few people seemed fully present, and one of them was Ben. He had a certain presence that drew you in with the steady pull of a sun's gravity. Before you knew it, you'd talked about nothing in particular for ten minutes, but it *felt* important. It felt like he saw who you were. And when he offered to meet with you, he said it in a quiet way that made you know it was genuine.

Meanwhile, Gabriel and Mason continued memorizing verses. It was Gabriel's least favorite activity of the week, but he didn't know how to get out of it. And for some reason, the words wouldn't stick in his head. It didn't make sense. He'd memorized whole chapters before, and lines for plays. Maybe what made it difficult was his strong desire *not* to memorize the verses. Maybe he didn't care about that anymore. It never seemed to change anything. Or maybe it was the frozen feeling he got around Mason.

Near the end of September, Gabriel worked at his desk, headphones in as he tried to forget his meeting with Mason. He was so focused he nearly jumped out of his chair when Mason appeared at his side and tapped him on the shoulder.

"Ready?" Mason asked, Bible in hand.

Jason looked them over. He was watching TV at his desk. Gabriel shut his computer and slouched out of the room. For an agonizing four minutes, Gabriel stumbled through the ten verses. Mason kept correcting him, and he didn't miss a word when he went.

"Let's add eleven through thirteen next week," Mason said. "See you in a bit."

"Alright," Gabriel said.

Entering his room again, Jason looked up. "What was that about?"

"Mason and I have been memorizing verses."

"Cool," Jason said.

Gabriel shuffled through the papers on his desk. "Are you going to Steven's testimony?"

"I don't think so. I have to finish some homework," Jason said.

Gabriel looked at him, then the show on Jason's computer. "Tough assignment."

"Very important stuff," Jason said.

Gabriel rolled his eyes as he left their room to join the people truly pursuing God.

ALTHOUGH GABRIEL FELT he was getting a handle on his classes, the only ones he truly cared about were Spiritual Formation and English.

Gabriel spent most of the initial weeks working on his theme essay for *Calvary*. It took so long because he wasn't sure how to talk about the film's content. He had a difficult time hearing the word *semen*, much less writing it out and analyzing the wealth of struggling characters in that story.

Through it all, Gabriel didn't have a lot of extra time. Besides classes, there always seemed to be something going on. Mason's ultimate frisbee. Sand volleyball. Bible studies. Watching movies in Andy's room. It was hard to choose what to do because he wanted to spend time with everyone. He wanted to make everyone happy.

Nearly a month in, Gabriel found the list of goals he'd set for the first semester.

He balked at all of the things he wasn't doing.

He hardly worked out. It was just the occasional push-ups and crunches, but no running. He was *sort of* memorizing verses, but he didn't *want* to, and that was the whole point. He didn't have a consistent sleep schedule, and he'd hardly opened a book to read for fun. Not to mention, he had no job, and he didn't feel ready to date.

It felt like he was already doing so much, but when he saw this list, it didn't seem like he was doing nearly enough.

HOMECOMING

October snuck up on Gabriel.

His first major assignments were in, and the air was crisp. He'd gotten an eighty-three on his theme essay for English. When Professor Davis returned them, Gabriel looked at the number in disbelief. He'd done everything required *and* turned it in on time. He snuck a look at the girl's paper next to him—an English major. He saw *79%* scrawled on the last page.

"Overall, you guys did a pretty good job," Professor Davis said as he finished handing out the papers. "I've included notes on the back for things that can be improved, and I hope you consider that for your next essay."

After class, the students around Gabriel compared their grades. Most were in the C range, but there were a few Ds. Gabriel saw one girl leaving the room in tears. The only person who seemed to have gotten a better grade than him was a girl in the first row, and she'd gotten an eighty-seven. Gabriel tucked his paper into his backpack, feeling slightly better about himself, but also wondering how he could possibly get an A.

By Homecoming weekend, he was thoroughly exhausted from

getting ahead on homework so he could spend time with his parents. They arrived Friday morning, just in time for chapel. Gabriel introduced them to Jenna and Luca, and they all talked vibrantly while Gabriel faded into his seat, tight and still. He didn't have all that much to say to them. He didn't particularly miss them, either.

Until now, he didn't realize how much he'd enjoyed being away.

"How do you like college so far?" His mom asked at lunch.

"It's good," Gabriel said. "I'm making friends. English is tough, but we get to write all our papers about a foreign film."

"Which one?" His mom asked.

"Mine's *Calvary.*"

"What's that about?"

Gabriel framed it in the best light possible. "An Irish priest gets a death threat. It's pretty dark."

His mom grimaced, and his dad picked up the conversation. "Have you met any cute ladies yet?"

Gabriel shrugged. Jenna flashed in his mind, but he wanted to take that slow. He wanted to get to know her before they did anything. "I don't know."

"What about Jenna? She seems like a nice girl."

Of course they'd noticed her.

"We're just friends," Gabriel said.

"Don't cut off the possibility too soon. Give it time," his dad said.

Gabriel pursed his lips.

"Did you hear James Ali is trying to sell his boat?" Gabriel's mom asked.

"Really? Why? It's still the fishing season," Gabriel said, forgetting his food.

"He wants something bigger, for longer trips."

"But he's still going to fish, right?"

"I don't think he'd stop if you gave him the world," his dad said.

Gabriel grunted in agreement.

After all his classes, he showed his parents his room. Their hall bustled with voices as parents and students walked up and down. Jason was studying at his desk. Across the hall, Andy was playing music and wrestling an overflowing trash bag out of the waist-high can.

They looked around Gabriel's room, browsing the arrangement of things and Gabriel's bookshelf. He tensed when his mom traced a finger on the book spines, going over the Bibles and textbooks. She didn't notice *The Perks of Being a Wallflower,* or she didn't care, or didn't remember what the story was about. When the moment passed, Gabriel felt pathetic for his fear. Why would they care what he read now? And if they did, how could they enforce it?

His parents left after an hour to attend a reunion with their class. On their way to dinner, Gabriel's family met up with Luca, his parents in tow.

Luca's dad was tall and had a severe expression. Black hair combed back, high cheekbones, and a sweater over a collared shirt. Luca's mom wore a cream blouse and suit pants and kept her hair in a tight bun. Her lips were full and red, and she towered over the women they passed.

Luca and Gabriel brought up the rear as they walked toward the Union. Luca stood straight and stiff and didn't meander with his words. He hardly spoke the whole evening, and his leg bounced under the table as they ate.

Gabriel missed his quiet brightness.

CORRUPTION, INDEED

"I PASSED BITCH!" Andy yelled, storming into Gabriel's room two weeks later. Gabriel jumped at the intrusion. "SEVENTY-TWO LET'S GO!"

"Your engineering mid-term?" Gabriel asked, tingling with adrenaline from the scare.

"*Hell* yeah!" Andy ducked his head into the hallway. "Smash Bros tournament in my room this weekend!"

Doors opened, people shouted back, and soon the date was set. It took up the entire Sunday after church, and Andy bought soda, chips, and pizza. As he and Gabriel sat in a corner of the room, everyone screaming at the final round, Andy sighed. "God, I could go for a drink right now."

Gabriel looked over at him. No one else seemed to have heard. "I could, too."

Andy just smiled like he already had a plan. The following Friday, Andy texted him to ask if he wanted to go on a hike after class. Gabriel hid his phone under the desk as Professor Davis got distracted from the lesson and shared about his time in Japan.

Let's do it, Gabriel sent.

Andy replied a minute later. *Cool, Kyle's coming too.*

Gabriel had talked to Kyle a few times, mostly during movie nights in Andy's room. He was a Junior Marketing major and sold thrifted clothes online. Kyle picked them up outside their dorm in his cherry red Jeep. Gabriel sat in the middle of the back row and leaned forward.

"What's the plan?" Gabriel asked.

Andy grinned. He opened Kyle's backpack and showed Gabriel the contents. Inside was a bottle of Smirnoff Vodka and a liter of Sprite.

"There's more," Andy said. He rummaged in the front pocket and pulled out three cigars.

Gabriel internally recoiled. According to his parents, smoking was a disgusting, vagrant activity.

"You haven't lived until you've lit up a cigar in the woods," Andy said.

"You cool with all this?" Kyle asked as they rounded a bend in the road.

"Yeah, I'm good," Gabriel said casually.

"He's cool, man," Andy said. "He goes down too if he says anything."

Gabriel didn't speak in his defense. He didn't want them to change their minds. Negotiations like these were delicate, and the less obnoxious you were, the more likely they were to trust you.

They drove another five minutes before stopping in a nearly empty parking lot, thick trees beyond.

"Someone's going to catch us," Gabriel said, looking around.

"Nah, we do this all the time," Andy said.

He retrieved a white, half-gallon Nalgene with a drinking spout. It rattled with ice. He removed the lid while Kyle unscrewed the vodka and poured half the bottle inside. Gabriel's eyes widened at each additional *glug*. Kyle poured the Sprite, topped it off with lime juice, and stirred it up with the straw. They did it all without saying a word.

Andy took a deep pull from the bottle. His face twisted. "Shit, that's strong."

"Let me try," Kyle said, taking a drink. He grimaced. "Might have put in too much vodka."

He handed it to Gabriel, and Kyle and Andy looked at him expectantly. Gabriel took the bottle and wiped the straw. God hadn't struck him down for drinking before, so why would he now?

And if He did…well, that was that.

Gabriel shrugged and took a long drink. He shuddered, handing it back.

He waited a few seconds.

Nope.

No lightning from heaven.

"Atta boy," Andy said, giving him a fist bump. He gave Gabriel another, smaller bottle to carry. "This is water."

They jumped out of the car. Kyle wore the backpack, and Andy carried the cocktail. Gabriel smacked his mouth and drank from the water bottle. It wasn't *terrible*, but he couldn't imagine they made drinks like that at a bar.

They walked the trail single file and passed the drink back and forth. Oak trees spread their branches high above. Orange and yellow leaves twisted in the chill air. The path dipped and rose as they passed over streams and skirted boulders. Dirt and moss mingled in the air.

Gabriel soaked it in, content in the quiet. He could sense the reverence for this place. No one spoke. And when they approached a gate with a red and white sign saying, TRAIL CLOSED, Kyle skirted it without glancing back. Andy and Gabriel followed.

After ten minutes, they came to an opening between two massive rocks, a small shore ahead. The river lazily trickled by. Kyle sat down on the shore's edge, back against the rock. Gabriel propped himself against a mossy boulder.

"Now this," Kyle spread his arms, breaking the silence, "is living."

He tossed the Nalgene to Gabriel and retrieved the cigars from the backpack. Gabriel took another drink. It was going down smoother now. He leaned his head back, all of a sudden giddy and warm. The world tilted as he reached for a cigar. It didn't seem like such a bad idea now.

The cigar was the diameter of a penny. Gabriel cut the end and put it to his lips, tasing a cherry sweetness. A few tobacco flakes went into his mouth. He spat it out as Kyle kneeled in front of him with a lighter.

"Don't breathe it in," he instructed. "Just keep the smoke in your mouth."

Gabriel had many questions about what that meant, but Kyle had already lit the end of his cigar. He puffed in. Smoke seared his lungs. Gabriel doubled over, coughing violently. Andy burst into laughter.

"Do the opposite of that," Kyle said.

The opposite? He'd hardly done anything.

Gabriel had to drink from the Nalgene to calm his burning throat, and then he took a tentative puff. Held it. Breathed out. A billow of smoke filled the air. He took another, bolder pull and felt the smokiness rolling over his tongue. Gabriel exhaled in a small cloud. He smiled.

He sat back again, puffing the cigar.

"No one's going to smell this, right?" Gabriel asked.

Andy and Kyle exchanged a look, then a shrug. "Probably not.

We're pretty far from the open trails," Andy said.

Before, Gabriel might have worried. But *right now*, he couldn't think of a reason why that should ruin this moment. He reached for the Nalgene, nearly toppling over as the world shifted.

"Oh God…" Gabriel said, flipping the spout. The others laughed.

"Could you imagine if Grant could see us right now?" Andy asked with a grin.

"He'd probably have a stroke," Gabriel said.

"That guy needs to loosen up," Kyle said.

"He's probably reading his Bible right now—"

"And trying not to masturbate for the fifth time today," Andy said, cutting Gabriel off. They laughed, and Andy added, "I'm serious."

"Wait, what?" Gabriel said.

"I'm pretty sure he masturbates in the bathrooms," Andy said. Gabriel's eyes widened. "He goes into one of the stalls with his iPad and headphones and doesn't come out for *thirty* minutes. He literally takes off his shorts and bunches them on the ground by the door. You can hear his muffled breathing, like he's trying to have a quiet orgasm."

"What the *fuuuck*," Kyle said, rubbing his forehead.

"I was brushing my teeth once and he came out of the stall, and he looked super guilty. I didn't know what to do. I tried to pretend he wasn't there."

"I feel like I've seen that before," Gabriel said. "I thought I blocked that out, so thanks for reminding me."

"That's why I'm here," Andy said humbly. "I just think it's funny how he's always preaching about purity, and I *guarantee* you he's jerking off in the bathrooms."

"You know what they say, you preach hardest against your biggest sin," Kyle said.

"I don't think that's a saying," Andy said.

"But it's true, yeah? Look at all the pastors who get busted with hookers, often *men*, too," Kyle said.

Gabriel nodded. He'd seen enough stories like that to make him pause and think something wasn't right. He took another drink from the Nalgene. "Do you guys masturbate?"

"Here and there," Kyle said.

Andy nodded. "Everyone does."

"Yeah, same," Gabriel said. He blinked. He'd never admitted that before, and for some reason, it didn't seem like such a terrible thing. "Why do people say it's so bad?"

"If it makes you happy, it's a sin," Kyle said.

"Ha!" Andy barked.

"The more miserable for God, the more righteous you are," Kyle said.

Andy continued smiling, and Gabriel folded his arms around his knees. That was exactly it. Sometimes, it felt like a competition to see who struggled the most.

"Have you ever had sex?" Andy asked.

"God no," Gabriel said.

"Just hand stuff so far," Kyle said.

Gabriel laughed, but Andy grimaced. He found a stick on the ground and began digging into the mud and pebbles. "I have. A few weeks ago…my first time…" He kept his attention on the ground.

Shame thickened the air, louder than any rebuke. All attention snapped to Andy, and he seemed to know how wrong it was. He didn't meet their eyes. Gabriel kept his expression neutral.

"Dude, that's great. Why'd you wait so long to tell me?" Kyle asked.

"I didn't know how to say it."

"Was it bad?"

"No…"

"And?"

"*And* I don't regret it, that's the thing. It seemed *right*, but every-thing I know says it's the worst thing I can do," Andy said, emphatic now.

Gabriel shrank. He knew that feeling, but saying anything might expose him. He drank from the Nalgene.

"Then last week, I told Grant and Mason after the Bible study," Andy said, tapping his cigar to remove the built-up ash. "They had a whole intervention. People like them make me feel so guilty, but *mad*, too, you know? Grant acts so high and mighty, but he's in a porn addiction group."

"Woah," Gabriel said.

"I shouldn't have said that," Andy said.

Kyle coughed. "I joined one of those as a freshman because I was convinced it was the only way I could be saved."

Andy took a long drag on his cigar. "I don't want to feel like that anymore."

Kyle gave a slow nod. Gabriel did, too, and everything he hadn't said clamored to break free. He clenched his jaw to keep anything from slipping out.

Andy reached for the Nalgene. It rattled, nearly empty. He chomped on his half-smoked cigar and refilled it. There was an inch of vodka remaining in the bottle.

"You want to shoot the rest of this?" Andy asked.

"Yes, obviously," Kyle said.

Andy took a swig and then passed it to Kyle, who raised it in the air. "To our corruption."

There was a quarter inch remaining when it got to Gabriel. He tipped it back, gagged, held it in his mouth another second, and swallowed. Shivering, he gulped down water. He leaned back again, feeling lighter with each passing minute.

Was it really so bad to like who you wanted?

In this moment, it didn't feel wrong at all.

For a while, he focused on puffing his cigar and watching the smoke trickle from his mouth with aimless swirls. He found himself grinning at nothing.

To their corruption, indeed.

POLAROIDS

SNOW FILLED THE air as Gabriel and Luca walked the town of Meridian. It was the closest city to campus, but it was barely a blip compared to any of the Boston suburbs.

Luca was bundled in a knit sweater. It had large squares in muted grays and greens. When he first saw it two weeks ago, Gabriel jokingly asked Luca to give it to him for his birthday. Luca scoffed at the idea but suggested they go thrifting in Meridian instead. They hadn't planned on the snow, but it added a playfulness to the day.

They spent an hour flipping through racks, trying on things they would never wear. Gabriel held a brown corduroy jacket. He smiled as he put it on, zipping it up and running his hands over the fabric.

"I love it," Luca said over his shoulder. "You should get it."

"I don't know," Gabriel said. Even Luca saying that wasn't enough. People would stare if he wore it. He wished he had the strength not to care so much what others thought.

He put it back.

It felt like he was losing something.

They navigated to an antique shop. Every inch of the floor-to-ceiling shelves were filled with soon-to-be-discovered treasures. He couldn't help but touch random objects. Road signs. License plates. Stereos. Rocking chairs.

Luca was a few steps ahead. He gasped and dove into a shelf. Gabriel came close to his side, and Luca showed off a Polaroid camera. He flipped it open, revealing the flash bar and bubble lens.

"This is incredible," Luca said, face radiant. He brushed off a layer of dust. The surface was still dirty, and the cartridge took some work to remove.

"Do you think it works?" Gabriel asked.

"No idea."

"How much?"

"It says ten on the sticker."

"You have to get it."

Luca nodded. "I just need to find film for it."

They split off again, content to browse on their own.

Gabriel went up and down every aisle, fingers playing over mugs and sculptures and carved boxes. That's when he saw the typewriter, and longing sprang to life in his spirit. It was old, the kind with metal keys and exposed struts. He tried pressing a key, but it didn't budge. He pressed them all. Only a few weren't stuck. Gabriel's visions of writing his assignments on this machine fell apart. He checked the price tag. $43.

That didn't matter. He needed it. He didn't know why, but he needed it. He carefully picked it up as Luca rounded the corner.

"There you are," Luca said, the Polaroid and two boxes of film in hand. His jaw dropped. "Please tell me you're getting that."

"Absolutely."

"Does it work?"

"Kind of."

"Maybe you can fix it."

Gabriel agreed. They paid at the counter and walked back to Gabriel's car, snow peppering their faces. Luca examined the sky, flakes catching in his hair. Gabriel smiled, chest full and warm. He locked the typewriter in the trunk, and they returned to walking. Luca kept the camera on him, determined to get it working.

"Have you ever used one of these before?" Gabriel asked.

"Not this version, but they're pretty simple," Luca said, examining the cartridge slot.

They made it to a candy shop. Luca slung the camera over his neck with the strap and stowed the new film in his pocket. They filled up two bags, tasting a bit as they went. Then they got hot chocolate at a café and sat at a small table in the back.

Gabriel dug through his bag of candy and chewed a sour rope. Luca was wholly absorbed with the camera. He pursed his lips, brow furrowed, blue eyes focused on removing the old cartridge at the bottom of the camera. Fingers straining, he yanked it out with a *crack*.

Luca looked up, eyes wide. "If I broke it, I'm going to cry."

"Well, I'm here if you do," Gabriel returned.

Luca's mouth twitched as if holding in a smile. He used the hem of his sweater to clean the opening. It was suffocatingly warm in their corner, and Luca had rolled up his sleeves at some point. Luca's muscles shifted as he worked, and this was the first time Gabriel remembered seeing Luca's bare arms. His skin was tan, but there wasn't a visible reason to keep himself covered—no scars or tattoos or birthmarks.

Gabriel rifled through his bag again, pulling out a piece of black licorice.

Luca glanced up. "I don't know how you eat that."

"Are you kidding? I should have gotten *more*."

"You disgust me."

"Just try it."

"No."

"Come on."

"Only psychopaths eat black licorice. And my hands are dirty. I might get infected or something."

"God, you're such a baby. Here." Gabriel leaned forward, shoving a piece up to Luca's mouth. He twisted away, but Gabriel persisted, leaning further over the table. "Hold still."

Luca was leaning as far away as he could, chair tipped back.

"If you try it, I'll buy doughnuts on the way back," Gabriel said.

Luca scrunched his nose, and Gabriel's insides weakened. Luca finally opened his mouth enough to bite the candy. Gabriel went back to sitting normally as Luca chewed uncomfortably. Gabriel smiled with satisfaction and sipped his hot chocolate.

"Huh," Luca said, frowning. "That wasn't as bad as I thought it would be."

"Ha! I knew it."

"I didn't say I liked it."

"Well, I know the truth."

Luca finished unwrapping the new film cartridge. It was a small black tray, about half an inch thick. He snapped it in, and they heard a whir as the camera charged. Their eyes met at the same time. Luca brought the sight to his face, putting Gabriel in the frame. Gabriel froze, and the camera *clicked*. Moments later, a three-inch Polaroid emerged from the bottom. Luca grinned, immediately flipping it upside down so the light wouldn't ruin the image.

"Here, let me take one," Gabriel said, their fingers brushing as he took the camera.

"It's the button on—" Luca began, hand up, cut off by another *click.* "Unbelievable."

Gabriel flipped over the picture and returned the camera.

"How long do we have to wait?" Gabriel asked.

"A couple minutes. Not long."

It felt like an eternity. Gabriel's foot bounced. He drank more hot chocolate. When the time came, they examined the polaroids. The one of Luca was a bit blurry, and he'd been frozen in the middle of instruction, but it was candid and vibrant.

"You can have that one," Luca said, handing it back.

Gabriel examined the polaroid again before tucking it into his pocket. Luca did the same with the one of Gabriel. They didn't share a word about it. They both knew the significance of the moment.

When the time came, they headed back to Gabriel's car, and Gabriel did as promised, buying doughnuts on the way back. Gabriel didn't want the day to end. It felt better than the ones they shared on campus. It was calm and joyful and *free*—just them and the snow and no one else to watch.

In his room, Gabriel set the typewriter on the corner of his desk. It was a bit crowded with the lamp, cup of pens, and his stack of textbooks, but it was the best he could do now.

He retrieved the Polaroid from his pocket. Smiling, he scanned the room for a place to put it. He couldn't display the photo. People would ask questions. But he didn't want to hide it away and forget about it. His eyes settled on his copy of *The Perks of Being a Wallflower.* He removed it from the shelf and taped the picture to the inside of the back cover.

Perfectly content, he returned the book to its place.

SINS OF THE FLESH

Throughout October, Mason preached to Gabriel about the importance of sharing one's testimony. It was a regular subject during their verse memorizations and on their walks to and from The Gathering.

"When do you think you're going to give yours?" Mason asked on their way back from the latest meeting at Ben's house.

Gabriel's insides squirmed at the question. "I don't have much of a story to tell."

"We *all* have a story. You just need to be honest with yourself."

"I haven't gone through anything crazy."

"It just needs to be true."

Gabriel nodded as if he understood, but his blood ran thick with fear. He clenched his hands at his sides as they walked. The last thing he wanted was to give his testimony. There *were* things he could talk about, but he couldn't say any of it aloud.

He had to get away from this.

The never-ending conversation about God and sin was fraying his mind. Mason intended well, but it was too much. He couldn't stand it anymore.

For the next week, he made excuses to get out of their regular breakfasts, and he planned a movie night with Luca to get out of testimony night. But he couldn't escape entirely without confronting it head-on. He finally got up the courage once he and Mason finished reciting James 1 in the dorm hallway. Gabriel knew he had to end it before they began another passage.

"There's too much for me to do right now," Gabriel said after their final recitation. "I don't think I need another thing to work on, you know?"

Mason listened intently, disappointment creeping into his eyes. "Why?"

Why?

"I mean, I need to focus on classes."

Mason's eyes bored into Gabriel's. "I thought you liked memorizing verses."

Gabriel's mouth worked. "Um. It's *good*, but I need a break."

"You skipped last week's testimony, too," Mason said, letting the statement hang in the air. "Have you been spending time with God, otherwise? What's going on?"

Gabriel fidgeted with the hem of his shirt. Why did Mason care so much?

"I'm good," Gabriel said. "But I'd rather focus on other things."

Mason tilted his chin in the air, and his gaze traced the ceiling. He nodded once, shoulders slumped. There was hurt in his eyes when he looked at Gabriel again, and Gabriel felt awful for letting him down. "Alright, I get it."

"Yeah?"

"But you have to come to my testimony this week."

"Sure."

"It's going to be good."

"Okay."

"And then you can give yours!" Mason said.

Gabriel just laughed, more tense than ever. He backed toward his room. "I'll see you then."

"See you," Mason said, still watching him closely.

Gabriel didn't look back. He could feel Mason's eyes on his back the entire walk to his room.

That Wednesday, everyone crowded into Mason and Grant's room. Two people sat on the top bunk, three on the bottom. Others sat on desks and dressers and leaned against the wall wherever they found space. Gabriel wedged himself between Ricky and the foot of the bunkbeds, back against the wall. He had to wrap his arms around his knees to make room for the people in front of him.

Mason sat near the middle, propped against his dresser, Grant and Stephen on his sides. He thumbed through his Bible while everyone got settled. Jokes and separate conversations filled the room. Mason closed his Bible.

"I guess we can get started," Mason said, looking around the room. "Thank you all for being here." He let out a shaky laugh. "I'm nervous."

Understanding smiles greeted him. Grant squeezed his shoulder. "Whenever you're ready."

Mason's life unfolded in snippets over the next twenty minutes.

"I grew up in upstate New York...

"...my mom stayed home with all the kids...

"...dad speaks at conferences and has written some apologetics books...

"...he wasn't home often, so me and the older kids had to step up..."

Gabriel shifted every few minutes as Mason continued. Most of these testimonies weren't all that interesting. His mind wandered, settling on his Biology quiz tomorrow.

"I always felt close to God as a kid, but I started to drift away around high school. It was bad movies and vulgar music. I wasn't reading my Bible or praying. I just felt *bad* inside, and I didn't know what it was."

Gabriel leaned his head against the wall to stare at the ceiling. It was virtually the same story as everyone else. They always drifted away from God over basic 'sins,' but they always found their way back by the present day.

"It's funny because the thing that has brought me closer to God again has actually been the most difficult thing I've had to deal with."

Gabriel squashed a smile. Mason went quiet long enough for Gabriel to look at him, intrigued.

"This is really hard to say," Mason said with a half laugh.

"It's alright, we're all here for you," Grant reassured him.

Mason nodded. His hands kept folding over each other. His eyes were downcast, fixed on nothing. "Growing up, I've never been all that interested in girls…"

Gabriel bristled as if stuck with a thousand safety pins.

"It made no sense. They're so beautiful," Mason continued, and Gabriel refrained from rolling his eyes at the qualifying statement. "But for as long as I remember, I, uh…I guess I'll be completely honest…" Mason's confidence had bled away until his voice trembled like a branch about to snap.

Sick anticipation turned Gabriel into a statue. He knew what was coming next. Some of the others must have picked up on this, too. Gabriel could see it in the stiffness between shoulder blades and the twitch of jaw muscles. It was in the claustrophobic silence. No one dared move as they focused on Mason's drowning form.

He closed his eyes and took a steadying breath. "I've been struggling with same-sex attractions for a long time, my whole life, really."

And now, the tension in the room coalesced into a tangible thing. It hung there, dark and pulsing and deformed, dripping with the ooze of fear.

The shape of repulsive truth.

Gabriel wished he could sink into the floor.

Mason barreled forward. "The more I noticed it, the more I pulled away from God. I was going down a terrible path, but I opened my Bible on a whim and came across this passage from Jeremiah twenty-nine." Mason flipped through his Bible with shaking hands. A few heads nodded at the chapter reference.

"'For I know the plans I have for you,' declares the Lord, 'plans to prosper you and not to harm you, plans to give you hope and a future. Then you will call on me and come and pray to me, and I will listen to you. You will seek me and find me when you seek me with all your heart.'"

Mason looked at the open Bible as if reliving that defining moment. It took a while for him to speak again.

"When I read that, I knew God had a plan for my life. All I needed to do was pursue Him with everything I had. I realized He *hates* my sin, but He *loves* me. I knew that as long as I didn't act on these feelings, I'd be okay. I truly believe that God can heal anything, *any* sin. I believe when the time comes, I'll be able to have a family of my own."

*Amen*s and *yes God*s sprinkled the room.

Gabriel felt nauseous.

"I'm still tempted, but that's my burden. I would sacrifice everything, endure whatever God places before me because I *know* this journey is worth it. This life is temporary, a mere *blink* compared to an eternity in heaven."

Gabriel knew that desire. He'd made the same promises.

Nothing had changed for him either.

"I find a lot of comfort in *Job* because God tested him to see if he was loyal in the worst times, and my struggle is *nothing* compared to what Job went through. I'm happy to bear this burden and show it's possible to overcome our sin with God's strength," Mason said, emphatic. He met eyes everywhere, conviction in his voice. Gabriel saw a vision of Mason preaching in front of thousands. He pictured young people hanging on every word.

It hurt to imagine, but he couldn't place exactly why.

"I guess that's it," Mason said. He dropped his eyes to his Bible.

The room exhaled. People uncurled themselves and dropped their invisible torches and bricks. Mason was fighting it. He was one of them.

"Wow," Grant said, stroking his beard. "Thank you for trusting us with that. It's an incredible journey. Can we pray for you?"

"Please," Mason said.

Hands reached out to touch him on his shoulders, arms, and knees. The people who couldn't reach him raised their hands in his direction. Gabriel mechanically did the same.

Grant began. "God, thank you so much for my brother in Christ, Mason. His devotion and faith are beautiful inspirations to everyone in this room. I know this struggle has been incredibly difficult, but there's no sin worse than another. We are all sinners. We're all born filthy, but you wash us clean."

Gabriel opened his eyes to see nods all around. His lungs weren't working like they were supposed to. It was like he was burning from the inside out.

"Through faith, there is healing. God, I pray you would come down right now and heal Mason if you desire. Mason, I know God has an incredible plan for your life, and I believe he's preparing a beautiful bride for you right now."

Amens.

What if they were wrong?

Mason trembled. Tears streamed down his cheeks.

"It's a battle every day, but we're living today for eternity tomorrow, and I believe the hardest battles produce the strongest warriors. You are a *warrior*, Mason. Don't forget that. Amen."

Heads rose. Hands tucked themselves away. Mason brushed tears from his face. Stephen handed him a box of tissues. He went through three before he could speak again.

"Thanks for being here," he said.

"We love you," Grant said. "There's nothing we can't get through together."

Affirmations swept the group, and the first hints of regular conversation crept into the room. Within two or three minutes, you wouldn't have been able to guess what had just transpired. Everyone seemed to be doing a good job pretending Mason hadn't just confessed to the worst of all sins.

Gabriel stood up, forcing himself to smile along. He glanced back at Mason, who was still being comforted by Grant and Stephen. Gabriel stepped over legs and chairs, panic crawling up his throat. He slipped down the hallway and into his room. It was empty. Good. He locked the door and closed the blinds.

This was it.

The first time he'd met someone who was struggling with this particular sin.

He shook with adrenaline.

Wasn't he the same?

No no no…

Gabriel pinched his eyes shut. Every cell of his body wanted that to be false.

He knew the truth. He'd known for a very long time.

I like men.

Shit.

He'd never admitted that to himself before.

I like men.

In general. Plural.

Fuck.

Adrian was just one person. It felt better when it was just one person. It could be an isolated incident, then. He could convince himself he liked Adrian as a friend. Nothing more. Nothing else. Not actors or characters or…or…

No, *that* was too much.

Gabriel paced the room, throat closing with tears.

"I like men," he said, barely a whisper.

A whisper was enough to make it true.

Now, it was real. It was an awful reality, but it was here and real and present, and there was no escape. He knew the fate that awaited him if he continued down this path. But keeping it in was tearing him apart.

"I like men…and that has to be ok," Gabriel choked out. He clenched his teeth and squeezed the bridge of his nose. "I have to be ok with that."

Gabriel let out a full sob, terrified of what that meant for his future. For his family.

For his eternal fate in either heaven or hell.

THE REST OF YOUR LIFE

"DID YOU GUYS hear that Mason's gay?" Jason asked the room at large.

Gabriel was on his bed, journaling, desperately trying to clear his head. Jason and Arlo were playing cards on the carpet. Hunter had settled at Gabriel's desk, taking notes from a textbook.

The question drew all attention to Jason. Gabriel squeezed his thighs. He'd been in a fog the last two days. Admitting how he felt sickened him, and all he knew was dread. It twisted through every inch of his body. It was like being diagnosed with a terminal illness. Before, he'd just *thought* something might be terribly wrong. Now, all he saw was inevitable doom.

"Seriously?" Arlo asked.

"He told the whole dorm," Jason said.

"Not us," Hunter said, turning around to put an arm on the back of his chair.

"No shit, he didn't tell us," Jason said.

"When was this?" Arlo asked.

"During their Bible study," Jason said. "Andy told me about it yesterday."

"Yeah, I was there," Gabriel spoke up. Everyone looked up at him.

"What did he say?" Hunter asked.

Gabriel hesitated, not sure if this was something he should be talking about. "He actually said he was same-sex attracted."

Hunter snorted. "He's gay, dude. He's just in denial."

"I'm pretty sure he has a girlfriend," Gabriel said.

"*Her?* The long-distance one? She's a three, *tops*," Arlo said.

Jason laughed. "For real? I need to see her."

"One second," Arlo said, diving into his phone.

"People only say that when they're in denial," Hunter said. "'Oh, I'm afflicted with Same Sex Attractions.' What does that sound like to you? He's fighting it."

"Should he not?" Gabriel asked.

"It's the wording," Hunter explained, adjusting his glasses. "Saying you're struggling means you don't want it to be a part of you. He just needs to admit it."

"He did."

"Yeah, but he's not accepting it. That's the only way you can actually be at peace."

Gabriel frowned.

Was it?

"Found her," Arlo announced, and all attention turned to him. "I stalked everyone in the dorm a while ago and saw this photo on his Facebook."

"*That's* his girlfriend?" Jason covered his mouth. "She's like…a frog. Just a plain…brown frog."

"Shit, Jason," Hunter said.

"She's probably got a *great* personality," Arlo said.

"What do you guys think about it?" Hunter cut in. "Should he accept it?"

"I don't really care," Jason said. "That's for him to figure out."

"Whatever makes him happy," Arlo said.

Gabriel couldn't believe what he was hearing. He felt the room closing in. How could they just *not care?*

"Isn't it supposed to be a sin?" Gabriel asked, speaking up. His mouth went dry at continuing the debate.

"Maybe, according to a few verses in the Bible," Hunter said.

"It's pretty clear on that," Gabriel said firmly.

"But is everything in the Bible true?" Hunter asked, more a question than a challenge.

It left Gabriel sputtering for a defense. "It's supposed to be the inerrant word of God. You can't toss one thing out because you want to."

"I just think some things need to be re-evaluated. The Old Testament was used to justify the Crusades and other conquests. People used the Bible to advocate slavery. They use it now to crucify gay people." Hunter removed his glasses to polish them. "I don't want to get into a fight. I just think being gay isn't a crime. It just *is.*"

"Are you trying to tell us something?" Arlo asked with a mock-serious voice.

"No, I just…" Hunter seemed to struggle with what to say next. "I know someone who is, and I can't get them in trouble."

There were a few seconds of revelatory silence as they processed that information. Gabriel kept very still. Did Hunter know about him?

"Oh, no, is it Arlo?" Jason asked with a smile. "I support that."

"And they were roommates," Arlo said.

The three of them dissolved into laughter, but Gabriel was too fraught with tension to smile. He turned back to his computer, even more tangled up than before.

IN THE FOLLOWING days, Gabriel tried to figure out the impossible: If his mere existence was an abomination. All the while, he had the constant, sick-to-his-stomach thought of, *I like men, I like men, I like men…*

Sometimes, he whispered it to himself in the mirror in his room. He cringed at the words. He couldn't say them with conviction. He couldn't say them without shame.

He couldn't imagine telling another person.

But he didn't have to. They didn't need to know.

If he could just find a way to lock away his thoughts—

Wait…

Did thoughts send you to hell?

Shit.

Wait, no, that couldn't be it. *Everyone* had bad thoughts. That was just part of being human.

And maybe admitting you were same-sex attracted was alright as long as you didn't say you were gay. If you used that label, was that being unrepentant? Was that agreeing with sin?

Maybe, still, the label didn't matter so much as never acting on your feelings.

For your entire life.

Decades of denial.

Could he do that?

And what counted as acting on your attractions?

Lusting? Masturbating? Gay porn?

If that's what condemned someone, he was already doomed.

But maybe it was only physical relationships that were condemned. But how physical? Was holding hands wrong? What about cuddling? Or kissing? Or was it *sex itself* that cut you off from heaven? What if you only did it once, never again, and repented afterward?

Would you be condemned *then?*

There were so many nuances that could mean an eternity of paradise or torture, but how could you possibly know what single action was deemed unforgivable? Especially when the Bible was so unclear?

The more Gabriel poured over different passages, the less certain he was. And the more sources he read, the more sides to the argument there were. Some people said the few verses on homosexuality referred to pedophilia and sexual abuse, or the Greek and Roman custom of pederasty—the coupling of boys with men. Some said the word *homosexuality* wasn't used in any Bible translation until the 1940s when they substituted it for *young boys.* Other scholars said those ideas were deliberate misinterpretations of the Bible, and the most straightforward understanding was the right one. In other words, take it at face value.

But by that logic, shouldn't every thief have their hands cut off and every person who lusted gouge out their own eyes? Why didn't people take *those* verses seriously?

Online comments were worse, and everyone pushed their ideas with venomous language. Gabriel had to stop reading after a week because he struggled to do the simplest things. He wasn't sleeping, and he'd begun skipping his morning classes. He couldn't get out of bed, and the stress made it hard to eat.

It didn't escape Luca's notice.

"Are you alright?" Luca asked before a quiz. "You look off."

"I don't know," Gabriel said, wishing he could shrink to nothing.

"Well, I'm here," Luca said quietly.

Gabriel couldn't bring himself to look in Luca's direction. That might have been too much for him to handle, and he might have broken down in the middle of class.

Through it all, a single thought wouldn't leave him alone:

If God's love was supposed to be boundless and unconditional, why were so many people trying to put it in an angry little box?

POWERFUL STUFF

GABRIEL SKIPPED THE next testimony to do homework. He could have spared an hour, but after Mason spoke the previous week, it felt like that room would swallow him whole. Walking the hall, he swore he felt people's eyes on him, trying to read his thoughts.

He skipped the following week, too.

He had no plans to return.

IT WAS JUST Gabriel and Andy at lunch in early November. They sat by the cafeteria windows, grey clouds turning the sky into soup.

"So, have you and Jenna gone out yet?" Andy asked.

"What? No," Gabriel said quickly. "I thought I made that clear."

And he *had*. Whenever the subject of Jenna and dating came up, Gabriel brushed it off. He had more important things to think about.

"Come on, you'd make a great couple!"

"You hardly know her."

Andy shrugged. "I saw her in the Union a few days ago."

"And?"

"*And* she asked about you."

"So what?"

"You're an idiot. She likes you, obviously."

Gabriel rocked back. What had he done to get her to like him? Did he even deserve it?

And did he like her back? Was it finally time to act?

"You should ask her out," Andy said.

"I don't know."

"Why not?"

"I'm not sure if I like her that way."

"You're just nervous."

"Yeah, probably…" Gabriel said, picking at his plate.

"Just think about it."

Gabriel did. For the next two weeks, it was at the forefront of his mind. He tried thinking about everything he wanted in a wife, and Jenna *did* check many of those boxes. She was witty and good-looking. She liked movies and books and music. She was a strong Christian but wasn't in your face about it. And he enjoyed talking and doing homework together, but did that mean he *liked* her?

It had to, right? How else was he supposed to feel?

A part of him yelled that he *did* know how it felt to like someone —and it wasn't Jenna. Gabriel refused to listen to that voice. It led down a path he couldn't go. And so, a week before Thanksgiving break, Gabriel had lunch with Jenna.

"I talked to Andy a while ago," Gabriel said as they settled at the end of a long table. "I was wondering…" He trailed off, cheeks growing warm with embarrassment. "Are you interested…in me? At all?"

Jenna picked at her food. She nodded, keeping a smile at bay. "I do like you."

Gabriel met her eyes for the briefest moment, somewhat nauseous. He knew he had to say it back. After all, that's why he'd asked to get lunch together.

"Nice, me too," he said quietly.

Jenna smiled at him.

Was that a lie?

He didn't actually *say* he liked her; he just reflected what she said and let her fill in the blank. Was that worse?

It didn't matter.

They decided on next Saturday for their first official date.

AN HOUR BEFORE Gabriel left to pick up Jenna, Andy knocked on his door and waved him into his room. Kyle was there, too, and he closed the door.

"Want any?" Andy asked, waving the Nalgene.

"I'm actually going on a date," Gabriel said.

Andy nearly spit on the floor. "With Jenna?"

Gabriel nodded.

"I told you she was interested! Are you excited?"

"Nervous, really."

"Try some of this. That'll help."

Gabriel considered the Nalgene. He took a drink. It was better than last time. "I don't know how interested I am…"

"Just go for it and see what happens," Kyle said.

"That's what I was thinking," Gabriel said.

He spent another fifteen minutes with them before returning to his room to change. He opted for a cream sweater, navy pants, and a black wool jacket. Spraying a dash of cologne in the air, he walked through the cloud, then spent twenty minutes coming up with the perfect playlist for a six-song drive. He did pushups to help clear his head.

His hands shook the entire drive to Jenna's dorm. He parked, texted her, and waited. One minute. Two. The seconds dragged. He squeezed the steering wheel.

What were they going to talk about?

Was she going to expect a kiss afterward?

Did he have time to back out?

Sweat trickled down his armpits.

Shit.

Shitshitshit.

Jenna came through the entrance of her dorm. She waved, smiling wide. She wore black jeans, a dark green turtleneck, and a blue jacket to top it off. She hopped in, and Gabriel smoothly pulled away, letting himself sink into the music. Letting it calm him as he mouthed the lyrics. They chatted about their days and ignored the first date tension.

Her floral perfume filled the car. Was *his* cologne this strong?

"You look good," Gabriel said, feeling awkward at the compliment. He had to say it, though. She had to know he noticed her.

They talked easily the rest of the way, and Gabriel worried he'd run out of things to say before they even got to dinner. How did people do this? How did they spend so much time with one person and never tire of them?

Gabriel parked. There was still a bit of sunlight in the sky as they walked the town. They went to the thrift store, trying on outfits. Gabriel searched for the corduroy jacket. It was gone. Disappointment threatened to overtake him. He settled for a grey sweater and bought overalls for Jenna.

"Thank you," Jenna said, looping her arm in his as they left the store.

"Of course," Gabriel said. He kept up a smile, but he felt a stone of unease settle in his gut. Did they have to be so close? Why didn't he want to hold her back?

Where was the spark of desire?

They stopped in the antique shop next. Jenna examined the shelves, Gabriel slightly behind. She passed over the cameras. Gabriel stopped, picking one up, suddenly struck with the memory of having the same evening with Luca just a few weeks before. Only that time, he didn't feel nervous. He wasn't constantly searching his brain for things to say. He hadn't been worried about the silent moments because, with Luca, they didn't seem like spaces to be filled. More like spaces to explore.

"Where'd you go?" Jenna asked, appearing around the corner.

"Look at these cameras!" Gabriel said. He pretended to take her picture.

"Yeah, they're cool," Jenna said. "The owner told me they're closing, though."

Gabriel put the camera back. "Want to get food now?"

"Yes, I'm dying."

They settled on Thai Village. It was nestled between an Irish pub and a pizza place. Gabriel was glad for the food because it meant they didn't have to talk the whole time.

"So, what's your favorite movie?" Jenna asked.

Gabriel dug into his Pad Thai. "Tough question. *Gladiator* is up there."

"Amazing movie."

"Maybe *Braveheart*, too," Gabriel said, and Jenna nodded. "But my all-time favorite is probably *The Perks of Being a Wallflower*."

Jenna tilted her head to the side. "I'm not sure how I feel about that one."

Gabriel's jaw dropped. "Are you serious? It's *incredible*."

"It's good, sure, but it's almost too…" Jenna waved her hands as she searched for the right words. "I don't want to say *worldly*..." Gabriel's chewing slowed. "It just felt forced, like it was trying to push too much."

"What do you mean?" Gabriel asked carefully.

"The whole *Rocky Horror Picture Show* was over the top. The cross-dressing in it, *that* was too far...and I don't know why so many movies now have to be about gay people."

Gabriel twirled his noodles, looking intently at his plate. He betrayed nothing. He wore a mask of stone.

"We get it, they exist, but do we have to celebrate it? I don't want it shoved in my face, you know?"

All Gabriel could do was nod. But he wasn't scared. No, all he felt was a sudden, burning anger. He fought to keep his voice level. He said, "That's not what the story's about. It's about Charlie."

"But the gay characters are so prominent."

Not really. Gabriel swallowed the comment. "I guess."

"I just don't want to see it."

"Shouldn't they have their own movies?" Gabriel asked. He didn't mean to say that. It just slipped out.

"They do!"

"Not many. How many gay movies can you name?"

Jenna looked affronted. "I don't know, *Love Simon*..." There was a stretch of quiet before she added, *"Brokeback Mountain."*

"How many rom-coms can you name with Julia Roberts alone?" Gabriel asked. He could think of three off the top of his head.

Jenna bit her lip in irritation. "Fine, maybe not so many movies, but you can't get through a show nowadays without being forced to watch a gay kiss or something."

"Powerful stuff," Gabriel said quietly.

"I just think society is losing its morality, and no one wants to stand up for traditional families anymore. Everyone's scared of being canceled for not saying the 'correct' thing—"

"Or they could just let people exist."

"But who's going to stand up for the truth?"

What truth?

Gabriel barely kept himself from blurting out the question. "I don't know if gay people see it that way."

"What way?"

"That your truth is theirs too."

Jenna laughed. "There's no debate! Subjective morality doesn't work! Without the Bible, who's to say you can't rape kids for fun? That could be their 'truth,' and who will stop them?"

"Wow." Gabriel sat back. He looked at his food, sick. "I don't think you have to be a Christian to know that's wrong."

"Ehh," Jenna grimaced. "Those people justify anything. There's no morality anymore."

Gabriel used his straw to stir the ice in his glass. He had nothing left to say.

"Good discussion," Jenna said after a minute.

"Yeah."

"I like debating big topics."

"Sure."

"That's why I like you," Jenna said, and Gabriel looked up. "You're a thinker."

Gabriel scanned the restaurant. "Over-thinker, really."

Jenna leaned back in amusement. Gabriel paid for the food, and they finished the night by walking the town. Deep inside, there were fractures of doubt spreading through the walls he'd built. He patched them up with smiles and laughter so Jenna wouldn't notice, but he continued to sink with each passing minute.

Did she really believe what she said?

Could he trust her with his most vulnerable self?

All of a sudden, they were parked in front of Jenna's dorm. Gabriel gripped the steering wheel in confusion. He didn't remember a single thing about their drive back. Not any of the turns, or what songs they listened to, or anything they might have said.

Jenna stepped out of the car. Gabriel followed. They stood before each other, and Gabriel's mind went blank. He searched the sky, forcing contentment onto his face as if that was better than words.

"That was fun," Jenna said.

Gabriel glanced at her—at her lips—in the streetlight glow. "It was."

Jenna just stood with a half-smile, watching. Waiting.

Was he supposed to kiss her now? He winced at the thought. It was hard to imagine them together like that. He didn't know if he'd like it.

The space between them stretched.

"Well," Gabriel began, hands in his pockets. "I guess I'll see you later."

"Yeah, see you," she said, still not turning away. She tilted her chin up, her lips poised for Gabriel to move in.

Shit.

Gabriel spread his arms in an obvious hug. He squeezed her quickly and backed toward his car. "Have a good night."

Jenna's face drooped, and he closed the door. He didn't look at her as he drove away, overwhelmed with the feeling that he'd done the exact wrong thing.

JUST LIKE THAT

THREE EMPTY CAMPUS Safety sedans were parked in front of Gabriel's dorm. Gabriel skirted the cars and entered the building. Students milled just inside the entrance, whispering to themselves. Some leaned over the second and third-floor balconies.

Gabriel passed two officers as they talked to the RD in his office. The door to his hall was propped open. He ducked inside. People milled outside their doors. Grant and Mason talked with an officer in front of their room. Stephen and Rickey hovered near the conversation. Jason, Arlo, and Hunter were halfway down the hall. One officer stood at the very end.

Shit.

"What happened?" Gabriel asked, pausing in front of Jason's group.

"I think Andy and his friend got busted for alcohol," Jason said.

Gabriel's stomach dropped.

"Who caught them?" he asked.

"Who do you think?" Arlo said. "Fucking Grant…"

Gabriel's eyes flashed to Grant, who spoke to the officer in a low voice. "What are they doing now?"

"Searching Andy's room."

"They're done," Hunter said, shaking his head. "They'll be kept somewhere tonight and be gone tomorrow."

A minute later, there was a ruffling of voices and a barely controlled, "I'm going, Jesus!"

Andy appeared in the hallway, toting a duffle bag and his backpack, flanked by a security guard. His face was red with focused rage, and he stalked the hall like a predator. The milling students flattened themselves against the walls as he passed. No one said a word. Andy didn't look at any of them. His eyes were locked on Grant.

Ten feet away, Andy flipped him off with his left hand. "Enjoy porn therapy, you fucking *rat*."

"Hey! Shut it!" The guard following Andy yelled.

"Keep jerking off in the bathrooms like no one notices!" Andy shouted, reaching the dorm entrance.

"Shut up!" The guard barked.

"EVERYONE! GRANT JOHNSON IS ADDICTED TO STEPMOM PISS PLAY!"

Andy's thunderous last words echoed in the hallway. Deafening silence filled the air. Grant's face had gone ashen. His eyes darted frantically up and down the hall. "I have no idea what he's talking about."

"He'll say anything to distract people from his actions," Mason agreed.

"We can talk in the room," Grant said to the officer. His hands shook as he opened his door.

"I *knew it!*" Arlo said, a monstrous grin on his face. "Have you guys noticed how he takes forever in the bathrooms?"

Hunter nodded. "And always takes his iPad?"

"Hypocrite," Jason said.

Disbelief rooted Gabriel in place. It hit him, then.

There would be no more late-night video games. No more movie nights. No more drinking and cigars.

It was over, just like that.

CAN'T DENY IT

GABRIEL TEXTED ANDY as soon as he woke up the next morning.

What's going to happen?

*Kyle and I have a hearing with the
Dean and President this afternoon. I
doubt we'll be here much longer*

Shit

Yeah

Gabriel turned off his phone and stared at the ceiling. He eventually forced himself to shower and get ready for church. He didn't want to go, especially not with Grant. He didn't even like that church.

Maybe he'd skip today.

There was too much to think about anyway.

Gabriel filled his backpack and marched down the hall. Grant was outside, waiting for the usual group to arrive. Gabriel looked right past him.

"You joining us today?" Grant asked casually.

"I have homework," Gabriel said, not stopping.

Wind cut underneath his jacket, but the sun was out, making it bearable. He turned right, heading for the diner. He didn't know what the feeling was at first, but by the time he arrived, a quiet sadness had soaked through his being.

He got a small table by a window facing the street. For a minute, he just watched the cars go by. He ordered quickly and went back to watching the world outside, hands around a steaming mug of tea.

He ate in silence—just him and the background chatter and the storm beneath his ribs.

It was the mournful knowledge that Andy and Kyle would be gone soon, and fear that the school would find out that he had drank with them. And in the midst of it all, he couldn't shake the memory of Mason's testimony or the terror of admitting how he really felt. Or the date with Jenna, and how he left things.

The sun had disappeared, and wisps of snow danced in the air as Gabriel took a winding route back to his dorm. Jenna texted him, saying she was glad they'd gone out. Gabriel ignored it for now, focusing on the soupy sky, squinting as the snowflakes battered his face.

The longer he walked, the quieter things became. It was as if the snow could freeze time, and maybe his reality, too. He just needed to stay ahead long enough to figure out what to do next.

On his third lap around the lake, Gabriel spotted a figure on the steps of the Biblical Studies building, looking over the water. He skirted the steps, only giving a quick glance at the person—

Ben?

Gabriel had never seen him alone, much less wandering the

campus on a Sunday afternoon. Gabriel halted.

"Hey, what's up!" Gabriel said, offering a half-wave.

Ben started, and his attention focused on Gabriel. His brow drew together. Confused? Gabriel trudged up the steps.

"I've gone to The Gathering a few times—" Gabriel began.

"Gabriel?" Ben asked.

"Didn't think you'd remember me."

"I remember."

Gabriel faced the lake. "How's it going?"

Ben shuffled his feet. "Just thinking."

They stood in silence for a while.

"What about—"

"What time is it?" Ben cut him off. "I left my phone at my place."

Gabriel dug his phone out of his pocket. "Almost four."

"Shoot, I have to go," Ben said.

"Oh."

Ben squeezed Gabriel's shoulder. "I'll see you at the next Gathering, yeah? It's the first week back after Thanksgiving."

"I'll be there."

"Alright, have a nice break," Ben said.

He trudged down the stairs, shoulders gathered up to his ears against the cold. Gabriel watched him leave, feeling like he should have said more. But what? He hardly knew Ben, and he clearly didn't want to talk.

Gabriel thought about calling after him—asking if he wanted to get dinner later. He opened his mouth. Hesitated. Then Ben was too far away. Then he was gone.

ANDY TEXTED HIM that evening: *We're done. I'm leaving in the morning.*

Gabriel knew it was coming, but there had always been that stupid hope that something would change the inevitable. Gabriel skipped chapel in the morning to help Andy pack. They didn't talk much. There wasn't a lot to say.

At Andy's car, they hugged.

"Give 'em hell," Andy said.

"Will do," Gabriel returned.

Andy got in his car and drove off. Gabriel watched him go, hands in his pockets.

Another thread in his chest *twanged* and broke.

Gabriel walked the campus again. It felt like the only way to clear his head.

He finally responded to Jenna. *Sorry I'm just getting back to you, I was really busy today. I had fun too! See you at chapel tomorrow.*

By now, he was sure he'd overreacted to what she'd said. He must have heard her wrong. He was just confused with so much going on. And he didn't *actually* like men. That was absurd. His moment after Mason's testimony felt like someone else's nightmare. Maybe he *had* dreamed that...

Jenna was friendly at chapel and nudged him with an elbow. "We should hang out again."

"Yeah," Gabriel said. "Maybe after break?"

"Okay," Jenna said.

Luca watched silently, his face unreadable. Gabriel looked at him, and Luca turned his attention to the stage, jaw set.

In Biology, Gabriel couldn't stop staring at Andy's empty seat. In his dorm, he kept wanting to play video games with Andy and Micah, but he wasn't all that close to Micah, so he just lay on his bed and stared at the ceiling.

THURSDAY MORNING, GABRIEL woke up in a fog. It had crept up on him slowly since Andy left. He didn't remember it was his birthday until he looked at his phone.

His parents called to say they were planning a small celebration for when he returned Friday night. Chloe sent him a long text with a bunch of emojis, saying she couldn't wait to catch up. Mason threw a small party in his room. They played board games and ate melting ice cream cake.

The best gift came from Luca. He showed up with a square package wrapped in brown paper. Gabriel excused himself from the party so they could open it in the privacy of his room.

"You didn't have to get me anything," Gabriel said.

"I wanted to," Luca said, barely containing a smile.

Gabriel carefully unwrapped the paper. He grinned sheepishly, wondering what Luca had found for him. He removed the single strip of tape that held the box closed.

There were two items, and Gabriel felt the sudden urge to cry.

He didn't. That was weak. And this was Luca. He couldn't cry in front of Luca.

Folded neatly on the right was the corduroy jacket Gabriel wished he'd gotten from the thrift store. On the left was one of Luca's sweaters—the one with large squares of grey and green.

Gabriel looked at them in disbelief. "How…"

"I had to go back for the jacket," Luca said quickly. "And I know how much you liked the sweater, so I thought you'd like—you do like it? Please tell me you like it…"

Gabriel gathered both items in his arms and held them close. "I love it. I don't know what to say."

"No need," Luca said. His smile was contained, but his eyes shone bright enough to chase away the worst kind of darkness. It was infectious.

Gabriel hugged him. "Thank you." It came out muffled against Luca's shoulder.

"You're welcome," Luca said quietly.

Gabriel didn't want to let go. In this moment, everything was *full* and exactly as it should be. It was like he'd found the thing he'd been looking for, after all this time.

Gabriel pulled away. They stood for a moment. Gabriel found his eyes drawn to Luca's lips. He looked down and gathered his fingers in the sweater.

"I didn't get a chance to wash them yet," Luca said.

"That's fine," Gabriel said.

Walking back to Mason's room, Gabriel felt light again. Maybe it wouldn't last, but it was here now. And as he watched Luca out of the corner of his eye—his hands pulled into the sleeves of his sweater—Gabriel knew the cause.

He'd never felt this kind of affection before.

Not even for Adrian, because Adrian awoke something anxious and desperate in Gabriel, and it didn't seem like love. It was an ache that had burrowed deep inside and might never go away.

But with Luca, there was calm. And joy. And gentle desire.

And he couldn't possibly deny it any longer.

THREE

SINKING

GABRIEL MADE IT home Friday evening. He parked on the street, retrieved his suitcase and backpack from the trunk, and surveyed the neighborhood. A few houses had already put up Christmas lights, but not his parents. His gaze settled on the Ali's across the street. Warm light streamed from the front windows.

Gabriel steeled himself and entered his house through the garage. The smell of chicken filled the air, and then his mom exclaimed from out of sight, "Gabriel?"

"I'm back!" Gabriel said. He set his things down as his mom rushed around the kitchen island to hug him.

"How are you feeling? Are you hungry? I have dinner almost ready," she said, hardly getting one thought out before the next.

"I'm starving. All I had for lunch was a bag of chips."

His mom swatted him. Gabriel smirked. He took in the house, pausing at a handful of presents on the living room table. A chocolate cake was also on the counter, halfway through being frosted with a chunky coconut and pecan glaze. Despite it all, he couldn't help but feel underwhelmed. He'd half expected some of his siblings to show up. Or even the Ali's.

He felt terrible for thinking that.

"Where's dad?" He asked.

"He's getting changed from work. Look at all your presents!" She said, pointing to the table.

Gabriel nodded emphatically. Heavy footsteps came from the stairs, and Gabriel's dad appeared around the corner. "Happy late Birthday!" They hugged, and his dad squeezed his arms. "You feel strong! Have you been working out?"

"A bit."

"How are you doing?"

"I'm good, just tired. Hungry, too."

"School's been fun?"

"It's great," Gabriel said, hardly thinking about the words. If he did, he would have known that wasn't quite true. Not that things were terrible, just complicated. It was better for everyone if he said what they wanted to hear. "It's been busy keeping up with all my classes. But it's been good. I've got a few good friends."

One less, now, with Andy gone. Two, if he included Kyle. But Gabriel didn't mention them because he could see the line of questions leading to how they got kicked out and the inevitable ones about whether he'd participated in the drinking. He talked about Jenna and her group but didn't mention the date. He *did* show them the sweater from Luca, but he said he found the jacket at a thrift store, which was technically true. It would have been suspicious if he'd gotten two gifts from one guy.

From his parent's perspective, it must have seemed like he was overflowing with things to share. He just didn't want silence because silence preceded deeper questions he might not be able to answer.

"Do you know how to run a business yet? Maybe you can take over for me, yeah?" His dad said, smiling.

Gabriel snorted halfheartedly. "Not yet. It's just basic classes so far. I don't know if I want to own a business, though."

His dad cocked his head. "Really?"

"I'm not sure I'd like it," Gabriel said, spearing a piece of broccoli. "I'd rather do something more..." he waved his hands uncertainly. "...creative? I don't know."

Gabriel's dad shoveled potatoes into his mouth, muffling his words. "I come up with creative solutions all the time."

"Don't talk with your mouth full," Gabriel's mom jumped in.

"What?" His dad said, cheeks bulging.

"Smaller bites, hon," she said with a sigh. "We want to be polite at dinner, not see what's in your mouth."

She laughed, but Gabriel's dad shrank in his seat. He chewed a good twenty seconds before swallowing, his excitement muted. Gabriel picked at his plate. His dad leaned on the table to continue the business lesson, but his mom cleared her throat.

"Elbows," she said, dramatically putting her hands in her lap.

Gabriel's dad gaped at her. "I'm trying!"

"Well, *we're* trying to have a nice dinner," she said, looking at Gabriel as if they were in on a joke. He just looked down, not wanting to be a part of this.

There were three or four minutes of relative silence while everyone focused on their food.

"You'll find a good job," Gabriel's dad finally said.

"I just want something I like," Gabriel said.

"Sure, but you need something that pays well, too."

"I don't really care about money."

Gabriel's dad laughed. He put his elbows on the table again. "Providing for your family is more important than doing something you like. It's about sacrifice, *responsibility*. Strong foundations,

Gabriel."

Gabriel slouched in his chair and sipped his water. "Yeah, sure."

What if he didn't want a family?

What if he didn't particularly want kids? Or a wife?

What if he wanted a husband?

What then?

Really, what happened then?

Gabriel got up to clear his plate. Out of sight from the dining table, he gripped the kitchen counter and took steadying breaths. After clearing the rest of the table, he sat back down. His mom hovered over the cake on the counter, inserting candles.

"Happy Birthday to you…" his parents sang.

Gabriel fidgeted in his seat, that familiar guilt tugging at his smile. His mere existence felt like a disappointment. The song ended, and Gabriel stared at the flickering candles, trying to clear his head enough to think of a simple wish.

He just wanted things to get easier.

Gabriel blew out all the candles in one try. He couldn't help but grin self-consciously as smoke stung his nose. He barely finished his small slice and a single scoop of vanilla ice cream. They moved on to the presents, and Gabriel unwrapped a grey peacoat, leather gloves, and a Jules Verne collectors set.

Brilliant things. *Expensive* things. Too expensive.

He didn't deserve any of this, for who he really was.

Gabriel hugged his parents, thanking them profusely as he gathered everything into his arms and headed to his room. Then he grabbed Luca's sweater and laid on his bed, nose tucked into the fabric. It smelled faintly woodsy, like pine trees after a rainstorm.

He closed his eyes and drifted away.

THAT SMALL VELVET BOX

THE NEXT EVENING, Gabriel jogged to the Ali's for dinner at their place. Everyone was home. Chloe and Adrian from school, and Mr. Ali from the ocean. He'd closed out the fishing season two weeks before.

"He barely smells normal again," Mrs. Ali quipped as they gathered around the kitchen island.

"We went through a *lot* of soap," Mr. Ali said, then winked at his wife. "Didn't we?"

She smacked his arm. Gabriel laughed.

"Alright," Adrian slapped the table and stood up. "Didn't need to hear that." He tugged Gabriel's arm. "I have something to show you."

Gabriel looked back as Mr. Ali raised his hands in defense. "What? It was a joke." A pause. "Kind of."

"Stop!" Chloe groaned.

Adrian led the way to his room, where he rummaged in his nightstand. The bed was made, but Adrian's suitcase spilled clothes all over the floor. Adrian turned around, a black velvet box in hand.

Gabriel took it, looking up. Adrian seemed ready to burst with excitement. "Open it."

Gabriel did, revealing a diamond ring. It was small. Elegant. A skinny, silver band with one diamond in the center. The pit in Gabriel's stomach deepened, but he threw on a smile.

"Of course I'll marry you," Gabriel said. "But I don't need a ring."

Adrian laughed heartily. "I'm going to propose to Savanah before Christmas."

Gabriel struggled for words. "That's incredible."

"What do you think?"

"I love it. It's simple, but perfect…"

"I think so."

"That's so exciting. I'm really happy for you," Gabriel handed the ring back, and Adrian looked at it, face beaming. That allowed Gabriel time to compose his expression, to chase away the strain at the edges of his eyes.

"You're the first person I've told besides my family," Adrian said.

"Wow…" Gabriel managed to get out. "When are you going to propose?"

"I'm thinking Christmas Eve. We'll probably go out to dinner, then I'll ask after that."

"That's great. I can't believe it."

"I can't wait."

"I bet."

Adrian returned the ring to his dresser and they went back downstairs.

Gabriel was a churning sea.

He'd hardly thought about Adrian since that sermon before college. He'd blocked it all out. He couldn't deal with the unresolved feelings or knowing nothing could ever happen between them. And it's not like he wanted that anymore, but after all these years, those feelings had nestled into his very soul. Only now—with the time apart—could he recognize how it really was.

It was a racing heart before they saw each other. Restlessness in his presence. The need to say something meaningful, to feel that *connection*. And every time it became about 'Adrian and Savannah,' he felt a stab between his ribs.

Gabriel spent a minute in the downstairs bathroom. He shook out his arms. Washed his face. Smoothed his shirt.

Rejoining the others, Mr. Ali opened a bottle of Chardonnay. He emptied it into five glasses. Chloe and Gabriel took theirs with mature thanks. Mrs. Ali kept her disapproval to a quiet frown. Gabriel swirled his glass.

"Did you show him?" Mr. Ali asked Adrian.

"The ring? Yep," Adrian said, eyes alight.

"I thought he was proposing, but the diamond wasn't big enough," Gabriel said.

Chloe choked. All the air vanished from the room. Eyes snapped in his direction.

"Oh my God…" Gabriel whispered. Shame crushed his lungs. "I didn't mean that at all."

Chloe continued coughing. Mr. Ali shifted uncomfortably, and his wife looked like she'd been slapped. Adrian stared into his glass.

"I…I'm so sorry," Gabriel persisted. His face burned. "I was trying to make a joke…"

"It's fine," Adrian said, forcing a laugh. "I know what you meant."

"It's an incredible ring."

"Thanks."

"She'll love it."

"I hope so."

Chloe gave a final cough, then laughed. "You're so dumb." She hugged him from the side. "That's why we love you. I *missed* you, Gabriel."

The tension cracked and slipped away to something small. It was still there, but it hid in the shadows. Gabriel knew he wouldn't stop thinking about it the entire night. For the next few days, probably. He leaned close to Chloe and nudged her with his elbow.

"What's new?"

"Not much," she said. "I'm trying not to go insane with all the engagement talk."

Gabriel bit his lip. He watched Adrian and his mom go back and forth about the intricacies of picking out rings. Mr. Ali busied himself with pulling a casserole out of the oven, a pleasant smile on his face. They seemed to have recovered from his thoughtless comment.

Gabriel didn't believe it.

He knew he had to re-earn their affection.

"Yeah, I get that," Gabriel said, sipping his wine. He carefully set it down. The last thing he needed was to break something.

"It's *literally* all they've talked about today. And as soon as we have people over, they'll ask when I'm getting married."

"I never know what to say to that."

"We've barely started college."

"And there's so much else going on."

"Like what?"

Gabriel caught himself. He tugged his shirt collar and looked at Adrian. He tore his gaze away and realized Mr. Ali was watching him and Chloe. Dropping his attention to his hands, he said, "I don't know. Everyone seems so happy…"

Mr. Ali had turned away again. It took Chloe a few moments to respond. "I understand."

She didn't.

They talked about school, but Gabriel couldn't focus on the conversation. He felt like an imposter. He wondered if they knew.

Adrian drifted to the living room fireplace to take a call from Savanah. Chloe and her mom put the finishing touches on the dinner by running items to the dining table. Mr. Ali broke out another bottle of wine, nodding at Gabriel's empty glass.

"Want another?"

"If I can, thanks."

"Sure," Mr. Ali said, refilling their glasses. "Are your parents cool with this?"

"We don't really talk about it."

"I don't want to overstep my bounds."

"I mean, it's your house, right?"

"It's more about trust with them."

"They didn't stop me at Christmas."

Mr. Ali dipped his head, conceding the point. "Anyway, how is it being away?"

"It's great. I can finally breathe."

"That's good. Making friends?"

"I think so, I…" Gabriel grimaced, teeth set. Mr. Ali's brow raised. "I have one friend who was kicked out for drinking on campus. It was just a few days ago, so that's…tough."

"I'm sorry."

"It's fine."

Mr. Ali shrugged in a way that said it wasn't. "How do you feel being back?"

Gabriel hesitated. He touched his neck. His shirt felt too small. "It's great to see everyone, but it's nice to be away."

Mr. Ali sipped his wine. "I feel the same, sometimes, being on the ocean. You're someone else out there, you know?"

Mr. Ali's attention drifted through his house. Gabriel stared into his glass.

"Dinner's ready!" Mrs. Ali called from the dining room.

"Hey, I'm always here," Mr. Ali said.

"Thanks."

"If you want to get breakfast before you go back to school, I'm free."

"Yeah, maybe."

"Boys! We're waiting!" Mrs. Ali called again.

"We're coming," Mr. Ali returned. He squeezed Gabriel's shoulder and led them to the dining room. "Whatever you need."

It sounded genuine.

Gabriel couldn't imagine saying exactly what was on his mind. Mr. Ali might be able to understand. But there was a chance he wouldn't. Gabriel couldn't risk that. This was too precious of a relationship to lose if things went wrong.

Something settled over him that evening, heavy and thick—slowly at first, so he hardly noticed, and then it was all he felt. It was like the fog after Mason's testimony and the night with Jenna. After watching Andy drive away.

It was in the walls of his parent's house, too, in the very foundations. It was in the recollection of nights better left alone.

It was all the things he'd never said.

And in just a few hours, he'd completely forgotten what it was like to exist outside of this feeling.

THE FOG

GABRIEL WOKE UP bright and fresh, just after nine.

He thought back to last night and was ashamed for feeling so bad. It didn't make sense. It was almost like he'd been making it up. Maybe he was.

Gabriel read for half an hour, did three sets of push-ups and sit-ups, then showered and made breakfast. He was halfway through planning the rest of his day when his mom clomped downstairs and said they would leave for church in twenty minutes. He reviewed his list. He'd forgotten it was Sunday, so church wasn't on it. He hardly had time to do everything as it was. Time at bookstores and coffee shops couldn't be rushed.

Everything tightened when Gabriel entered his parent's church. He warily navigated the sanctuary, hoping they wouldn't run into Pastor Evans. After the sermon, his family drifted to the potluck line, which meant they'd be there for at least another two hours. The Alis left early, forcing Gabriel to fend for himself amongst the people dying to hear about his first months of college.

They made it home just after three. By this point, there was no use in trying to salvage the day. He didn't have the energy for that anyway. His mind was stuffed with cotton, and an invisible hand had been pressing against his ribs again. He decided to take a nap. Then it was dinner and watching TV until he could no longer keep his eyes open.

It WAS A bit harder to wake up the next day.

He stayed in bed for a long while. He knew he should read, but he didn't particularly feel like it. He didn't work out, either. Those were distractions. He needed to focus.

Today, the most important thing was getting out of the house.

It wasn't as easy as people made it out to be. It took thirty minutes for him to decide to make scrambled eggs with a side of toast and another twenty to muster the energy to clean everything up. Then he sat in his car for nearly ten minutes, trying to decide where he wanted to go first.

He went to a coffee shop and sat at the corner of the community table. He tried to read, but his attention kept drifting. Most of the time, he just sat and stared. Fatigue set in by noon, so he scrapped the bookstore plan and went home to sleep it off.

The next day, he filled his backpack and went downstairs but never made it outside.

The fog had gotten worse. He'd pushed it to the side before, but it refused to budge today. It was like everything was slowly closing in, and he felt sad for every reason but for nothing in particular.

He just wandered the house, observing all the little things that had accumulated over the years: Childhood crafts on top shelves, fifteen-year-old glue art on the dining room window, stacks of magazines behind the living room easy chair.

He browsed the bookshelves without direction and paused before the small collection of parenting books. There were a lot about raising boys.

Gabriel pulled *Raising a Modern Day Knight* off the shelf and thumbed through it. The cover was of a tacky, bejeweled sword.

He smirked.

If only his parents knew. If only they understood how far he'd fallen. So much for their books and prayers and hopes. He put the book back.

And then he understood a deep truth, and there was nothing but guilt.

These books weren't for Gabriel or his siblings. They were for his parents, to teach them how to build a family. They were looking for answers too, and the last thing they wanted was to do something wrong. Of course they didn't.

But Gabriel was screwing that up. He hadn't tried to disappoint them. It was happening anyway. Gabriel settled on the couch, knees pulled up to his chin.

You're nothing.

Gabriel ducked his head. He found it hard not to listen when there was so much evidence against him.

You're not the kid your parents wanted.

That much seemed clear.

At least they have Jacob.

Yes. At least they had Jacob.

Gabriel heard the rumbling of the garage door. He jolted to his feet and dashed to his room, backpack in hand. His mom plodded inside, and Gabriel heard the telltale sound of her unloading groceries. She shouted upstairs to say she was home. Gabriel shouted back.

He opened his computer and sat on his bed. Maybe he'd just watch TV today. That seemed to be the only thing that kept the clouds at bay.

By Thanksgiving day, there was nothing but numbness. Gabriel covered it up nicely with the sweater from Luca.

By late morning, the house was bustling with activity. Everyone but Isaac was present, and there was hardly any room to move. Gabriel couldn't go two feet without squeezing past cousins and aunts and uncles—all on his dad's side. They still lived in Boston. Most of his mom's family was in New York and Vermont, so they didn't see them as much.

Three of Heidi's kids screamed and ran in circles before someone kicked them outside to play in the snow. She carried her fourth on her arm. He was eight months old and stared at everything with blank shock. Rachel's first—two-year-old Emily—soared the house on Uncle Marshall's shoulders.

Jacob soon cornered Gabriel on the couch, wine in hand. Gabriel's drink was apple cider, but he kept glancing at the open bottles of alcohol.

"When do you think you're going to get a girlfriend?" Jacob asked.

Gabriel grimaced. "I'm just focusing on school right now."

"That's good. You need to set yourself up for a future first."

"That's the plan."

"But when you do find someone—and it'll probably be unexpected—you should be intentional. That's one of the biggest things I've learned with Nancy. Girls love to be pursued."

Did Luca count as unexpected?

"Make sure you're going on regular dates. Really take your time to get to know her."

"Sure," Gabriel mumbled, scanning the room.

"It's great, *really* great."

"What is?"

"Marriage. Dating is awesome, but man, being married is *incredible*. Being so tied to another person, trying to figure things out together. It's a lot of work, but it's so good. It's so worth it."

"I bet."

"You'll love it."

"Yeah," Gabriel stood up. Jacob wasn't taking the hint. "I'm going to get another drink."

"I better be the first person you call when you find a girl!" Jacob called after him.

Gabriel clenched his jaw and navigated to the minibar in the dining room. There were a handful of open bottles of wine. Whites and reds. A few of champagne on ice. There were juices, sodas in a bucket of ice, and some bottles of sparkling cider.

Gabriel hovered at the table as his cousin Sarah chased a screaming Emily through the room. Grimacing, he reached for the champagne and poured himself a generous glass. It was almost the same color as the cider, so it should be easy enough to hide. Taking a sip, he walked into the kitchen and was immediately kicked out by his mom. She frantically went from stove to oven to counter, dancing around Rachel and Aunt Lilly.

Every open surface was covered with food. Sweet potatoes with brown sugar. Garlic green beans. Deviled eggs. Two large turkeys. Pecan and pumpkin pies. Everyone ate when and where they could. Sitting down as a group was too much hassle, and they simply didn't have enough room to set up extra tables.

Gabriel filled a paper plate and squeezed onto the living room couch to watch the Detroit Lions game. He chose this spot to avoid personal questions, and he knew enough about football to talk vaguely about the standings and most of the league's big players. His dad and Uncle Marshall stood to the side, keeping half an eye on the game as they talked about work.

Gabriel refilled his champagne at the end of the first quarter and got a third during halftime. By his fourth, someone had opened the second bottle, and he was able to comfortably drift from one conversation to the next. Now, he didn't feel as claustrophobic, and the heaviness had been gone for at least an hour.

"How do you like school so far?" Aunt Lilly asked as Gabriel hovered over the dessert table.

"It's good! It's fun being away," Gabriel said, selecting a chunk of pumpkin pie crust.

"That's great. Have you met anyone special yet?"

Gabriel shrugged. "I went on a date with this girl, Jenna, but I don't know if we'll go out again."

"Aww, that's too bad."

"It's ok," Gabriel said, floating through the house again. When Uncle Marshall asked the same question, Gabriel was more forthcoming with the details. "We went thrift shopping and got dinner. It was fun. She's really cool, so we'll see what happens."

"I'm really happy for you!" Uncle Marshall said. "We've all been waiting for you to find someone."

Gabriel swallowed uncomfortably. He ducked his chin into Luca's sweater.

"I hear rumors you've met someone?" Uncle Roger said.

Gabriel ground his teeth. Why did everyone care so much?

"Tell me about her," Uncle Roger said.

Him, you mean?

Gabriel almost blurted it out. And then he was grinning for some reason, even though everything ached inside. Maybe he'd had too much to drink…

Gabriel swirled his glass, trying to compose himself. "Yeah, *she's*…really great."

But she doesn't like gay movies.

Who did, really?

But…

Wait.

He liked them, right?

Did that make him a bad person?

"We'll see what happens. I'm not sure if we're going to date," Gabriel said. "I might have my eye on someone else."

Gabriel froze.

Shit.

Uncle Roger's brow furrowed in concern.

"I'm kidding!" Gabriel waved a hand in the air. "She's great, there's just a lot going on."

Stop talking.

Gabriel gulped down the rest of his champagne. "I think I'm going to help with the dishes."

Gabriel stumbled upstairs for his headphones because cleaning was always better with music. He chugged a glass of water and laid on his floor, trying to convince his body to sober up.

He really *did* intend to help with the dishes, but he fell asleep before he got the chance.

A SINGLE MAN

THE HOUSE WAS empty again by Saturday night.

Gabriel sat on his bed, browsing movies on his computer. And then he saw it: *A Single Man*. His eyes widened. This was one of Luca's favorites—the one he made a poster for. They hadn't discussed it since they met, and Gabriel kept forgetting to bring it up until he'd forgotten about it altogether. He pressed Play without reading what it was about because sometimes it is best to be surprised.

And this movie…

Well, this movie shook the foundations of his world.

It was the opening violins and Colin Firth's naked body writhing underwater, struggling for air.

It was the awful screech and *smack* of a car accident. A flipped car and a body on a snowy road—Firth approaching with careful steps, then lying next to the dead man.

It was a final, gentle kiss between the two, and the way he *gasped* awake. The way he touched his lips, distraught, and his narration of "*Waking up begins with saying* here *and* now. *For the past eight months, waking up has actually hurt.*"

It was the way he mechanically prepared for the day. The perfect arrangement of notes and letters on his desk and floor. The proclamation to himself in the mirror, *"Just get through the goddamn day."*

And, finally, the line that cut through Gabriel's soul: *"After all, my heart has been broken, and I feel as if I am sinking. Drowning. Can't breathe."*

The film was *everything*, and everything Gabriel wanted in love. The banter and devotion and quiet moments between George and Jim. The yearning. The grief and joy and the discovery of *life*.

And when it was over, all he could do was wipe his eyes and stare at the ceiling and sit with the ache in his chest.

FOUR

A BRILLIANT STUDENT

GABRIEL SKIPPED CHURCH Sunday morning to drive back to school. The further away he got, the lighter he felt. While he drove, he listened to the soundtrack for *A Single Man*. He couldn't get the movie out of his head. He longed for what George and Jim had.

He couldn't wait to tell Luca.

Parking in front of his dorm, Gabriel hoped for a good end to the semester. And then—walking down his hallway, suitcase in tow—it struck him again that Andy was gone.

His shoulders deflated.

Clouds built and darkened in the back of his mind.

GABRIEL ARRIVED AT Spiritual Formation before Luca, and when Luca showed up, all Gabriel wanted to do was hug him. They fist-bumped instead.

"How was break?" Gabriel asked.

"Good! Probably gained ten pounds, can you tell?" Luca said, patting his stomach.

"Looks more like twenty," Gabriel said.

"Harsh."

"Yeah, well, you still look good."

"I always do," Luca said. He leaned back, hands folded in his lap.

Gabriel tapped his pencil on the table. "I watched *A Single Man* over break."

Luca's eyes snapped to Gabriel. "Yeah?"

"It was incredible. The music, colors, *everything*…" He looked at his hands. "You remind me of Jim. I liked him."

Luca just scratched his nose, mouth half open in the way you did when you were trying not to smile. For a minute, there was silence. Not the bad kind, but the kind that held space for all the things that couldn't be said aloud.

"I can send you a list of other movies," Luca said.

Gabriel met his eyes and felt a flutter. "Like this one?"

"Similar," Luca said vaguely.

"I'd love that," Gabriel said, and that was that.

At chapel, Jenna and Gabriel hugged and exchanged questions about their time off. They'd hardly texted the whole time. Gabriel was relieved by that. Maybe if he didn't initiate, nothing else would happen.

But did he really want that? Could he make a relationship with her work?

Gabriel ran out of things to say by the time the band took the stage. He mouthed the songs without much gusto, and he was ready to leave when Dr. Stone marched to the podium.

"I hope you guys had a nice break. Just a few more weeks, so finish strong," he said, somber. He rubbed his face, taking a few seconds to continue. "I have heavy news to share with you all. As some of you know, we lost an incredible student last week. Ben Salazar passed away right before Thanksgiving."

Gabriel stiffened.

No…

"He was a brilliant student, truly a light on campus, and he was a wonderful friend. There will be a memorial service this weekend in Grandview, open to any student. We ask that you please respect his family's privacy as they navigate this difficult time."

Gabriel studied the picture of Ben in disbelief. His broad, genuine smile dominated the screen. There wasn't a hint of confusion or heaviness behind his eyes. So different from the person he'd seen on the steps of the Biblical Studies building.

No no no…

How could he be gone?

There were whispers of what might have happened in the back of his mind, but he shut them down. He couldn't think about that.

The message that day was on the fragility of life and the need to minister to others. To be a light. To build each other up.

Had Gabriel failed at that?

Guilt weighed down his limbs. The rest of the day, Ben was the only thing people cared to talk about. Back in their dorm, Gabriel and Jason played Galaga in Micah's room. Jason had just started a new round.

"Did you guys know him?" Gabriel asked.

Micah shrugged. "Not really, but I think one of Andy's friends lived with him off campus."

"Yeah, I've been to their gathering a few times," Gabriel said.

"I don't think I met him," Jason said. "Still feels weird, though."

"Do you know what happened?" Gabriel asked.

"I heard he did it to himself," Jason said. *"Shit!"* His ship exploded.

Gabriel stared at him, but the whispers inside echoed the speculation. "Really?"

"That's just what I heard," Jason said.

"I heard that too," Micah said.

"It's probably just a rumor, right?" Gabriel asked.

It had to be. If he'd been one of the last people to see Ben and hadn't helped him…that would be too much to bear.

"I don't think so," Micah said. "He and Mason were friends, and Mason won't talk about it. If it's a car accident, you say it's a car accident, you know?"

In a cold and detached way, Gabriel understood. There was no reason to hide something if there was nothing to hide. But why would Ben do it? He seemed so put together. So full of purpose.

What caused him to throw that away?

What caused *anyone* to throw that away?

THE WEIGHT OF IT ALL

THE FIRST GATHERING after the break was heavy with the loss of Ben.

There might have been eighty people packed into the house, making it hot and hard to breathe and nearly impossible to move. Gabriel drifted through the crowd, not wanting to stop and talk about the things straining for the surface. He gave tight smiles and nods and went off to find a quiet corner.

Everyone was here because of Ben. It seemed they all wanted to be a part of the aftermath, to show they'd been present at this significant time. Girls dabbed their eyes, and a few were outright crying. Guys reminisced about late-night antics. They all had something to say, but Gabriel wondered how many of these people Ben was actually close with.

Gabriel snagged a spot on the living room couch long before the evening events started. He'd lost track of Mason some time ago. Three others squeezed in next to him as the room continued to fill. He tried to make himself as small as possible, leaning on the armrest. The rest of the living room was packed with people sitting on the floor, knees pulled up to their chests. Others spilled around the corners and into the kitchen and hallway by the front door.

Pressed against the far wall, a blonde-haired girl led them in worship with her guitar, and a guy behind her played a percussion drum. People raised their hands in the air and closed their eyes in reverence. Half of them seemed on the verge of breaking down.

After three songs, one of Ben's roommates—Joseph—came up to speak. He paced the five-foot strip of floor that wasn't occupied.

"I don't know exactly what Ben was facing, but if I did, maybe I could have helped him," Joseph said, staring at a point above Gabriel's head. He came back to himself and walked his stage again. "I think this is a wake-up call. We need to be honest with each other about what we're facing in our lives. You can't hide it anymore."

Gabriel covered his mouth with one hand. His leg bounced.

"I know people in this room are dealing with things they haven't talked about. I know some people here are holding onto things they are too afraid to say. But that's the *Enemy* talking. The Devil wants you to stay silent."

Gabriel swallowed. It felt like there was glass in his throat. Failures plagued his mind.

Getting drunk at Thanksgiving. The way he felt for Luca and how he just wanted to be in his presence. His lack of trust in God. The bad movies and music. The porn.

Not checking on Ben.

He was a terrible person.

Joseph went on like that for twenty minutes, and Gabriel continued to sink.

"The only way we can move forward with God is to come clean about our pasts. It comes through confession and repentance. True faith requires action, and we need to act in this battle against the Enemy," Joseph said, motioning for the band to return. "As they play this last song, I want you all to partner up and pray for each other."

Dread compressed Gabriel's lungs. Heads turned left and right, searching for victims. Some people shuffled around the room to find different groups. Gabriel became a statue. Maybe if he didn't move, they would think he was part of the furniture—

"What's your name?" The guy next to Gabriel asked.

"Gabriel," he said.

"I'm Jonathan."

"Okay."

"Is there anything I can pray for?"

Gabriel tried opening his mouth to speak, but terror closed it. The instinct to sprint from the room surged in his legs. "I don't know."

"What's on your mind?"

Gabriel shrugged. He had to say *something*. "I don't know, I've been a bit anxious recently. About school, life…" Gabriel scratched his nose, willing his emotions to stay under control. "I guess I've been kind of sad too."

Kind of?

"What else?" Jonathan asked.

How did he know? Could he see his guilt? His pain?

Gabriel dug his nails into his arms. "And I've been struggling with some things…"

"What things?" Jonathan asked, eyes hungry to know the sins of the flesh and to cast them away.

Gabriel wanted nothing more than to jump off the couch and escape this place. Fervent prayers of those around him filled his ears. His heart hammered in his chest. His vision flickered. He couldn't think.

"I guess I've been struggling…with my…" Gabriel licked his lips. Adrenaline weakened his limbs, and he teetered on the edge of no return. The moment he opened his mouth, his life would never be the same. He just didn't think he could keep it inside anymore. His eyes filled with tears. "…with my sexuality—for as long as I can remember, and I don't know what to do."

There.

It was done.

He thought he might throw up.

Jonathan didn't move.

Gabriel refused to look at him. He didn't dare meet his eyes.

"Alright," Jonathan began, "I can pray if you want."

Gabriel wiped his eyes and nodded. He tensed when Jonathan placed a hand on his shoulder. They bowed their heads.

"Dear God, thank you for Gabriel. Thank you for his bravery to admit to the struggles he's facing. God, you say that if we confess our sins to one another, we will be healed and cleansed from all unrighteousness. I want to declare that over Gabriel right now, that he would be healed from his afflictions and that you would show him this is just a condition of our broken world. And just as some of us struggle with anger or lying, all sin is the same to you…"

GABRIEL CRUMBLES.

Jonathan drones on, unaware.

The wrong words can break a fractured heart.

These are the wrong words.

Regret can destroy a trembling soul.

There is nothing but regret.

This is what it means to be Gabriel Moore, right now.

JONATHAN REMOVED HIS hand from Gabriel's shoulder. "I really felt God's presence, didn't you?"

Gabriel nodded in a numb, disbelieving kind of way. He had vainly hoped that being honest would relieve some of the pressure.

He felt infinitely worse.

And Jonathan was wrong. They *all* were—Grant, Mason, Pastor Evans.

Not all sin was the same.

You could choose not to rob a bank. You couldn't choose who you liked. That was something you *did*. This was something you *were*. And with no way to separate your soul from your sin, the only option was to hate the very core of yourself.

Gabriel stood and shoved his way out of the room, dodging legs and arms and confused looks. He thought he heard someone call his name. He didn't stop. And after a second, there was nothing but rushing water in his ears.

He emerged outside and immediately took off to the right, not knowing where he was headed. Every breath was more difficult than the last. The air was icy, but he hardly felt it. He cursed his weakness for opening up. It had just confirmed his worst fears—that they were just as scared of this as he was.

But *why?*

Why was it so terrible when it had never been used to hurt anyone? What if it was genuine, like George and Jim? Why was that so wrong?

And as much as he wanted to accept himself, did they know he never would have chosen this? Did they know the agonizing fear that your very *thoughts* might send you to hell despite your belief in God? Did they know about the pleading for God's healing? Or the hopelessness when it didn't happen?

Did they know nothing ever changed?

Because no matter what he did, the weight only grew worse. And worse. Every day, worse.

Of course they didn't know. It was just another sin to them, yet simultaneously a scourge to be eradicated. They didn't care, and they cared too much. But they never tried to *understand*.

Gabriel didn't know how long he could hold out. If God never healed him, he didn't think he could go his whole life fighting the desire to hold hands with a guy. Or kiss. Or more…

And maybe his only option was to kill himself before that happened. Because he *would* slip up. Maybe only once, but that was enough. So, maybe God would forgive suicide if it were done to prevent something worse—

Shit.

Shitshitshit.

He squeezed his temples with both hands and took frantic breaths. He was in the woods now, a mile south of school—

Maybe he *should* end it.

STOP.

He was falling apart.

Why did God make him this way?

If He didn't make mistakes, why did He make people gay? Or crippled? Or stuck with abusive parents? If everything happened according to God's plan, why the *fuck* were people punished for things *He* designed for them?

"It's not fair…" Gabriel hissed to himself. The final threads holding him together snapped. Volcanic anger rose from deep within, and he screamed into the void. "I've done everything you wanted, and you don't *fucking* care! You know what, *FUCK YOU!* Fuck you, you *goddamn* cunt bastard!"

And there it was. The unforgivable sin.

Cursing God Himself.

Sinking to the ground, Gabriel let out a quiet sob. Despite what he'd just done, he felt incredible relief. He was going to hell now. He knew that. But that was probably guaranteed already, considering the path he was on.

GABRIEL'S RELIEF LASTED all of five minutes.

It faded with his anger and was soon replaced by the terrible realization of what he'd done. He'd messed up. Horribly. There was no way God could forgive him for this.

He prayed anyway. Slow at first—calm and ashamed. Before he knew it, his prayers morphed into desperate pleading. "I'm so sorry, I didn't mean it. Just let me find a wife, and I'll be happy. You can take anything else away. I'll do whatever you want...I don't care. Just forgive me, I'm so sorry..."

Gabriel lay sprawled on the forest floor, hands digging into the leaves and rocks and muddy earth. Uncontrollable sobbing wracked his body.

He rocked back and forth in the darkness for a long, long time. He ignored the cold and the way jagged rocks dug into his knees. It felt like an eternity before the tears slowed and the panic subsided enough for him to breathe again.

Gabriel adjusted to a sitting position and brushed the dirt off his legs. He retrieved his phone and put on a worship playlist, then laid on his back and let the music take him far away.

GABRIEL MADE IT back to his dorm three minutes before curfew.

The first thing he did was wash his hands and face in the bathroom. The mirror revealed an awful sight, and Gabriel almost started crying again. His eyes were so red it looked like he'd popped a blood vessel. Underneath, they were puffy, like he'd had an allergic reaction.

Gabriel turned on the leftmost sink as the bathroom door opened. He splashed water over his face.

"Gabriel, you're back," the intruder said. Mason. *Shit.*

"I went for a walk," Gabriel said, sparing a glance in Mason's direction. He was in his underwear with a towel slung over his shoulder, shower caddy in hand.

"Are you ok?"

"I'm just tired, and I have a lot on my plate right now."

Mason stood there long enough for Gabriel to know he didn't completely buy the act. "Alright, well, I'm here if you ever need to talk."

"Sure, thanks," Gabriel said.

Mason nodded and headed for the showers. Gabriel dried his face and stared at his reflection. He smiled. It just looked hollow.

He couldn't even fake it.

THE EDGE OF ETERNITY

WHEN YOU MIGHT have doomed yourself to hell, there is terrible fear, and that fear is a sickness. It corrodes every good thing until there is only the dark.

This dark is complete and total.

IT WAS WITH Gabriel when he woke up and when he crawled into bed at night. It was there in class and chapel. It was there no matter who he talked to or what he did, and it took away his appetite.

It seeped from every cell. It pooled in his lungs and coiled around his heart, and it *squeezed* with everything it had.

Only two things seemed to help.

First, TV kept the world at bay. He knew he just needed to get through each day, and hours of screen time made things just a little easier. If he got through enough days, maybe, eventually, things *might* get better.

He hoped.

Second, sleep erased the world. It was a place of nothingness, the closest thing to peace. When he laid down, hours drifted away like the wisp of smoke from an extinguished candle.

For weeks, he did the bare minimum to pass his assignments, and he skipped classes when he could, often missing the entire day, including chapel. Every time he stepped into a classroom, it felt like the walls were closing in. Sometimes, he'd sit outside, bundled in a jacket but hardly feeling the cold or the bite of snow. Sometimes, he jogged around campus, the physical action letting his mind detach. The only bright moments were spent with Luca in class or studying in one of their rooms.

He still participated in movie and game nights in his dorm, but he only went so they wouldn't question his absence. These nights were hard to enjoy. He could never completely block everything out, and every time he laughed, it cut off too short.

These changes hadn't failed to attract attention. Mason stopped by his room one evening as Gabriel watched a movie on his computer, sitting on his bunk.

"I just wanted to check in to see how you're doing," Mason said, one hand holding the door frame.

"I'm alright," Gabriel returned. Mason pursed his lips, evaluating him calmly.

"I knew Ben since we were freshmen, and what happened..." Mason trailed off as he looked at the ceiling. "It didn't have to happen. And I don't want you to feel like you're alone."

Gabriel was careful to keep his face emotionless.

"My door's always open," Mason said.

"Sure," Gabriel said quietly. "Thanks."

They let the silence hang in the air. Mason soon left the room and closed the door. Gabriel shut his computer and curled into a ball on his bed, feeling like he was being torn apart piece by piece. No doubt he could talk to Mason, but could he trust him?

Maybe.

Probably not.

And he didn't want to talk. Not after Jonathan at The Gathering. Mason would just make things worse.

He'd have to keep this quiet.

Just get through the goddamn day, George said in his mind.

Gabriel thought back to the movie. The ending. The *feeling*. And Luca.

Yeah, well, some days are harder than others.

THE LAST WEEKEND before finals, Jason planned a camping trip with Arlo and Hunter. Gabriel had to stay back because he had too many assignments to catch up on.

The Friday Jason was set to leave, Gabriel skipped English to spend the afternoon at the coffee shop in town. He fully intended to start working on his paper, and he'd brought his Biology textbook to begin a study guide for the final exam, but neither happened. Instead, he found himself lost in his journal, desperately trying to figure out where he stood. What he wanted. Who he was. The kind of life he hoped for.

If anything even mattered.

On his second hot chocolate, he figured it out. Kind of.

He wanted to fall in love. He wanted someone kind and gentle. Someone who could understand the things he didn't and heal what he couldn't. A person to hold in the emptiest of nights, and someone for the good times.

He wanted to be like the people in the movies who weren't afraid to go after what they wanted. He wanted what George and Jim had.

He wanted to be happy and not feel this pain anymore.

And maybe that could be Luca. Or someone else. Just someone, really.

But the more people he saw who had what he wanted, the worse it felt because it wasn't an option for him. He wasn't allowed to have that kind of life and abandon what he believed. He would lose everything. He would lose his friends and family and be condemned forever—if he wasn't already.

And Gabriel knew something else: He *would* slip up one of these days. No matter how hard he tried, he knew he would fall because he didn't want to fight it anymore. It was too exhausting a battle. There was terror in that realization, and he couldn't escape the feeling that once he did stumble, there would be no coming back.

Gabriel packed up his things and left the coffee shop in a daze. He stopped at the bridge a block away. A stream trickled below, the banks packed with ice. He leaned over the edge. It wasn't a far drop. Fifteen feet, maybe. Probably not enough.

He turned back and examined the street. Cars trundled by. He bounced on his toes, watching them pass, trying to gauge their speed. The signs said twenty-five miles per hour, barely more than a crawl. He watched the tires.

Even a slow car can crush things.

He hissed to himself and walked toward campus. Vague thoughts of laundry detergent and Ibuprofen filled his head. He kept his eyes down as he navigated his hallway. Composed, mind blank, he entered his room. Jason was in the middle of packing his duffle bag.

"Any plans this weekend?" Jason asked, stuffing in a jacket.

Gabriel skirted his roommate and removed his backpack, struggling to keep his voice even. "I'm not sure. Probably just going to be nice and quiet." Gabriel set his backpack on his chair and flipped open the top, his back to Jason.

"That's cool," Jason said. "I can't believe the semester's almost over."

"Yeah…" Gabriel said.

He removed his computer. His notebook. Water bottle. Lined them up on his desk. He reached in one more time for his computer charger. For a long moment, he looked at it, fingers running over the thick rubber cord.

Jason zipped up his duffle bag. "You alright?"

Gabriel set the cord down. "Just thinking about all the homework I have left."

"That's why I'm putting it off for a few days."

"Love it," Gabriel said. He removed his shoes and jacket, stepped on his desk, and crawled onto his bed. "I'm going to lie down for a bit."

"Sure," Jason said. "I'll be quiet."

Gabriel didn't respond. Jason had settled at his desk and was typing on his computer. Despite his exhaustion, Gabriel couldn't find sleep. His thoughts kept returning to the computer charger.

Out of everything, it seemed like the simplest option.

Would it work?

Gabriel pinched his eyes, keeping his breathing level. He kept hearing Jason's sporadic movements. It was both comforting and aggravating. He desperately wanted him to leave but was terrified of what being alone might bring.

It's a strong cord.

A phone buzzed. Jason stood up and shuffled around the room. Gabriel remained perfectly still.

It's not like he had to do it. He just wanted to see if it was possible. Just in case. Was that so bad?

There came the sound of a crumpling jacket. The swish of laces being tightened. A small grunt at the lift of a duffle bag. Then the opening of a door.

Gabriel longed to say something to stop him from leaving, but of course he stayed silent.

The door clicked shut.

He was alone. Finally. He peeked over the edge of the bed. The charger was still there.

Waiting.

Gabriel curled back up into a ball, willing his mind to go blank. Willing all the inescapable thoughts to disappear somehow. He kept trying to get himself to cry, but the emotion he couldn't always control around others was nowhere to be found by himself.

No. That wasn't entirely true. It was there, just lodged inside his throat. Stuck. Like a rock jammed in the sole of a boot...

The next time he opened his eyes, the room was nearly dark. It was probably time to get dinner, but Gabriel wasn't hungry. He rubbed his eyes.

Just try it.

Gabriel flipped onto his stomach and buried his face in his pillow. His hands clawed at the mattress.

It won't get better.

He stayed there as long as he could, lungs screaming for air. He raised his head and took a desperate gasp. The relief only lasted a few moments, and then everything was crashing over him again, many times worse.

Gabriel sat up, rocking back and forth.

It'll be easier than you think.

Gabriel dropped to the floor. He tried not to listen. He did a few jumping jacks, then pushups. He moved to the window and lowered the blinds. He did more pushups, but they weren't clearing his head this time.

He snatched the computer cord from his desk, examining it. It had three parts. The thin cord that plugged into his computer, the adaptor in the middle, and the thicker section that plugged into a socket. Each piece was detachable.

He wrapped the thin part around his neck, tightening it against the skin. It wasn't enough to impede his air, but he felt pressure build in his head from the restricted blood flow.

Shit.

Gabriel released the cord and circled the room, feeling his jugular and carotid with one hand. They pulsed angrily. He wrapped the cord again, leaving it a bit longer until his head felt wobbly.

Fuck.

Gabriel dropped the cord on the ground. He pressed his hand against the point where his neck and jaw met and was barely able to wheeze out a breath. He circled the edges of the room. He stepped carefully, his front heel brushing the toes of his back foot.

When this failed to keep his attention, he peeked inside the closet and tested the bar inside. It creaked under the weight of one hand, already sagging from his clothes.

The bunk was better. Each corner post extended a few inches higher than the headboards. Gabriel detached the thick part of the cord and looped it over the post, letting his weight sag. The bed creaked but seemed plenty steady.

Gabriel paced the room again, squeezing his head in his hands.

Just try it. See if it's possible.

Hardly aware of what he was doing, Gabriel wrapped the cord around his neck and tucked the plug underneath. He adjusted it to rest right under his jaw, then tucked in the adaptor side, forming a big loop above his head. His back to the post, he guided the cord to catch the edge. Lowering himself just enough to keep it from popping free, he tightened the cord to block the blood flow.

And he waited. Four seconds. Five. He grimaced against the building pressure in his head. Adrenaline flooded his limbs. He trembled.

Seven.

His mouth tasted like metal. His heart skittered in his ribs like a rabbit in a cage. It knew what was happening.

And now, he let himself slowly sink until his knees nearly touched the ground, allowing the weight to cut off his air.

At ten seconds, his head started to swim. He felt himself drifting. Floating. Blood rushed in his ears, but it was strangely distant.

It's working.

For a few moments, there was eternity. And in that eternity, there was utter calm.

A door slammed in the hallway, and Gabriel's eyes snapped open. Everything spun. Black spots danced in his vision.

A distant part of him thought maybe he shouldn't be doing this.

This was supposed to be a test, right?

Right?

His whole body tingled, and that thought was lost to the void.

Gabriel stood up. Or…he tried.

His legs barely responded enough to send him twisting to the left. That's when the true panic hit. Gabriel summoned his arms into action. They sluggishly responded, and when he touched the cord above his head, it felt like he was wearing astronaut gloves.

No…

Gabriel's mind flashed with a vision of his hanging body. Then the fleeting image of Luca's shattered face.

Gabriel fought harder. His right foot pushed against the ground, and he was suddenly falling forward. The side of his head hit the floor. His fingers scrambled to untangle the cord. He pulled it apart with all his remaining strength, and then the pressure was gone.

Gabriel took a starved breath.

He lay on his side as his oxygen-depleted brain sent euphoric shockwaves through his body. It took two or three minutes for this to pass. He didn't move. Feeling came back to his extremities with stinging needles. The floating subsided, and his head throbbed. His neck felt the ghost of the cord.

He didn't even cry.

How could you, really, after something like that?

He just lay very still in the shadowy room, completely overcome by two simple things.

First, it had worked, much easier than he initially thought.

Second, he didn't want it to end this way.

THE TRUTHS OF GABRIEL MOORE

OUTSIDE OF TIME and location, there is quiet.

It feels something like eternity.

In this stretch of nothingness, the person who is Gabriel Moore becomes aware of three simple truths. These are deep understandings woven into the very fabric of his soul. Even *he* hardly knows of their existence, and if he could have put words to the indescribable, it would have been something like this:

One, he truly, madly, *desperately* wanted to live. He just didn't want to be in pain.

Two, he still hoped to fall in love.

Three, the faith he claimed since birth demanded something he could not give without destroying himself. Maybe, now, it was time to step away.

In this blank, eternal stretch, outside of time and location, these are the truths of Gabriel Moore.

THE HEART OF LOVE

GABRIEL SLOWLY SAT up.

Quietly, with embarrassed movements, he reattached his computer cord and returned it to his desk. He surveyed the room, arms crossed protectively over his chest, his shoulders hunched. He crawled into bed. This time, he fell asleep quickly, overcome by an exhaustion that had been building for a very, *very* long time.

ONLY A FEW slivers of light came through the shades when he awoke. Gabriel rubbed his eyes. He couldn't help but notice how quiet things seemed. It was like waking from a dream.

He recalled the frantic moments leading up to the swinging and floating. That couldn't be real. He would never do something like that. Would he?

Of course not.

Gabriel touched his neck, feeling his pulse. There was soreness all the way around and faint pressure in his head.

Oh.

Not a dream, then.

But what did it mean?

He hadn't *actually* tried to hurt himself, right?

He was just testing a theory, and he hadn't been injured, so it wasn't serious. He could keep this to himself. No one would understand anyway.

Gabriel slipped from his bed and plugged in his Christmas lights, filling the room with a warm glow. He examined his snacks and took a handful of peanut butter pretzels. He only ate five before putting the rest back.

Was there a future for him?

He could imagine one with a male partner, but that was different than reality. If he really wanted a life with a man, he'd have to tell people and not be ashamed.

Shame was all he knew.

He circled the room as he wondered who he could tell. None of them felt right. Not Mason. Certainly not Grant. Jenna would be a bad idea.

Andy? He wasn't here anymore, so a poor reaction wasn't the end of the world.

And, of course, there was always Luca.

He was the one person Gabriel thought might be able to understand. But the last thing he wanted was to try—having misread the signs—and be proven wrong. That might break him.

The longer he paced, the more restless he became. Tendrils of panic crawled from the ground and wrapped his ankles. He shook his hands at his sides as he walked. Then he was counting the bulbs of his Christmas lights. They kept blurring together. He wiped his eyes, starting over.

Forty-seven.

That couldn't be right. It had to be fifty. He must have missed a few.

He wiped his eyes again.

He was drowning.

He had to do something.

Gabriel paused long enough to send a short text to Luca. *Do you want to come over for a bit? I know it's late, so don't worry if you're busy.*

There. He'd reached out and given Luca a way to say no. With any luck, Luca would be getting ready for bed, doing homework, or watching a movie he didn't want to interrupt.

Gabriel was in the middle of organizing his desk when his phone buzzed. He reluctantly picked it up, seeing Luca's message: *Sure! I'll be down in a minute.*

It felt like forever before Luca arrived. Gabriel trudged down the hall to let him in. He was wearing a dark green, cable-knit sweater.

"What's up?" Luca asked.

"Not much," Gabriel responded casually. "I was bored. Jason's camping this weekend, and I was just sitting around."

"Maybe we could watch a movie or something."

"That could be fun," Gabriel said as they entered his room. Gabriel smiled. It was strained. Too wide.

Luca examined him. "What's going on?"

"Nothing," Gabriel said, smiling again. It cracked. He looked away. "It's nothing," he repeated, widening his eyes and yawning to fight off the torrent below. He went to his bookshelf and removed his new copy of *A Single Man*. He handed it to Luca. "I got this in the mail a few days ago. I figured I should give the book a shot."

Luca looked it over, and Gabriel bounced on his toes. He turned away and pinched his eyes with two fingers. He realized Luca was staring at him, no longer distracted by the book.

"I just have a headache," Gabriel explained. He scrunched his face and yawned again. "And I'm tired. It feels hot in here. Do you feel that?"

Gabriel rolled up his sleeves and stretched his arms above his head. He glimpsed the computer cord on his desk and unconsciously touched his throat. Luca returned the book to the shelf and stepped in front of him. Gabriel couldn't meet his searching eyes. Tears bubbled up despite his best efforts to keep them inside. And when the first ones fell, the rest seemed desperate to follow.

"Gabriel," Luca said. "Tell me what's going on."

Gabriel shook his head, arms crossed. "I can't...I just..." The words stuck in his throat. "I don't know." Luca touched his arm, face lined with deep concern. "I just feel like I'm suffocating, *constantly*..."

Luca pulled him into a tight embrace. "Can you tell me why?"

It was a simple question, but it shattered Gabriel's defenses. And there, in Luca's arms—a place of comfort and stillness—he finally let go.

All his buried guilt and hurt came tumbling out, and for a while, there was only muffled sobbing. Luca just held him, and that was exactly what he needed.

Minute by minute, the waterfall slowed.

Gabriel pulled away, head down. He grabbed a tissue from the box on his desk and blew his nose. He took deep, shuddering breaths.

Eventually, he turned around, his blood electric. Luca sat on the edge of Jason's desk, brow creased.

There was no escape.

He had to face this.

"The truth is," Gabriel began, "I...like you. A lot."

There was an infinite, utter silence.

Gabriel stood, a sculpture of possible regret. Luca sat casually, a portrait of the quiet longing to be a helpful presence.

Six feet apart.

A chasm.

And then Luca's lips pursed with a tiny smile, and his light blue eyes glimmered brightly.

"I like you too," Luca said.

"No, I *like* you."

"Same."

Gabriel wasn't sure if he'd heard that correctly. "What?"

"Maybe you *are* as dumb as you look."

Gabriel choked out a laugh. "That's possible."

"I thought it was obvious." Luca stepped close. He reached out and grasped Gabriel's hands, stilling their movements. Gabriel looked down, warmth seeping into his body at the touch. Luca's grip was firm but gentle. "Do you think I'd give anyone my second favorite sweater?"

"It's your second favorite?"

"Behind this one."

Gabriel's eyes went to where he'd sobbed into it. "Sorry about using it as a tissue."

"That's what it's for, sometimes," Luca said.

Gabriel's eyes drifted across Luca's face, taking in all the little details. The earnest blue. The soft lashes. The bit of stubble on his jaw and his faint, woodsy cologne.

He saw, too, the heaviness at the corners of his eyes. It formed in tiny creases when he smiled. He saw caution in the way his lips fought to stay in line, lest he show a full, revealing smile and invite disappointment. And there was an honesty in the way his brow drew together when he was thinking, or concerned.

Every part of Gabriel longed to be in Luca's presence, to know what Luca didn't trust himself to say. He wanted to lean close and be the one to make him laugh and sit in the same room without having to say a word.

This is the moment he understood the mystery of love.

Gabriel leaned in, heart thundering. Their lips met. Luca's were soft and warm. Their mouths shifted, and Gabriel's head swirled as he waited for God to strike him down. When that didn't happen, he waited for that ravenous desire for *more*. Instead, it was like a low flame, steady and quiet.

They pulled apart. Gabriel hugged Luca, their cheeks pressed together. It was here that he experienced the full flood of warmth and *rightness*. He never wanted to let go.

"You make me feel at peace," Gabriel said, the truest thing he could.

Luca took a bit longer to respond. "I feel safe with you."

As they held each other, none of the pain or doubt or guilt could find him. A part of him knew it would come later, but for now, it held back.

For now, that was enough.

A TERRIBLE IDEA

THE MOMENT LUCA left, it was as if Gabriel had been split in two. One half screamed that he was doomed to hell. The other part wanted to fall asleep with Luca in his arms.

But the fear…

Oh, how the fear gnawed at his soul.

And his mind? Well, his mind shut down every time he returned to when he'd nearly—

Blank.

He couldn't even think it.

He knew he could never tell another person. They would just get worried he'd try it again.

He wouldn't, right?

Of course he wouldn't.

GABRIEL MADE PLANS to meet Luca for lunch the next day, and he bounced on his toes while he waited outside the cafeteria. His pulse shot up every time another student looked at him. Could they see his guilt? Could they see the sin he'd committed written on his face?

And now that he and Luca shared a secret, it would be that much harder to ignore. But maybe it would be easier to bear between the two of them—

Luca bounded up the stairs to the second floor. Gabriel jolted. Luca waved and smiled, and Gabriel's tension melted away.

After lunch, Gabriel went straight to the library. He had a mountain of assignments: Spiritual Formation paper, revising his cultural analysis for English, studying for Biology and American Literature exams, preparing his final speech.

Luca joined him, even though he'd already done most of his studying.

"I *actually* have to do homework," Gabriel said.

"I wouldn't *dare* distract you," Luca returned playfully.

He was true to his word. Luca disappeared into a book for American Government, only looking up occasionally. Gabriel focused on his paper.

Ever since Professor O'Brien announced the assignment, Gabriel had been thinking about his essay and the impossible question: What *did* he believe? He'd considered and dismissed dozens of topics. Nothing resonated except for one terrible idea. It sank claws into his mind and wouldn't let go.

It started as a trickle, just a few tentative sentences. Then a paragraph. Then it was deleted. He started again. And again. And then it finally *clicked*. The rest exploded from somewhere deep inside. He couldn't write fast enough. His fingers pounded the keyboard, misspelling every other word in his haste to get everything down. He felt this strange, manic excitement every time he perfected another sentence.

The aftermath was like gasping for air after a lifetime of holding your breath.

He couldn't imagine turning in what he'd written. He couldn't imagine turning in something else.

Saturday became Sunday, and he had no other ideas. Monday morning, Gabriel stood outside the classroom, his essay clutched in sweaty hands.

Sometimes, the truth is the only way out.

He ducked inside the room. Only a few others had arrived so far. Professor O'Brien typed on his laptop at the podium.

"Where can I put this?" Gabriel asked.

Professor O'Brien looked him over. "Next to the sign-in sheet, thanks."

Gabriel dropped off his essay and found his seat, overcome with the feeling that he'd made a terrible mistake.

The following two days passed in a blur of frantic studying, dread building as he waited to hear from Professor O'Brien. He almost asked about it on Wednesday, but he froze before class and didn't have time to bring it up after.

He got an email from Professor O'Brien on Thursday afternoon.

Gabriel trembled as he read.

Gabriel,

I wanted to reach out because your essay was an unexpected but wonderful read. You brought up some great questions, and I appreciate your vulnerability. I want to assure you I won't share it with anyone else. If you ever want to talk about it, I'd love to sit down and hear your story. I want you to know I support you.

Would you be willing to let me read it aloud to the class on Friday? I would change a few details to keep you anonymous, but I won't share it if you don't want me to.

I hope you're having a good day.

Sincerely,

Professor O'Brien.

Gabriel turned off his phone and took sharp breaths. Professor O'Brien knew. *Really* knew. If he said yes, everyone else would, too. That might be exactly what he needed.

It took an hour for Gabriel to reply. He retyped his message countless times. It was just one sentence: *Yes, you can read it.*

GABRIEL DRIFTED TO his final Spiritual Formation class in a daze. He'd brought an energy bar, but he'd only eaten two bites the whole walk. Professor O'Brien stood next to the sign-in desk, greeting each person. Gabriel bent down to sign his name.

"How are you doing, Gabriel?" Professor O'Brien asked, the question full of many others.

Gabriel straightened. "I'm alright."

He knew he could have said not to read the essay. It was a terrifying prospect. But a desperate part of him wanted everyone to hear it. He wanted the whole school to know. The world, really. Maybe this was the only way to do that.

Gabriel took his seat. He set up his name card but left his pen and notebook in his backpack. They were watching the second half of a movie today, having started it Wednesday.

Luca appeared and tapped him on the arm. "Almost done."

"So close," Gabriel said. His leg bounced. He kept looking at the clock at the front of the classroom.

"You alright?" Luca asked.

"Huh?"

"You seem nervous."

"Just thinking about finals," Gabriel said. He took out his phone and texted Luca.

Professor O is reading my essay in class

Is that bad?

*I said he could, but it might ruffle some
feathers*

Perfect. I love divisive literature

Gabriel huffed. Luca's eyes twinkled. They returned to talking normally with the people around them, sharing about their finals and what they were looking forward to upon returning home.

Professor O'Brien soon greeted the class and started the movie. Gabriel fidgeted the entire time. When the credits rolled, they had eight minutes left. Professor O'Brien shut down the projector as people began packing up their things.

"Hold on, I have one more thing before I let you go," Professor O'Brien said. Groans sprinkled the room as he retrieved a paper from his satchel. "I got permission from a student to read their essay in class. I want you all to really listen."

"Better be good," the girl next to Gabriel muttered.

Professor O'Brien placed Gabriel's essay on the podium. He cleared his throat. The room quieted. Gabriel became an unblinking statue as Professor O'Brien began.

ALL THIS HURT

THIS IS THE essay of someone who has nothing left to give:

*I think I believe in God, but I wish I didn't. I wish I didn't believe in hell, but I fear that's where I'm going. Here's why: I kissed someone a few weeks ago. The problem is, we're the same gender.**

That would be alright if I weren't a Christian, but church is all I've known. Growing up, my family rarely missed a service. I did everything that was expected of me. I prayed, memorized verses, and went on mission trips. But no matter what I did, it never seemed to be enough. I could never escape the feeling that I was doing something wrong somehow. That I was wrong, just for being alive.

This is what I was taught to believe. I was taught that from the moment I was born, I was corrupted by sin. That every action I took was tainted. Every thought was vile. Every desire was from the Devil. I was taught that I couldn't trust myself, only God. That pain was a test, and the worse I felt, the more righteous I was.

---

* In Gabriel's original essay, he wrote, *The problem is, it was another guy.* Dr. O'Brien must have changed the line to help conceal Gabriel's identity.

People I know take comfort in the book of Job *because he lost every-thing but never lost his faith. All I see in that story is a man being tor-tured over a bet, and we're supposed to praise God for letting this man's entire family be killed? We're supposed to look up to Job for his unwaver-ing loyalty to a callous master?*

We like to say that God is loving, but why would a loving God initiate the slaughter of hundreds of thousands—again and again and again? Why would He perpetuate slavery? Why would He let a man be tortured to prove his loyalty?

We like to say that God is loving, but these actions are the opposite.

To answer the prompt, I think I believe in God. I see the world, and it's beautiful. It feels right that someone created it. The 'why' of my belief is harder to figure out. At first, I thought it was because it's what my parents believed. It's what my siblings believed, what my friends believed. And that's part of it. But the real reason is something much deeper. It's something I've felt since my earliest memories.

Fear.

It was the terror of stepping out of line. The torment of never know-ing when God might strike me down.

My belief in God was never about love and devotion. It was entirely about the fear of being condemned to hell. The fear of eternal torture for what I can't control. I did all the right things because I was terrified of doing one thing wrong and being punished forever.

I often wonder where the line is, the definitive point of no return.

It depends on who you ask and what sources you read. Even within one church, many people believe different things, and everyone thinks they know the truth. When this is the case, how can they all be right? And does any of it even matter? Are we all missing the point?

After all these years, the faith that was supposed to bring me comfort has overwhelmed me with pain. The love that was supposed to bring destruction and shame is one of the few things that makes me feel at peace. When I kissed that person[†], things felt right for the first time since I could remember.

I know this now: I can't fight my feelings anymore. I wouldn't survive it, and I do want to live. I would rather learn to accept myself and risk hell than live a short and miserable life for a heaven I'm not sure exists. I don't think you can understand that feeling until you've reached the very edge.

Again, I think I believe in God, but I don't know if I want to. I want my belief to be out of love, not fear. I just don't know if that's possible for me.

[†] Another of Dr. O'Brian's changes, this time substituting *guy* for *person*.

WHAT COMES AFTER

Professor O'Brien looked up. The classroom was deadly silent. Gabriel didn't move.

Professor O'Brien returned the paper to his briefcase. "Think about it. Let it sink in and inform how you interact with others. Otherwise, thank you for being an amazing class. I hope you all have a wonderful holiday."

The classroom came back to life. Mutters became hushed conversations as everyone discussed the essay with those around them. Gabriel heard a few comments of *who do you think it was* and *I wonder if they're alright*.

Luca caught his eye, face unreadable. Gabriel sank with worry at how Luca would react. They left class together, unable to say everything at the forefront of their minds. There was so much Gabriel wanted to share, but he didn't know how much he could say with so many others around. By the way Luca kept looking at Gabriel and opening his mouth, then closing it again to look at his feet, he must have been thinking the same thing. They paused at the turn-off for their respective classes.

"I'll see you later," Gabriel said.

"Before we go home, yeah?"

"Okay," Gabriel said. He wanted to say more. He didn't dare risk it. "I'm already late for class."

"Me too."

Gabriel backed away, Luca still standing in the middle of the concrete path. Gabriel clenched his jaw, tears welling up. He brushed them away with his sleeve, cursing himself. He breathed through his nose, taking purposeful strides as he bullied his fears and doubts back into the corners of his mind.

THEY MET UP after class at a picnic table in the snow-covered field next to the Student Union. Even here, they might be overheard, but at least they could see people coming in time to change topics. Luca sat on the table's surface, his feet on the bench. Clouds of fog puffed in front of his face. Gabriel stood in front of Luca, shivering. His feet crunched snow.

"Hell of an essay," Luca said. "I kind of wish you'd shared it with me, though."

Gabriel bit his lip, full of guilt.

"I don't really have the right to ask, but…" Luca scanned the lake. "It's a big deal, revealing that…"

"I'm sorry," Gabriel croaked.

"I know, it's just…it involves me too."

"I'm sorry."

Luca picked dirt from under his fingernails. He nodded. He looked up, searching Gabriel's face. "Do you regret it?"

Gabriel had to think for a long time. There was a lot he might regret in the last weeks. He shifted his weight. His toes were slowly going numb.

"I'm glad I wrote the paper. I'm not sure about having it read aloud," Gabriel said. He focused on Luca's hands. "And what happened in my room…I don't think I regret that either."

"Neither do I," Luca said, and he opened his mouth as if to say more, but nothing came out. He leaned forward, arms against his knees. "I just…" His face twisted and he shook his head. "I don't know if I can do it again."

"Oh." Gabriel rocked on his heels.

"It's not you," Luca said, squeezing his thighs. Gabriel had never seen him so restless. It hurt to watch, but he couldn't place why. "It's, uh…I don't think I'm ready for *that*, yet…"

Gabriel didn't even know if *he* was ready. It was almost a relief to hear. He still couldn't believe he'd kissed a guy. Did he want to do it again? He knew he wanted Luca, but did he want *that?*

"Okay," Gabriel said, shifting his weight again.

Luca looked up, still hunched over. Relief flashed across his face. "Okay?"

"Sure," Gabriel nodded, rubbing his arms. "Are you cold?"

"I'm freezing," Luca said, getting to his feet.

They hardly talked on the way back to their dorm, but it was the kind of quiet that let them get lost in their thoughts. Just inside the entrance, they faced each other again.

"I'll see you after break," Gabriel said.

"After break," Luca echoed.

They hugged tightly. Gabriel cherished the closeness—the scent of Luca's cologne.

"I'll miss you," Gabriel whispered.

"You too," Luca said.

They pulled apart. Luca started up the stairs, and this time, it was Gabriel's turn to watch part of his soul walk away.

FIVE

YOU CAN TELL ME ANYTHING

GABRIEL DROVE HOME in silence.

Every few minutes, another crack split through the walls he'd built. The tops were already crumbling. Their whole foundation shook.

Gabriel put on a practiced smile when he walked into the house, his mom greeting him from the kitchen. The air smelled of chicken broth and onions. Gabriel hugged his mom and carried everything to his room. It was unchanged, but white Lillies were in a vase on his desk.

All Gabriel had energy for was lying on his bed and scrolling through YouTube on his phone. Over and over, he clicked videos, stopped them a few minutes in, and returned to the homepage. Then he spotted a coming-out compilation from recent TV shows. He clicked it immediately.

He teared up at a few. Smiled at some. Laughed at others. Ached at them all.

He didn't know if he had the strength to tell everyone he knew. He could dream, though.

A few minutes into dinner, his mom frowned at him. "You look tired. Are you feeling alright?"

Gabriel looked up with a dismissive scrunching of his face. "I'm good. Finals were tough."

"Well, you can relax now."

Gabriel just nodded. He went upstairs straight after dinner and fell down a rabbit trail of coming out videos for the next three hours. Head reeling with stories and advice from strangers, he turned off his phone and lay in the claustrophobic quiet.

DURING THE DAYS, Gabriel did his best to wake up at a reasonable time, but he just ended up watching movies all afternoon. He quickly made his way through the list of queer-themed films Luca sent him, and he usually supplemented this activity with long naps, but they never cured his exhaustion. He kept at it, if only to block everything out for a few hours.

He occasionally spent time with the Alis, and he went shopping with Chloe three days before Christmas. He found a tin of chocolates and an apron for his mom, two plaid shirts for his dad, and books for his siblings. It was the best he could come up with.

"So, do you like college?" Chloe asked as they headed back to her car. The sky was dark with clouds that promised snow.

"I think so."

"*That's* not convincing."

"No, it's great," Gabriel amended. "I like being away."

"Yeah, me too."

"But sometimes it's hard."

They reached Chloe's car. Gabriel stowed his gifts at his feet.

"You're going out with someone, right? How's that?" Chloe asked, looking over.

"It was just one date."

"More than you've had in a while…or ever, really," Chloe said.

Gabriel bristled even though he knew she hadn't meant it as a barb. "We haven't really talked about the date. I think we're leaving things be. I'm not sure."

"Oh, ok."

Gabriel fidgeted with his jacket zipper. Chloe changed lanes, one hand at the bottom of the wheel.

"How are you doing? Really," Chloe said.

Gabriel bit his lip. "I don't know. I feel like there's a lot going on…" He trailed off, and Chloe glanced at him but said nothing. "I just feel like there's a lot I haven't talked about."

"Like what?" Chloe asked softly.

"I can't…"

"Why not?"

"No one will look at me the same. I just can't do it."

"Gabriel, we've been best friends since we met."

"This is different."

"I swear," Chloe said, sincere and slow. "Nothing will change how I see you. You can tell me anything."

Gabriel desperately wanted to trust her. He bit his knuckle, unable to stop tears from welling up in his eyes. He looked out his window.

"It doesn't matter what it is. Hell, I'd even help you cover up a murder—oh, shit! You killed someone, didn't you?" Chloe asked, and Gabriel chuckled.

"Not quite," Gabriel said. He wiped his eyes. "I'll be fine."

Chloe rubbed her nose in a way that said she didn't quite believe him, but she didn't press for details. He might have told her if she did. He wanted nothing more than to share with someone who might understand, or at least be kind. They didn't talk much on the rest of the drive. When Chloe parked in front of her house, Gabriel gathered up his gifts, only hesitating for a moment.

"You can tell me anything," Chloe repeated.

"I know," Gabriel said, opening the door. "I know," he repeated quietly to himself. "I'll see you later."

He kept his head down as he crossed the street to his house.

NEW YEAR'S EVE

THE DAYS LEADING up to Christmas adopted a frantic air.

All the movies and coming-out videos circled endlessly in Gabriel's head. It was no longer a question of whether he started talking, but how long he could hold himself together before every-thing came spilling out.

Opening presents Christmas morning, he dug his nails into his palms to keep himself grounded. At breakfast, his legs never stopped bouncing under the table. And he could hardly breathe when he had conversations at Ali's party that night. He focused all his energy on not passing out because he was so lightheaded.

All the while, he prepared speeches in his head for every possible question and reaction if he *did* slip up and mention Luca or *A Single Man.* He spent hours pacing his room, staging arguments in a manic haze. He pictured every person he would talk to. Saw every look of shock and fear. Imagined all the verses and books they'd beg him to read.

When this became overwhelming, he considered posting on Instagram and leaving it at that. It would be so simple, but it would be just as easy for everyone to dismiss him—to cut him off and never speak to him again. He had to take a different approach. It had to be personal. They needed to know he'd analyzed every possible option. That meant sitting everyone down and explaining it all. Then, he was back to arguing against himself into the late hours of the night.

In the days following Christmas, he walked his neighborhood for hours, squashing panic attacks before they could gain a foothold in his mind. On New Year's Eve, he spent the entire morning pacing his room. He didn't know if he could face another gathering without completely falling apart.

Gabriel managed to get dressed by eleven, and he scoured thrift stores to find an appropriate outfit. This year, the Ali's annual New Year's party was 1920s-themed, so he needed a vest or newsboy cap to tie the look together. It took three stops to find a tight, beige vest.

The rest of the day, he locked himself in his room. He was so restless he couldn't even watch TV. The party felt like his inevitable end. It couldn't be avoided. It was crushing him.

He paced at the foot of his bed. Before he knew it, he was gasping for air again. He buried his face in Luca's sweater. He'd worn it so much it had lost Luca's scent.

His phone rang. He froze. It rang again. *Chloe*. He snatched it from his bed.

"Hey, what's up?" Gabriel said.

"Want to come over early to help set up? We could get a head start on some drinks. I stole a bottle of champagne," Chloe said.

"That sounds fun," Gabriel said. His voice only had a slight waver, but he couldn't do anything about his breathlessness.

"What are you doing?"

"Just working out. Getting a head start on those resolutions, you know?"

"Alright, well, you should come over when you're done."

"Yeah, sure."

There was silence on the line. Gabriel bounced on his toes. He peered out his window toward the Ali's house.

"Are you alright?"

"Yeah, I'm good."

"You sure?"

"Incredible," Gabriel said, then clamped his hand over his mouth. Tears streamed down his cheeks. He removed the phone from his ear and took a sharp breath. He fought to compose himself. "I don't know. I'm just thinking, you know?"

"Tell me about it," Chloe said gently.

Gabriel's heart sprinted. He squeezed his free hand at his side. It felt like everything inside him was collapsing. His vision blurred. "I don't know…" Gabriel said between a sob. "I've just been holding everything in for so long…"

And now he was crying without restraint.

Why did he have to answer the phone?

He wanted to hang up, but she'd just call back, even more concerned. He was trapped. There was no escape.

He felt like screaming.

"Basically…I'm…I'm not straight…and I don't really know what that means, and I've been dealing with that for years…I just can't hold it in anymore—"

"It's ok," Chloe said. Gabriel couldn't respond. He just muffled his sobbing with his free hand. *"That's fine. It's ok."*

"But it's *not*," Gabriel choked out the words. "It's *wrong*, it's a sin, it's—"

"Stop, Gabriel, it's alright," Chloe persisted. Her voice was edged with an authority that struck down his defenses. *"Don't think about that. You're you, and that's perfectly fine."*

Gabriel broke down again. He locked his door in case his parents heard and tried to barge in. Then he slumped to the ground at the foot of his bed.

"How long have you known?"

"Nine, ten years, maybe. I don't know."

"That's a long time to keep something to yourself."

"But I didn't really notice until a few years ago."

"What do you feel?"

"I guess…I like guys," Gabriel said, cringing. It felt gross to admit, even to himself.

"Would you say you're gay?" Chloe asked.

His whole body revolted against the word. He couldn't be *gay*, could he? He couldn't possibly be one of *them*.

Maybe he didn't want to be. Maybe he didn't think he *was*.

Maybe he thought he could still marry a woman and pretend none of this happened.

"I don't know," Gabriel said after a while. "It's not like I'm attracted to people very often. And I don't know if it's always guys. I just feel different around certain people. Like I want to be with them, but I don't know if I really want to *do* anything. But sometimes I do, you know?"

Chloe was quiet for a moment. *"Not really."* She laughed. *"But I don't have to. You can't completely understand another person."*

"You're probably right."

"I don't think you need to have everything figured out right now."

"I guess," Gabriel said, but it felt the opposite. Any doubt on his part made it so much harder to talk about. Why would he open up when he wasn't sure?

"So…" Chloe began, and Gabriel already knew what she was leading to. *"Do you like anyone?"*

"I think so," Gabriel said, rubbing his forehead. "His name's Luca, but I don't know how to feel about it."

"Yeah, ok," Chloe said, controlled excitement in her voice. *"I can't wait to hear more when you're ready."*

"Yeah."

"When you're ready."

"Of course."

"So, want to come over and get drunk? Show your parents how it's done?"

Gabriel laughed. "Maybe. I don't know. I need to get cleaned up."

"No problem. Come over whenever," Chloe said. There was a long stretch of nothing on the line. *"Thanks for telling me, for trusting me with this. I'm really happy for you."*

"Just don't tell anyone."

"I won't."

Gabriel knew she wouldn't, but he feared the possibility all the same. It wasn't his secret anymore, and the more people he let in, the more likely the wrong people would find out before he was ready.

"I'll see you soon," Gabriel said.

"Don't be too long."

Gabriel hung up. Vertigo twisted the room, and he was suddenly looking at his body from above.

Could he skip the party?

He cycled through possible excuses. He could say he was sick or didn't sleep well or had eaten something he was allergic to. But that probably wouldn't work. Everyone would know something was up.

He had to face it. He had to face them all and smile and laugh and pretend he didn't have a jagged hole inside, a terrible wound being torn open every other second.

Gabriel watched himself enter the bathroom to examine his face in the mirror. His eyes were bloodshot with dark circles underneath. He turned on the faucet and let the water run over his fingers before splashing his face. He dried off and practiced his smile. It cracked. He tried again. It shattered.

He clutched his chest. Each inhale stabbed him like he had broken ribs.

He focused on getting dressed. He buttoned his shirt. Pulled on his grey wool pants. Tied his canvas dress shoes.

The trouble came with the tie. He had it in his hands and suddenly forgot how to loop it together. He frowned, confused tears rising. Finally, the pattern came together, but it was four inches too long. He ripped it apart. This never happened. It took another three tries to get mostly right. Donning his vest and sports coat, he reviewed himself in the mirror.

He straightened his tie and smoothed his jacket. Touched up his hair. Threw on a practiced smile.

And his appearance was flawless.

He took deep, cleansing breaths and shoved everything else out of his mind. And for a while, it was as if nothing at all was wrong.

It was just another night. He would talk and laugh. He would impress everyone with his clothes. Even the thought of meeting Chloe wasn't so scary. He could laugh it off. They didn't have to talk about it. They didn't *ever* have to talk about it. It wasn't something he needed to share anymore. He was better now. Bottled up.

In control.

Gabriel floated downstairs to meet his parents. He gave a flourished spin to show off his outfit. His dad wore a black vest with a black tie, a gold chain in the pocket. His mom had put on a cream dress and had pinned up her hair in her best imitation of the 20s fashion.

She clapped her hands at his appearance. "You look so good!"

"Very suave," his dad said.

Gabriel hardly gave them time to admire his outfit or scrutinize his face before he snatched up the Tupperware of cookies on the counter. "Come on, we're late!"

Gabriel marched across the street. The Ali's house was already filled with bodies shifting in front of the windows. Cars packed the sides of the road. Gabriel bounced on his toes in front of the Ali's front door, waiting for his parents to catch up.

Chloe knows.

Gabriel's spirit lurched. His walls trembled. There were fissures everywhere.

He wasn't going to make it.

Once inside, he dropped off the cookies in the kitchen.

"Gabriel!" Adrian shouted, coming in from the living room.

"What's up?" Gabriel said.

They hugged.

"You look so good," Adrian said.

"I had to go all out tonight."

"I love it. Hey, we're starting a ping pong tournament in the basement."

"Ready to lose?" Gabriel asked, falling perfectly into the role he was supposed to play for the night.

They traded insults on the way to the basement. Someone played music on a speaker. Gabriel surveyed the room. Seven or eight people were there, but not Chloe. Relieved, he zeroed in on the bucket of drinks in the corner of the room. Cracking open an IPA with the highest ABV, Gabriel stood against the wall to watch Peyton and Sean finish their game. He downed half his beer by the time Peyton won.

"Gabriel and I have next," Adrian said.

Gabriel selected a paddle and spun it twice. He and Adrian volleyed for a minute to warm up.

And then his mind was perfectly clear.

THIS IS HOW it feels to be in complete control:

You serve first and go up 4-1. You nick corners. Return impossible backhands. Slam the ball again and again, unable to miss.

It's transcendent.

Nothing exists outside of this moment.

You win 21-13, open a second beer, and another victim steps up.

Peyton.

Easy.

You stalk your side of the table like a panther. Five minutes later, you win again. Your body is electric.

The others try to take your paddle. You refuse to give it up. This is your *moment*.

They let you play Sean.

"Last game," they say.

Yeah, yeah.

Feet clomp down the stairs.

You serve.

Chloe appears from nothing, red wine in hand.

Fear guts you like the butcher it is.

SEAN WON.

It was no contest.

Gabriel couldn't hear with the roar in his ears. He tossed the paddle on the table and shook Sean's hand. He retrieved his beer, nauseous. Chloe raised her hand in greeting. Her hair was pinned up, and she wore a pearl necklace and a gold dress. They hugged.

"Hey," Chloe said.

"Hey," Gabriel repeated.

"How are you doing?"

All Gabriel heard was, *I know your secret.*

"I'm good," he said.

No, you're not. You're a dirty faggot, she said in his mind.

"I like the outfit. It looks good," Chloe said.

"All part of the facade," Gabriel said jokingly, then sucked his teeth. Chloe squeezed his arm, compassion in her eyes. He said, "You look great, too."

"Thanks," she said.

They watched the next ping pong game, and Gabriel opened a third beer. Unable to stay still, he trudged upstairs, already swaying. Chloe followed him up. He wasn't hungry, but he browsed the trays of food anyway. Someone had brought a platter of Chick-fil-A nuggets. He chewed one mechanically, hands shaking. He gripped the edge of the counter to steady himself.

In the following hours, Gabriel swayed on a tightrope. Every time he glimpsed Chloe, he felt like he might turn into a puddle. Every time he remembered what she knew, another knife pierced his body. And so, he kept himself moving, never staying in one spot or conversation for more than a few minutes. He wandered the house, keeping up appearances with quick smiles and witty comments.

It wasn't working.

He was coming apart at the seams.

The tie around his neck felt like it was cutting off the blood to his head. He loosened it, then undid the first button. For a moment, he could breathe, but the vest was constricting him, too. His lungs couldn't expand as much as they needed. He stood in a corner of the house, clutching his chest, feeling his heart slamming against his ribs.

It was barely 9 p.m., and he was already exhausted. The carefree laughter of those around him closed his throat with emotion. Tears bubbled in his eyes.

Gabriel rushed to the nearest bathroom and locked the door. He held his head with both hands as tears slipped down his cheeks. He couldn't stop them. They just kept coming.

He yawned and shook his head and widened his eyes. He undid the buttons of his vest.

He patched himself up again and again. Told himself to suck it up and get through the night.

He broke every time.

The mirror was his enemy. It mocked him and showed him exactly who he was.

He couldn't bear seeing his haggard appearance—his sloppy tie and unbuttoned collar and vest. His aching, red eyes.

He couldn't face them like this.

Taking sharp breaths, his remaining strength fractured.

Gabriel left the bathroom and dashed for the front door. He didn't look to his left or right. Didn't listen for his name.

The second he was outside, his walls turned to rubble.

Consuming panic crawled from his toes to his lungs, taking away his air. His very cells seemed to be imploding. The more he tried to control his sobbing, the more desperate it was to escape.

He walked the neighborhood as the last month flashed before his eyes.

The date with Jenna. Losing Andy and Kyle. Ben's death. Confessing to Jonathan at The Gathering. Swinging in his dorm room. Kissing Luca. Hearing his essay being read aloud in class.

Discovering what he really wanted.

She knew.

She knew.

It wasn't his secret anymore.

Chloe knew, and he could never take it back. Never ask her to forget. It would be all she thought about when they saw each other. How could he have been so weak as to let her in? He vowed not to let it happen again. And maybe he could tell her it was all some misunderstanding. He could say he was under a lot of stress, but he was fine, and they never had to mention it again.

But how did this *happen?*

He had no idea. He couldn't have predicted this. If he traced the threads of his life, they would go back years, not weeks and months. They would go all the way back to before he was born. Back to the way his parents were raised.

And he would know things happened just *because*—because that's how life has always been. Things happened, and you had to deal with it the best way you knew how.

That's why Isaac never came home and Jacob knew he was 'right' and Gabriel shut down to keep it all away.

He'd never been prepared for this.

This wasn't how his life was supposed to go.

He felt terrible grief for the person he had become.

Most people would hate him when they found out. The thought of losing his friends and family was overwhelming. He had to convince them he was still the same person, that he still mattered and deserved to be a part of their lives. And if he had to beg, that was fine too. He just didn't want this to get in the way of them loving him.

And it wasn't *that* bad, was it? He just liked men, sometimes, and only one in particular. Was that so terrible?

Gabriel paused at the cross street three blocks away from the party.

Damn.

Maybe it was that simple.

Gabriel wiped his eyes and headed toward the Ali's. Maybe he could face them now, just long enough to say goodbye. A block away, he pictured the seething crowd, and he was drowning again. Sobbing, again. Gasping for breath.

Again.

He just liked one guy, but it wasn't that simple.

His whole world could change. It could end. It could be taken away, just like that.

He cried, and cried, and there were no answers. And he cursed himself and laughed bitterly at his weakness. He needed to be stronger. People wouldn't accept him like this.

He walked right past the Ali's house. He kept his head down, barely sparing a glance at the glowing windows and the people shifting in and out of the frame. He was so focused on his steps that he hardly noticed the figure one house down, digging something out of the passenger seat of their car. Gabriel skirted the person, not even looking at them or their car. He couldn't draw attention to himself. He just needed to put himself together enough to say goodbye to the required people—

"Gabriel?"

The voice cut through his thoughts. He kept walking. He didn't even recognize who it was. If he kept moving, maybe they'd let him go—

"Gabriel!"

This time, he glanced back. *Shit.* Mr. Ali.

Gabriel ducked his head and continued walking. He couldn't deal with this right now. Mr. Ali's feet pattered on the concrete as he jogged to catch up. Gabriel picked up his pace. Mr. Ali came up beside him.

"I was just grabbing the cigars I bought today," he said, flashing a plastic package that glimmered in the street lights. Gabriel didn't respond. He dried his face with his sleeve, keeping his eyes on the ground. "What's going on? I've hardly seen you all night. "

Gabriel couldn't speak. Mr. Ali's hand found his shoulder, bringing him to a stop. He stepped in front of Gabriel.

"What's wrong?" he asked.

Gabriel couldn't meet his gaze. He was trapped. Again. But things were already bad, so he might as well say it. Couldn't get any worse.

"I think I'm gay," Gabriel said, point blank, staring at the center button of Mr. Ali's shirt.

"Oh," Mr. Ali sounded.

Gabriel found his mind drifting away from his body. His mouth kept talking. "Or something. I just know I like this guy…and it's all so confusing…" Gabriel's words kept stumbling over each other. There was so much to boil down to just a few sentences. "I told Chloe, and I don't know how to face her, or anyone else. And I'm terrified of what this means and what's going to happen, and I feel so *guilty*…all the time…and it's all too much to deal with right now—"

Before he knew it, Mr. Ali had wrapped him in a tight hug, ending his ramblings. That was just as good since he had dissolved into tears again. He clutched Mr. Ali's jacket, warmth seeping into him one fraction at a time.

"Hell, Gabriel, I thought you'd done something bad like sink my boat or run over a kid," Mr. Ali said, humor touching his voice. "You didn't do that, did you?"

"No," Gabriel said, voice muffled.

"Not even Mrs. Mullen's little nightmare?"

"Nope."

"Damn, that might have been a good thing." Mr. Ali pulled away. He held Gabriel's shoulders and caught his eye. "I don't see what the problem is."

"What?"

Mr. Ali surveyed the street. He stroked his beard, and Gabriel thought he saw a watery glint in his eyes. "I love you like my own kid. Probably more than the ones I have, to be honest…"

Gabriel couldn't help but give a stilted laugh.

Mr. Ali smiled. "I just want to help."

"Thanks," Gabriel said.

Mr. Ali put an arm around his shoulder, leading them toward the party. "How did Chloe react?"

"She was good."

"Have you told anyone else?"

"Just a few people at school."

"Not your parents?"

"No."

"Not even Adrian?"

"Definitely not."

Mr. Ali went silent. He looked to the sky, and then his eyes widened. He chuckled.

"What?" Gabriel bristled.

"It's nothing."

"*What?*"

"It just makes sense now," Mr. Ali said with the kind of smile that came from solving a nagging puzzle. "I could tell something was going on…and I just had this thought, seeing you and Adrian together…"

Gabriel stiffened, yet there was incredible relief knowing someone else knew, and he didn't have to say it. "I didn't think anyone had noticed."

"I'm probably the only one who did. The people we know…" Mr. Ali shrugged. "This isn't something they consider."

"Feels obvious to me."

"That's because you see, and you *understand*. For others, it's easier to live in a bubble than to challenge what they believe."

"Yeah, maybe."

"Not enough people are willing to change their minds."

The night was still. Gabriel looked past the streetlights to take in the blinking stars.

"How are you feeling?" Mr. Ali asked.

"Better," Gabriel said, and he realized he wasn't lying. He was exhausted and raw, but the panic had found someone else to torment. "A lot better, thanks."

"Good. Do you want to go back inside?"

"Not really."

"That's fine. Are you fine being alone? Want me to stay, or grab Chloe?"

"No, I'm good. I'm just going to go to bed."

Mr. Ali looked him over, lips pursed. "Alright."

"What will you tell them?"

"I'll say you weren't feeling well and went home."

Gabriel nodded. "Thank you."

"It's going to be alright," Mr. Ali said, giving him another tight hug. "Maybe it doesn't seem like that, but it will be alright. Let Chloe or I know if there's anything we can do to help."

"I will."

They parted, and Mr. Ali trudged up the steps to his house. Gabriel crossed the street and returned his attention to the sky. He wrapped his arms around himself, feeling clear for the first time in a long while. Moving forward wouldn't be easy, but he had a few people on his side. Maybe that's all he really needed.

WHAT IT FEELS LIKE

GABRIEL WOKE UP to a text from Adrian.

> *Where'd you go last night? I heard you*
> *weren't feeling good*

> *I think I got a bug. Maybe it was slam-*
> *ming those beers*

> *Sorry, man. Feel better. We need to hang*
> *out before school starts again*

> *Absolutely. I can't wait to beat your ass*
> *in ping pong again*

> *You wish. I'd already had a few so I'm*
> *blaming losing on the alcohol*

When Gabriel saw his parents for the two minutes it took to prepare a bowl of cereal, he told the same story of feeling sick but left out the part about the alcohol. They didn't question him. He *did* look ill, after all. His eyes were dark and bruised from crying, and he stayed in his room most of the day, lying down to watch TV.

Despite how well Chloe and Mr. Ali reacted, he still wished it had been a terrible dream. He still carried the sinking knowledge he could never take it back. This would shape his life, forever.

His phone buzzed with a text from Chloe.

So…Ryan Gosling or Jake Gyllenhaal?

More like Hugh Jackman

Wait, hold on. HOLD ON. Oh my god
HUGH JACKMAN THAT'S WHY
YOU LOVE X-MEN SO MUCH!

Gabriel laughed aloud to himself. It felt good to do that. Life wasn't so scary when you could laugh at it.

Even Mr. Ali reached out.

Thanks for opening up last night. I'm
really proud of you. I hope you're doing
alright today

Thanks for being there. It means a lot

Call me anytime, seriously

Gabriel choked down the lump in his throat. *I will, thanks,* Gabriel sent before returning his attention to the show *Sex Education*. He'd already finished season one and was two episodes into the second. And then, in the fourth episode, a certain *revelation* hit him square in the chest.

Florence had a problem. She didn't want to have sex. Ever.

No one understood.

"I think I might be broken," she said, voice cracking. She sat in Dr. Jean Milburn's office at school, tidy and desperate in her yellow hat and curly red hair.

Then, the piercing, measured question from Jean. *"Do you know what asexuality is?"*

And everything was different.

Gabriel turned to the internet as soon as the episode was over. He read articles and watched videos and finally *understood*. It was like the clicking together of a years-old mystery.

It made sense now, why he rarely noticed people—why he'd never really pictured sex, despite the deep longing to share his life with someone else. Maybe that's why hugging Luca felt better than the kiss. And the kiss wasn't bad, it just wasn't the thing he wanted most.

But he still wanted *Luca*—to be around him and dress up and go out and sit close.

Maybe he'd want more, later. Maybe not. It didn't matter either way.

But he'd figured it out.

Gabriel sank to his bed, lightness in his bones. He laughed to himself.

It was going to be ok.

He knew what he wanted now.

And despite all he still had to face, it would be ok.

Right?

It had to.

It *had* to.
There was no other option.
It truly, simply, *had* to be alright.

SIX

THE MEANING OF UNCONDITIONAL

GABRIEL'S PARENTS WERE extra attentive to him in the days before he returned to school. They kept asking how he felt, and his mom wanted to know if he was happy.

"I'm good. I'm just thinking about a lot right now," he said, putting on a practiced smile. "I'll let you know."

His mom studied him, nose scrunched. "Well, I'd love to hear about it."

Gabriel nodded. He felt like he might burst in that moment, but he kept himself together until he got on the road Saturday morning. As he neared campus, he couldn't escape the knowledge he had to tell them soon enough. And no matter when it happened, it would never be an easy conversation.

Maybe the best option was to get it over with now.

Gabriel parked in front of his dorm. His hands trembled as he picked up his phone and found his mom's contact info. His finger hovered above the call button. Clenching his jaw, he leaned his head against the seat. He pressed the button, plunging himself over the edge. Lightning surged in his blood. He put it on speaker, and the angry ringing filled the car.

"Gabriel, what's going on? Did you get to school?" His mom asked.

It took a moment for Gabriel to find his words. He pinched the bridge of his nose. "I just pulled in. I wanted to let you know."

"Oh, well, I appreciate that."

"Of course."

"I miss you already."

"Yeah, me too." Gabriel picked at a crack in the steering wheel.

"I guess we'll see—"

"Is Dad th—sorry."

"No, go ahead."

Gabriel dug his nails into the plastic of the wheel. "Is Dad there?"

"He's in the office."

"Alright, I just wanted to talk to you guys for a bit."

"Oh, ok. I'll grab him," his mom said.

Gabriel set his phone on the seat next to him.

"Fuck," he hissed to himself.

It was happening.

He didn't know if he had the strength to follow through, but the thought of Luca, Chloe, and Mr. Ali made this mountain a fraction less daunting.

He heard his mom mumble something on the other line, his name, and then his dad saying, *"Hey, Gube, what's up?"*

"Hi, Dad," Gabriel said, picking up the phone again. "Alright, well…so, I've been thinking about a lot recently, these last few months. And I've been trying to figure out some things."

"Like what job you want?" his dad asked.

"That's part of it, and some other life stuff," Gabriel said. He looked out his car window, watching someone enter the dorm. "So, um…for a while actually—the last few months—I've been pretty anxious." Gabriel's voice trailed up at the final word, almost breaking.

Almost a question. "Just about school and classes, and all that…and that's why I left the New Year's party. I was too anxious to be around people that night."

"*Ohhh, honey,*" his mom cooed over the phone. "*I'm sorry. How are you doing now?*"

"I, uh…I still feel it. It doesn't really go away," Gabriel said. And this time, his voice *did* break. He covered his mouth as he choked on the lump in his throat.

"*I'm sorry. We could tell something was going on,*" his dad said.

"*Thanks for letting us in.*" This from his mom.

"Yeah…and I guess I've been a bit sad too. It's been hard, figuring everything out," Gabriel said. A *bit* sad? He flashed back to swinging in his dorm.

"*What are you trying to figure out?*" His mom asked, tentative.

Gabriel swallowed hard.

Don't do it, don't do it, don't do it.

His heart thundered.

"I think I'm bi," he said.

No no no, shit!

"*What?*" His mom asked.

"I think I'm bisexual, or something," Gabriel said, doubling down with another statement that sounded more like a question. *Fuck.* He hadn't meant to use that label. He'd intended to use *gay*, but he'd panicked as the words slipped out.

Fuckfuckfuck.

Maybe this would soften the blow.

Seconds ticked by with no warm assurances. He felt like he was balancing on the edge of a razor blade as he waited for their response.

"*What do you mean?*" Gabriel's dad asked, breaking the silence.

Gabriel composed himself. "I guess…I like guys sometimes. And maybe girls, too, not as often. I don't really know."

"*I just, I don't—*" his dad began. "*I'm confused how this happened.*"

"How this happened?" Gabriel echoed quietly.

His mom picked up the thread. "*We just want to know why, what caused this? What did we do? I just remember you were so happy as a kid...*" Gabriel's mom broke off, emotion overtaking her voice.

"Nothing *happened*," Gabriel said.

"*How long have you felt like this?*" His mom asked. "*Since you left for school?*"

Gabriel's jaw dropped. *Months?*

"Eight, nine years, I don't know," Gabriel said.

"*Oh...*" his mom breathed.

Gabriel's dad cut in. "*How do you know?*"

Every second chipped away at Gabriel's resolve. He said, "I don't know how to explain it."

"*So you're...*" There was discomfort in his dad's voice. "*...attracted to guys?*"

"Sometimes, I guess," Gabriel said, hot embarrassment running through him.

"*But you still like girls, right?*"

"I don't know. I—"

"*You said you do, right?*"

"I'm not sure. I'm still figuring it out."

"*Well, Gabriel,*" his dad said, tired. "*That's important for you to know, for your future family—*"

"*Yes, and what your dad is saying is that it's ok to feel...*" his mom trailed off. Gabriel pictured her waving her hands in the air for the right words. "*...how you do...just that you can still meet a girl.*"

"*Exactly, and have a normal family.*"

"*And kids. Don't you want that?*"

"I know someone who's had homosexual feelings before," Gabriel's dad said, and Gabriel cringed. *"He's a great guy—strong Christian—but he's married, and he has four beautiful kids and an incredible wife. Maybe I could give you his number and you can talk to him about how he overcame that. He'd be able to understand and maybe have some advice."*

Meanwhile, Gabriel had dropped his phone on the passenger's seat and was bawling into his shirt, taking stifled breaths every few seconds.

"That's a good idea. Have you thought about talking to Pastor Evans?" His mom asked. *"He offers counseling services. He's an incredible man. He loves God, and I know you do too. I think it would be helpful to talk to someone like him."*

Gabriel found it impossible to speak. He ran his hand over his face.

"Gabriel?" His mom asked. *"Are you still there?"*

"I don't want to talk to them," Gabriel said.

They're not safe, is what he wanted to say.

"Are you sure? It could be really informative," his mom persisted.

"I'm good."

"What about James Ali? He's known you forever."

Gabriel broke into a tearful smile. If only they knew. And then that smile collapsed because Mr. Ali accepted him without a second thought. There was no doubt or fear or attempts to direct his future.

Not even his parents could accept him.

This realization lodged something dark and hopeless in Gabriel's spirit.

"Yeah, maybe I'll talk to him," Gabriel said.

"Good," his mom said, relieved.

"So…" his dad said. *"Are you…with anyone? With a guy?"*

"No, definitely not," Gabriel said hastily.

It wasn't even a lie. Not really. He liked Luca, but they weren't dating. And even though they'd kissed, that was the last piece of information he wanted to admit to his parents.

But maybe that would have made things easier. Maybe they would understand Gabriel wasn't as uncertain as he sounded. Or maybe that would increase their desperation to intervene. For all he knew, they might show up the next day and demand he pack his bags to head home or send him off to some conversion camp.

He really *didn't* know what his parents were capable of as they reacted to the news, and that was the scariest feeling of all. He just hoped telling them here, *now*, would give them time to warm up to the reality.

"That's good," his dad said. *"That's really good. Keep fighting to stay pure. God will help you through this as long as you pursue Him. I know it can be confusing for people your age, especially now, but you've hardly developed! You know? You can't possibly know what you want yet. Just stay strong. God will send you an incredible woman very soon."*

Gabriel wanted to throw his phone and punch his hand through the driver's window. He wanted to scream at the top of his lungs until his voice gave out.

He wanted to point out how Jacob had gotten married when he was a year older than Gabriel was now, and that Adrian had already proposed to Savanah.

How come no one said they were too young and undeveloped *then?*

Instead, he swallowed the pain once again and offered a mournful "Sure."

"Gabriel, we love you no matter what. We just want you to be happy, to have a good and long life," his mom said.

Homosexuals don't get that, is what she might have said.

"*Thank you for opening up about this struggle. We're here to help,*" his dad said.

Thank you for sharing your affliction. We're here to fix this.

"Yeah."

"*We want to know what's going on in your life. Don't be scared to call and talk about anything,*" his dad said.

"Ok."

"*Alright, we love you,*" Gabriel's mom repeated.

"Mmm," Gabriel sounded. "I'll talk to you later."

Gabriel hung up. He dropped his phone on the seat. For five or six seconds, all he did was stare out the windshield. His vision blurred.

"*FUUUUCCK!*" he screamed.

He pounded the steering wheel until his palm was purple and aching. He leaned his forehead against the wheel.

"…fuck…" he whispered to himself, defeated.

IF THE PANIC after telling Chloe was bad, it was nothing compared to the hopelessness in his gut after talking to his parents. It was a confirmation of his worst fears. They believed something was wrong with him, and their first thought was to have a pastor and a married *homosexual* talk him straight.

Gabriel didn't know what to do.

He skipped lunch to try and sleep, weighed down by a fog that would no doubt obscure the following weeks. At 4 p.m., he forced himself to get out of bed to find his new classes. By dinner, he was hungry enough to stop by the cafeteria. He ate half a burrito before he couldn't stomach another bite. And for the next hour, despite the icy air, Gabriel walked the campus as the light faded from the sky. He was completely drained, and every few minutes, his stomach sank with the remembrance of the call with his parents.

Just after seven, he got a text from his dad he wished he never read:

> *Thank you for sharing with your mom and me, but I don't think you're bi or gay, or whatever it is. I think you just need to face your fear of being rejected. I think you need to make the leap and ask girls out. Be confident. I believe you will have no trouble finding a date. This will allow you to discover how wonderful it is to be in the company of women, but no relationship should start sexually. Treat her like you would your sister. College is the perfect time for this kind of experiment. Don't let it go to waste. This is God's will. I'm proud of you and I love you no matter what*

Gabriel sank to the grass. His phone slipped from his fingers.

This is God's will.

Was it? Who could really know the will of God, especially for someone else?

I love you no matter what.

Did he?

Unconditional love doesn't accuse you of being afraid. It doesn't invalidate your experience. It doesn't try to make you into something else.

It simply takes things as they are and holds nothing back.

There is no fear in love.

Gabriel reread the text, hand over his mouth to keep himself from sobbing. It felt like he'd been shot in his soul. It was deep and agonizing and *permanent*. Something he wasn't sure he'd ever recover from.

A TREACHEROUS MIND

GABRIEL WAS TERRIFIED to return to his empty room. He didn't know what might happen if he gave the darkness any precedence in his mind.

He went anyway.

When he arrived, he immediately crawled into bed. He could have called Chloe or Luca, or even Mr. Ali, but his ever-present fear whispered that this was a bad idea.

You see, unspeakable pain has a way of twisting your mind against itself. It shuts down any thought of reaching out for help. It convinces you that even though your closest friends would give anything to hear from you, your doubt and guilt and shame tell you it's all too much for them to bear.

You've already asked too much of them, and you will *not* be a burden.

This is why Gabriel doesn't make a call.

HE'S LUCKY, THIS time, because he fell asleep within minutes of lying down.

It wasn't an easy morning.

Gabriel reread the text from his dad while lying in bed. He still hadn't responded. He didn't plan on doing so any time soon. That afternoon, he skipped church to sit at the coffee shop in town. When he returned to the dorm that evening, he caught the tail end of Grant talking to Stephen.

"…not returning this semester," Grant said.

Gabriel turned on a heel, thumbs looped in his backpack straps. "Who's not coming back?"

"Mason," Grant said curtly.

"What? Why?" Gabriel sputtered. Mason had given no indication he was leaving at the end of last semester.

"Personal reasons," Grant said vaguely. "I think he wanted to take some time off."

"Huh," Gabriel said, setting off for his room.

Micah's door was open, and he talked with Jason in hushed tones.

"Yo, Gabe, did you hear?" Jason asked.

Gabriel looked down the hall before answering. "About Mason leaving?" They nodded, and he entered the room. The three of them stood in a loose circle. "Grant said it was to take time off."

"Grant's a liar, we all know that," Jason said.

Micah huffed in agreement.

"What happened?" Gabriel asked.

"He got kicked out," Jason said in a conspiratorial way.

"You can't be serious, he's the perfect student," Gabriel said, jaw slack. Jason laughed.

"You're not going to believe this," Micah said, leaning in. "But one of my friends said he and another guy were caught *making out* in the dorm during break."

Gabriel covered his mouth with both hands. "*What?* I mean, I know he was…um…"

"Gay?" Jason supplied.

"Sure, but he's so against it I doubted he'd actually try anything," Gabriel said.

"Apparently it was going on for the last month," Andy's roommate said.

"Oh my God," Gabriel said, trying to keep himself from grinning. That was a terrible reaction, but he couldn't help himself. He laced his fingers behind his head. "Oh my *God*. I don't know what to say…"

"I know, it's wild. Hey, what are the odds Grant gets kicked out next?" Jason said.

"God, I wish," Micah said.

Gabriel just laughed along with them, still trying to process the fact that Mason was gone. For kissing a *guy*, no less. Gabriel wasn't particularly sad, just shocked into stillness.

He went to bed a few hours later, mind still turning over the news. He felt bad for it, but it was a relief to be thinking about someone else for a change. He wondered how Mason was doing. Probably terrible.

Maybe he should reach out. It was the least he could do. He just needed to think of what to say.

THE ART OF CONFESSION

GABRIEL WOKE BEFORE his alarm and pulled his covers tighter around his chin. His first thought was about Mason and how alone he must be feeling. He spent the next hour composing a text.

> *I heard you're not coming back this se-*
> *mester. Hope you're doing alright. I just*
> *wanted to say that I think I like guys*
> *too, so you're not alone. Thanks for be-*
> *ing open about your story*

He sent it before he could stop himself, but he felt good about reaching out. He didn't expect a response any time soon, so he began preparing for the first day back.

This semester, he had loaded his schedule with Monday/Wednesday and Tuesday/Thursday classes, leaving Fridays free for whatever he wanted. But that meant every class was an hour and fifteen minutes, and he had four on Tuesdays and Thursdays. Gabriel hoped it was worth it.

Unfortunately, even though they had two of the same classes,

Gabriel and Luca were never in the same classroom at the same time. At least they'd be able to study together.

The first time Gabriel saw Luca was right before chapel. They agreed to meet outside the auditorium and walk in together. Luca was wearing a sweater Gabriel hadn't seen before. It hugged his form a bit more than usual. The sleeves were green, the torso blue, and the cuffs and collar were white.

Gabriel suppressed a grin.

The clogged atrium faded. Or maybe Luca was more vibrant than the others. Luca saw him and waved, a full smile taking over his face.

They hugged, and Gabriel took in the faint scent of pine on Luca's shirt. Gabriel thought there might be some awkwardness, especially since they'd hardly talked over the break—since they'd kissed—but Gabriel felt perfectly at ease. More steady, in fact, with Luca by his side.

"I missed you," Gabriel said, pulling away.

"You missed *me?* I'm flattered," Luca said playfully. Gabriel swatted his arm. "Missed you too."

"Nice sweater," Gabriel said, catching the fabric of the arm between his fingers.

"I mean, I had to show off a bit," Luca said, mouth open in a suggestive smile.

Gabriel raised an eyebrow, looking around the atrium. No one paid them any attention, as far as he could tell. Gabriel had to admit he liked the subtle flirting, but they had to be careful no matter how normal it felt. Mason was just one example of what could go wrong.

And then Gabriel paused with realization.

He wasn't scared to flirt with Luca. He enjoyed it. It was *comfortable*. It felt right. More importantly, in this moment, nothing felt *wrong*.

That was the power Luca held.

They entered the auditorium, scanned their IDs, and trudged up the stairs to their section of the balcony.

"How was break?" Luca asked.

"Uh," Gabriel sounded, rubbing his chin. He shrugged, unable to come up with an adequate explanation. "I don't know."

"And people say you have a way with words," Luca said, shaking his head.

Gabriel resisted the urge to hit him again. He sighed. "A lot happened."

"Good? Bad?"

"Most of it? Not great…"

Luca nodded as if he knew, but he didn't say anything because they'd arrived in their section. They all exchanged their usual hugs, and Jenna peppered Gabriel with questions about what he'd gotten for Christmas.

The band took the stage, and soon the whole auditorium was on their feet, worshiping along. Gabriel's hands rubbed together in discomfort. He hardly mouthed the words. He glanced at Luca. This was the only time his presence faded.

After two songs, Dr. Stone greeted everyone with his usual exuberance and well-wishes that they'd enjoyed their Christmas break.

"Today, I wanted to step away from my usual Monday teachings and invite a guest speaker on stage. I know, I know, you're all sorely disappointed you won't be hearing me for the hundredth time." He paused as the smattering of laughter faded. "But we have a great message planned for you—especially relevant in this day and age. So, give it up for the brilliant Doctor Anderson!"

Cheers and whistles pierced the air. A man walked up the steps with measured strides. He shook hands with the President and adjusted his notes on the podium. He wore a black blazer and pants, a light blue button-up with the top undone. The screen behind him revealed his upper half. He wore black glasses and had close-cropped brown hair, pale skin, and a short, trimmed beard.

"It's good to be back, Morrison!" He said to pointed applause. "I'm honored to be here today to kick off the semester. And today will be a bit different than the sermons I've shared in the past. After talking to Doctor Stone these last weeks, we thought it would be good to share a more personal story."

He paced the stage. Gabriel glanced at the others in his row. "Do you know who this guy is?"

"No idea," Luca said.

Dr. Anderson began talking as he looked at his feet, one hand waving in the air to illustrate his story. "My parents were farmers. We raised all sorts of animals in my childhood. Cows, chickens, pigs… *me*." He paused as the auditorium laughed. "I was a mess. Picture me playing in the pig pen at six years old, utterly convinced I was born into the wrong family." Dr. Anderson shook his head with remembrance. "My parents were horrified when they found me all covered in *you know what*, so they promptly used every bar of soap on the farm and sent me off to school to learn how to be a normal human."

Gabriel settled back in his seat, hoping it would just be a long story today.

"I liked school," Dr. Anderson continued, pausing at the right side of the stage. "I liked the structure, learning new things, *reading* about animals instead of pretending to be one—much to the relief of my parents."

Scattered laughter.

"But as the years went on, I began to realize I wasn't quite like the other boys."

Gabriel cocked his head, getting the vague, sinking feeling he knew the topic of the message.

"I was more interested in books than playing baseball at recess. I was sensitive, quiet, and studious. God had given me those wonderful gifts, but Satan worked to twist and destroy them. For years, I was ostracized for being effeminate."

Gabriel stiffened. There it was—just like he'd thought. A direct response to Mason, and a message to anyone like him in the audience. He waited for the big reveal.

"The first time I remember having same-sex attractions, I was ten years old, and I was at a classmate's pool party," Dr. Anderson said.

Gabriel became a statue. He clutched his knees and closed his eyes. The oxygen had been sucked from the auditorium. No one moved. Air was like nails in his lungs.

Dr. Anderson continued his story about attending college and walking away from God. "I was partying, pursuing the world for all it was worth. Encouraged by everyone around me, I was having countless sexual interactions with people I didn't even know. Multiple a day. Doing drugs, everything.

"When I came out to my parents after graduation, they were completely shattered. They didn't understand how I could have fallen so far from what they taught. You see, I'd already bought into the lie that homosexuality was an inseparable aspect of who I was as a person."

A few people in front of Gabriel wrote down this piece of wisdom. Dr. Anderson took a moment to gather himself. His eyes glimmered with pain. He rubbed his face and took a drink of water. Gabriel was shaking. All he wanted to do was grab Luca's hand and leave the auditorium.

"I didn't talk to my parents for three years. I kept partying and sleeping around. I pretended to be the office funnyman, but I was crumbling inside. I kept trying to fill this *void* in my life, and that's when I got the phone call that my mom had died in a car accident."

Sharp inhales punctuated the auditorium.

"That news broke me. I'd never reconciled with her, and now I never would. At her funeral, my dad shared the hope of the gospel with such grace and love. I think that's the first time I *heard* the message of Jesus. I talked with my dad about God for hours a day after that. I couldn't learn fast enough, and I knew I'd reached a turning point."

Dr. Anderson paused, looking over his captive audience. "I could abandon God again and let my *feelings* dictate who I was, or let go of the homosexual lifestyle by *liberating* myself from my feelings and live as a follower of Jesus Christ."

Gabriel's lips drew together. The skin of his eyes tightened.

"After all these talks with my dad, my decision was clear and obvious," Dr. Anderson paused for an infinite moment. "I chose God."

The tension at the beginning of the message broke. He chose God. He was still saved. Of course he was. That's how God worked.

He redeemed the most lost and broken people.

The worst of the worst.

Gabriel fought to keep his lips from turning into a painful sneer.

"I realized then, my feelings did not define my identity. Just as I pretended to be an animal as a kid, playing in the muck of the pig pen, I was deceiving myself. It only brought me harm."

Wow, Gabriel mouthed, eyebrows raised.

"My sexuality is *not* an inseparable aspect of who I am as a person. And it is *never bigger than God.*"

The auditorium rippled with *amens.*

Gabriel twitched with anger.

He knew this logic. He'd used it too. It had kept him in line all these years. It kept him afraid of inevitable punishment.

Don't trust your instincts, it whispered. *The pain you feel is good; it glorifies God. This is how you know you're holy.*

Only now did Gabriel realize how clever this manipulation was.

"I share this story with a heavy heart, but also with understanding. *I know what it's like.* And I know that it never fulfills you. It only leaves you more broken and empty than before." Dr. Anderson paused for a long moment. He examined the crowd before him, squatting to get a more eye-to-eye view. "And I know some people in this very room might be dealing with the same things. Or maybe it's some other sexual sin. Pornography. Or lust. It could be something else entirely, but God hates it all the same. No matter how hard you fight," he said quietly, almost a whisper, "it's never enough if you're not with God.

"I think this school has an incredible generation of believers. But that means the Enemy will try even harder to bring us down. I want to see this school be at the forefront of a spiritual revolution, something to change the world. That starts *right now.*"

Someone shouted, "AMEN!"

More people clapped. Dr. Anderson nodded.

"You can cheer for that," Dr. Anderson said. At his prompting, the auditorium erupted into hoots of affirmation. Dr. Anderson smiled, eventually quieting the crowd by waving his hands lower and lower. "This means helping your brothers and sisters, not tolerating sin. If you see your brother in sin, confront him about it. Go to an authority figure. Make it known because sin cannot thrive in the light."

Gabriel balked. Did he just call for students to report their friends?

"For all those people struggling right now, I can sense the Spirit moving, tugging you into action. And for everyone who wants to rededicate their lives to God, I want you to come up to the stage right now."

There were frozen seconds as everyone realized what they were being asked to do. This was not the typical 'bow your heads' closing statement. It required action. Demanded it.

The audience stirred, uncertain.

"No one will judge you for repenting. In fact, we should welcome anyone so humble as to accept their desire to reconfirm their salvation." Dr. Anderson pursed his lips, eyes searching for the first brave soul to stand. "That fear you feel is from the Enemy. It's just you and God right now. Are you willing to do what it takes to truly follow Him, or will you keep wallowing in a half-hearted faith?"

The first student stood up in the second row from the stage. A girl rose to her feet a couple of rows behind. Then five more were on their feet, shuffling to the aisles.

And then it was a flood.

Jenna stood up, passing over Luca and Gabriel. Gabriel watched her descend the stairs, and the aisles were already clogged with students. He felt desperate to join them, to be a part of the crowd. He didn't want to be left sitting in his seat and have everyone know he hadn't made a move to become closer to God.

And Gabriel understood something else at that moment.

If the guilt didn't force you to take action, the fear of being left out would probably finish the job. When it felt like the only way to receive forgiveness was to get up and prostrate yourself at the stage, who could keep themselves from joining?

Of course, there were plenty of people who hadn't gotten up.

These would be the ones utterly convinced they had enough salvation. Or the ones too scared to move.

In three minutes, nearly half the seats had been vacated. People crowded the aisles. They rocked back and forth, desperate prayers on their lips, tears in their eyes.

Gabriel sank lower in his seat, crossing his arms. He glanced at Luca, who only clenched his jaw. Gabriel turned his gaze to the ceiling and felt himself floating out of the auditorium. He closed his eyes and pictured the ocean. Imagined the gentle waves lapping on the shore.

Hand in hand with someone he wasn't allowed to hold.

And things were quiet.

FEAR LIKE NO OTHER

EVEN THOUGH THERE was minimal teaching that first week, Gabriel didn't know how he made it through his classes.

Sometimes, he'd walk into a building and forget where he was going, or what classroom he was supposed to be in. Those were the worst moments because Gabriel would just stand there, confused, as other students streamed around him. And then he would step to the side, a bit panicked and suddenly fighting the urge to cry over nothing at all.

Gabriel's dad texted him again on Monday, saying he hoped Gabriel was having a good start to the semester. When Gabriel still hadn't responded, his dad called on Tuesday. Gabriel ignored it, and when the voicemail appeared in his inbox, he deleted it without listening.

His dad texted him again on Thursday: *Call me back. Please.*

Gabriel sucked his teeth, primal anger rising in his throat. He returned his dad's call on the way to his next class.

"Gabriel! Thanks for talking," his dad said.

"Yeah, sure."

"What's going on?"

"I'm heading to class."

"I can call back when you have more time."

"This is fine. I'm really busy this week."

There was silence on the line. His dad's voice came back on, pained. *"Alright, well, I just wanted to check in to see how you're doing."*

"I'm fine."

"Is that it? Nothing else going on?"

"What do you want me to say?"

"I'm trying to talk to you! How are you doing?"

"I don't know!"

"Try explaining it to me."

Gabriel wanted to throw his phone. "I don't have anything to say to you."

Silence, again.

"I hope you know I love you."

"Okay."

"I really do."

"I have to go, sorry."

"Oh, well, thanks for calling."

"Yeah."

"I love you."

"Yep. I have to go."

Gabriel hung up, full of irrational, burning anger.

OVER THE NEXT week, there were rumors that two students had left because of sexual sin violations. From what he overheard in the cafeteria, in class, and from Jason's group, they were reported by their peers.

The first Friday of the first week, Gabriel received a text. He was walking into chapel when it buzzed in his pocket.

Mason.

Gabriel's insides lurched. He'd almost forgotten he'd reached out. He opened the message.

> *This is Mason's mom. Mason is attend-*
> *ing a prayer retreat to cleanse his sin*
> *and you should too. Don't ever contact*
> *him again*

Gabriel stopped in his tracks. His knees nearly buckled. Students parted around him like water around a boulder. He didn't see their irritated glances. His vision narrowed. Fear like he'd never experienced squeezed him with everything it had.

Immediately, his mind flashed to the students who had been kicked out, overcome with the horror that he might be next. And then he remembered coming out to Jonathan at The Gathering, and wondered if he would report him.

Gabriel started walking again, going past the Ministry Center. He fought the crowd. People kept throwing glances at him. Gabriel stared straight ahead, right hand pressed over his ribs.

He didn't know where he was going. He just needed to walk.

GABRIEL HAD LOOPED around the Athletic Center by the time Luca texted him.

> *Skipping chapel today?*

> *I just needed some time to myself*

> *Nice. My roommate's staying at home*

*this weekend. Want to watch a movie
tonight in my room?*

That sounds great

Sending the text, Gabriel shut off his phone. And walked. And tried
not to think for as long as he could.

TO REMEMBER IS TO HURT

LUCA AGREED TO watch *Calvary* even though Gabriel had already seen it twice, but only after promising they'd see *A Single Man* next.

"You'll love it. It's your kind of movie," Gabriel said as they walked back from the Dollar General off campus, plastic bags bulging with snacks. "It's moody and dark—"

"Uh!" Luca scoffed, swatting him. *"Rude."*

Gabriel grinned. "And *mysterious.*"

Luca softened. "I like mysterious."

As they neared campus, they lapsed into silence, and both could feel the tension of things unsaid.

"What happened over break?" Luca asked.

Gabriel ducked his chin into the collar of his jacket as a gust of wind hit them. He watched his feet and avoided the cracks in the uneven sidewalk. "New Year's Eve, I came out to my best friend back home," Gabriel said. Luca's head spun to look at him, mouth open. "And then her dad, which went pretty well. And then I called my parents Saturday when I got back to school…" Gabriel scanned the campus, avoiding Luca's eyes. "But that one didn't go so well."

"Wow," Luca said, gazing at the naked tree branches above their heads. "I'm sorry."

"But the first person I ever told is here on campus, and I'm kind of terrified he's going to turn me in." Gabriel's voice cracked.

Luca just kept walking. He didn't offer false assurances that it wouldn't happen, or that the school wouldn't kick him out. They both knew it was possible.

When Luca spoke, it was calm and tender. "Whatever happens, I'll be there for you."

They paused in the middle of the sidewalk, no one else around. Gabriel met his eyes. "I don't want to drag you into this."

"I want to help."

"Why?"

"Because I like you, and being alone with something like that…it just gets worse."

Gabriel thought about that for a while, examining Luca's earnest face. "I didn't tell anyone here about you, just so you know."

Luca cocked his head. "But you told the ones back home?"

A tiny smile escaped Gabriel's lips. "Maybe."

Luca's eyes twinkled. They started walking again.

"I told someone about you, too," Luca said.

Gabriel couldn't express how warm that made him feel. Back in Luca's room, they settled on his roommate's couch, not too close but close enough to feel the spark of connection.

"Fair warning, it has a shocking beginning," Gabriel said, mischievous weight to his eyes. "But I don't want to spoil anything."

"Hmm…" Luca mused. "I'm ready."

Once again, Gabriel was breathless at the start. Luca covered his mouth during the entire scene in the confessional booth, and when Gabriel glanced over, Luca's eyes were watery. They hardly shared a word the whole time, and Gabriel took that as a sign of the film's captivating story. When the credits rolled, Gabriel held his hands close to the upper part of his chest. He looked over at Luca. He was crying, fully this time.

"Luc," Gabriel said.

Luca removed his glasses and wiped his face. He seemed ready to say something, but he covered his mouth instead.

"It's an intense movie," Gabriel said. He reached over and squeezed Luca's shoulder. Luca tensed. Gabriel dropped his hand. "Hey, what's going on?"

Luca brought his feet onto the couch, knees against his chest, and buried his chin in the crook of his arm. Shakily, he said, "I wasn't ready for that."

Gabriel remained quiet, not sure what to say because he now understood that there was more going on than he initially thought. He stared at the TV. "We don't have to talk about it."

"No," Luca said, muffled by his sweater. He propped his chin on his arm. "No, it's just…that happened to me…"

"What?" Gabriel said. He heard the words but couldn't make sense of them.

"Not *that*, but similar."

"Stop…"

"I was thirteen…scared and confused that I liked guys, so I told my youth group leader."

"No," Gabriel whispered, gripping the collar of his shirt.

"And he…touched, and, and…" Luca broke off, face cracking. "…for two years…and he said I'd go to hell if I…if I said anything."

Luca turned away, shaking. Gabriel had never felt so helpless. He desperately wanted to comfort Luca, but he had no idea what to say, or if he could touch him. Deep pain carved through Gabriel's chest. Horrible guilt churned his stomach over forcing Luca to relive the trauma. And Luca hadn't said a word. He just watched, helpless. Paralyzed.

"I'm so sorry," Gabriel said, knowing the words weren't nearly enough. "I'm so *so* sorry, that's horrible. I wouldn't have suggested this movie if I'd known—"

"It's alright," Luca choked out.

"No, it's not."

"You didn't know."

"That doesn't matter."

"I needed to remember, to finally say something."

"But—"

"I've never said that before," Luca said, looking in Gabriel's direction. "You're the only one who knows."

Gabriel was struck by that admission, by the weight of being the first to know something so immense. He bit his lip, tears forming in his own eyes.

"Can I…" Gabriel said, tentative. "…hold you? Is that okay?"

Luca thought this over and gave a slow nod. Gabriel scooted closer on the couch and put his right arm around Luca's shoulders. Luca melted into him, and Gabriel held him tight.

"I'm so sorry," Gabriel repeated.

Luca didn't respond. He just cried into Gabriel's shirt, body trembling. It felt like such a futile gesture, but there was nothing else Gabriel could do. It tore him open to imagine Luca's pain, and he felt awful for his part in bringing it up.

But he was glad to be here, glad to be trusted with Luca's most vulnerable moments.

"Luc, whatever it is," Gabriel said softly, left hand rubbing Luca's back, "I'm here."

HOW TO MEND A HEART

THREE MORE STUDENTS left in the following week, and Gabriel's constant, high-alert anxiety had transformed into background static. It crackled under the surface of every action and thought, but there weren't so many peaks and valleys.

He'd been going to the gym most days in the first two weeks, or running the paths around campus. It was the easiest way to cope with the fear of being found out at any moment. He was just doing push-ups, sit-ups, and bicep curls, but the simple exercises were already working. He could feel his abs coming in under his shirt. Even so, he didn't pay too much attention to his progress. That's not why he went.

On the second weekend of the semester, Gabriel and Luca did homework for Politics and American Culture in Gabriel's room. It was just them. The door was closed, and they sat in the middle of the floor.

Luca looked up from his textbook. "Gabe."

"Hmm," Gabriel mumbled, writing a definition on a notecard.

"Gabriel."

"What?"

"I need to say something."

Gabriel looked up, tapping his pen against the palm of his other hand. "Alright."

Luca's face was creased with sadness. "I don't know if we're going to work out."

"What?"

"I don't think I can give you what you want."

Gabriel opened and closed his mouth. He squeezed his pen. "What do you mean?"

"What...*happened*...to me, I don't know if I can," Luca's eyes scanned the ceiling, "be *physical* with anyone."

"Oh," Gabriel said.

"I don't know if I'll ever want that, or if it will just take time. I don't want you to miss out on someone else who can give that to you."

Gabriel's face softened over how deeply Luca cared. Enough to tell the truth. Enough to want him to find someone else. Someone better.

He'd never found someone better.

Gabriel scooted closer to Luca, keeping his hands to himself. "I don't know if I want that either. I can't say I've ever wanted that." Gabriel looked into Luca's face. "I just want to be around you."

"You don't get—"

"I understand. It's alright. This is more than enough," Gabriel said. He fidgeted with the fabric of his pant cuff. He didn't know what else to say or do, so he returned to his textbook and discarded notes.

"Okay," Luca said. He flipped the page of his textbook. "And we can still hold hands, or..."

Gabriel glanced up. Luca's cheeks were pink.

"We don't even have to touch. I just want to be close," Gabriel said, his face flushing. "Just like this."

Luca's eyes twinkled. "Alright."

Gabriel just nodded and tried to focus on his notes.

He failed.

He smiled.

THE PATH OF RESTORATION

WEDNESDAY AFTERNOON OF the third week back, Gabriel sat by himself in the upper section of the cafeteria, enjoying a slice of pizza and an Arnold Palmer. He checked his phone and saw an email from Dr. Adam Clark, the Student Life Dean. The subject read *Enrollment.*

Gabriel froze. Enrollment?

Stomach sinking, he clicked the email.

Mr. Moore,

I hope you're doing well at the start of the semester. Would you stop by my office this afternoon to discuss an enrollment matter? My office is in the President's Hall, 104. I'll be there until 5 p.m., and it looks like your classes are done, so it should fit into your schedule.

Blessings,

Dr. Clark.

The skin around Gabriel's eyes tightened.

Why had Dr. Clark gone through the trouble of looking up his schedule? Was it that serious? Was this the email other students received before being kicked out?

He set his phone down and stared ahead, paralyzed. He was no longer hungry, and he'd actually been enjoying his food today.

What if he didn't go? He could pretend he hadn't seen the email and make Dr. Clark track him down if it was truly urgent. But that's exactly what would happen. He couldn't just ignore a message from the *Dean*.

The group three tables away laughed at something. Their actions were foreign to Gabriel.

Invisible hands squeezed from all sides, and he sat for twenty minutes, hardly moving. Hardly daring to breathe.

GABRIEL TRUDGED UP the five steps to the President's Hall. It was a small building on the southwest tip of campus, only a few minutes from his dorm. A steeple pierced the sky, and stone pillars stood on either side of the entrance.

The interior looked like it was from the early 1900s, and Gabriel's shoes sank into the plush carpet. The walls were carved cherry wood with glass paneling for the office windows. He passed Dr. Stone's office, and the President was sorting through a stack of papers on his desk. He glanced at Gabriel, expressionless. Gabriel moved on.

Dr. Clark stared at his desktop computer, chin propped in his left hand. His square glasses reflected unreadable images as he scrolled. Gabriel knocked on the open door, and Dr. Clark looked up. "Come in."

Gabriel hovered just inside the doorway. "I got an email about enrollment," he said, and at Dr. Clark's blank look, he added, "I'm Gabriel Moore. You asked to see me today."

Dr. Clark's face lit up with recognition. "Right, Gabriel, of course." He stood up and extended his hand. Gabriel shook it. "Sorry about the late notice. Thanks for stopping by."

"Sure," Gabriel said, taking an uncomfortable seat in the chair across from the desk. He set his backpack at his feet and kept his hands in his lap.

Dr. Clark sat, a pleasant smile on his face. He had a short brown beard that was patchy on his cheeks and thinning brown hair that was gelled to a point.

"You said it was about enrollment?" Gabriel prodded. "Why isn't academics bringing this up?"

Dr. Clark's smile faltered. "Yes, well, it *could* be an enrollment issue. I just wanted to chat with you first. Informally, of course."

Gabriel didn't respond.

"Well, you know how much we value our principles at Morrison, the code of conduct, following the example of Jesus..." Dr. Clark said. "We have a special mission here, trying to raise a passionate generation of Christians to go into the world—"

"Why am I here?" Gabriel cut him off.

"Well, recently," Dr. Clark grimaced, lacing his fingers together, forearms on the desk, "there have been some *events* on campus that needed to be addressed. For everyone's privacy, I can't speak on specifics, but they were in regards to violating school policies. Things clearly outlined in the student handbook as harmful behavior."

Dr. Clark looked expectantly at Gabriel, but Gabriel didn't give him anything to latch onto.

"Some students had violated our alcohol policy. We have zero tolerance for drinking while enrolled as a student. And others..." Dr. Clark shifted uncomfortably. He twisted his gold wedding band, eyes darting behind Gabriel's head. "...have engaged in *homosexual* activities, which is a violation of the sanctity of marriage, clearly outlined in the Bible. We think different violations require different responses, and we fully believe in restoration and healing. Otherwise, none of us would be here, right?"

Dr. Clark smiled as if they were in on a joke, but he watched Gabriel closely. Gabriel kept his face impassive. He didn't even fidget. He wouldn't crack until he had to.

"And?" Gabriel prodded.

"And we know you've been in contact with Mason Gram."

This time, Gabriel twitched. This was about *Mason?* He was about to ask why when he remembered the text he'd sent after finding out Mason had left school. And then the response from Mason's mom. Everything tightened inside.

There was a feral glimmer at the corner of Dr. Clark's mouth. "The reason I wanted to talk was because Mason is a homosexual offender whom we've attempted to rehabilitate in the past," Dr. Clark said, and Gabriel coiled up at the wording. Dr. Clark shuffled a few papers around, then slid one across the desk toward Gabriel. "And we received this screenshot a few weeks ago."

It was of Mason's screen, Gabriel's name as the contact at the top, and the offending text: *I heard you're not coming back this semester. Hope you're doing alright. I just wanted to say that I think I like guys too, so you're not alone. Thanks for being open about your story.*

Gabriel squeezed his hands together, reading it a second and third time, mind spinning as to how he could twist his words so they weren't so bad. But the *I think I like guys too* portion would sink him. The only redeeming part was his uncertainty. It didn't say he was gay, which would have been a damning statement. Gabriel swallowed and looked up, waiting for Dr. Clark to direct the conversation.

"What was the nature of your relationship with Mason?" Dr. Clark asked, clinical.

"We were friends."

"Just friends? But you knew about his predispositions."

"He shared his testimony with the dorm last semester, so we all knew."

"Did you ever take advantage of that?"

"What?"

"Try to be physical, or watch people…"

Dr. Clark let the implications fill the air.

Gabriel furrowed his eyebrows. "I wouldn't do that."

"I need you to be honest if we hope to move forward here."

"I am."

"It's ok, Gabriel, you can share with me. I'm here to help." Dr. Clark leaned forward. He adopted a soft expression, probably something he thought was warm and comforting, but there was conflict underneath. "Have you ever engaged in sexual activity with another male?"

Gabriel prepared his lie.

The trick was to tell a version of the truth, one layered with enough honesty that you could genuinely believe what you were saying.

"I've never been sexual with *anyone*," Gabriel said, unwavering. He pressed into his confusion as if the very thought was repulsive.

It *was* true, in layers. The kiss with Luca was more about comfort and curiosity than anything else, which didn't seem like the illicit activity Dr. Clark sought. And he hadn't touched a girl, so he was honest there.

And yet, he could never reasonably deny the text to Mason.

"But I think I've been…same-sex attracted, and I don't know what to do." Gabriel covered his mouth with one hand. He didn't even have to fake his shame. It was real and present and hot on his cheeks.

Dr. Clark nodded deeply, fingers steepled under his chin. "I'm glad you're able to admit this, Gabriel. That's the first step toward healing."

"I just don't want anyone to know," Gabriel said. And that *was* true. He couldn't let this get out to the campus at large.

"Privacy is my top priority," Dr. Clark said. Apparently, that didn't apply to Mason. "And if you're willing to work with us on a plan of healing, I don't see any reason why you can't have a long and fruitful time at Morrison."

Gabriel's mind raced. "What do you mean?"

"We fully believe in restoration, that healing is available *and* necessary. And I'm glad we've caught this so early," Dr. Clark said. Gabriel twitched again. "Once someone acts on their feelings, it's far more difficult to set them on the right path."

"That makes sense," Gabriel said carefully.

"And that's what you want, right? You want to get better?"

Gabriel nodded, latching on to how 'better' meant changing his feelings. Maybe he didn't want to change. Maybe he didn't want to lose Luca. But he could share something else, no less true. "I want to be happy."

Dr. Clark smiled. "Good. We want that, too." He leaned back in satisfaction, his swivel chair creaking. "So, based on our conversation, I think I can recommend our counseling center. It's an excellent resource for whatever you're going through."

"Do I have to?" Gabriel asked, tentative.

"Of course not," Dr. Clark said, his uncomfortable smile returning. "We want to give you all the options, but this one is the most private for *you*. It's paid for by the school, so there's no need to involve anyone."

Meaning, not tell his parents. Or anyone else. Could he trust that?

"And we want to provide a safe environment for you to talk about whatever's going on. Inside...or at home." Dr. Clark peered inquisitively at Gabriel. What did his home life have to do with this? "We want you to thrive, to discover your purpose. And we want everyone at Morrison to feel comfortable with other students."

Gabriel clenched his jaw at the underlying message.

Keep it to yourself until it's fixed.

"Otherwise..." Dr. Clark raised his hands in a regretful gesture. "There's not much we can do. As long as someone is enrolled as a student, we want them to be a vibrant part of our community, but that means embodying our values. Does that make sense?"

Gabriel dug his nails into his thigh under the lip of the desk. He understood. There was no real option. It was conform or leave. Conform, or be disgracefully kicked out, with everyone talking about your misdeeds in dorms and classrooms.

He couldn't let that happen. He couldn't face the ridicule. He couldn't face his family or the Ali's or anyone else he knew.

He couldn't fail them.

Telling a few people about his life was one thing, but ruining his reputation and college career was something else entirely. Dealing with the aftermath would be too much to handle.

He only had one choice if he wanted his life to be anything close to normal. He had to look at the bigger picture. This didn't mean he was hiding. He was just biding his time while he figured out what to do.

Maybe if he got through this semester, he could transfer schools.

And so, Gabriel swallowed his pride and truth and pain like he'd done for many years, and he said, "When do I start?"

THE ROOM WITH THE BLUE COUCH

THE PLAN WAS to start Friday, and he would continue going weekly through spring break. If all went well, he would have monthly 'upkeep' meetings on a declining basis until all parties involved felt like he'd thoroughly dealt with his predispositions.

Dr. Clark presented the plan like they'd come up with it together.

Gabriel left the meeting in a haze. His consciousness floated a few feet behind his body and watched him stand, confused, twenty feet outside President's Hall. He did a slow spin, trying to figure out where to go and what to do.

Was this really happening?

Rehabilitation. Restoration.

Pleasant words for something awful.

Gabriel went back to his dorm and took a three-hour nap, then he watched TV for the rest of the evening. He did the minimum work to complete his assignments for the following day. He didn't care about his grades this semester. He just needed to pass.

GABRIEL WAS TOO busy with classes on Thursday to dwell on his upcoming counseling session. It just hovered in his mind, waiting to take over. He felt somewhat accomplished that no matter how bad it got, he never panicked enough to rush out in the middle of class.

Friday came, and he lay paralyzed in his bed. He didn't exactly know what to expect from the session, but it couldn't be good. He stayed in bed until well after 10 a.m., skipped chapel, and eventually wandered the campus, nibbling on an energy bar. By noon, he's circled campus twice, laid down in three different fields to settle his aching stomach, and finally made his way to the counseling center located in the Union.

The entire walk there, it felt like he was heading to his death. Each step sent jagged fear knifing through his ribs. His mind kept trying to detach, but he desperately needed to plan what he would say. He needed a minute to think. He needed a few seconds to breathe.

He just needed *time*.

Everything was collapsing. Closing in. Squeezing him from every direction. It was like he'd been wrapped in cellophane and was about to be dropped in a lake.

Lightheaded, he steadied himself against the bridge's railing leading to the Union. Physical pain went through his gut, angry at him for only eating half an energy bar today. Gabriel straightened up and continued walking.

The counseling center was a small subsection of the Student Union on the second floor. Three other students filled the leather couches of the waiting room. A girl had a clipboard in her hands. Two guys fidgeted with their hands and shirts, staring at everything but not focusing on anything for too long.

Gabriel approached the front desk, thumbs looped into his backpack straps. The woman behind the desk looked up from her computer. She was in her forties and had straight black hair, greying at the roots. She wore a cream blouse and silver flower earrings.

"Hi, how can I help you?" She asked warmly. Her name tag read *Lydia*.

"Hi, uh, I'm here to sign up," Gabriel said.

"For counseling?" She asked as if there were other options.

"Yes, um…" Gabriel scratched his nose. "I'm Gabriel Moore. Doctor Clark should have contacted you."

The girl with the clipboard looked at Gabriel. There was something dark and heavy behind her eyes. Gabriel returned his attention to Lydia before he could dwell.

"Yes, Gabriel…" She said absentmindedly. "I got that note Wednesday, I think…"

Gabriel shifted his weight. "Probably."

"Alright, why don't you fill out these, and we'll schedule you for an evaluation." Lydia handed Gabriel a clipboard and a pen, then returned to her computer.

Gabriel surveyed the open seats. He took one on a diagonal from the girl who'd looked up when Dr. Clark's name was mentioned. He did his best to focus on the paperwork. He filled in the easiest information first.

Name. Phone number. Birthday. Medications.

And then there were the hard questions.

Why are you seeking counseling?

Gabriel tapped his pen against his knee and bounced his foot on the floor. Writing out his three-sentence answer took him at least five minutes.

Dr. Clark sent me. I've been struggling with my sexuality and some anxiety. I think I'm depressed too, and I don't know what to do.

Gabriel took tiny breaths. He couldn't tear his eyes from his handwritten *sexuality*. It felt so real, seeing it in writing.

And there was a personal background check.

Have you experienced any of the following?

Anxiety. Depression. Suicide. Eating disorder. Bipolar disorder. Sexual abuse.

Gabriel looked up at the other students once more. They could be dealing with any of these things, or multiple at once. He would never know by looking at them. But they were here for a reason. Whether that was forced or voluntary, they were here for a reason.

Gabriel thought of Luca and how he might fill out this form. Suddenly, Gabriel's problems seemed so much smaller. And yet, he was so torn up inside he couldn't possibly imagine what Luca experienced on a daily basis. How much worse was it for him?

Did he feel as bad as Gabriel? Did he feel like he was constantly suffocating?

Gabriel bit his knuckle so hard the joint flared in pain. He clenched his jaw, eyes tight, trying vainly to swallow the lump in his throat that wouldn't move.

He checked the box for anxiety. After a few minutes of deliberation, he checked the one for depression. He paused at the box that said *suicide.*

It made him freeze up. Deep down, he knew the truth. He knew the reality of the things he'd done and thought. And no matter how much he pretended they weren't real, they'd still happened.

His hands trembled as if he'd witnessed something terrible. Adrenaline weakened his muscles. He tasted copper, like he'd sucked on a penny.

Gabriel checked the box.

Fuck.

He squeezed his temples between his palms.

He didn't even consider the question about eating. That wasn't his problem. Being unable to eat because of stress wasn't the same as simply *not eating*, or having too much, right?

Of course it wasn't.

He stared at the shaky scrawl covering the paper, knowing it was over. All of it. Starting now.

He couldn't ask for another form. He couldn't take back his text to Mason. He couldn't make New Year's Eve a happy night. He couldn't rewind the call to his parents or pretend his dad hadn't sent *that* text. He couldn't erase any of the moments leading to this point.

He'd done the best he possibly could, and that brought him here. It made him even more scared to move forward. He simply didn't know what future action would cause the next cascade of terrible events.

Gabriel sat another ten or twelve minutes with his clipboard, reviewing the information. He held his entire past in his hands. His entire future.

He got to his feet and stopped in front of Lydia's desk. He knew the moment the paperwork left his hands, his life would be forever changed.

It already was.

GABRIEL RETURNED TWO hours later, terror in his bones.

He checked in, sat down, and watched the clock. Every second dragged. The minutes flew by. A door opened, and Gabriel jerked. A middle-aged woman stepped into the waiting room. "Gabriel?"

He nodded, standing up to face her. They shook hands. She was a head shorter than he was. She had dark brown hair cut in a bob and black glasses with strings on their ends that looped behind her neck. She had a plump body, covered partially with a red cardigan.

"I'm Marci. It's good to meet you," she said.

Gabriel didn't trust himself to speak as he followed her into her office. She closed the door, and he nestled into the corner of her blue fabric couch, displacing an embroidered pillow. He pulled it into his lap, taking shallow breaths.

The walls had been decorated with signs in cursive writing. Each one was a Bible verse or said things like *Pray* and *Trust God*. On the desk was a picture of Marci with a man and two small kids between them. She had a calendar covered in sticky notes and a bookshelf on the left wall filled with writings from Christian authors.

Marci settled in her swivel chair across from Gabriel, a clipboard in hand. *His* clipboard. His entire life boiled down to a few check-marks and barely legible sentences. Things he'd never admitted to another person. But *she* knew, now.

The room swayed out of focus.

"How are you doing today?" She asked, pushing her glasses up her nose.

Gabriel thought he might pass out. "A bit nervous."

"That's alright, I'm here to help," she said with a warm look that failed to set Gabriel at ease. "Today, I want to focus on your paperwork and getting to know each other. How does that sound?"

"Fine."

"So, what brings you in today?"

"Doctor Clark referred me."

"Yes, that's right. I see on your form you said you think you've been struggling with your sexuality. Could you talk about that? How long has that been going on?"

Gabriel dried his palms on the pillow. Sweat trickled under his arms. "A while, probably since I was I was ten or eleven. I didn't really notice until high school."

"What is it you're struggling with? Who are you attracted to?"

"I'd say I'm mostly attracted to, um…" Gabriel swallowed. "…to guys. And maybe girls, I'm not sure."

"Well, that's to be expected."

"What?"

"Same-sex attraction is more common than you'd think. It affects many young men your age," Marci explained. "This is a critical time for the development of men, and there's bound to be confusion and uncertainty when it comes to sexuality. I want to help you figure out the root cause. It's quite often that sexuality can be traced back to events in the past or family relationships."

"What do you mean?" Gabriel asked, sinking at the implications of her words.

"Young men can be affected by many things. Absent fathers might lead someone to seek that connection in other men, which develops into attraction. An over-parenting mother prevents the son from developing into a self-assured man. It could be confidence issues."

"Oh."

That was the same thing his dad insinuated: Something happened to make him this way. What if he just *was*?

"Would you say you're attracted to women, too?"

Gabriel fidgeted with the corner of the pillow. "I don't know. Maybe."

"Ok, that's good," Marci said encouragingly. "That means there's something to work with. And it's less necessary to diminish how you feel about men so much as bringing out those fruitful attractions towards women."

And now Gabriel understood. He should have known sooner.

This wasn't meant to help him find peace or acceptance. It was meant to shape him into what the school wanted. It was obvious the way Dr. Clark described things, but Gabriel held out hope his counselor would be different.

But she was a Christian counselor. At Morrison. And Morrison believed in Biblical marriage. There would only ever be one solution here.

Rehabilitate the bad. Restore the good.

Gabriel watched the door from the corner of his eye, hoping someone would come barging in. Or the fire alarm would go off. Or *something*. Anything to get him out of this room.

"We can get into that during future sessions. I want to continue reviewing your form," Marci said. She turned over the paper. "I see you have contemplated suicide."

It was a statement. A fact.

Gabriel dug his fingers into the pillow.

Shame flooded him. He was so weak. He shouldn't have checked that box.

"How are you feeling today?" Marci asked.

"I'm good," Gabriel said, measured.

"When was the last time you thought of suicide?"

When *was* the last time?

Maybe that night with the computer cord—

Gabriel blinked, and the thought was gone.

Or maybe Christmas Eve when he couldn't stop staring at the kitchen knives, and how he—

Gone.

Or how he could twist the wheel driving—

Gone.

But the thoughts weren't quite erased. If he looked, he could have found each one. He just stayed very still and kept his mind very blank.

"Gabriel?" Marci asked, leaning forward. "When was the last time?"

He went with the most obvious answer. "At the end of last semester."

"And what happened then?"

Gabriel squirmed in his seat. He couldn't meet her eyes. "I, um, I put my computer cord around my neck…"

The corner of Marci's mouth twitched. She wrote this down.

Gabriel continued because that's what he thought she wanted. "And I looped it around my bunk. And I hung there a bit, but I stopped myself."

"So you've attempted suicide, then."

Another statement. Marci's eyes flashed pity. Gabriel looked away, biting back tears.

It felt like he was imploding.

It was too much. He couldn't do this. Was there no escape?

And then he was suddenly floating above his body, and he was no longer himself.

Gabriel's mind drifted to the window, light and free. He examined the cobwebs in the corners of the ceiling. He dove under the desk and found a black ant hauling a breadcrumb three times its size.

All the while, the counselor prodded the poor student with questions.

What brought you to that point? The counselor asked.

I just wanted to test it, the student said.

Why test it?

To see if it could work, I think.

Have you thought about suicide since?

Not like in my dorm.

Can you elaborate?

I've thought about knives.

What about the knives?

I put one against my skin, just once.

Where did you put the knife?

Gabriel watched the student trace his index finger over his left forearm and the right side of his neck. The counselor wrote all this down. Gabriel wished he could offer help, but all he could do was float and watch, and the student was doing valiantly on his own, anyway. If only he knew.

The counselor opened the office door a while later, and the student left. Gabriel followed him out. The student talked with the receptionist about his next appointment and left the building, head down, shoulders hunched.

Shattered.

No one else could tell how bad it was.

But Gabriel knew. He saw it all.

GABRIEL BLINKED IN the sunlight, unsure where he was or how he'd gotten there. He had a grey folder in his hands. Inside were pamphlets for counseling retreats, tricks for anxiety, and clinical resources.

He frowned.

It took a few minutes, but the details slowly came back, along with the black hole of dread. He remembered the waiting room. Meeting Marci. Her relentless questions. And then…nothing. Just him standing outside with no direction.

Gabriel looked around again, recognizing the Student Union behind him and remembering his dorm was somewhere ahead, beyond the lake. He went in that direction.

As he walked, the session didn't become clear, but his body was jagged and raw like he'd been sliced apart and put back together, but not quite in the correct order.

He knew what the meeting had been about, but it felt like it had happened to someone else.

And yet, it was like he'd been stripped bare.

Exposed.

Just…violated.

He took a sharp breath, wrapping his arms around himself.

And this was only the beginning.

THE VIEW FROM ABOVE

GABRIEL SPENT MOST of the weekend sleeping in his room. He went
to the cafeteria for lunch on Saturday and nibbled on snacks throughout Sunday. He considered going on a run, but that seemed like too
much effort. He was *tired.* He could hardly get up and go to the
bathroom as it was.

As Old Testament wrapped up on Thursday, Gabriel just sat
there, staring at the wall but not really seeing it. He vaguely registered
students packing up and leaving. Like a phantom, Professor Rosenthal materialized from thin air and sat on the desk in front of Gabriel.
He scratched the stubble on his cheek, bald head reflecting the ceiling
lights.

Gabriel returned to himself and stuffed his notebook into his
backpack. Where'd his pencil case—

"What's going on, Gabriel?" Professor Rosenthal asked.

"Sorry, I'll get out of your way," Gabriel said. He rummaged in
his backpack, finding the zip-up bag.

"Hold on a second. Are you alright?"

Gabriel shrugged, not meeting his eyes. "Just a bit stressed, I
think."

"I can tell. Your work has been rough."

"I know, I'm sorry."

"It's alright, but I know you have more potential."

"I'll do better."

"No, Gabriel, that's not the point. I want *you* to do better."

"I'm trying—"

"Hey, you can't be good at school if you're not good inside."

Gabriel stopped packing his backpack. It was done anyway. He looked up.

"If I knew what was going on, maybe I could help. Or we could work something out for your assignments. I'll let you rewrite your last paper."

Gabriel felt guilty for the generous offer. "I don't know if I have the energy for that."

Professor Rosenthal pursed his lips. "Think about it."

"Sure," Gabriel said, attention drawn to the door as a student entered for the next class. "Thanks."

"Of course," Professor Rosenthal said, standing up.

Gabriel left the classroom, eyes on his feet until he was outside. His next class started in two minutes. He looked to his left, then right, then headed for his dorm. He'd had enough school for the day.

AS GABRIEL WALKED to the next counseling session, he slowly detached from himself. It was easier to deal with things when he wasn't quite there. He watched from above as the student entered the counselor's office and settled on the blue couch.

I want to follow up on your attractions, the counselor said, getting started.

Okay.

What are you attracted to in men?

I don't know.

What draws you to them?

It just happens.

And how does that feel?

Like I want to be around someone? Warm, maybe.

What do you think you are looking for in these relationships?

I don't know.

Are you sure?

The student shrugged.

I'll need you to dig a bit deeper if we're going to discover the root of your attractions. Have you ever acted on these homosexual feelings?

Their voices droned on, and Gabriel checked in with the ants behind the trash can. They swarmed over a dusty raisin. They couldn't see him, but he smiled at them anyway.

Do you want to continue telling people about yourself?

Gabriel zipped back to the couch at the question. Had he missed anything big?

I'm not sure.

What's your goal? What do you want?

I don't want to think about it all the time. I don't want it to be a big deal.

We can work with that. There are several ways we can approach this. I would like to continue meeting, of course, but you might be interested in additional programs. I have a list of local support groups and a few summer retreats.

Gabriel and the student shivered at the same time.

Retreats?

They're for people who experience same-sex attractions.

I don't want…conversion—

Oh, no, it's not conversion therapy or anything like that. The coun-

selor huffed, almost a laugh. *It's for people to learn about sexuality from a Biblical worldview. They dive into the past to address the root causes of things.*

The student burrowed deeper into the couch.

I can refer you to a few places, and you can check them out on your own time. I have friends who have benefited from these programs. They're happy, with families…

Gabriel had heard enough. He floated to the window to wait for the session to end.

AFTER, GABRIEL CRASHED back into his body, and he was assaulted with a searing pain in his chest. He couldn't breathe. Why couldn't he breathe? Tears flooded his eyes. He turned his head as he passed a group of girls headed toward the Union.

Claustrophobia rose from the depths of his being. It was like countless hands had gripped his limbs and were dragging him down into nothingness.

Gabriel pressed his eyes, breathing in through his nose and out his mouth. He spun on the sidewalk, then stepped off the path into the grass under a tree. He laced his fingers behind his head.

He couldn't keep doing this. He was going to break. He was *already* breaking.

He tugged at his hair. It was all too much.

Then he had his phone against his ear with no memory of how it happened or who he was calling.

"Gabe, what's up?" Luca's voice said.

Gabriel barely choked out a response. "Hey, are you free?"

GABRIEL TOLD HIM everything, *everything,* and it took the whole evening. Luca drove them around in Gabriel's car so they didn't have to worry about people overhearing.

"It's the best way to think, anyway," Luca said. "Whenever I can't figure something out, I drive."

Talking to Luca wasn't as awful as with Marci, but it was more difficult. More vulnerable. His mind wouldn't let him drift away. Maybe it knew more than him the need to be present for something like this.

It was excruciating, like pulling clumps of barbed wire from between his ribs and untangling it from around his heart. He couldn't look at Luca as he talked about what happened the night before their kiss, or the counseling sessions, or the call with his parents and the text from his dad.

There was still an ocean of shame when he finished, but there was a lightness, too, having finally let some of it out.

"I know what you need," Luca said in the aftermath, squeezing Gabriel's hand.

Gabriel didn't have the energy to be curious, so he just waited for the reveal. And when they stopped in the candy store in Meridian, Luca bought Gabriel an entire bag of black licorice.

"Never speak of this again," Luca said, handing it over but smiling all the same.

"Only if you have some, too," Gabriel said.

Luca grimaced, taking a piece. "Only for you."

Gabriel stopped and hugged Luca in the middle of the sidewalk, face buried in his shoulder as he fought back tears. Luca rubbed his back. Gabriel melted.

This was it, the kind of love he'd hoped for all these years:

Something pure and simple and perfectly at ease.

HOW TO UNDERSTAND

Sunday afternoon, Jenna asked Gabriel to lunch.

Just us, if you can make it, she texted.

I'll be there, Gabriel sent back.

He was still ragged and anxious, but he showered and donned Luca's sweater to show the world he hadn't given up yet. They met outside the cafeteria entrance, got burritos because it was a moderately short line, and sat in a back corner away from most of the commotion.

"Thanks for coming," Jenna said, settling into her seat. "I feel like it's been forever since we did anything together."

"Seriously, I miss hanging out," Gabriel said, and he meant it. They only saw each other during chapel and lunches, and they never made time to do anything more. They'd both been busy.

"Me too," Jenna said.

"What's up?"

"I just wanted to see you, check in," Jenna said, taking a bite from her burrito. She gulped down iced tea. "I'm trying to be more intentional."

"I'm not very good at that."

"You just get distracted," Jenna said with a knowing smile. She straightened her glasses. "Is that why we never went out again?"

Gabriel's chewing slowed. He should have known she'd ask at some point. "I don't know. I'm just trying to get through my classes."

"I get that. But did you want to again?"

"I…" Gabriel glanced up. "I don't know if it felt right to me."

"Okay." Jenna rubbed her nose.

"I'm sorry."

"No, it's alright. I think I like someone else."

"Oh!"

"I just wanted to make sure you were alright with that."

"Why wouldn't I be?"

"I just wanted to check."

"I think it's great."

"Okay," Jenna said, smiling.

"So…who is it?"

Jenna shrugged, cheeks turning pink. "His name's Dante."

"Dante…" Gabriel thought. "I don't know a Dante."

"We have biology together."

"Sure, 'biology,'" Gabriel said, doing air quotes with a wink. "Lots of hands-on work, then?"

"Uh!" Jenna reached over the table and smacked the top of his head.

"Ow!"

"You're mean."

"I try."

Jenna returned to her food. "But I'm glad we're friends."

"Me too."

They ate quietly for a while.

Jenna's smile slowly transformed into something pained. "You know about my grandma, right? The one with MS?"

Gabriel eyed her warily. "Sure."

"She's been pretty sick these last few weeks. My parents think she might need hospice care soon."

"Shit."

"Yeah."

"I'm sorry."

Jenna removed a wilted piece of lettuce from her burrito. "I'm just scared I'll never see her again."

Gabriel reached for his water. "Can you fly home?"

"I want to, but if I can't in time…" Jenna's voice choked up.

They sat in heavy silence.

"She's not a Christian," Jenna eventually said. "So when she's gone, she's *gone*. No heaven."

Gabriel nodded solemnly. "I'm sorry."

"I mean, I think she believes in *God*, but she mixes in other things too. And she doesn't think you need to be saved."

"But if she believes in God—"

"It's not the same."

"Why not?"

"It just doesn't work. 'I am the way and the truth and the life. No one comes to the Father except through me.' Jesus said it right there. Repenting of sin and belief in Jesus is the only way to salvation."

Gabriel picked at the tortilla of his burrito. It was beginning to fall apart. "What if you're wrong?"

"If?"

"Yeah, what if there's another way?"

"I don't believe there is."

"How can you be so sure?"

"What's with all the questions?"

"It just feels like I'm missing something."

Jenna examined him, but Gabriel didn't shrink away. She touched her glasses and took a bite from her burrito. "I'm sure because God is the only constant in my life. He's been the only real comfort, and I've *felt* Him, you know? I *know* He's real, and I *know* the Bible is true. It's not just something I do on Sunday."

Gabriel didn't know what to say. He'd yearned his whole life for that kind of belief. Why—from the very beginning—had it never happened for him?

"That's why I'm so convinced," Jenna said. "It's why I take the Bible seriously and everything it teaches."

"Okay, I get it," Gabriel said. He really did, and he couldn't blame her at all.

He understood conviction.

He knew what it was like to love a man. She knew what it was like to feel the presence of God. It was all the same, really, just not something the other understood.

"I hope you find the time to see her," Gabriel said.

"I might go next weekend."

"You should."

"Okay."

"And *after*," Gabriel said, meeting her eyes, "I hope you see her then, too."

Jenna gave a small smile. "Me too."

FURTHER CORRUPTION

ON THE WAY to Old Testament Tuesday afternoon, Gabriel's phone
buzzed with a message from Andy.

> *What are you doing?*

> *Heading to class*

> *Skip*

> *Why?*

> *Because I have beer and cigarettes and*
> *I'm five minutes from campus*

Gabriel stopped on the sidewalk. He looked around. The sun was out,
making it a pleasant day in the forties. The Biblical studies building
loomed ahead. Gabriel turned on a heel and walked back toward his
dorm.

Pick me up at Milton

FUCK YES

Gabriel smiled. Andy's white Camry was already waiting, the engine growling with age and missed oil changes. Andy pounded the steering wheel, a grin splitting his face as Gabriel approached. He tossed fast food wrappers and plastic cups into the back seat to make room.

"DUDE!" Andy said. He sported a black sweatshirt and had abandoned his buzz cut for a short mullet; the sides shaved to nothing. "What's up!"

"Same shit."

"I hear that."

Andy punched the gas, and the Camry lurched forward. He turned up the music, some Indie band, and peppered Gabriel with questions about everything he'd missed.

"How's Grant? Still jerking off in the toilets?"

"Oh, for sure, he doesn't even close the door now. Great show."

"*Love* that."

"And he's still not dating anyone."

"As expected. Does he still look like an overflowing muffin?"

"Absolutely."

"Gotta love that chunky son of a bitch," Andy said. He flicked his turn signal. "What else did I miss?"

"Mason left."

"Really?"

"They caught him making out with some guy in his room, so they kicked him out."

"OH FUCK."

"Yep."

"I did not see that coming."

"None of us did."

"I guess all that testimony shit didn't work out, after all. Have you given yours?"

"I stopped going."

"Yeah, I wasn't the biggest fan," Andy drummed the steering wheel, head bobbing with the music. His eyes lit up. "Oh! How's your girlfriend?"

Gabriel shifted in his seat. "We only went out once."

"*Once?*"

"Once. I don't like her like that."

"Well, you tried."

"Kind of."

"Anyone else? Come *onnnn*," Andy reached over and shook Gabriel by the shoulder.

Gabriel couldn't help but laugh, Luca flashing in his mind. "I don't know."

Andy spared a glance at him as they careened around a corner, forcing Gabriel to grip the door handle. "AH! I know that look!"

Gabriel didn't know why he was smiling so wide. He couldn't squash it. It could have been Andy's unabashed enthusiasm. Or maybe it was the *fuck it* urge to blurt everything out and see what happened, despite the terror inside. It's not like he had much to lose.

"Who is it?" Andy asked.

"You can't tell anyone—"

"I knew it!"

"—but I'm kind of in love with Luca."

Andy blinked. Then blinked again. "Luca…"

"From the third floor."

"Luca? Hold on. That doesn't—WAIT…"

"Yeah."

"Oh my God! You guys are…?"

"Yep. Kind of."

"DUDE!" Andy smacked his forehead. "I've been throwing girls at you like a dumbass and you already had a guy, wow. That's great, man."

Gabriel leaned back in his seat, relieved. "It's good."

"I bet you're the gross kind of cute, too. The kind they make romance movies out of," Andy said.

Gabriel laughed. "Probably."

"Nice."

Andy wheeled into the parking lot for the Adawa County Trailhead, and the atmosphere changed in the subtle way it does when there are deeper things to talk about. There was a reverence in this place, with the trees and quiet and the promise of their continued corruption. Only one other car was present.

Andy filled his backpack with far more cans of Coors Banquet than they should drink, and relegated Gabriel to carrying the blankets. One went in his emptied backpack, and he wrapped his arms around the other. Andy cracked open a beer and took three long gulps before handing it over. Gabriel took a swig and tucked it under the blanket. They followed the same path as the last time, Andy up front and Gabriel behind.

"How's Kyle doing?" Gabriel asked a few minutes into the hike.

"I think he's thriving, actually," Andy said over his shoulder. "He's just thrifting all day and selling everything online, planning pop-up shops for the summer."

"Nice," Gabriel said. "What are you up to?"

"I'm working at a restaurant. It's good money, and it keeps me out of the house."

"I hear you."

"It's not bad."

Gabriel took a long drink from the beer. "How was it, leaving?"

Andy was quiet long enough to make Gabriel think he hadn't heard the question. He glanced back, holding out his hand for the can. He stopped, downed the rest, crushed it, and removed his backpack. He handed a fresh can to Gabriel and took another for himself.

"It was shitty," Andy said. "My parents lost it. They're forcing me to attend AA."

"Damn."

"Guess it hasn't taken yet," Andy said, raising his beer in the air.

"Yeah, well, I keep going to chapel, but it hasn't made me straight," Gabriel said

"Five days of chapel a week isn't *nearly* enough. Have you tried praying?"

"Every time I masturbate."

"Good," Andy grinned. "If God doesn't listen, make him watch."

If God doesn't listen or speak back, can He blame you for leaving?

"They're making me go to counseling," Gabriel said, and he discovered he wasn't all that scared to tell Andy "They found a text I sent to Mason after he left."

Andy twisted around. "Are you serious?"

"Sadly."

"Why?"

"I'm broken, apparently," Gabriel said, staring at the beer in his hand. "And if we can discover the 'root cause,' I'll be fixed, or something."

Andy looked him over. He rubbed his hand over his hair, shaking his head. "That's fucked."

"Yeah."

"Do you have to go?"

"Only if I want to stay at school."

Andy started walking again. "And you *want* to stay?"

Gabriel thought about this for a long while. "I don't really have the option to leave."

"Why not?"

"It's the family school, and I can't leave in the middle of the semester."

"You *can*, though."

"But then I'd have to restart somewhere else. Retake the classes I'm in now."

"But you wouldn't be *here*."

"I'd rather stick it out."

"That sounds shitty."

"Not as bad as leaving now. Then everyone will be concerned, and I'll have to tell them exactly what happened."

"So you're just going to roll over and take it? Let them grill you with counseling and all that bullshit?"

Gabriel bristled, but he had no response. That's exactly what he was going to do. "If I can make it to the end of the year, maybe I can transfer."

"Hey, it's up to you, but sometimes you need to stand up for yourself."

Gabriel thought about this as they reached the hidden boulder by the stream.

To stand up for himself was to risk expulsion. He couldn't face the ridicule of leaving. He couldn't disappoint his parents more than he already had.

He had to stick it out.

After all, it was just one counseling session a week.

ON THE SURFACE, it is just one counseling session a week.

You show up. You talk. You leave.

Done. Easy.

Kind of.

It is just one counseling session a week, but the whole is so much larger than that.

It is an entire life with the underlying pressure to perform, to become the person of faith you believe you need to be. It is out of reach standards and your inevitable failure. It is the shame of that failure that drives you to try again and again. And again. Leaving you more desperate and ragged every time.

It is a system built for control.

It is everything.

It is just one counseling session a week.

ALL THINGS END

GABRIEL WOKE WITH a headache the next morning, mouth dry, throat burnt from cigarettes. He and Andy had stayed out past dark, and for a while, there had been nothing but the giddiness of alcohol and the buzz of nicotine in his blood. For a while, the unrelenting pressure was nowhere to be found.

But, of course, all things end.

He felt it happening before it was really over. It was fading elation after the first two or three drinks. It was trembling hands from too many cigarettes and the vague, terrible realization he reeked with smoke—that he might be caught, that he *will* be caught and *how could he be so stupid?*

Dread seeped into his body, and it remained all night. It was still there in the morning because this is the kind of dread that will no longer be ignored.

He knows it is only a matter of time before the inevitable catches up, before he must accept defeat and all the plans it has for him.

Such is the fate of sinners like him.

WHEN ALL THAT'S LEFT IS CRAZY

GABRIEL HELD OUT as long as he could.

He went to all his classes for the rest of the week and didn't skip any assignments. He even went for a run on Thursday. There were stretches of normalcy where he played video games with Micah and did homework with Luca in empty classrooms.

But his body knew it was an act. Exhaustion reigned. The promise of his next counseling session weighed heavily on his mind.

The walk to Marci's office was one of resignation. When he sat down on her couch, he didn't float away. Marci was filled with vigor and invasive questions, saying things like, *do you have anger toward your father?* and *why have you sought a relationship with Mr. Ali over your dad?* and *so much time spent with just the mother can influence a young man's identity.*

On and on it went. The questions should have been more painful, but there was a numbness spreading through Gabriel's being, making them easier to accept.

"I think your situation is understandable," Marci said near the end of the session. The clock above her desk showed twelve minutes to the new hour.

"Situation…" Gabriel whispered to himself.

"What?" Marci looked up from her clipboard. "Oh, I mean to say it makes sense why you've developed certain ways of interacting with the world, why you might desire connections with some men. It's understandable, and I think we have a lot to work with moving forward." Marci scanned her notes. "Tell me more about Jenna. It sounds like she can be a good influence, and you did say she was pretty."

Gabriel stared through Marci. He ignored her prompt. "What if there's no reason for how I feel?"

"I'm sorry, I don't understand."

"What if there's no root cause?"

"What do you mean?"

Gabriel dug his nails into his palms. "What if nothing made me this way, and I just *am*, and there's nothing to fix because nothing's wrong?"

Marci pursed her lips and pushed her glasses up her nose. "Gabriel, we're not trying to fix you. We're trying to help you discover the fullness of life the way God intended."

"That sounds like the same thing."

Marci sighed. "Don't you want a fruitful life? Don't you want to experience all the *good* God has planned for you?"

"I want to be happy," Gabriel said quietly.

"And you can have that. God is the source of all joy, but He requires devotion—"

"I've been devoted my whole life and I have nothing to show for it."

Marci leaned forward. "God sees you. He *knows* you. You just need faith in His plan."

Gabriel licked his lips. "If this is His plan, I don't want to be a part of it."

"What are you saying?"

Gabriel shifted, eyes drifting to her window. Marci peered over her glasses at him. Gabriel knew the truth. He'd known it since their first meeting.

"I don't think this is working for either of us," Gabriel said.

Marci blinked at him. "It's never easy at the beginning."

"It's not *going* to work."

"We just need time. You'll see a breakthrough soon."

Gabriel rubbed his hands on his pants. "I don't think I can keep doing this."

Marci gave a heavy sigh. "Okay." She checked her watch. "It's clear we've done all we can today, so I'll let you go early. But I *will* see you next week, okay? We can't give up just yet," she said with a tired smile.

Gabriel saw no point in arguing. He just stood up and opened the door without a word. He didn't bother making an appointment for next week.

The dominos were already set up. They had been for months. Now, the first one teetered and fell.

GABRIEL AND LUCA went out to dinner the following evening. Luca chose a place thirty minutes from school that specialized in seafood and pasta. They both felt the need to escape campus even though they couldn't entirely escape its problems.

"What's the plan, then?" Luca asked after they'd been seated in a booth in the lounge.

TVs hung over the bar top, patrons crowding on stools. The din of conversation and music forced them to lean close to hear each other. Gabriel liked the shimmer he felt as their arms brushed. And yet, he couldn't help but feel like people were watching them. He wondered if this would ever feel normal.

"I'm not sure," Gabriel said, picking up a menu. "I just don't know how much longer I can do it."

"We're almost to spring break. Dr. Clark said they would cut down your sessions after, right?"

"I said they *might*, and I doubt they'd do it now. Not after yesterday."

Luca scrunched his nose and examined his menu. Their waitress stopped by to take their orders and drop off complimentary garlic bread.

"I'll figure it out," Gabriel said. "And I'd rather not talk about it tonight, anyway."

And so, they watched the bar patrons, making up stories about why each person was there. Two men in suits were in the middle, probably discussing stocks or something. A trio of thirty-something guys on their right shouted at the hockey game on TV. Gabriel said all three *almost* went pro, but injuries and girls got in the way. On the left end of the bar, four women gathered and pestered the bartender for martinis. They wore glittery dresses with lipstick and eyeshadow on so thick they could have been anywhere between thirty and fifty years old. Luca guessed they were here to celebrate a birthday and maybe take some men home, too.

Once their entrees arrived—chicken Alfredo for Gabriel and grilled salmon for Luca—they hardly talked until they were halfway through. Gabriel devoured his food, not realizing how hungry he'd been. It seemed, away from the troubles of school and with Luca by his side, he wasn't so worried tonight. He could eat when he wasn't worried.

Hardly two minutes later, Dr. Clark strolled past their booth, eyes scanning the bar top. Gabriel choked on his Arnold Palmer. Adrenaline pumped into his blood.

"What?" Luca said. Gabriel coughed, ignoring him.

The Dean of Student Life zeroed in on an empty chair at the very end of the bar, right next to the group of women. He raised a finger at the bartender, leaned forward to share his order, and relaxed into his seat. He wore a white button-up and a blue blazer on top.

"*What?*" Luca repeated.

"End of the bar," Gabriel squeaked out.

One of the women bumped into Dr. Clark. She turned and did one of those dramatic, full-body *I'm so sorry*s, her hands pressed against his chest. Her breasts practically spilled out of her tight red dress as she laughed. He laughed back. The bartender dropped off a shot and a beer in front of Dr. Clark. He downed the shot, gulped a third of his beer, and pointed to the empty shot glass and raised two fingers.

"Smooth," Luca said.

"Fun fact," Gabriel said, queasy, "that's Doctor Clark."

Luca looked at the man and laughed. "Nahhh."

"...of all the fucking places..."

Luca looked at Gabriel before squinting at Dr. Clark. "The guy trying to get *wasted?* No way."

Gabriel sank into the booth, unable to respond. The bartender dropped off two full shot glasses. Dr. Clark and the woman clinked and drank.

"You're serious," Luca said. "Shit."

"If he sees us, we're screwed."

"Think so?"

"Do we *look* like we're just friends?"

"Probably not." Luca absentmindedly folded his napkin into a small square. "Well, if we're caught, you'd have a therapy partner. We could do group sessions!"

Gabriel almost laughed.

Luca dropped his napkin on his plate. "We can get the check."

In the eight minutes it took to flag down their server, Dr. Clark had a second beer in hand, and the woman was practically sitting in his lap for how close she stood. She kept leaning over to talk in his ear and laugh, and his eyes kept drifting to her breasts. Only once did Dr. Clark look in their direction, and Gabriel frantically ducked under the table. By the time Luca signed the bill, the woman was running a drunken hand through Dr. Clark's hair. He grinned up at her.

"There's no way that's his wife, right?" Luca asked.

"Doubt it," Gabriel said.

"This is gross," Luca said, mouth half open in a prolonged grimace. He began to scoot to the edge of the booth. "Let's go."

"Hold on," Gabriel said, not moving. "Oh my God, hold on…"

He scrambled for his phone, started a video, and zoomed in. He recorded for two minutes, heart pounding, ducking out of sight every few seconds. From where they sat, the quality was grainy, and people kept blocking the view, but it had to be enough. He couldn't risk exposing themselves for a better shot.

"Alright," Gabriel said, tucking his phone in his pocket. "Let's go."

They rushed out of the restaurant. Outside, Gabriel laced his fingers behind his head, smiling.

"What?" Luca asked.

"This might be my way out."

"Of what?"

"Counseling."

"How?"

Gabriel waved his hands in the air, talking fast. "I'll go to him and say I can't do it anymore. If he doesn't listen, I'll hit him with the video—"

"You're going to *blackmail* him?"

"Why not?"

"That's insane."

"Why?"

"They didn't even kiss!"

That *was* an unfortunate detail. But Gabriel had recorded at least three moments of the woman's hands on Dr. Clark's face and chest. If he could screenshot those—

"This is crazy," Luca said.

Gabriel bounded the rest of the way to his car, smiling a wide, manic kind of smile.

Maybe it was. But crazy was all he had.

THE NATURE OF POWER

LATE THAT NIGHT, tucked under his covers, Gabriel poured over the video of Dr. Clark and his budding affair. He scrubbed through every frame, screenshooting anything that looked halfway deceptive: Hands on each other, whispers in ears, leering eyes.

There wasn't a lot to use.

Half the video was obscured by someone's head or shoulder, and taken out of context, none of the subsequent photos looked all *that* bad except one. It was of the woman undoing the second button of Dr. Clark's shirt, his eyes locked on her breasts.

It wasn't much, but Gabriel knew what he saw, and Dr. Clark would know he'd been discovered. That's what mattered. Men like him would do anything to cover this up.

Gabriel didn't want money in return for keeping quiet. He just wanted to be left alone.

GABRIEL'S ZEAL FOR the truth faded in the night, and the morning brought fear.

Did he really have the strength to confront Dr. Clark? How stupid was it to try? What would happen if the Dean didn't listen?

Maybe he should forget the plan and stick it out with Marci. It wasn't all that bad. He could just pretend he was a movie character. Maybe he'd even learn to—

His whole body shuddered, revolted at the thought.

You can't go back, it said.

He knew this was true.

FRIDAY AFTERNOON, THE moment came. Gabriel lay on his bed, paralyzed. Soon enough, Marci would know he wasn't showing up. Maybe she already did. Then she would report his absence to Dr. Clark. He knew it would be best to beat her to the reveal.

And yet, he couldn't move. His heart thrummed. His whole body tingled with the promise of confrontation.

He lay there another hour.

When he became desperate to use the bathroom, he took this opportunity to force himself to leave his dorm. Clouds drifted in front of the sun. Icy air cut through his jacket and bit his nose and ears. Gabriel trudged up the steps of President's Hall.

Dr. Clark was in his office, typing on his desktop. Gabriel stopped in front of the propped-open door. He knocked. Dr. Clark looked up, frowned, and motioned for Gabriel to enter.

"Come in," he said. "Remind me…"

"It's Gabriel."

"Right! Of course. How can I help?"

Gabriel sat in the leather chair opposite Dr. Clark's desk. "So, um…" Gabriel didn't know how to start the conversation. "You know how I've been meeting with Marci?"

Dr. Clark's full attention found Gabriel. His hands laced together. "Of course, how's that going? I've been meaning to reach out to check up on things."

"It's alright."

"I'm glad you're settling in. Do you feel you're making progress?"

Gabriel rubbed his thighs. "I don't know. It's tough."

"Well, it takes time," Dr. Clark said kindly. "I'm glad you're trying."

"That's just it," Gabriel said. "I was wondering if there's any way I could stop?"

Dr. Clark blinked. "Stop?"

"I think it would be best."

"So soon? It's only been a few weeks."

"Three. Today would be four."

"Did Marci send you? I've received her initial assessment but not an updated report of your progress…" Dr. Clark clicked a few times with his mouse, his eyes on his desktop screen. "You met with her today?"

"No, actually…" Gabriel grimaced. "I came here instead."

"Instead?"

"I don't want to keep going, so I was hoping to withdraw with you—"

"Hold on, Gabriel," Dr. Clark said, face serious, leaning forward. "You didn't go today?"

"No."

"Why not?"

"I don't want to go anymore."

"That's not…" Dr. Clark sighed. He scratched his beard. "You can't just decide not to go. It's a process where we *all* determine where you're at—"

"Even me?"

"Yes—"

"Well, *I* don't think I need to go anymore."

"You don't *think* you need to go or don't *want* to?"

"Both, I guess."

"Gabriel, we can't do everything we want. Otherwise, I'd eat doughnuts for every meal," Dr. Clark laughed. "And when dealing with this particular sin, we *certainly* can't do what the flesh wants."

"That's not—"

"I'm just saying purity requires discipline. It's a battle every day. We can't just decide when we want to take a break."

Gabriel laughed, then covered his mouth with a hand and coughed. The memory of Dr. Clark at the bar flashed in his mind.

Dr. Clark's eyes narrowed. "What is it?"

"Nothing."

"Gabriel."

"Just a cough, I'm sorry. Keep going."

Dr. Clark straightened a stack of papers. "I want to know that you're taking this seriously."

"I am."

"Okay, that's good. Do you believe you are ready to stop seeing Marci?"

"Yes."

"Why, then? *Why* are you ready after only three sessions?"

"I don't think there's anything left to address."

"I find that hard to believe."

"Why?"

"Homosexuality is a big deal, Gabriel. It can take *years* to root out, not weeks."

"But it's *my* experience, and I'm ready to stop."

"Would Marci agree with your assessment?"

Gabriel gave a show of thinking it over. "Probably, yeah."

"You're *sure?*"

"Yes."

"I'll have to confirm with her first, of course. Until then, you should reschedule today's appointment."

"I don't know if I can this week. I have a lot of homework."

Dr. Clark evaluated him, mouth a thin line. "Alright, but make an appointment today for next Friday."

Gabriel didn't say anything. He didn't nod.

"Alright?" Dr Clark said. When Gabriel didn't respond, the Dean drove a finger into the top of his desk. "Make the appointment, Gabriel."

Anxiety throbbed in Gabriel's veins. "I don't think I will."

Dr. Clark's head tilted like he didn't hear correctly. "Come again?"

"I'm not going anymore."

"That's not your decision."

"Well, I'm making it."

"I feel like we're going in circles," Dr. Clark sighed. He leaned forward to meet Gabriel's eyes. "By withdrawing from counseling without mutual agreement from Marci and me, you will be in violation of Morrison's rules of conduct regarding homosexuality. Do you understand this?"

Gabriel didn't move.

"As such, you will no longer be allowed to continue at Morrison," Dr. Clark said. "Gabriel, do not throw away this opportunity. Everyone here wants you to succeed. We want you to have a fulfilled life, a *family*. Don't you want that?"

Gabriel gave a slight nod.

"Then continue meeting with Marci."

"I don't want to fight this anymore," Gabriel said in a small voice.

"That's the nature of this fallen life! It's not easy, but we need to lean on God to make it."

"I like who I am."

"Gabriel, God can't love you when you're blatantly living in sin."

"I don't think it's wrong," Gabriel said. He didn't know if he believed that yet, but he wanted to. He *needed* to.

Dr. Clark rubbed his forehead. "There's hope for you, but only if you don't give up. Think of the rewards of heaven. Do you want to throw that away? The trials of life are a blink compared to eternity. An eternity separated from God, *tortured*. Hell is torment."

Gabriel set his jaw. Could that be worse than what he'd already gone through? "I'm not going."

Dr. Clark looked at him for a long time, disappointment in his eyes. "Then we can no longer have you as a student."

Gabriel knew it was coming. He'd waited for those words the whole conversation, but they slapped him across the face all the same. Now, there was only one option.

He scanned the bookshelf behind Dr. Clark's desk, settling on the picture of him and his wife in a wood frame. Her hand was on his chest, ring on full display. She had blonde hair and was more than a head shorter than him. Certainly *not* the woman at the bar.

"Is that your wife?" Gabriel asked, measured. Casual.

Dr. Clark frowned at the abrupt change in topic. He glanced at the picture. "It is. You could have that, too."

Gabriel nodded to himself and wiped his palms on his pants. He met Dr. Clark's eye. "How long have you been cheating on her?"

Dr. Clark's smile froze. Then cracked. Then slipped completely from his face. A dangerous glint appeared in his eyes. "Excuse me?"

Gabriel allowed himself a small smile. "I like how you put it. 'God can't love you when you're living in sin.' Or does that not apply to you?"

"I don't know what you're talking about," Dr. Clark said, voice edged like a knife.

"She was tall, red dress, big breasts…"

"I've never cheated on my wife."

"Maybe a picture would help you remember," Gabriel said.

He opened his phone, selecting the picture of the woman unbuttoning Dr. Clark's shirt. Gabriel zoomed in, and Dr. Clark's face paled.

"I have a video of you together, but I don't have to share it," Gabriel said, putting away his phone. "I'm not going to leave in the middle of the semester, and I'm not going to counseling anymore. If you try to make me, these get out."

Dr. Clark stood up, and Gabriel thought he might try to wrestle his phone away from him. Instead, he strolled to his office door and closed it. He sat down again. "I don't know what you're trying to do, but that's not me."

"It clearly is."

"And it's blurry."

"Doesn't matter."

"It *does,* though. It doesn't look like me, and there's nothing going on in that photo. Two friends having a drink? Come on, you have to do better than that."

"I have a second witness."

"So what."

"*So what?*"

"No one will believe you."

"I have *proof.*"

"Not enough," Dr. Clark said. "And who will listen to you, anyway?"

He stared at Dr. Clark, slack-jawed.

"Release the video. See what happens." Dr. Clark spread his arms wide. "What will people think when they find out you're a *documented* homosexual lashing out because of his sin?" Dr. Clark leaned forward, a feral smile on his lips. "You can't touch me. You have no power here."

And that's when Gabriel knew he didn't stand a chance—that he'd made a terrible mistake. Dr. Clark was right. The people who mattered would sweep it under the rug and concoct a story, throwing Gabriel to the wolves.

After all, the truth rarely mattered when your power was threatened.

It was over.

Nausea overtook his body.

Dr. Clark looked at Gabriel with satisfaction. "You are no longer welcome at Morrison University. Please pack your things and leave by the end of tomorrow."

Gabriel sat, stunned, regret and terror flooding him.

It hadn't been a good plan, but it was all he could do. That was the hardest part. There was absolutely nothing else he could—

Wait.

He blurted out the next part without thinking. "I'll go back to counseling."

Dr. Clark balked at the response. "What?"

"I'll go back, just let me finish out the year," Gabriel said, practically begging, now.

Dr. Clark tapped his index finger on his desk, eyes squinted. "You are clearly consumed by sin and will do anything to escape correction. I think it will be best for everyone involved if you leave."

Gabriel swallowed. That was it, then.

How could it fall apart so quickly?

He stood up slowly, legs wobbly. He paused at the door and turned around. "Do you have kids?" When Dr. Clark didn't respond, Gabriel said, "I hope not, because you'd be a terrible father."

"Get out," Dr. Clark hissed.

"I hope your wife cheats on you so you know how it feels," Gabriel said, cringing.

That might be the most awful thing he'd said to another person.

Dr. Clark abruptly stood up, veins in his neck bulging. He stalked around the desk, hands balled into fists. Gabriel looked at them warily, a final, stupid idea flashing in his brain.

"Did you at least buy her dinner that night? Before you fucked her in your car, I mean," Gabriel said. He had no idea *what* Dr. Clark had done that night. It was just a guess.

Dr. Clark's right hand clawed the air a few inches from Gabriel's neck. The man's eyes burned with rage.

Gabriel licked his lips and met Dr. Clark's eyes. "Do it, *bitch*."

Dr. Clark's body coiled, and Gabriel braced himself for the punch. The moment stretched. Three seconds. Four. Dr. Clark stepped back. He shook his head, exhaled, then went back to sitting at his desk.

"Have a nice day. Please leave," Dr. Clark said.

Gabriel cursed himself for being unable to goad Dr. Clark into assaulting him. Now, he was truly out of options.

Gabriel left without another word. There was nothing else to say.

GABRIEL SAT IN the grass under a tree behind the Biblical Studies building.

He was done. Just like that.

Was he really so weak he felt the need to stop counseling? And to confront Dr. Clark? Of course this was the outcome.

How could he be so *goddamn* stupid?

And how the *fuck* was he going to explain this to his parents? To his dorm? To everyone back home?

His life might actually be over, and he'd caused it to happen. This was all on him.

Gabriel wrapped his arms around his knees and gasped for air. His body shook. His mind had nothing left to give. He closed his eyes and imagined he wasn't real.

And in that stretch of nothing, he *almost* didn't cry.

SEVEN

THANK YOU AND GOODBYE

LUCA HELPED GABRIEL pack the next afternoon while Jason was away at lunch. Gabriel couldn't hold a conversation. He just directed Luca here and there with gathering his things. He moved mechanically, the bare minimum to accomplish each task. He removed his books one by one, and he picked up *The Perks of Being a Wallflower*. He thumbed through it, seeing the polaroid of Luca in the back. He'd forgotten it was there. Gabriel dropped the book on his desk, swallowing hard.

When his suitcase was stuffed and the clothes basket was filled with loose items, Gabriel knew it was time to start moving everything into his car. The problem was, he couldn't get *himself* to move. Things weren't so bad when it was just him and Luca silently organizing, but the thought of trudging down the hall, his arms full of his possessions, felt like the worst kind of shame.

He didn't know what he'd say to anyone who asked. He didn't know if he had the energy to lie or the strength to tell the truth. And he certainly didn't think they'd accept his silence for an answer.

He sat on the floor, holding his face, his eyes peeking out. A part of him wished he could stay in this moment forever. But that only suspended the inevitable.

A knock came on the door. Gabriel's attention snapped to the disturbance. The door opened, and Grant stepped inside.

"I just wanted to check in to see how you're doing, if you need any help," Grant said.

Luca examined Gabriel, then Grant. "I think we're good."

Grant looked over the scattered belongings on the ground. He scratched his patchy beard. "Alright. I'm sorry about all this."

Grant closed the door. Gabriel just sat, staring blankly. Luca stood in front of the typewriter, one hand in his pocket, his other testing out the keys. *Tap tap tap*s resounded in the room.

Gabriel looked up, face wan. "I don't know if I can do this."

Luca glanced over his shoulder. "Yeah."

"But there's no choice."

"No."

Gabriel took a deep breath and stood, adrenaline flooding his limbs. Luca stepped in front of Gabriel and straightened the collar of his shirt.

"Chin up, no fear, yeah?" Luca said.

Gabriel blinked weakly. "What?"

"You're brave," Luca said, looking deep into his eyes. There was a warmth there, and comfort, and an earnestness that Gabriel desperately wanted to believe. "Show them."

You're brave.

No.

Was he?

No.

But he could try.

Gabriel pocketed his car keys, picked up his suitcase, and shoved aside the terror clawing up his throat.

He opened the door.

No fear.

Yeah, sure.

He huffed.

If only it were that simple.

JASON WAS THE first person he saw in the hallway, and he was leaning halfway into Arlo and Hunter's room. He held a styrofoam cup and a to-go bag from the burger spot in the Union.

"Going home for the weekend?" Jason asked.

"Forever, actually," Gabriel said.

"Nice," Jason said, turning back to Arlo, then back to Gabriel. "Wait, what?"

"They kicked me out."

"What?" Jason sputtered.

"No way," Arlo said, peeking out of the doorway.

"What did he say?" This was from Hunter deeper in the room.

"They kicked him out," Arlo said.

"What? Why?" Hunter appeared in the hallway.

Gabriel was nearly at the dorm entrance. He twisted around, walking backward a few steps to shout over Luca's head. "Because I'm FUCKING GAY!"

Gabriel shoved through the door, Luca right behind. He felt a strange relief at the proclamation, and he had the sudden urge to take a megaphone to the cafeteria and start a riot.

"That's one way to do it," Luca said when it was just them.

"They were going to talk anyway. Might as well own it," Gabriel responded.

He tossed his suitcase into the trunk of his car, then the clothes basket. He circled the parking lot and parked in front of the dorm.

Inside, people had gathered outside their doors, congregating in small circles. Conversations hushed, and all eyes turned toward Gabriel as he entered. Gabriel paused, taking it in. Grant watched silently from his doorway. Micah had joined Jason's group.

Gabriel slouched down the hall, avoiding eyes. He worked quickly, gathering all the shirts and jackets from the closet in his arms, then set off down the hall again. Next time inside, Jason's group followed Gabriel to his room, offering their help. The room was cleared in minutes.

They all stared at him, shuffling their feet, not knowing what to say. Goodbyes took less than a minute. It was just short hugs and wishes of good luck.

Outside, Gabriel and Luca stood in front of his car. For a while, all they did was observe the other. Gabriel wanted to reach out to bridge the gap between them.

"You can bet some of them are watching," Gabriel said.

Luca's eyes flicked toward the dorm. "Probably."

"I'm sorry about all this."

"It's not your fault."

"Feels like it."

"But they forced it to happen."

"I guess."

"You have to believe that."

Gabriel bounced on his toes. Luca removed his glasses to polish them with the hem of his shirt. His eyes glimmered with moisture.

"Want to run away with me?" Gabriel asked.

"I wish." Luca huffed, thoughtful. "My parents would cut me off if I did something like that."

"I get it," Gabriel said, bowing his head.

"Doesn't mean I don't want to go."

"But if they caught you with me—"

"They'd probably try to send me to some conversion camp, even though they can't do that since I'm over eighteen."

"Shit."

"At least you can go back home."

Gabriel's jaw clenched. For all they didn't understand, and probably never would, his parents hadn't cut him off yet. That was more than a lot of people had. According to the text from Mason's mom, Mason was at a camp like that. Voluntarily, too, since he was twenty-one.

"I saw the Polaroid today, packing," Gabriel said, shuffling his feet. "I think that was my favorite day—" Gabriel's voice broke. "—favorite day this year. I wish we could go back to that."

Luca shifted, seemingly at war between wanting to comfort Gabriel and risking public affection. "Me too," he said.

"So, is this it?"

"Of what?"

"Us."

"No, I don't think so."

"That's good," Gabriel said. He stuffed his hands in his pockets. "Thanks for being there."

"Of course."

"I mean it."

"I know."

"I don't think I would have made it without you."

Luca bit his lip pensively, lines on his forehead. He gave a single nod. He knew. He understood.

Luca met his eyes. He opened his mouth. Grimaced. He turned his face to the sky. "And you…" Luca covered his mouth and let out a stifled sob. "…thank you for being so good to me…with everything…"

Gabriel felt his spirit tearing, and he touched Luca's arm. Luca unfolded himself and hugged Gabriel.

"I'll always be there," Gabriel said

"Me too," Luca returned.

They pulled apart. Gabriel studied Luca's face for a long moment, taking in the little details, drifting over his lips and jaw and the blue in his eyes, knowing it would be a while before they saw each other again. Luca stepped backward as Gabriel sat in the driver's seat and turned the key.

Driving away—knowing what was ahead, watching Luca grow smaller in his mirrors—Gabriel thought he might completely fall apart.

THE INEVITABLE OUTCOME

GABRIEL SPENT THE first minutes on the road in complete silence, a mess of dread and shame and heavy guilt. He didn't know if he could face what lay ahead. He didn't know how to break the news to his parents and if they'd kick him out. He wondered how many friends he'd lose once everyone knew.

Gabriel watched the road through slits in his eyes. He directed the steering wheel with the thumb and forefinger of his left hand.

Had he just ruined his future? All because he couldn't keep it bottled up?

Maybe he had.

But maybe this was the only way.

He traced his mind through the past months, settling on the text to Mason as the point that led to this moment. He wished he hadn't sent it, but how could he *not* reach out? He'd already done too little for Ben, and maybe he was dead because of Gabriel's lack of effort.

No, he would have always sent that text, so this would have happened anyway. Maybe it didn't need to happen like it did, but it *had*. And now, he had to face that reality.

The storm inside slowed and settled. He just felt sick now, like there was a black hole in his chest.

Road signs and cars were blurs of color in his window. The road curved. Gabriel's head lolled with the momentum. He struggled not to blink too long, to just close his eyes and see what happened.

But then Luca would never see him again.

That wouldn't do.

Gabriel switched hands on the wheel and bit his knuckle, elbow propped on the window ledge.

No, that wouldn't do at all.

For him, right now, the only way out was through.

HUSHED CONVERSATIONS

UPON ARRIVING AT his parent's house, Gabriel sat in his car for a long while, unable to move. It was like he was back in his dorm, waiting to make the leap to talk to Dr. Clark. Only now, his fate was set. It wouldn't change no matter what he did. His parents would still regret they had a son like him.

Gabriel peeled himself out of the driver's seat and went through the garage, not taking anything with him. His mom's car was present, but his dad's was gone. That would delay his reveal. They had to find out at the same time.

Gabriel skirted the hallway to the kitchen, wary. His mom wasn't there or in the living room or front office. He sighed with relief and opened the fridge. Nothing looked good, so he opened all the snack cupboards before returning to the fridge in case he missed anything. He didn't. He stood at the kitchen island, hands on the marble countertop.

Energetic footsteps plodded down the stairs, and Gabriel's mom appeared around the corner, humming to herself. She stopped abruptly. "Gabriel!"

"Surprise," he said.

"A wonderful surprise!" She said, rushing forward to hug him. "How are you doing? How's school?"

There were a hundred other questions all wrapped up in that one. They hadn't talked since he came out to her over the phone. Uncertainties thickened the air. Gabriel bit his lip as he navigated to the jar of roasted pumpkin seeds.

"I'm alright," Gabriel said, taking a handful. He just needed something to do with his hands. "I need to talk to you guys about that. Where's dad?"

His mom gave him a suspicious once over. "He's at the library but should be back any minute."

Gabriel responded by munching on some seeds. He crept over to the windows overlooking their backyard. His mom made feeble attempts to get him to talk about his classes or the Boston Bruins. Gabriel couldn't keep the small talk going, and they settled for silence like that was normal.

The garage door thrummed. Gabriel flinched and braced himself. His dad clomped into the house, boots falling heavily on the wood floors.

"Hey, is Gabriel back?" He called from out of sight. Gabriel turned from the window as his dad entered the kitchen, zeroing in on him. "Hey, Gabe, good to see you. What are you doing back? Why's all your stuff in your car?"

Shit.

Gabriel's mom looked up from the spices she was sorting through on the counter. "You brought your stuff back? What's going on?"

Gabriel shuffled to the island to sit in one of the bar seats. His dad came up beside his wife. Gabriel wrung his hands under the lip of the counter.

He stared at the marble. "They forced me out of school."

There was utter silence for two seconds. Three.

Gabriel's mom shrieked, *"What!"*

Gabriel cringed. His dad's eyes flickered with anger.

"They found out…about me," Gabriel said, shame thickening his voice. "I had a choice to go to counseling or leave—"

"And you *didn't go?*" His dad spat.

"I did! I went for a *month!*" Gabriel shot back.

"And?"

"And it was awful!"

"So you quit? You *throw away* school? Just like that?"

"I didn't—I can't…you wouldn't understand—"

"Make me understand, Gabriel."

"They were trying to change me. I couldn't keep going."

"I can't believe this," his dad said, squeezing the counter's edge. His mom was crying, not daring to intervene. "Do you know how much money we're paying for you to go to school?"

"Yes," Gabriel croaked.

"It's a *lot of fucking money*, and you just decide to piss on it—"

"Robert!" Gabriel's mom yelled, smacking his arm. "He knows!"

Gabriel's dad sucked his teeth, a portrait of barely controlled fury. The muscles of his jaw clenched. He pushed away from the counter, said, "I can't do this right now," and headed for the garage. The door slammed behind him.

His mom dabbed her eyes. "I can call the school tomorrow. Try to talk to them."

"I'm not going back."

"You have to give it a chance, Gabriel. It's a *good* school."

"They want me to be different."

"What do you mean?"

"They want me to fight this."

"Isn't that what you want?"

"I've been fighting my whole life! Nothing's changed!"

"Gabriel, we just need to pray—"

"All I've done is pray!" Gabriel shouted. "*This is who I am, Mom!* I like men. Okay?"

His mom started crying again. Gabriel stood up.

"It's just not how I thought your life would go," she said.

"Well, it's my life."

"I know," his mom nodded. Her eyes and cheeks were red. "I love you, alright? No matter what."

Gabriel rubbed his nose and left the kitchen. He set to work unloading his car. It took twenty minutes, and when it was done, he curled up on his bed, arms wrapped around his knees. At dinner, no one spoke except to say things like *pass the salt and pepper* and *this salmon is perfect* and *it's beginning to feel like spring.*

Gabriel ate quickly and disappeared into his room. His parents let him go without helping clean up, and he began to unpack despite his exhaustion. He didn't even listen to music.

Desk lamp in hand, he froze.

Was that his name?

Gabriel listened at his door, trying to pick out the muffled voices from downstairs. Nothing. He frowned, tucking the lamp under his bed for now—

Gabriel perked up. He'd definitely heard his name this time. He crept to his door and gently turned the handle. His parent's voices became louder but were still too muffled to make anything out. Gabriel crept down the hall in his socks, expertly avoiding the creaky floorboards. Even at the top of the stairs, he could only catch snippets of the conversation, but they were *undoubtedly* talking about him.

…just don't understand how this could happen…

…thinks it's a sure thing, that it can't change…

…keep praying…

…God, please reveal yourself to our son…

…doesn't give in to temptations or lies…

Gabriel sank to the floor.

Is this what they really believed? That he'd been deceived? That enough prayer could change him?

Yes. Most likely.

After all, hushed conversations reveal the heart. The truth always finds a way out when you think you're alone.

Gabriel's dad visited his room later that night. Gabriel held his breath as his dad hovered just inside the doorway. He looked exhausted, drained of fight and energy.

"I'm sorry for reacting how I did," he said, mournful. "It was a shock to hear. And I'm still trying to get used to you, being…" he couldn't finish the sentence.

Gabriel ducked his head. "I'm sorry."

"It's a lot to wrap my head around, and I don't know what you'll do for school. Maybe they'll take you back. Maybe you can find a different counselor—"

Gabriel coiled up. "They won't take me back."

"You have to try."

"I don't want to go back."

"Gabriel! What are you going to do for school?"

"I don't know," Gabriel whispered.

"Well, we need to figure that out."

"Can we wait *one* day? I just want to go to bed."

His dad rubbed his cheeks in frustration. "Fine, we'll make a plan in the next few days."

"Ok."

There was a ten-second stretch of nothing. Gabriel didn't move.

"I'm just upset because I care, because I love you."

"I know."

Gabriel's dad patted the frame of the door. "Alright. We'll figure it out. I love you."

Gabriel didn't say it back. His dad left.

Sleep eluded him that night. His heart pounded, and his mind churned in a delirious state. He tossed for hours, checking the clock periodically until it was just past 4 a.m. He finally retrieved his computer and sat up in bed, watching *The Perks of Being A Wallflower* until the first hints of dawn crept through his window.

TAKE ALL THE TIME YOU NEED

When Gabriel's mom woke him up to go to church, Gabriel managed to convince her to let him keep resting. He curled up under his covers as endless footsteps circled downstairs. Finally, the garage door opened, and his mom's car surged down the street.

Only *then* did the tension release.

He fell asleep until the garage churned in his dreams, shooting him upright in bed. Gabriel sprang to his feet and dashed for the shower. If they found him still in bed, they'd start yelling again. He had to come up with a story for how he used the morning. Maybe they'd want to hear about him praying and reading the Bible.

When he went downstairs for a bowl of cereal, his parents greeted him with smiles. Gabriel squinted at them in return. As he drank the milk from the bowl, his mom announced that the Ali's were coming over for dinner. Gabriel's stomach lurched.

Had they planned this for a reason? Had they told James and Robin about why he'd left school? Was this an intervention? And if it were, what would Mr. Ali say? Maybe he'd changed sides in the last few months. Maybe he'd realized how sinful Gabriel really was.

Gabriel found it hard to breathe, so he slipped upstairs, changed into running clothes, and circled the neighborhood until he was too exhausted for worry.

GABRIEL GREETED THE Ali's at the front door. Mr. Ali hugged him tightly and wore a genuine smile.

"Great to see you," he said.

Mrs. Ali smiled, too, but her eyes were tight, and her hug was cautious.

The tension of unsaid things laced the evening.

The Ali's didn't mention why Gabriel was back or ask questions about how school was going, which meant they knew. They would only avoid the subject if they'd been told not to discuss it.

How much they knew was the real question.

As much as his mom enjoyed lamenting wayward children, Gabriel was sure she'd be too ashamed to admit the truth of his situation.

Gabriel's hands shook as they ate, and he hoped no one noticed he did little more than move his food around his plate with his fork. After dinner, Gabriel's dad worked on starting a fire in their wood stove, and the moms were in the kitchen putting away the extra food, talking in hushed voices. That left Gabriel and Mr. Ali at the dining table.

It was suffocating.

"Did you tell her about me?" Gabriel asked, voice low.

Mr. Ali's brow furrowed. "What?"

"Does Mrs. Ali know?"

Mr. Ali swirled his water glass. "I had to tell her. She's my wife."

Gabriel pressed his lips together, looking down.

"I'm sorry. I should have asked your permission."

"It's fine."

"I should have asked."

"I get it."

Mr. Ali mulled over his next words. "What happened at school?"

Gabriel traced his finger over the edge of the table. "What did they tell you?"

"That you left because it was too much strain."

Gabriel wasn't all that surprised by the vague answer. "They forced me to leave, actually."

"No..."

"I sent the wrong text. Then I was in counseling. Then I was out."

"I'm...so sorry," Mr. Ali said, barely a whisper.

"Fire's blazing!" Gabriel's dad called from the other room.

Gabriel stood. "Me too."

There was nothing else to say, so they all gathered in the living room to once again pretend nothing was wrong.

GABRIEL WAS TOO stressed about the looming conversation with his dad about his future to *actually* start planning for it, so he spent the next few days sleeping, distracting himself with TV, and avoiding his parents as much as possible. It didn't always work, though, and familiar dread snaked in every time his attention drifted from the computer screen.

To his credit, Gabriel's dad waited nearly four days before confronting him at breakfast.

"Have you started thinking about what's next?" His dad asked, digging into a large bowl of oatmeal.

Gabriel stirred his cereal. "I'll probably go to community college or something."

"Community college?"

"Maybe, I don't know."

"Well, you can get caught up if you take summer classes, then go somewhere better in the fall."

"I guess."

"What will you do until then?"

"I don't know."

"You should get a job in the meantime. Keep busy," his dad said, nodding to himself as if it were settled.

Gabriel chewed slowly. "I want to take some time off."

His dad shoveled oatmeal into his mouth, making his cheeks bulge. "Maybe a week, sure."

"I was thinking until the summer."

His dad stared at him. "No," he said flatly. "You need to get moving."

Gabriel pushed his bowl away. "Why?"

"Why?"

"Why is it so important I jump into the next thing?"

His dad laughed, showing chewed-up oatmeal. "You can't just sit around and do nothing. You need *action*."

Gabriel got up to wash out his bowl. "Forget I said anything."

"Wait. Gabriel, we're not done," his dad said, facing him.

"I'm done."

"We're in the middle of a conversation. You need to listen to me —"

"You need to listen to *me!*" Gabriel spat. His dad stilled. "I need a break! Let me have that."

Gabriel grabbed his jacket off the island barstool and started for the front door.

"Hey! We're not done—"

Gabriel slammed the door behind him, cutting off the rest of what his dad had to say. Rage strangled him as he stalked the icy morning.

AT DINNER, GABRIEL ate as quickly as possible, then went straight to his room and turned off his light so he wouldn't be bothered.

It didn't work. His dad barged in just before 9 p.m., forcing Gabriel to turn on a light and listen to a tangled apology.

"I talked with your mom, and you can take as much time as you need," he said. "We're here to support you."

"Sure," Gabriel said.

His dad left, and Gabriel locked the door behind him, a knot of doubt inside.

As much time as he needed? It was a nice sentiment. He just didn't trust it.

His dad would change his mind in time.

He always did.

A POUNDING HEART

GABRIEL WALKED ON eggshells the entire week, and he left the house for extended periods at a time. Sometimes, he would go to the library or a restaurant, but his favorite thing was wandering the Massachusetts Bay to explore the docks and to look at the boats.

He rarely talked with his parents, and everyone seemed content to ignore the obvious. The second Sunday home, Gabriel knew he couldn't reasonably avoid going to church, so he reluctantly attended a service for the first time in months.

He wasn't ready for the claustrophobic feeling of stepping inside the building. He wasn't ready for the endless volunteers greeting people with painted-on smiles. And the last thing he was ready for was seeing all the families and parents he'd known for years, especially when *they* knew he was supposed to be in school.

Over and over, he told the story that he'd withdrawn and was taking a break. Everyone seemed to buy it. In their eyes, he had no reason to lie. His mom hovered as he talked. She fidgeted and jumped in occasionally, as if her absence would cause Gabriel to do something drastic and blurt out the truth.

At the Miller's worship night, Gabriel disappeared into a corner to keep eyes off him. At dinner with the Porters, Gabriel ducked his head, hunched his shoulders, and focused on the food on his plate— moving it all around, building shapes, and taking small bites. He could almost lose himself in this tiny world.

He wondered if any of them noticed he hardly ate more than a few bites. He wondered if any of them cared.

Did they know how hard it was to breathe when they were in the same room?

Did they know how ashamed he was of his existence?

Did they know?

Did they?

No, of course they didn't. They never would. No matter what he said or how well he explained, they could never understand. They would always be ignorant because they were either too blind to see it or too afraid to acknowledge it or too insulated in their perfect lives to really know what it was like.

The weeks passed, and the walls closed in. The longer he kept up his unaffected front, the harder it was to move and think. Every second felt like it might be the one that tipped the scales into chaos. It was a house of cards that could collapse any minute without reason or warning.

Sleep was sporadic. One night, he suddenly inhaled like he hadn't breathed in ten or twelve seconds. He closed his eyes and tried to clear his head. A minute later, he jerked upright with a desperate gasp, and he realized he *hadn't* been breathing.

It was like he'd been holding his breath, but this wasn't voluntary like when you dive underwater. It was unconscious, like his body had simply refused to do its most basic function. It didn't make sense. That's not how the body was supposed to work. It couldn't just quit on you like that, could it?

This happened four more times before Gabriel turned on his lamp and sat up to keep himself awake. As he sat, he focused on his thudding heart. It never slowed. But this night, it wasn't the speed that caught his attention. It was the way it pounded. Desperate, clamoring to get out. Like it was throwing itself against his ribs with everything it had.

THUD THUD THUD.

Gabriel clutched his chest. He wondered if his heart would stop without warning. He wondered if it would burst or tear or simply sputter to a halt. It had been this way for months, and it seemed inevitable that one day soon—any minute, maybe—it would just give up.

THUD THUD THUD.

Gabriel leaned his head back, eyes closed.

It didn't matter if he took deep breaths or shallow ones. It still pounded at its cage. And every time he did breathe, it was like his lungs were fighting against a space that was far too small for them. They *pressed* and strived to expand, but they never got enough air.

THUD THUD THUD.

He felt tears come to his eyes. It was just too much. He felt lightheaded, but also a headache coming on. He wasn't getting enough oxygen. Maybe his brain was shutting down, too. It certainly felt like it.

He'd abused his body long enough. Maybe it was finally calling it quits.

Gabriel didn't move. He didn't make a sound.

THUD THUD THUD.

And now, the tears were flowing freely.

Because, after all, there was absolutely nothing he could do.

BRING ANYONE YOU WANT

For spring break, Chloe took a trip to Maine with friends, but Adrian returned home. Neither Gabriel nor Adrian had texted each other since Gabriel had left Morrison. They'd hardly talked since the school year began. But this week, Adrian suggested they get lunch on Saturday before checking out Mr. Ali's new fishing trawler, *Queen's Dream II*. Adrian drove.

"Bro, how's it going?" Adrian asked.

"Not too bad," Gabriel said.

"I heard you're not in school anymore."

"Yeah, I've been home a few weeks."

"Sorry I didn't reach out. It's just been so busy."

"Don't worry about it," Gabriel said. "What's going on?"

"School, and weekends with Savanah. Finding housing for next year. Wedding planning. It's crazy."

"That's a lot."

"But it's good, you know?"

"When's the wedding?"

"July fourth, for the fireworks. But there will be some other fireworks that night, *if you know what I'm saying*," Adrian said, pounding his fist against the steering wheel. "God, I can't wait to have sex."

Gabriel looked out the passenger window, not caring to have this conversation. He still felt obligated to join in. "You haven't yet?"

"No, of course not. We want it to be special. It's sacred, meant for marriage, you know?" Adrian said. He rubbed his chin with one hand, then gave a slight shrug and a sigh. "But we've been close a few times. Never without clothes or anything like that. I've always had my pants on, but I've…" Adrian waved his free hand in the air. "… finished, I guess? We've never actually *had sex,* though."

Gabriel raised an eyebrow. That *wasn't* sex?

Sure, he knew the clinical definition, but couldn't it be more than that? Not that Gabriel cared, but was Adrian really fooling himself into thinking he hadn't broken the sanctity of marriage?

"Are you going to bring anyone to the wedding?" Adrian asked. "You get a plus one."

"Probably not."

"No girls in your life?"

"Nope."

"That's disappointing. You need to find someone so we can go on double dates."

"Yeah," Gabriel said, halfhearted. He held the door handle with his right hand as the road curved. "I mean, I could bring a guy." Adrian snorted. Gabriel chewed his lip. "I could, though, right?"

"Bro, you can bring whoever you want. Could you imagine? Our parents would freak out."

"I should do it for fun, just to see what happens."

"That would be hilarious. I support that."

Gabriel removed a piece of lint from his thigh and watched it float to the ground. "I like guys."

Adrian laughed and glanced at Gabriel. "Sure you do."

"I'm serious."

Adrian glanced at him again, smile faltering. "Nahhh."

Gabriel folded his hands together, tracing his thumbs over each other.

"Wait, you're kidding, right?" Adrian said.

All the humor had been sucked from the car. Gabriel just looked out the passenger window, chin in hand, heart thudding in his ears. If there was a way to drive a car tensely, Adrian was doing it. It kept jerking here and there to stay in the correct lane.

"No, I'm not kidding," Gabriel said.

Adrian exited the highway.

"Wow," Adrian said, running a hand over his face. "What does that mean, though?"

"I just like guys, I guess."

"So you're gay?"

"I don't know."

"But do you want to be?"

"What?"

"Do you want to meet a guy? Or try to find a girlfriend? What's your plan?"

Gabriel tried not to linger on the subtle meanings behind Adrian's words. "I would like to meet someone…most likely a guy."

Adrian nodded, face taught. "Anyone in mind?"

"Maybe," Gabriel said.

Could he tell him about Luca?

It felt too intimate to reveal to Adrian just yet. He couldn't explain why, he just knew it wasn't right. Adrian didn't press the matter, but he asked other questions.

How long have you known? Have you ever kissed anyone? How do you know you like guys? Who else knows? Why didn't you say anything sooner? Are you still a Christian?

Gabriel answered as best as he could. It felt like he was back in Marci's office.

"You know this doesn't change anything, right?" Adrian asked as they found a parking spot.

Gabriel looked over, and their eyes met. His chest blossomed with the pain of unresolved feelings he'd never really looked at. "Thanks."

"I still believe in the Bible and everything," Adrian said.

Gabriel's relief soured. "Of course."

"And sin, and all that. And I think some things are wrong to live in, but that's just our world," Adrian said dismissively. "And we're not going to agree on everything in life, but I'll be there no matter what."

Gabriel got out of the car, feeling sick. He stretched his hands above his head, but the pain was tearing at his seams now. His mind whispered that Adrian was lying, and his back-and-forth words did nothing to suggest the opposite.

Frigid air blew off the bay, cutting through Gabriel's jacket. The ocean pulled to him, promising adventure and escape. He longed for the freezing air in the mornings. For the spray of the water and the salty air. For the stories and camaraderie and *closeness.*

They met Mr. Ali at a restaurant a few blocks from the boat. He bought them lobster and shrimp and cod. It was much too expensive, but Gabriel was grateful.

"She needs some repairs and updates, but she's a great ship," Mr. Ali said, cracking open a lobster shell. "It'll take a few months to get everything ready, so we'll miss the beginning of the fishing season. I'm hoping to get on the water by the end of May if possible."

"What do you have to do?" Gabriel asked.

"We need to replace some radio equipment and overhaul the freezers. Repaint. Fix up the bunks. It'll keep me busy for a while."

Gabriel nodded along. He couldn't help but smile at Mr. Ali's enthusiasm. After lunch, Mr. Ali gave them a tour of the ship. It was a blue and white, forty-two-meter freezer trawler—twelve more than *Queen's Dream.*

Mr. Ali talked, and Gabriel listened intently, taking it in. He touched everything he could. The bays of rope on deck. The freezers and processing room. The wench and net drum that would trail in the water, hauling in the catch.

It was big enough for a crew of twenty with sardine bunks and tiny lavatories. Up one deck was the galley and a small lounge. At the very bottom was fish processing.

Gabriel returned to the top deck to look over the harbor—boats of all sizes filled docks across the way. Buildings and roads crept up to the water's edge. To his right, the ocean expanded. The soupy sky blended with the water, but Gabriel found it beautiful.

"Hey, I have to be back soon for my suit fitting," Adrian said from behind.

"Yeah, ok," Gabriel said, not moving away from the rail.

He didn't want to go back just yet. He just wanted to stay and take in the cleansing air. Somehow, surrounded by docks and boats, he felt an elusive kind of hope. He wanted to hold onto that as long as possible, knowing what lay ahead.

When Adrian returned a few minutes later, Gabriel still hadn't moved. Mr. Ali was with him, carrying a full trash bag in one hand.

"Let's go!" Adrian said from the ramp to the shore.

"Do you *really* need a fitted suit?" Gabriel called back, half joking. "I feel like staying here is a better use of time."

Adrian threw his hands in the air. "Savanah would kill me if I didn't go. Maybe if you were getting married, you'd understand."

Gabriel rubbed his nose, shrugging in acknowledgment. Would he ever get married? Adrian shifted, not meeting his eyes, probably thinking the same thing.

"I'll be here a few more hours," Mr. Ali said. "I can take you back when I'm done."

"Sounds good to me," Gabriel said.

Mr. Ali gave him a thumbs up and started down the ramp to dump the trash.

Adrian hovered a moment. They were still ten feet apart. "Alright, I'll see you later."

"See you," Gabriel said.

Adrian seemed like he wanted to say more, but he backed away and walked down the bridge. Gabriel faced the water again. He sat down and draped his legs over the edge of the boat, arms folded over the railing, chin resting on the back of his hands.

The thought of Adrian's wedding made everything hurt. He didn't even know if he wanted to go. Mr. Ali appeared to his right and leaned on the railing with his elbows to peer down the side of the boat. He scanned the surrounding docks.

"It's nice out here, isn't it?" Mr. Ali asked.

Gabriel took a while to respond before giving a slight nod. "Feels like nothing else is going on."

"The water's even better," Mr. Ali said. "Hauling in a catch, nothing but the job on your mind…"

Gabriel imagined that.

An entirely new world. Being so far out to sea, you could barely see the shore. The rocking of the boat. Choppy water. Storms pounding the hull.

You were so small out there, entirely at the mercy of nature.

Nothing else mattered, then, when the ocean could swallow you whole on a whim.

"How have you been recently?" Mr. Ali asked, looking down.

Gabriel examined the railing he held and picked at the cracking paint. "I really don't know."

Mr. Ali accepted this, letting the silence prod Gabriel into speaking if he felt like it. Gabriel let a strip of paint flutter to the water below.

"I came out to Adrian on the drive here," Gabriel said.

Mr. Ali appraised him thoughtfully. "Good for you, that's big. How'd it go?"

"I'm…" Gabriel trailed off. "…not sure."

"Yeah?"

"I think he's fine with it."

Mr. Ali thought for a moment. "It's not really his choice to be fine with."

"I guess." Gabriel went back to resting his chin on his hands. "I don't know why it's so hard to talk about."

"Because it's personal. It's *you*," Mr. Ali said, looking over again. "And if people don't like that…"

"It feels personal," Gabriel supplied. "Like I'm the one who's wrong."

"Exactly."

"And yet, not talking about it is starting to feel even worse. Everyone knows I left school, but I can't say why. I don't know what to do."

Compassion filled Mr. Ali's face. His eyes softened, and he sat on the deck a few feet to Gabriel's right.

"But you have good people to talk with, right? If not me, you have Chloe. And Adrian, in time. And I know your parents care…"

Mr. Ali trailed off.

"It's not the same with them as it is with you. But there's Luca, I guess," he said, the words slipping out before he could stop himself.

"Who's Luca?"

"Someone at school."

"Huh."

Gabriel peeled another strip of paint off the railing, and Mr. Ali regarded him with a slightly irritated *really?* kind of look.

"Luca's a guy," Gabriel said.

"Ah," Mr. Ali said knowingly. "Tell me about him."

Gabriel didn't know how to respond. Words came to mind, but the more genuine they were, the more ashamed he felt.

"He has blue eyes," Gabriel said, tentative. "And a good smile when he lets himself. He's always wearing a different sweater, like the best ones from thrift stores. And I feel like nothing is wrong when I'm around him."

Mr. Ali nodded along ever so slightly, a tiny smile underneath his beard.

"It feels normal with him, but *special,* like I've found something priceless." Gabriel dropped his eyes to the railing and peeled another strip of paint off the rail. "But we haven't talked much since I left, and I don't want to jinx it and lose—" Gabriel steadied himself. "—lose him."

Mr. Ali scratched his chin. "I hear you." He took a moment to think, then looked at Gabriel. "I don't think something like that fades so easily. It's scary because it means something to you. I think that's how you know it's real. I don't think you need to be afraid of it."

"I just don't want to try and have it not work out."

"Sure, a lot can go wrong, but consider this: What's the *best* thing that can happen?"

Gabriel let himself lay down on the deck, hands on his chest, legs still over the boat's edge. "I guess…I could be happy. I could be with the person who changes everything for good."

Seagulls called in the air. Two circled lazily high above.

"That's what you should look toward," Mr. Ali said. "Don't give up on that."

For a brief moment, Gabriel let himself imagine how it would feel to build a life with Luca. He saw them living together, cuddling under a blanket as they watched a movie, having people over, being unashamed and unafraid. Unburdened. No more weight.

No more feeling like he was less than human for being who he was.

He smothered a smile, trying not to give in to the romance of the idea. He couldn't let himself imagine that kind of happiness for too long because it seemed so far away. He had so far to go, and there was only one way to ensure it happened.

Gabriel sat up. "I think I'm going to start telling more people."

Mr. Ali looked over, left eyebrow raised. He smiled and squeezed Gabriel's shoulder, then ruffled his hair. "That's good, I'm glad. Let me know if I can help."

IMAGINE THIS

HOME AGAIN, IT took twenty minutes to make a list, two days to refine it, and a week to muster the courage to take action.

Gabriel stared at his phone. He reread the names. Some he'd have to call. Most, he'd have to meet in person.

He wanted no part of this plan. But he was suffocating, and this was the only way out.

He closed his eyes and drifted into the future he so desperately wanted.

GABRIEL FLOATS, BUT the feeling remains.

This is what it's like.

Imagine it.

You have something buried inside, and you have a list of twenty-three people.

It's everyone you're close with.

Siblings. Friends. Their parents.

It's everyone who has to hear the truth directly from you. You believe you owe them a full explanation.

An Instagram post is not an option. People will be desperate for answers. They will be confused and shocked and hurt by what you have to say, and no paragraph online will ever suffice. More importantly, it will be there forever. It might affect your search for a job.

So, the only option is to take that list of twenty-three people and explain everything face-to-face. This will allow you to share all the details of your darkest moments to build sympathy—which you'll desperately need—and to show you didn't suddenly 'decide to be a homosexual.' This way, you can explain to everyone you're still the same person and convince them they have nothing to fear.

You *have* to do it.

There is no other way to keep these people in your life.

You are utterly convinced that this is true.

IMAGINE THIS, TOO.

Before every conversation, your body tries to fall apart. Sometimes it does.

Everything shakes.

Your heart *THUD THUD THUD*s in your chest.

There are needles under the skin of your palms, and you have the continual, gut-churning sense of falling.

Your stomach hurts. Sometimes you're hungry, but you can hardly eat.

Your mind is full to bursting. You can't think. There is only static.

There is no relief.

No matter who it is—even with the people you *know* will be accepting—the anticipation is just as bad as the time before, if only a little more numb. Every time you arrive early at a coffee shop or restaurant, you have to fight the urge to escape and disappear forever.

You have to bully yourself into submission. You have to strangle the instinct that this might be doing more harm than good.

Over and over, you must convince yourself this is the only way to make them love you.

This is the only way.

This is the only way.

ONE AFTER ANOTHER

GABRIEL RETURNED TO himself and picked up his phone.

His body tried to collapse.

This is the end, it whispered.

GABRIEL CALLED ISAAC first because he knew his brother would take it well.

"I'm happy for you," Isaac said after Gabriel's rambling, choked-up speech. *"You need to visit me in New York sometime. Lots of gay guys out here, and away from mom and dad…"*

Gabriel couldn't help but smile. "I actually like someone."

They talked about Luca for a bit, and things felt almost normal, but there was still an inescapable distance between them. It was all the years apart and the ten-year age gap. It was Isaac staying away from the family after college. It was Gabriel never reaching out.

Maybe they'd become actual friends someday, not just blood. Maybe this was that start.

AFTER ISAAC, GABRIEL figured the simplest thing would be to call the rest of his siblings one after another.

Heidi hardly talked the whole time Gabriel explained. Soft crying came from her line, but she managed to get out the requisite question of whether he still believed in God.

"I need space to figure it out," Gabriel said.

And she asked if he had a boyfriend.

"I don't…feel comfortable talking about that…" Gabriel said.

"I won't be telling any of the kids just yet," she said. *"They're a bit too young for all this. You understand, right?"*

He wasn't sure he did. When the call ended, he sat in heavy silence.

RACHEL WAS KIND.

"I just want you to be happy, however that looks," she said. *"Are you happy?"*

There was a quiet stretch as Gabriel clutched his phone, *ache* pouring out of him.

"I don't know," Gabriel said.

It felt wrong to admit, and it felt like his fault. He'd been given so much in life. He should be doing better than this.

"You'll get there," Rachel said.

Gabriel did his best to believe her.

OF ALL HIS siblings, Jacob was the hardest to tell, and he assured Gabriel he'd meet a girl when the time was right.

"What if I don't want to?" Gabriel asked.

"It'll be alright," Jacob said, sidestepping the question. He was in full pastor mode now. He probably relished this opportunity. *"You just need to lean on God and focus on the next thing. He's the one to seek when we face trials. Can I pray for you?"*

Gabriel agreed because he didn't feel like he was allowed to refuse.

"God, please bring Gabriel comfort in this difficult time…"

THEN IT WAS quick calls to Peyton and Sean, lunch with Alec Thomas, and afternoon coffee with Uriah Dunn.

On a whim, Gabriel sent a text to Adam Miller. They hadn't talked in nearly two years—ever since Adam and Jacob fell out. All Gabriel knew about the situation was that a girl had something to do with it.

Apparently—about two years ago—Adam had been sleeping with his girlfriend. Jacob found out and staged multiple interventions because "Christian men don't sleep around."

"He said that?" Gabriel asked, eyebrows raised as he loaded his fork with hash browns.

"Something like that," Adam said with a shrug. "But he got Adrian and Josiah to help stage an intervention one night. It didn't take. They kept trying to get me to stop seeing Helen, then they tried to force me to break up with her—"

"What?"

"It was crazy." Adam nodded with vigor. "And when I proposed *instead,* Jacob cut me off. He didn't go to my bachelor party. Adrian told me he didn't even want to go the the wedding."

"Jesus…" Gabriel breathed, leaning back.

Adam picked at his food. He set his fork down after a minute and reached for his coffee. "To be honest, I'm a bit surprised he didn't do the same to you."

"Yeah, well, I haven't brought a guy home yet, so there's still time," Gabriel said. "He gave me a nice sermon, though. I'm sure there's more coming."

"There's *always* another sermon with him."

They laughed, and Gabriel knew there was nothing to fear in this friendship.

They made plans to spend the next weekend writing music and watching movies. Gabriel hadn't realized how badly he needed friends like this until now.

AFTER TWO WEEKS, Gabriel had crossed off half the names from his list. He didn't know how he'd made it this far. It felt like he'd run out of gas a long time ago. But now that his friends were out of the way, he had to tell their parents. This phase would be worse. They'd be less accepting. More set in their ways. Harder to convince that he was worthy of love.

When Gabriel asked the Greysons if they could meet to 'talk,' they took him to a nice dinner. It was a place with dim lighting and where the servers were dressed in all black.

Gabriel arrived early, and the Greysons ran late. He scanned the menu but was unable to understand any of the words. They didn't blur together so much as seem like a different language. He flipped it over and scanned the wines, but that page was clearly in gibberish.

When they arrived, Gabriel's stomach flipped because Mr. Greyson looked even more handsome than usual with his blue sweater, grey temples, and a quiet, easy smile.

Gabriel dove into his confession after they ordered. Ten minutes in, Mr. Greyson asked, "Why are you telling us?"

Gabriel froze.

Why are you telling us if you don't want help?

Why did you have to ruin our perception of you?

Gabriel leaned forward, flashing each of them a quick glance. "I care about your family. I thought I'd let you in."

Wasn't there another reason? Something about Mr. Greyson and his handsome—

Gabriel killed the thought, feeling like a fraud.

GABRIEL CONTINUED THROUGH the list of his friend's parents.

Mr. Rhodes was the most understanding, but he suggested Gabriel should seek God with everything he had and see what happened. That's the moment Gabriel withdrew.

Mrs. O'Mara was skeptical from the beginning, and it didn't take long for her to suggest a few books about Christian sexuality. Mr. Evanston and Mrs. Miller suggested books, too.

They all looked at him with sadness and regret.

ALL THE WHILE, texts tricked in each day. Sometimes after conversations. Sometimes from people he never expected would reach out.

Bad news travels fast.

*Thank you for being open. We all strug-
gle in this broken world*

*God has a direction for you, so please go
to Him for guidance. Please know I love
you*

*Do you think this stems from the rela-
tionship you have with your mom?*

*I believe God is the only way, and we
should live according to what the Bible
says*

What are you attracted to in men? Have

you ever acted on it? Are you attracted to women too?

Hi Gabriel, thanks for letting us know about the struggles you are facing. Don't give up on God. We love you and are praying for you

After each text, Gabriel found it harder to respond. Harder to feel like he was doing the right thing. They didn't seem to understand.

Through it all, only Mrs. Hudson refused to meet. She tried to explain in a text, but Gabriel could read between the lines.

My schedule is jam-packed this month! I'm so sorry! I'd still like to send you an excellent book. I'll have it shipped to your house!

Which book?

Holy Sexuality and the Gospel, by Christopher Yuan. It's all about finding your identity and purpose in God, and Christopher has walked this journey too. I'm just trying to share some solid Christian info!

I'd rather not read it.

I actually just sent it this afternoon!

Fucking hell. Did *no one* listen?

Maybe he'd burn the book and send her a video.

EVERY TIME PEOPLE asked if he had a boyfriend, Gabriel denied it.

Maybe this was because he wanted to keep Luca tucked away where no one could hurt him. Maybe, also, it was because he was afraid of the truth. Once they knew, there would be no going back, and not sharing about Luca might soften the blow.

That's what he hoped, at least. It only made people more confused. He could see the questions behind their eyes.

Why come out if you're not dating anyone? We thought you were a good kid. Why ruin how we see you?

Through it all, Gabriel rarely talked to his parents. He just told them where he was going and who he was talking to. When he got home again, all he said was that the conversation went well. They never asked for more information, and he wouldn't have shared if they did. But they did say a few times they were proud he was being such an *upstanding man* by respecting people with face-to-face meetings. And despite how much he hated going to church each week, he couldn't refuse.

"You attend as long as you live with us," his dad said when Gabriel tried to skip one week.

And so, he put on his mask and smiled and shook hands and gave hugs to all the people who now knew his secret. He almost felt worse now than when he started the process. The claustrophobia was as intense as ever, but the shame was overwhelming. He couldn't meet people's eyes, knowing *they* knew.

And after all that effort, nothing had changed. No one brought it up again. It was like they'd all agreed to pretend nothing had happened, to keep praying and hoping Gabriel would find the truth. The fact he went to church only seemed to feed the idea that he was still seeking God and wishing for a way out.

It was *here* that Gabriel discovered deep regret.

He should have posted on Instagram. No explanation. No pleading for acceptance. Just a photo of him and Luca and maybe *boyfriend* as the caption. Then he wouldn't have had to torture himself with meetings that never made things better.

But it was over, and he couldn't change a thing. He should have felt free. All he knew was defeat.

EIGHT

128.3

Every day for the next month, it was nearly impossible to get out of bed. And although he needed to find a job and start applying to schools, all Gabriel could do was sleep and watch TV. It was as if he'd been allotted a certain amount of energy for the year, and he'd already squandered it.

He wished he had the strength to call Luca.

They still texted—mostly about recent movies they'd seen—but they never really *talked*. Gabriel didn't know why he hesitated. Maybe because he'd already asked so much of Luca. He didn't want to wear anyone out. He refused to be a burden. And he *was* fine enough to do this on his own.

Barely.

A few times, Gabriel overheard his parents discussing ways for him to get back into regular life. Mr. Ali's name kept coming up, along with words like *trust* and *mentor.*

Every handful of days, they asked if he'd made a plan yet. Gabriel continued to avoid them. He just wanted quiet. He wanted everything to be still for a while as he caught up. He just needed one day where he wasn't in a dozen different pieces, failing to keep himself together.

The only consistency he'd found was working out. It was one of the only ways of escape. He craved it. And while working out in his room and running in his neighborhood was simpler, the gym took more and more of his time as the weeks slogged by. He could now do fourteen pull-ups in a row if he wanted. He could run three miles in under twenty minutes.

Sometimes, he checked himself out in the mirror. He was skinny around the waist, but his arms and chest had filled out more than he expected. His abs, too. He could see every muscle.

Near the end of April, Gabriel stepped on the gym scale to see how much muscle he'd put on. The last time he weighed himself had been sometime in November, and he'd been 143 pounds. He didn't expect a huge change, but he hoped he'd added some weight.

Gabriel looked down. The scale flashed in bold, black numbers, and a knife jabbed under his ribs.

128.3

"There's no way…" Gabriel whispered to himself, stepping off the scale. He let it reset so he could step back on.

Numbers fluttered up and down, moving crucial ounces.

128.3

Gabriel pressed his hand against his chest, taking shallow breaths.

There was no way he'd lost that much weight. How did he lose that much weight?

He shuffled to his locker and sat on the bench, dumbfounded. It didn't make sense at first, but really, it made the most sense of all. He'd spent so much energy coming out to people, and he hadn't been eating much. He *tried*, but that was hard to do when you were so anxious you never had an appetite. But it was more than just the last two months. It went all the way back to January. December, even.

He fought the urge to break down in the middle of the changing room. He barely kept himself together long enough to gather his things and leave.

NOT CLOSE ENOUGH TO LOSE

GABRIEL SKIPPED CHURCH on the last Sunday of April. He made up the excuse that he wasn't feeling well and wanted to sleep in. For a few hours, he was completely alone and light and *free*. He played music on his phone, made breakfast, and went on a short walk around the neighborhood.

The Sunday after that, Gabriel scheduled a meeting at a coffee shop. His parents thought it was with one of his old friends, but it was just him reading *The Perks of Being A Wallflower* for the third or fourth time. It wasn't even a lie. The book *was* an old friend.

He spent the entire day out of the house, getting lunch for himself and driving to the bay to walk along the water and watch the boats. He even brought a small sketchbook. Mostly, he just sat in the quiet, not even listening to music. Just taking it in.

The third Sunday, he hadn't had time to make up an excuse, and his alarm woke him up an hour before his family usually left. He turned it off and tried in vain to fall asleep again. Anxiety kept him brightly awake as his parents stirred across the hall and clomped downstairs. The sounds of breakfast being made filtered through the floor.

Ten minutes before they usually left, Gabriel heard the telltale sound of his dad's shoes coming up the stairs. He sprawled out, hoping it looked like he was dead asleep.

His dad knocked. "Gabriel, are you getting ready?"

"What?" Gabriel asked as groggily as he could muster.

His dad opened the door, and Gabriel rubbed his face with one hand, propping himself up on his left elbow.

"We're leaving for church in a few minutes," his dad said, looking him over. "Get dressed."

"I think I'm going to sleep in today," Gabriel said.

His dad looked at him, irritation tightening his face. "You've missed the last two weeks. It's not good to skip church. You need to feed your spirit."

Gabriel sat up and gathered his covers around his lap. "I don't feel like going today."

"Come on, get dressed."

"I don't want to."

"Why?"

"I just don't want to go."

Gabriel's dad sucked his teeth like he was arguing with a toddler. Maybe he was.

"How are you doing spiritually? I'm concerned you're not pursuing God like you need to," his dad said.

Gabriel fidgeted with the hem of his sheet. He shrugged, looking down. "I don't know."

His dad nodded as if confirming something he hadn't shared aloud. "I can tell, and that's exactly why you need to go with us. You won't have a good life if you're not feeding your spirit. This is for your own good. Get dressed, we're going to be late."

Gabriel shook his head. "I'm not going today."

His dad hissed, one hand resting on Gabriel's dresser by the door, the other propped on his hip. "Why are you suddenly defiant?"

"Because I hate going!" Gabriel snapped. "I can't stand it anymore! I feel like I'm suffocating. I always feel worse after. Every time I go, I'm reminded exactly why I don't like being there."

Gabriel's dad stared him down, unmoving. "Where is this coming from? You need spiritual guidance. How else will you get that if you don't go to church?"

Gabriel searched for words. His mouth opened and closed as he tried to find the best way to put this. "I don't want that right now."

"What are you talking about?"

"I don't want to go to church anymore. I need a break."

Gabriel squeezed his hands so tight his knuckles ached. His dad was a statue of controlled frustration on the edges of Gabriel's vision. If Gabriel studied him, he might have also noticed regret and fear for his soul. He didn't look. He didn't want to see.

"I'm not going," Gabriel said again.

His dad looked at his watch. "We'll talk about this later."

He left but didn't shut the door. Gabriel remained frozen in bed as footsteps plodded downstairs. Only when he heard the muffled voices of his parents did he spring into action. He shut his door and paced the room. He cursed himself. There would be backlash for his defiance.

Gabriel immediately got dressed. He threw on pants and a sweater, filling his backpack with everything he needed for a day out. The garage door rumbled, and Gabriel sat tensely on his bed, waiting for his parents to drive away. Once they pulled down the street, he scrounged a bowl of cereal and headed for his car. He didn't set a destination. There were too many options, and he just needed to get out.

He drove in silence.

RIGHT BEFORE NOON, his dad called to see if he wanted to get lunch and talk. Gabriel told him he'd already eaten. It wasn't true. He was journaling at a coffee shop and hadn't decided where to go despite his stomach growling at him for the last two hours.

Gabriel eventually *did* get lunch by himself, opting for an extravagant outing of fried shrimp and a salmon filet. He didn't have much money, but this was healing in a way only food could achieve. He ate it all and even got a small cup of ice cream after.

It wasn't until dark that he returned home. The closer he got, the worse he felt. Gabriel steeled himself as he entered the garage and quickly went upstairs.

He was about to shut his door when his dad emerged from his own room. "Gabe, you have a minute?"

Gabriel's body clenched. "Yeah, sure."

He entered his room and set his backpack on his desk chair, his dad following him inside. Gabriel proceeded to unload his backpack as his dad talked.

"I think it's time you find a job," his dad said.

Gabriel paused, setting his computer on the desk. This was an expected reaction. "Alright."

"Immediately. You need to start looking tonight."

"I'm not doing that now."

"Gabriel, look at me!"

Gabriel turned, face stony. *"What?"*

"It's time you start taking responsibility! I want you to get a job so you can start paying rent. And then you need to apply for schools."

"Is that all?" Gabriel asked. He knew it was a bad idea to goad his dad, but he couldn't help himself. "I'm sure you could think of more things for me to do."

His dad nodded aggressively. "Yes, actually, you need to start contributing—doing chores. I want you to vacuum every week."

"Fine."

"And sweep."

"Awesome."

"And fold clothes and do dishes."

"Perfect, keep it coming."

His dad's eyes burned. "I'm serious."

"Me too! I'll do it! Are we done?"

"No! I want you to listen to me."

Gabriel opened his mouth and spread his arms. "*How am I not listening?* I'll get a job. I'll pay rent. I'll do whatever you want around the house. I'll *fucking* do it, alright! What else is there to say?"

"You need to respect me," his dad said, voice trembling.

"What, and grovel at your feet? Is that what you want?"

"You need to be grateful for everything we've done for you."

Gabriel gripped the back of his desk chair. "I am."

"Well, you don't show it. That starts by giving back and paying your way."

"As I said, *I'll do it.*"

"That's all you've said these past months! But all I see is you lying in bed and watching movies. I don't want you taking advantage of me anymore."

"Wow." Gabriel rocked back on his heels. "I've needed this time to recover."

"From what?"

"*From what?* Are you kidding me?" Gabriel's anger closed his throat. "I was about to *kill myself* at school, then they forced me into counseling, then kicked me out. And then I was *convinced* I had to tell everyone every *goddamn* detail. You can't just *move on* from that." Gabriel's whole body was on fire. "I'll do what you want, but we're done."

"Gabriel—"

"We're done." Gabriel straightened up and faced his dad, fists clenched. Every muscle in his body tightened, ready for a fight. He longed for it. He wanted to *hurt* someone, to just unload everything he'd bottled up until his hands were broken and all the rage was gone.

All he needed was one more nudge.

Just one.

His dad took a step back. Another. Had he always been this small?

His dad left the room. Two minutes later, Gabriel was out of the house, walking the neighborhood. He went for miles, not returning for dinner.

He wished he didn't have to go back.

Ever.

THE NEXT MORNING, Gabriel took a shower, did some pushups, then started writing a resume. He still burned from last night, and it was a searing lump in his throat. There was a heaviness over him, too, but that never really went away. And, slowly, resignation set in. Soon, it would be an all-consuming fog.

The resume was nearly done when his dad arrived home from work. As expected, his dad stopped by his room. And, of course, Gabriel had to let him in.

"I'm sorry about coming down on you last night," his dad said, contrite. "I want us to be friends. I talked to your mom, and you don't have to pay rent yet. Not until you finish college."

Gabriel remained impassive, waiting for it to be over. That was a relief, at least. But who knew if it would actually last? He'd come up with a different solution soon enough.

"You still need a job. Have you figured anything out?" His dad asked.

"Working on it," Gabriel said.

"Anything you want to share?"

"No."

His dad shifted uncomfortably in the doorway. "Do you want to talk…about school?"

Gabriel shook his head.

"I'm always here."

Gabriel grimaced internally. "I need to get this resume done."

"I want to help however I can—help you find a job. You can work for me."

"I'll let you know."

"I don't want us to fight all the time. I don't want to lose you."

"Sure." Gabriel kept his face neutral. The truth was, they'd never been close enough to lose each other the way Gabriel feared to lose his friends. "I need to get this done."

Gabriel turned to his computer, tapping a key to wake the screen. His dad approached cautiously and put an arm around his shoulders. Gabriel stiffened.

"Alright, I love you," his dad said.

Gabriel just hummed in acknowledgment, staring straight ahead. He knew it was the wrong thing to do, to not say it back. He knew he was a bad son. He knew he was a disappointment, and selfish for holding back his affection. He knew he would never be enough.

But no matter how often his dad said he loved him, Gabriel wasn't sure if he would ever truly believe it. The text from his dad never left his mind. He wasn't sure if he would ever feel like an equal when they were in the same room or if he'd ever genuinely *want* to see his dad once he had his own life.

Gabriel stared at his computer screen until it went dark. He just looked at his reflection, sick to his stomach at these simple truths.

SOMETHING RIGHT

IN THE MIDDLE of May, Gabriel stretched on his front lawn, his running shoes on.

The Ali's garage was open, and their driveway was strewn with bikes and tools and overflowing bins of junk. Mr. Ali pushed out the lawn mower. He removed his ball cap and rubbed his forehead, surveying the mess. Seeing Gabriel, he waved him over.

"This looks fun," Gabriel said, coming up the driveway.

"I'm trying to get rid of some stuff," Mr. Ali said. "The minute you buy a house, random junk starts to accumulate."

"You should see our basement."

"Oh, it's *bad*, no doubt." Mr. Ali laughed, facing Gabriel. "How are you doing? We haven't seen you at church for a while."

Gabriel shifted on his feet. "I needed a break."

"Sure."

"I'll probably start going again soon."

Mr. Ali shrugged. "Only if you want to. Some people are better off not going."

Gabriel balked. In all his life, he'd never heard that statement from a Christian.

"I heard from your parents you're looking for a job," Mr. Ali said.

Gabriel grimaced. "They say it's time to get moving."

"What do you want to do?"

Gabriel shrugged. "Nothing."

"Don't we all?"

"My dad doesn't like me sitting around."

"Well," Mr. Ali said, hand on his hips. "Do you want to work for me this season?"

"Are you serious?"

Mr. Ali smoothed his hat. "I need to fill a few more spots, and you're familiar enough with the life."

"Wow."

"Think about it."

Gabriel didn't have to. "I think it would be awesome."

"Yeah?" Mr. Ali seemed surprised at the quick decision. "It's not easy work—long days, tough weather."

"I don't care."

"We'd be gone a week or two at a time."

"I can't stand being at home," Gabriel said.

Mr. Ali evaluated him in a way that saw his depths. He nodded. "Alright. We're not setting off for a few weeks. There's still a few things to fix up."

"That's fine."

"You can help me out if you want. I've got people working on the freezers and comms, but I need help painting."

"I can do that."

Mr. Ali smiled. "Alright, perfect. I'll be heading back out in a day or two. I'll let you know."

Gabriel smothered his smile. "See you then."

Gabriel turned away, excitement bursting alight inside. He could hardly believe it.

Something had gone right.

He started running.

Holy fucking shit, something had gone right.

GABRIEL SAT ON the job offer for the rest of the day, and it was like a massive stone had lifted from his shoulders. He didn't want to tell his parents too soon and spoil the relief he felt in this moment. He didn't need their praise or excitement or assurances that he was on the right path.

Monday morning, Gabriel and Mr. Ali drove to the docks together, hashing out the plan for employment. The pay wasn't all that much, and he'd start with the mind-numbing job of sorting the catch, but he'd get a lot of free meals—mostly cod or halibut. And, if his parents agreed, maybe he'd work the entire season and put off college until the new year.

DESPITE THE PROMISE of working with Mr. Ali, there were moments every day that nagged at him. He'd have the urge to blurt something out, but he'd stop himself just in time. Such as when watching the NHL playoffs with his parents and being unable to say Henrik Lundqvist was the best-dressed man he'd ever seen. Or stopping himself from talking about a recent movie that had a gay storyline. Or share that he wanted to wear eyeliner one day, just to see what it was like.

He didn't know what would happen if he followed through. Probably nothing good. Gabriel hadn't talked to his parents about his sexuality since being forced to leave school. And it's not like he *wanted* to talk to them, he just wished he felt comfortable with the possibility. He wondered if his silence was taken as a sign he was still fighting it. Maybe they thought if he were going to be a blatant homosexual, he would be dressing in skin-tight crop tops, painting his nails, and going out with a new man every night. In their minds, there couldn't possibly be more nuance than that, could there?

Sometimes, his parents asked how he was doing, and, of course, he said he was fine. Then he'd talk about how things were going on the boat and how he couldn't wait for summer. They accepted this and seemed happy for him.

It wasn't really a lie.

The last few weeks had been good. Well, better. And things would probably continue in that direction. He just didn't want to hope too much and have everything get bad again. He didn't know if he could handle that, and that's what scared him. If he had to go through everything again, he wasn't sure he'd be strong enough to make it out a second time.

Maybe that's why he'd never told the full story, why he didn't openly embrace himself by talking about Luca or gay movies or Hugh Jackman. He'd said the bare minimum to ensure his survival, and it had taken absolutely everything he had to get through the last handful of months.

He feared it would take the same kind of effort to attend an event with Luca and not shrink away. To own it. To really, truly own it. Because, then, there would be no turning back. Then, people would have to accept it. Then, finally, they would know who he really was.

He wondered if he would find that strength someday.

HOW LONG DOES IT TAKE?

TWO DAYS BEFORE *Queen's Dream II* set sail, Gabriel and Mr. Ali drove to the docks for a final inspection.

"How's it been these last months?" Mr. Ali asked a few minutes into the ride. "With all that's happened?"

Gabriel rubbed his nose. "I'm alright, I think."

"Just alright?"

Gabriel watched the road. He didn't quite know how to answer that question. "I feel like I should be happier than I am, have more things figured out…"

"Everyone has their own pace."

"I know."

"It takes time."

"I *know*, I just…" Gabriel tapped his fingers on his thigh. "I chose all this—this path, and I still feel like I'm failing, somehow. I chose this, so why am I not happier?"

Mr. Ali took a moment to respond. "Maybe you're putting too much pressure on yourself."

"Maybe. I want to prove to everyone I'm doing really well, like, 'Thanks for nothing, but I'm good now.' Otherwise, why did I come out? Why did I stop going to church?"

"Do you think you'd be happier if you didn't do those things?"

"I doubt it."

"Do you feel better than you did at school?"

"Yes."

"Then how could you possibly be a failure?"

I can manage, Gabriel thought.

Mr. Ali glanced at him. "You're not failing because you're at a different stage of life than everyone else. You're succeeding because you've come so far, and you're doing exactly what you need."

"You think so?"

"Absolutely. Nothing else matters."

"This might be the best I've been in a while. I just thought I would feel better after all this time. I'm still uncomfortable being open with people."

"About your sexuality?"

Even then, Gabriel winced. "It's like I did something wrong by *being*. And I want people to like me, so I never bring it up."

How long does it take to unlearn a lifetime of shame?

Months? That was unlikely. It would probably take the next handful of years. And, quite possibly, it would never go away.

Mr. Ali grimaced. He scratched his chin. "Honestly, that sounds like a bad way to live."

"I can't help it. I've survived by making myself invisible and being the person everyone wants me to be. And if people want to be around that version of me—"

"They wouldn't care for the real you."

"Exactly. But all the while, I have this…*anger* toward people for things that aren't their fault. They might make a comment that bothers me, but how can I be angry if I've never been honest? I feel like I'm going to explode."

"Maybe it's time to speak up."

"Then things would change again."

"Who cares what people think?"

"*I do.*"

Mr. Ali drummed his fingers on the steering wheel. "Have you ever considered therapy?"

Gabriel's insides clenched. He shifted in his seat.

Why would he ask—wait…

He'd never told Mr. Ali everything that happened at school. He never had to. Mr. Ali accepted him immediately, so there was no need to get his sympathy.

"I went for a month at school," Gabriel said.

"You did?"

And so, Gabriel told Mr. Ali the whole story of getting found out and the meetings with Marci.

Mr. Ali kept shaking his head as he talked, muttering to himself. He rubbed his forehead. "I'm so sorry that happened."

"Yeah."

"I wouldn't want to go back if that were me."

"No."

"Still, it's helped me a lot."

Gabriel looked over, intrigued, but he didn't say anything. He didn't need to pry.

"I've been going the last few years," Mr. Ali said, gazing into the distance. "I don't even see a Christian therapist. There's lots of people to choose from."

Gabriel fidgeted with the hem of his shirt. "It's too expensive."

Mr. Ali looked over. "I'll pay for you to go."

Gabriel spared a glance at Mr. Ali, then faced ahead. He didn't ask if he was serious because he had no doubt he was. Gabriel gave a small nod in acknowledgment. "Maybe."

They pulled to a stop.

"Think about it," Mr. Ali said.

Gabriel nodded again, feeling unworthy of such a generous offer. He'd already imposed enough. He would have to do this on his own.

"Gabriel," Mr. Ali said, turning off the car. He faced Gabriel, meeting his eyes. "Hear this: No matter what happens, you're exactly who you're supposed to be, and I couldn't be more proud."

REASONS TO BELIEVE

QUEEN'S DREAM II officially set sail on May 21—about a month behind most trawlers, but Mr. Ali was confident they would catch up to meet their quotas.

Everyone had their specific jobs on the boat, and Gabriel spent most of his time in fish processing. Sometimes that was sorting and sometimes packing and freezing.

Days lasted 16-18 hours, and the work made it easy to not think about school. Or home. Or anything else that grew the pit inside, that deepened the wound in his soul. But, sometimes, late at night, when everyone else was asleep, Gabriel felt storms of emotion fighting to break through. At these times, he would cover his mouth with a hand so no one would hear, and tears would trickle out the corners of his eyes.

He didn't like thinking about the last six months. Or the last year. Or the last three or four, for that matter.

Instead, he focused on the present moment. He focused on waking up. On despising his 5 a.m. alarm. On the serenity of being on deck at dawn, steaming tea in hand. He focused on the hope he felt in that moment.

He focused on the monotony of sorting fish. Of the thrill of watching a catch be hauled in and dumped into the vats by a crane. Of seeing another trawler on the horizon and the horn blasts in greeting.

He focused on the little conversations during their meals, crowded in the galley or on the deck. He focused on the icy wind and the torrential rain of the occasional storm. On the rocking boat and the choppy water.

There were times it didn't feel real, but in a good way. There were entire days, sometimes weeks, where Gabriel didn't spare more than a passing thought about what was going on at home.

That life couldn't touch him on the open sea.

HE SMELLED LIKE fish day and night, even after showering. Most days, he hardly had the energy to prepare for bed before passing out, then blinking awake the next morning after what seemed like just a few minutes. It was exhausting and dirty and physically taxing, but there was something beautiful about it. Something powerfully simple. Something so outside the normal functions of day-to-day life. They were in their own world, and nothing existed beyond the ship and the water.

On unloading days in the harbor, some of the crew went home to see their families for a night. Gabriel never went back. The uncertainty of who he would see and what they might ask him was too much to think about. He ate dinner with the remaining crew and slept on the boat instead.

During meals, the crew crowded the galley to get their portion, then spread out to eat. Gabriel liked to sit on the deck when the weather permitted it. The wind rarely died down, but as long as it wasn't raining, he could handle the cold.

They traded off cooking food. Most meals were fish, but Gabriel soon learned a dozen ways to prepare it. There was boiling and baking. Grilling. Frying. Chopping it into small pieces and making a patty.

He ate a lot. As much as they had to spare.

SOMETIMES, GABRIEL STAYED up after most of the crew had gone to bed. He liked to find a snack in the galley and stand on the deck under the stars. This night, Mr. Ali joined him at the bow, a glass of whiskey in hand. Gabriel held a Yeti filled with tea and honey.

There had been one question nagging at Gabriel's mind. Every time he came close to asking, it felt too vulnerable. He didn't know if he could handle the brutal truth. But he needed to know.

"Why did you accept me…" Gabriel began, "when I came out to you?"

Mr. Ali rocked back. "Why wouldn't I?"

"It doesn't make sense," Gabriel said. "Christians think it's wrong to be gay, don't you?"

Mr. Ali sipped his drink, mulling the question. "No, I don't think it's wrong to be gay. I see who you are, and it's *good*. You're kind, and you bring joy, not harm. And now, you're becoming the most authentic version of yourself. How could that possibly be wrong?"

"What about sin?"

Mr. Ali shrugged. "I don't think about that anymore."

"Really?"

"I see the Bible more as a guide, not a book of rules. It has generally good advice, but I don't think the same solution works for every person. And sin," Mr. Ali raised his hands in an uncertain gesture, "I see it more like this: If something I do is going to hurt me or someone else, I try to avoid it. If it will bring life and joy, I move towards that." Mr. Ali swirled his glass. "For example, collecting rare whiskey adds a lot to my life. It's a *good* thing. But it's bad for an alcoholic. That doesn't mean it's one or the other."

"It just *is*," Gabriel said, thoughtful.

"And how you use it." Mr. Ali nodded. "I think when the Bible says not to do something, that's because it generally brings harm instead of life. I don't think it matters who your partner is, but being unfaithful is wrong because it hurts everyone involved." He thought for a moment. "How did it feel to hide all these years?"

Gabriel gripped the rail. "Like I was dying, really."

Mr. Ali regarded him with quiet understanding. "And what's it like spending time with Luca?"

"Like I'm at peace."

"I would say that's good, then. Exploring that part of yourself, it's *good*. It's healing. Shoving it down is bad."

They let the silence stretch as Gabriel considered this reasoning. That's certainly how it *felt*. But for so long, he'd been programmed to doubt his intuition. Another inconsistency bubbled up in his mind.

"How do you call yourself a Christian if you don't believe in sin?"

Mr. Ali took another sip. He looked at the twinkling stars. "Maybe I'm not one, according to some people. I don't think it matters so much what you call yourself. I think it's more important who you *are*. It's about how you live and interact with the world."

Gabriel nodded at this.

"Can I share a verse with you?" Mr. Ali asked.

Gabriel involuntarily bristled. "I haven't read the Bible in a while."

"It's a good verse. I think you'll like it."

Gabriel evaluated Mr. Ali. It took a minute to trust he didn't have an underlying agenda. With anyone else, he wouldn't have said yes.

He nodded. "Alright."

Mr. Ali rested his elbows on the railing. "I'm paraphrasing, but when someone asked Jesus about the most important commandment, He said the top two were to love God with all your strength and love others as yourself." Mr. Ali smiled faintly to himself. "As far as I'm concerned, that's all that matters. It doesn't say anything about being gay. It doesn't say anything about going to church or converting people. It's not about avoiding specific sin or pointing it out in others or anything else we think is important. All Jesus said was to *love*, and I think that's what we need to focus on. Everything else is extra."

"Huh." Gabriel rocked back. He took a long while to respond. "I've never thought about it like that."

"I think true faith is simpler than we imagine, and God is bigger than the boxes we put Him in. And if we're wrong, I think there's more grace than we give Him credit for."

"Ever consider going into philosophy?" Gabriel asked.

Mr. Ali put up his hands with a chuckle. "Don't take that as scripture. Some people will call me a heretic. It's just what makes sense to me."

"I like it," Gabriel said. It was a comforting kind of belief. "Growing up, I thought it was all or nothing. I thought if you didn't believe everything the *exact* right way, you'd be tortured forever." Gabriel looked down to the ink-black water, flashes of the moon reflecting off the surface. "I don't know what I believe, but I think I'm still scared of that."

Mr. Ali hummed. "I don't think that's the heart of God. I don't think He's vengeful, or hurt, or threatened by us. Deep inside, I believe *some* version of God exists, but I don't think it's the fire and brimstone kind." Mr. Ali finished off his drink and shrugged. "Again, I could be totally wrong. Hey, maybe we'll be neighbors in hell."

Gabriel laughed.

Mr. Ali put his arm around Gabriel's shoulders, squeezing him. "It's going to be alright. It doesn't happen all at once, and it might take a few years, but one day, you'll look up and see how far you've come. And you'll be at peace."

Gabriel turned back to the water, resting his arms on the railing, chin on the back of his hands.

Despite the swirling uncertainty, there was a new sense of calm that things might be alright after all. Maybe he didn't need everything figured out. Maybe there was more room to explore than he thought. Maybe he didn't need a specific set of beliefs, and all that mattered was to do what Jesus said, to *love*.

Shouldn't that be enough?

When did everyone lose sight of that? When did it become more important to be part of the right denomination? To control lives with the fear of punishment? To justify pain, to *seek* it, to kill your intuition and sense of self—all for the glory of God?

When did all that become the reason to believe?

Gabriel couldn't stop thinking about the conversation with Mr. Ali.

He liked the message. He liked the shift in focus.

He just wasn't ready.

More than anything, he needed space. He needed distance. He needed time to clear his head and heart. There was too much to work out. Too much to process. Too much hurt he needed to face before going back to any sort of belief.

This was never more clear than when he sometimes listened to worship music in his bunk at night. He couldn't hear a single song without thinking about the attached sermon. He couldn't help but flash back to alter calls and condemnations by Pastor Evans. He kept returning to the first chapel after Thanksgiving break, the one where Dr. Stone announced Ben's death. Then the one that insinuated being *homosexual* meant living a life of drug addiction and sexual abuse.

All the music did was bring him back to those moments and remind him of a version of God who would never be happy, no matter how much he sacrificed.

He stopped listening to the music and anything else that related to church. He needed to learn how to breathe again without that pressure crushing his lungs.

Maybe, someday, he would find his way back.

Maybe not.

It didn't matter which.

THE FIRST TIME

MAY BECAME JUNE, which soon approached July.

With each passing day, it was easier to exist. He couldn't point toward why, it just *was*.

Gabriel usually had sorting shifts with Pavel. He was half French, half American. Tall and slim with a casual walk. He had sharp eyes and a perpetually concerned expression like he was solving a fundamental problem with the world. Pavel talked in clipped sentences, as if each word cost energy to say. Sometimes, they worked in complete silence, focused on the monotony of the job. When they did talk, there wasn't much fluff to their conversations.

"Why'd you join the crew?" Pavel asked one afternoon.

Gabriel shrugged. "I needed a job, and this got me out of the house."

"Gotta pay the bills."

"I still live at home."

"Wish I had that. Coulda saved a lot on rent. You should save while you can."

"I'll try," Gabriel said. "How old are you?"

"Twenty."

"Are you going to school anywhere?"

Pavel shook his head. "I'm teaching myself how to code and build websites. You don't need a degree if you're good enough. Tech pays a lot these days."

"Where's your family?"

"All around. New York. Pittsburg. I don't see them much."

"Damn."

"It's cool. I'm better on my own."

Gabriel didn't have much to say. He felt bad for still living at home despite everything. Having his parents pay for college. Not having to worry about making it on his own just yet.

"Are you in school?" Pavel asked.

"I'm taking a break."

"I hear you."

"I didn't like it much."

"It's not for everyone."

"I'll probably go somewhere else. I don't have much of a choice with my parents."

"Are they paying?"

Guilt.

"Yes."

"That's big. Don't waste that," Pavel said. He mechanically tossed fish left and right. "You have a girlfriend?"

Gabriel examined a limp fish. "I'm focusing on myself right now."

"Can't be good for someone else if you're not good for you, yeah?"

"That might take a while."

"Take your time is what I say. Only a special person should change your life."

"I'm not sure if I'll have that."

"Why not?"

The words slipped out before he could stop himself. "I like men."

"Cool," Pavel said without breaking from his work. It wasn't dismissive. Just a fact. Nothing to worry about.

"That's why I left school. They kicked me out."

Pavel stopped, looking up. "You serious?"

"I'm not the only one they did this to."

And before he knew it, Gabriel was sharing his entire story. Pavel nodded along, just as relaxed as before.

A sudden realization rocked Gabriel back on his heels.

This was it.

This was the first time he shared and didn't feel *wrong*.

The first time he hadn't been desperate to explain. The first time he felt truly comfortable saying exactly what was on his mind, and unworried about what might happen after.

Months ago, a moment like this would have left him catatonic.

But now…

Well, now it was just another conversation.

Just like that.

"What about you?" Gabriel asked, smiling to himself. "What brought you here?"

Pavel shrugged. "I left Pittsburgh when I was sixteen. Stole a car and started driving."

Gabriel's eyes widened. He didn't interrupt.

"Went to juvie a few times, was homeless for a while," Pavel continued. "Two years ago, I was hanging around the docks and met Mr. Ali. He offered me work, I don't know why. I'd never held down a job before." Pavel rested his hands on the lip of the conveyor belt, staring ahead. "Might not have made it without him."

Gabriel knew that feeling.

He watched Mr. Ali at dinner, and the man was utterly himself. Playful. Smiling. Completely unaware of the things he'd done to help those in desperate need.

One of these days, Gabriel wished to be just like him.

NINE

ALL THAT LIES AHEAD

HALFWAY THROUGH JUNE, Gabriel stood on deck, gripping the railing as the trawler dipped and rocked. They were on their way to drop off their latest catch in Quincy. The skies were bright blue, and seagulls floated in the breeze, calling to each other. The shoreline sprawled on their starboard side.

Adrian's wedding loomed heavy on Gabriel's mind.

He was already planning on skipping the bachelor party next week, even though Mr. Ali offered to let him take an extended break from work. Gabriel had no interest in taking a break.

These last months had been a sanctuary, a realization that there was another way of life outside everything he'd previously known. It was an insulation, too. He'd always felt like nothing could touch him on the ocean. It kept the bad out.

But if he avoided everyone forever, would he ever be free? And did he have the right to leave without saying goodbye?

Looking back, he hated the way he'd come out to everyone. He'd made such an effort to force all his friends and their parents to stay in his life, to not openly reject him. And that's what he'd done. Forced it. Met with people, not out of respect, as his parents said, but to manipulate their acceptance. To make them say *we still love you* as if that would heal his heart.

Only now did he realize what he'd done and how little he cared to have them around in the aftermath. He didn't miss anything about his old life. Not the dinners or worship nights or church. He didn't miss his family. He didn't even miss Adrian, but he ached all the same when he thought of his childhood friend. And he was angry, too, but he couldn't place why.

It was just so much easier on the ocean. It was so much easier being around Pavel and people like him, people with their own torn-up pasts and no judgment for anyone else's mess.

Mr. Ali appeared at his side. Gabriel glanced at him, then went back to watching the seagulls. They didn't talk for three or four minutes.

Gabriel faced Mr. Ali, his left forearm resting on the rail. "I don't know if I'm ready to see everyone again."

Mr. Ali twisted his silicone ring. "At the wedding? You don't have to."

"I kind of do."

"Maybe."

"It's Adrian's *wedding*. I can't miss that."

"It's your call."

"I think I'm scared," Gabriel said. He listened to the sound of water pitching against the hull. His knuckles were white from squeezing the railing. "I'm scared I'll have the opportunity to be honest and won't say anything."

"That makes sense," Mr. Ali said, regarding him with that steady gaze of his.

"I'm scared it will always be like that."

"It won't."

"What if it is?"

"At some point," Mr. Ali said, "what you need will matter more than what others might think. Eventually, you'll realize how much you don't care what they say—that it was all bullshit anyway—and then you'll start to live for *you*. *Then*, nothing will stop you because there will be no more fear."

Gabriel looked into the horizon. Was that future out there?

"It won't be easy, but you've already gotten through the worst of it," Mr. Ali said.

That was hard to imagine.

He knew this was the right path, but it felt like all he'd done was make his life harder. He wondered how much more difficult it would be to introduce Luca as his boyfriend. He wondered if he would ever be able to show public affection without the crush of guilt. He wondered if those nagging doubts in the back of his mind would ever be silent.

"Don't think about everything that hasn't happened," Mr. Ali said, squeezing his shoulder and bringing him back to the ship. Gabriel was convinced Mr. Ali could read his mind. "It'll be alright. Just be here, now."

Gabriel scanned the shoreline. The Quincy harbor was coming up.

"You know, you were the only parent who accepted me right away," Gabriel said quietly. Mr. Ali glanced at him, a small frown on his lips. "Everyone else told me to read the Bible and seek God. You just let it be."

Mr. Ali gazed at the sky, his chin tilted up. The breeze ruffled his collar. "Give it time," he said. "There's so many incredible people you haven't met. You can build your world from scratch. You can keep only what you need, *who* you need..."

Gabriel faced the water again.

He was tired.

It was that simple.

He was tired of being afraid—of trying to make others happy.

You can build your world from scratch.

Maybe he'd do just that.

And in the meantime…

He pictured attending the wedding with Luca and announcing their relationship through the microphone at dinner. He imagined Mrs. Hudson sputtering for words when he said he'd burned her book. He *hadn't*, but she didn't have to know that. He saw Mrs. Greyson going scarlet when he said her husband was a knockout.

Gabriel almost laughed. He smothered it, bending over the railing.

Maybe it didn't have to be that dramatic.

Maybe all he needed to do was show up.

Sometimes, that is the only way to start.

THE PATHS WE TAKE

FOUR DAYS LATER, Gabriel received a text from Mason that made him pulse with nervous energy.

> *Hi, Gabriel. I have my phone back. Do*
> *you want to call sometime?*

Gabriel reread the message in his bunk after turning out his light. He didn't know how to feel, or what to say, or even if he *wanted* to talk to Mason. He stared at his screen for a long while before turning off his phone to try and sleep. Each morning for a week, he thought of the text, then told himself he'd respond that evening. Every night, he was too tired to think of anything to say, even though he spent hours a day sorting fish, imagining their conversation. Everything they could share ran in circles in his head. It was a broken, endless loop.

And he did have time soon, which made it inevitable he would agree to talk. Mr. Ali was giving the entire crew a week off for Adrian's wedding on the fourth. It would be his only chance to catch up with people and see his family before another lengthy stretch on the water.

He finally responded, and Mason was quick to text back.

> *I'm free the first week of July. Let me
> know if that works*

> *Noon on the 1ˢᵗ?*

> *Sounds good, talk to you then*

JUNE 30ᵀᴴ, *QUEEN'S Dream II* docked in Quincy, and the crew dispersed. Mrs. Ali picked up Gabriel and her husband, and Gabriel felt instantly tight in her presence. He could already feel his walls going back up, and it wasn't about her or her endless questions so much as how relaxed he'd become on the water. Out there, he didn't have to be anyone but himself.

"Thanks for the ride. See you in a few days," Gabriel said as Mrs. Ali parked in her driveway.

Back home—his parents gone—the first thing he did was jump in the shower and scrub for twenty minutes to erase the fish smell. After a bit of cologne and deodorant, he could hardly notice it. Then he sat on the kitchen counter, eating directly from a tub of ice cream, part of him wishing he was already back to work.

GABRIEL SET OFF to walk the neighborhood just before noon the next day. He squinted in the sunlight, skin hot and unfamiliar with such calm and bright weather. It felt like a different world, passing all the houses he'd grown up next to—

He jolted, his phone vibrating in his pocket. He put it to his ear. "Hey."

Mason's voice crackled to life. *"Gabriel!"*

"How's it going, Mason?"

"I'm good, I'm good. It's nice to hear from you."

"You too."

"Thanks for taking my call."

"I'm glad I had time."

There was an uncertain pause. Both of them knew how much there was to say but not how to begin.

"What have you been up to?"

"I've been working on a fishing trawler this summer."

"That's cool!"

"It's good, I like it. It's nice to get away from everything."

"That sounds nice. I wish I could do that, too."

"I could probably find you a job," Gabriel said.

"If only…" Mason said. *"I have to be home, though."*

"Makes sense."

Another pause.

"Obviously, you know I left school?"

"You were gone? What?" Gabriel said, feigning shock. "I *knew* something was different this semester."

Mason chuckled. *"And I saw your text. Thanks for reaching out, by the way."*

"I had to check in."

"So…"

"So," Gabriel echoed. He rubbed his forehead, scanning the path ahead and behind him. He was alone. "I guess I'm…" he didn't know how to phrase it. "I might be gay."

Fuck, why was that so hard to say? Did he still believe he was anything *but* attracted to men?

"Who would have thought, right?"

"Not me."

"That's wild. I never picked up on that."

"You didn't?"

"Not at all, and I feel like I have a good sense of things."

"I guess I was keeping things close to the chest."

"I know what it's like," Mason said, and Gabriel grunted. *"Do you know why I left?"*

"I heard a few stories, but you don't have to talk about it."

"No, it's ok. I'm facing it. It's part of my story, you know?" Mason said. Gabriel imagined him on the other line, sitting on the edge of his bed, glancing occasionally at the Bible on his nightstand. He imagined notes in Mason's journal that updated his testimony. *"In short, I was in another guy's room the day after most people had gone home for Christmas break, so we thought we were alone..."* Mason's voice wavered. *"And the RD was doing room inspections and caught us kissing without our shirts. Then we had meetings with the Dean and the President. Then we were done."*

"Wow, that's...wow." Gabriel ran a hand through his hair.

"It was a lot."

"That's crazy, I'm sorry."

"That's just what happens, sometimes."

"Still hard to believe. And to be kicked out for that?"

"I hadn't exactly been on the straight and narrow," Mason said, and Gabriel snorted. *"And I was open about it, so the school knew, and I had chances before that."*

"Sure, but it's still drastic."

"I think it's a good thing. I needed something to get my attention. I think it was God reaching out, saying 'come back.'"

"Huh, alright. Maybe."

"I just wish I could have said goodbye to everyone."

"It was a shock to hear you'd left," Gabriel said. "And things went downhill after. You should have seen it."

"What happened? I haven't talked to anyone yet. I got my phone back a few months ago but just needed space."

"Makes sense."

"Tell me everything."

"Where to start?" Gabriel ran a hand through his hair. "Alright, get this. The first chapel after break, someone preached about how he'd 'lived as a homosexual' before denouncing it to follow God."

"Wait, was that Doctor Anderson?"

"I think so. I'd never heard of him."

"He has an incredible testimony. I kept thinking about his story as I was going through all this. It makes me feel like God can turn this into something good."

Gabriel frowned. All *he'd* heard from the message was how to betray yourself.

"Anyway, what happened?"

Gabriel dove back in. "As he was giving his alter call, I'm pretty sure he called for people to report each other. Specifically, people like us."

"Are you serious?"

"He said something like, 'Confront their sin or go to an authority figure if you have to.' Six or seven people left in January."

"Oh."

"I think it was because of what he said."

"That's…unfortunate."

"I couldn't believe he said it," Gabriel said. He shook his free hand at his side. "I have to say something before we go too far."

"Oh boy."

"Morrison forced me to leave too."

There was a half-second delay, then, *"And you just now tell me! What happened!"*

"Brace yourself."

"*Wait, did you kiss someone too?*"

"No." Gabriel laughed. "Well, kind of—"

"*Kind of?*"

"I *did*, but this isn't what caused it."

"*This is crazy. I'm on the edge of my seat.*"

Gabriel rubbed his face. "I hate to say this, but apparently, your mom sent a screenshot of my text to you to the *school*."

"*Stop…*"

"Yeah."

"*What the hell…*"

"I'm sorry."

"*No, I'm sorry. That's not right. I'll talk to her.*"

"Don't do that."

"*I will—*"

"It's done. There's no need."

Mason sighed. "*Fine.*"

"Anyway, Dr. Clark asked me to meet with him at the end of January. He showed me the screenshot and said I had to attend counseling or leave. I went for three weeks before I couldn't do it anymore. But get *this!*" Gabriel threw his hand in the air. "I was out for dinner with my friend, *and we saw Dr. Clark at the bar!*"

"*NO.*"

"He drank a beer and two shots in like *ten minutes!* And then he was hitting on this random woman, and she was touching his face and undoing his shirt buttons, and he was totally into it! It was insane."

"*There's no way.*"

"It was him. I took a video of it because he was obviously cheating—or about to. I went to him later that week to try and withdraw from counseling. When that didn't work, I showed him screenshots from the video and said I wouldn't share it if he let me stay—"

"You threatened to blackmail him?"

"Yeah, and it didn't work because I'm a fucking idiot. He said some shit like, 'You can't touch me. You have no power here.' And that's when he kicked me out."

"Wow. I don't know what to say…" Mason said, and there was a drawn-out silence on the line. Gabriel nodded at a woman pushing a stroller. *"I just…that's crazy. I can't picture Dr. Clark doing something like that—"*

"I'll send you the video."

"No, I believe you—"

"I'll send it, and you can decide his intentions."

"It's just hard to wrap my head around him doing something like that, saying all that…"

"That's the system."

Mason took a long time to respond to that. *"It's hard to see someone you admire mess up."*

"And his position at school! You can't do that."

"But we all fail, you know? Look at me. I might have done something wrong, but that's not who I am. And I understand that he messed up too—"

"But for him to do all that?"

"He definitely needs to do some work with God, but there has to be an opportunity for redemption, right? Otherwise, how are any of us supposed to get through life?"

"I don't know. It's about him being in control."

"I just think we need grace."

Gabriel paused on the sidewalk, thrown off by Mason's defense of Dr. Clark. "Well, it's done now, so we move on."

Mason didn't respond immediately. Gabriel pictured him standing at his bedroom window, watching the occasional dog walker pass his house.

"Anyway, how have you been?" Gabriel asked.

"Um…" Mason said. *"As my mom mentioned, I went to a Bible retreat for a while. I thought it would help me understand things, or shift my focus, or something."*

"Understand things?" Gabriel asked, but he surely knew the answer.

"It was focused on embracing Biblical sexuality."

"So…" Gabriel hesitated to say it. "…was that conversion therapy?"

"I didn't know. That's not how it's branded."

"But what did they do?"

"No phones or outside contact," Mason said. *"Lots of one-on-one meetings…group sessions…gender role activities…"*

"Why did you go?"

"I thought it could help."

"But *why?* Were you forced to?"

Mason was silent long enough that Gabriel realized he must have asked an ignorant question.

"I could leave at any time. But…" Mason's sigh fuzzed on the line. *"My parents thought it would be good. My whole family, everyone—they all want what's best for me. And with my dad being an author, talking at conferences…it's what's best for the family."*

Gabriel understood now, and it churned his stomach. Mason had the ability to choose but not the power. That kind of pressure only left one path forward.

"But I only stayed three months," Mason said. *"It was too much. I don't know if that's the right way to do things."*

"I don't think it's right at all."

"*But I understand what they're trying to do. And I admire that. But there's a better way.*"

"A better way?"

"*I think for people who want to change—change is the wrong word. For people who want to follow God, they can do things how they want. But so many people there were forced into it, and that's not good for anyone.*"

"Would you still have those places exist, then?"

"*I don't know. It's so murky. I think people should have the right to choose.*"

Gabriel found himself nodding. "No one should be afraid to live how they want."

"*I agree, but it's hard to find people who don't try to influence you.*"

"I know, trust me. I'm trying to learn to accept myself. I want to be proud of who I am, but for my whole life, I've felt this pressure to be something I *can't.*"

"*Expectations are hard.*"

"It's *suffocating.* Why can't I just love who I want?"

"*I get it,*" Mason said. "*I still think we should live a certain way.*"

"What do you mean?"

"*I think we should follow the Bible. We have it for a reason.*"

"Oh," Gabriel said. He didn't think he agreed with that anymore. "But we have to accept ourselves, right? Fighting who we are isn't living."

"*I don't know if our sexuality is who we are.*"

"How? We can't just *turn off* how we feel."

"*That doesn't mean we have to give in.*"

"But what if it's not a big deal? What if the only thing that matters is following the example of Jesus? What if all we actually have to do is love God and others? Jesus said that was the most important commandment—"

"*Sure, but that's only one passage. We have an entire Bible to follow. We can't overlook teachings on sin just because* that *verse doesn't mention it.*"

"Then why wouldn't Jesus mention it if it was so important?"

"*He doesn't have to.*"

"Why?"

"*The rest of the Gospel covers it. That's why we have to look at the whole.*"

Gabriel kicked a pebble on the path. It bounced and shot into a bush. He didn't know how to argue this.

"*As for sexuality,*" Mason continued, "*I believe in what the Bible says. It's the clearest path forward. It's not easy, but I think that's the best way to live.*"

"But you left that...*place.*"

"*That doesn't mean I'm abandoning God. I still want to follow Him. I just said places like that have it wrong. It's militant. The heart of it is wrong.*"

"What are you doing then?"

"*I'm seeing a different counselor. I'm just trying to make sense of it all.*"

"Yeah, ok," Gabriel said, though he wasn't sure if he understood. "What about us, then?"

"*What about us?*"

"Do you think people like us can be with who we want?"

"*I don't know...yes...I think so? But I believe in Biblical marriage. One man and one woman. I think that's what God intended from the beginning, not what we've come up with since.*"

Gabriel shook his head. "What does that mean for you?"

"It means I will either be celibate or—hopefully—marry a woman someday."

Even if it means an entire life of suppressing who you are?

Gabriel wanted to grab Mason by the shoulders, shake him, and yell, *Don't you see what they've convinced you of? You're killing yourself for them! You can be free!*

"Are you…are you doing this for you or your family?" Gabriel asked, low and quiet.

Gabriel pictured Mason pacing his room, tugging at his hair. *"It's the same thing. We all believe—"*

"It's not the same thing—"

"It is. There's no me without my family."

And now, realization enveloped Gabriel like fog off the ocean. Mason's family was his world, and they despised his 'affliction.' To ask him to embrace himself was to ask him to lose it all.

Gabriel could not do such a thing, and he could not blame Mason's decision. All he could do was watch and hope and ache for Mason to finally *get it.*

Something else slammed into his chest, and Gabriel sank into the grass of a stranger's front lawn.

Maybe that's exactly what his parents hoped for, too; that he would embrace life as *they* wanted it for him, just as he wanted it for *Mason.* Maybe they all had their version of the best way to live, and maybe those ideas would never quite line up, no matter how hard they tried to get the other person to understand.

Maybe this was the way of things, and all he could do was the best thing for *him,* because, after all, he was the only one who knew.

"That's just what I believe," Mason said. *"It could change, I don't know."*

"I get that."

"And what about you? What do you think? What do you want?"

Gabriel peered into the sky. He knew what he wanted. He'd known for a while, but he'd never said those words aloud—never *truly* admitted it. He breathed deep and let it out. "I want to be with a man someday."

He didn't think anything else would bring the same kind of wholeness.

"I think you should," Mason said. *"If that's right for you. If that's what you believe."*

It was. It really, *truly* was.

T-SHIRT AND A SMILE

WHEN THE CALL ended, Gabriel walked. And thought. And pictured what was next.

He didn't know if a big declaration was right, or what he might say. Maybe it could be a small step, something only he would notice.

That he could do.

GABRIEL CALLED LUCA before he returned home.

Luca answered on the third ring. *"Gabriel, hey!"*

He blurted it out straight away. "Want to go to a wedding in Boston?"

"Really?"

"It's on the fourth, for one of my friends."

"Oh, cool."

"You don't have to."

"No, that sounds fun."

"I know it's a bit of a drive."

"I don't mind."

"You can probably stay here overnight."

"Ooo, a sleepover."

Gabriel laughed. "Wear something nice."

"I always do."

"That's why I like you."

"The only reason?"

"Pretty much."

"Makes sense," Luca said. *"Is this a date? An official thing?"*

"I don't know. I don't think you'd be allowed to stay if my parents knew about us. My dad said a while ago I can't bring anyone home. His exact words were, 'I don't want *that* in my house.'"

Luca was quiet. *"Maybe it's best to keep it under wraps."*

"But I have a friend who'd take you in too, no questions," Gabriel said. Chloe *would*, right? "Oh! I have to show you the ship I'm working on. You need to come a day early."

"I could probably do that. I just have to get my shift covered."

"Whatever works is fine."

There was a pause.

"So, how have you been?"

Gabriel rubbed his face. "I'm good, I think. Sorry I haven't talked to you in forever."

"It's alright."

"I just had to work on some stuff."

"I get it."

"But…I came out to everyone, which was…kind of awful—"

"No way!"

"—then I started working on the boat, and I haven't seen anyone since May."

"Wow."

"Yeah."

"How does that feel?"

Gabriel quickly summarized the last months. He could have

talked and listened for hours, but he had to cut it short when his dad barged in to tell him dinner was ready.

"I have to go," Gabriel said after he left. "See you soon."

"I can't wait."

Gabriel hung up, bubbling with excitement.

On the dining table was a spread of grilled salmon, rice, and a salad with apples and almonds on top. His dad prayed over the meal. Gabriel stared at his hands and tried not to bounce in his seat.

"Who was on the phone?" His dad asked as they dug in.

"A friend from Morrison, Luca. You met him at homecoming," Gabriel said.

"Oh, right," his mom said. "He's got dark hair, glasses?"

Perfect eyes.

Gabriel nodded. "Anyway, he's going to be in town for a few days, visiting people, so I said he should crash Adrian's wedding."

His parents exchanged a look. His mom spoke up. "You'd have to check with Adrian. They have a set guest list."

"I know," Gabriel said. Now for the clincher. "He might need somewhere to stay if he can't find another place. Could he take Jacob's room or something?"

Another look between his parents.

"It's alright with me," his mom said.

Gabriel served himself a heaping spoonful of rice, trying not to seem too invested in his dad's response.

"If he can't find another place, it's alright," his dad said.

"Cool," Gabriel said. Inside, he was jumping up and down.

LUCA GOT HIS shift covered and arrived the day before the wedding. Gabriel was on pins and needles all morning while waiting for Luca to arrive. His hands trembled as he stretched fresh sheets over Jacob's old bed.

As soon as Luca arrived, Gabriel rushed down the stairs. His parents were out, so they didn't have to worry about re-introductions just yet. Luca stepped out of his Audi, hair gleaming in the sunlight. He wore black sunglasses with gold trim and a white and yellow T-shirt straight from the sixties. His biceps filled out the tight cuffs.

A T-shirt.

And he wore a full smile.

Gabriel threw his hands in the air. "You're here!"

"I'm here!" Luca returned.

Gabriel hugged him tight, face buried in his shoulder.

They pulled apart, and Gabriel straightened Luca's collar. "I love this shirt."

"Yeah, I'm…" Luca looked down at his exposed arms. "Branching out, I guess."

Gabriel just smiled.

They gathered Luca's backpack and duffle bag and headed inside. Gabriel gave him a short tour of the house, finishing in his room. Luca closely examined his bookshelf, fingers brushing the spines. He grinned at the typewriter on the middle shelf. He tried a few keys. It was still broken.

"Come on, I want to show you the ship," Gabriel said.

As Gabriel drove, they caught up on everything they hadn't had time for the other day.

"So, I…" Luca toyed with the hem of his shirt. "I started talking to someone."

"Already found someone better, unbelievable," Gabriel joked.

"No, it's not that…it's a therapist."

"Oh." Gabriel glanced over. "That's great."

"I got my job to pay for it, and it's online, so my parents don't know," Luca said. Gabriel just nodded. "I thought it might be time to talk about it all…what happened…"

"That's really good," Gabriel said. "Is it helping?"

"I think so. I'm kind of in shock still, but I think so."

"Good."

"Have you thought about going back?"

"To counseling?"

"Yeah."

"I don't know."

"It could help."

"Maybe."

"It doesn't have to be like the person at school."

Gabriel's body clenched at the memories of Marci's office. "I know."

"You don't have to go, but I think it will be good for me."

"Maybe I will," Gabriel said. He intended to think about it, at least. He knew he could trust Luca and Mr. Ali.

"Oh! I have news!" Luca said.

"Yeah?"

"I'm transferring to an art school in New Jersey this fall."

"No way!"

"I'm really excited. I'm surprised my parents agreed, but it *is* a much better program, so they listened to logic."

"That's amazing. You have to show me everything you make," Gabriel said. He looked over, and Luca was smiling, letting his hand drift outside his window.

"Absolutely," Luca said. "Are you going to go back to school?"

Gabriel shrugged. He exited the highway toward Quincy. "Probably community college in January. I think I'm going to finish out the fishing season. It ends in November."

"How do you like it?"

"I love it."

He told Luca all about life on a trawler for the rest of the drive. They parked and started walking. It wasn't a fancy port or city, but Luca looked around with awe. He took a picture of the ship before they climbed the gangplank to the deck.

"It's locked, so we can't go inside, but we can hang out here," Gabriel said.

He proceeded to show Luca around the deck and explain the equipment. When Luca ran out of questions, they just leaned against the railing to look over the harbor.

Luca reached over and held Gabriel's hand. Gabriel's spirit soared.

For a while, they were quiet. They didn't have to say anything to make this moment perfect.

SUMMER WEDDING, TAKE TWO

GABRIEL AND LUCA spent the following morning walking the city. They even held hands a few times. With so many people around, they were invisible. Or maybe no one cared.

Little steps.

"What if we went to the wedding as a couple?" Luca asked at lunch.

Gabriel looked across the table, dunking French fries in ketchup. "You're alright with that?"

"It could be fun," Luca said, wrestling his burger with two hands. "And I don't know anyone here, so it's not like my parents will find out."

"That's exactly what someone says before that happens."

Luca shrugged, taking a large bite. "Maybe it needs to."

Gabriel focused on his food for a minute. A part of him longed for the chaos they would create by going together. The fear of what might happen *after* kept him from embracing the idea.

"I don't know," Gabriel said. "You might have to find another place to stay if my parents find out."

"Because of your dad and the 'gay shit,' right? It *is* contagious, you know."

Gabriel laughed. "Makes sense to me."

Luca cleaned his hands with a napkin before grabbing his soda. "That's fine. Whatever *you* want is good with me."

Gabriel nodded, meeting Luca's eyes. He appreciated the sentiment. Even if he had no intention of acting on the suggestion, it was nice to have the option.

JUST PAST NOON, they returned to Gabriel's house to get ready.

Gabriel wore his grey suit, a white shirt and blue tie, and black shoes. He examined himself in his mirror, ensuring his tie was perfectly in line. It was tight around his neck. He grimaced, tugging at it. Without warning, he was back in the Ali's bathroom on New Year's Eve, filled with panic and desperately trying not to fall apart.

Gabriel sucked in a breath, pacing his room. Everything spun.

He yanked the tie off.

It took a minute to calm himself—to remember where he was and tell himself that things were different now.

There was a knock on his door. Gabriel smoothed his appearance. He turned the handle and Luca slipped inside.

"What do you think?" Luca asked, a nervous smile on his lips.

He was perfect.

Forest green suit. White shirt with the top buttons undone. All tailored. Cuffed pants that showed his ankles. Black, suede loafers, no socks.

"You're incredible," Gabriel said.

"Really?"

"You'll be fighting off girls all night."

"I hope not," Luca said, brow creased. He reached up and undid Gabriel's second button. Tugged the collar into alignment. Smoothed the front of his jacket. "You look amazing too."

Gabriel didn't know what to say. Luca just touched up Gabriel's hair, and Luca's woodsy cologne was the only air Gabriel wanted to be in. Their eyes met. Luca's swirled with life. There was a spark in them, more vibrant than how they'd been at school.

"I know it's not really your thing, but..." Luca said, fingers tracing Gabriel's jaw. "...can I kiss you?"

Yes yes yes.

Gabriel nodded. Luca leaned in. Their lips brushed, and Gabriel shivered, and when they kissed harder, Gabriel thought he might completely melt.

GABRIEL'S DAD DROVE, and his mom only corrected him twice about going the wrong way, but he took it with a smile. Good. The last thing he wanted was for them to fight in front of Luca.

The wedding venue was a stone mansion in the rolling hills outside Boston. It had arching windows and spires that pierced the sky. Trees filled the sprawling lawn, and there was a small lake in the distance. A sea of white chairs sat in front of the shore. A flower-adorned altar stood just behind.

Gabriel marveled at the sight. Luca stuffed his hands in his pockets, shifting his head left and right. He turned around and craned his neck at the mansion. On the patio were rows of tables with white cloths.

There were already scores of people rushing here and there, making last-minute preparations. The wedding party took pictures under a massive tree a hundred yards away. From this distance, they looked more like blurs of black and pink than people wearing suits and dresses. Shouts and laughter filtered from their direction.

Gabriel shifted his attention to the nearby crowd and searched for people he wanted to talk to. The list was short.

Chloe, but she had her hands full taking pictures as a bridesmaid. Mr. Ali, but he was talking to Mrs. Hudson at the moment, and Gabriel didn't want that interaction if he could avoid it. Peyton, but none of his family were in sight. They were probably running late. The Miller's had so many kids they never made it anywhere on time. But there *was* Mr. Greyson, nursing a beer on the patio's edge, one hand in his pocket as he surveyed the preparations.

Gabriel nudged Luca in that direction. Mr. Greyson turned and smiled, and Gabriel felt terrible for the way his heart stuttered. He feared he might always have that reaction to seeing the man. Mr. Greyson was wearing a cream suit and boat shoes. His hair was wavy and tinged with silver. His shirt was open, revealing a touch of chest hair.

Stop.

"Gabriel! Good to see you. How are you doing?" Mr. Greyson asked.

"I'm well, thanks," Gabriel said as they hugged. "This is Luca, a friend from school."

"Calvin," Mr. Greyson said, shaking Luca's hand. He looked him up and down. "Excellent suit."

"I was about to say the same," Luca said, taking him in.

Gabriel smothered a smile. Good. He wasn't the only one to notice. They exchanged small talk until Mrs. Greyson called for her husband from the lawn. Gabriel rubbed his chest, watching Mr. Greyson leave.

"Jesus, that might be the most attractive man I've ever seen," Luca whispered in Gabriel's ear. "No offense."

Gabriel grinned, squeezing Luca's arm. "Oh my god, *right?*"

"It's unreal."

"We should ask for a threesome."

Luca laughed. Gabriel smiled wistfully, then sighed, aching.

For the next hour, they navigated the thickening crowd. Twice, Adrian walked right past Gabriel. He didn't stop either time. Maybe he didn't see him.

As everyone started to find seats for the ceremony, Chloe dashed toward the mansion, a flash of pink. She turned around so fast she nearly fell on the grass. "GABRIEL!" She ran over and threw herself into a hug. "I have to go, let's talk later—who's this?"

"Luca, from school."

"Luca, nice, I'm Chloe. I have to go, I'm late, I'll see you later," she said, dashing off again. She stopped and whipped around. "Wait, LUCA! Oh my God, come here." She ran over again and hugged him too. "Good to meet you. I really have to go."

They watched her fly off before heading for their seats in the third row next to Gabriel's parents.

"She knows," Gabriel said.

"Clearly."

"And her dad, but they're the only ones I told. You'll like him."

Luca just nodded. They took their seats, and Gabriel's legs bounced as they made small talk with the O'Mara's in the row ahead.

The ceremony was long and filled with scripture. Pastor Evans performed it, and he looked like he'd put on even more weight since Gabriel last saw him. Gabriel didn't pay much attention. He just studied the backs of people's heads and counted how many people were crying. Seven, from what he could tell, and Savannah's mom was crying the hardest.

Lunch was a barbecue buffet, and Luca was relegated to a table of late arrivals. Gabriel had a table with Peyton and a handful of others his age. At least Adrian had been thoughtful enough to put him with people he liked. As they ate, there were dozens of speeches. Everyone wanted to talk about their special relationship with Adrian and Savanah.

It took just over forty minutes for Adrian and Savanah to make their rounds to Gabriel's table. Adrian hugged him from behind while Gabriel was still seated.

"Congrats!" Gabriel said.

"Thanks! I'm so glad you're here! I can't wait to catch up," Adrian said.

"Me too. It's been crazy…" Gabriel said, but Adrian was already talking to Peyton. Gabriel shut up. He unclenched his jaw and speared a piece of brisket with his fork.

After lunch, the waitstaff cleared half the tables to make room for dancing, and Adrian made no effort to find Gabriel. Gabriel didn't try either. Adrian had a new life now, and it didn't seem like there was room for Gabriel. That was fine. It hurt. But it was fine.

Sometimes, all you can do is move on.

Gabriel wandered, feeling alien around people he knew so well. He spotted Luca talking with Chloe and Mr. Ali on the lawn. He headed in their direction, weaving through the crowd.

Pastor Evans stepped into view, and Gabriel groaned internally.

"Gabriel, I thought that was you," Pastor Evans said.

He was a small planet among the guests. The skin of his face was pasty and pink. It jiggled when he moved. Gabriel fought to keep a grimace off his face. They shook hands.

"I'm glad you could make it," Pastor Evans said.

"Yeah, it's exciting."

"So," Pastor Evans said, dropping his voice. His beady eyes searched Gabriel. "I know things have been hard this year."

Gabriel's cheek twitched. "Sure."

"And I want you to know you can always talk to me."

"Ok."

"I've helped people with this…*problem* before."

Gabriel shifted his weight, attention drifting away. He didn't say anything.

"Whatever you do, keep seeking God. He'll help you get through this," Pastor Evans said.

Gabriel stared at him, unflinching.

Then he saw him. *Really* saw.

Pastor Evans was just a fat old man with too large of an ego. He didn't care. He just wanted to hear the roar of the crowd as he condemned the world.

Gabriel broke into a small smile. "I want you to know something. You disguise hate as truth, and I think Jesus would be ashamed."

Pastor Evans' eyes bulged. "Jesus would—"

"I don't care. Take it easy, big guy," Gabriel said.

He backed away, leaving Pastor Evans a sputtering mess. He only made it ten steps before Mrs. Hudson waved at him.

Goddamnit.

"Gabriel!" Mrs. Hudson said, walking up. She was a few inches taller than him in her heels and wore a yellow flower dress. "So good to see you! How have you been?"

"I'm good," Gabriel said, face neutral. He looked behind him to see if Pastor Evans wanted to get in the last word. He was out of sight. Good.

"That's great!" She said. "I'm so sorry I haven't been able to meet up with you. We've been so busy!"

"Sure."

"I'd still love to find a time to chat—catch up about everything!"

"Um…"

"Did you get the book?"

He nodded.

"It's such a good read. So important for young people."

"Hmm."

"Have you gotten a chance to read it?"

He *had* read it, and he disagreed with the message. Simply, it used deceptively kind language to manipulate only one response: Conform. Because, after all, hell was waiting if you didn't change.

"You didn't even ask to send it," Gabriel said, irritation spilling over.

"I just knew it would be a good resource," Mrs. Hudson said, giving a short laugh.

Gabriel didn't want to be a part of the joke. "I said I didn't want to read it, and you sent it anyway."

Mrs. Hudson's smile faltered. "I care about you."

"Yeah? For a whole month, you said you were too busy to meet," Gabriel said, looking around. "Everyone else found time."

Mrs. Hudson's mouth opened and closed.

Gabriel took a step away. "Hey, it was good to see you."

"I've got time this week."

Gabriel laughed, raising his hands in the air. "You missed your chance. I'll be on the ocean until November." He shrugged, trying not to smile too wide. "And I'm gay. What else is there to talk about?"

Mrs. Hudson looked like she'd been slapped. Gabriel turned on a heel, heart pounding in his ears. He took big breaths and smoothed his jacket. He couldn't believe he'd said that. He felt lightheaded and exhilarated at the same time.

Gabriel made it to the edge of the lawn just as Mr. Ali was heading for the mansion. Luca and Chloe were still talking in the distance. Mr. Ali spread his arms when he saw Gabriel, a big smile on his face.

He'd shaved down to a quarter-inch beard. He wore a Navy suit and a skinny black tie. He bounded up the steps to the patio.

"Want a drink?" Mr. Ali asked.

"Sure."

"What do you want?"

"Anything."

"So…"

"So?"

"Luca's great. Far out of your league, but…"

"Oh, I know."

Mr. Ali mussed Gabriel's hair. They reached the bar, and Mr. Ali signaled to one of the three bartenders. "I'll take a double Macallan Eighteen, neat, and a Coors Banquet six-pack."

The bartender nodded. Seconds later, the drinks were up. Mr. Ali handed Gabriel the six-pack. Gabriel felt self-conscious holding the beer. Parents watched him navigate past, eyebrows raised, disappointment etched on their faces.

"I'm amazed my parents still think you're a good influence," Gabriel said.

"I'm not?" Mr. Ali asked with an innocent expression.

As they neared the steps to the grass, Isaac appeared out of nothing, holding a can of Coors Banquet. Gabriel stopped in his tracks. Isaac's dark, wavy hair was nearly at his shoulders, and he had a silver nose ring, but his thick black glasses and mustache were the same.

Gabriel hadn't seen him since Christmas. They hadn't talked since he came out. Mr. Ali glanced at both of them and excused himself without a word.

"I thought you weren't coming," Gabriel said, shifting on his heels.

"I had some time off. Besides, who can pass up an open bar? And look at you, you little devil," Isaac said, playful. "A six-pack?" He looked over his shoulder at the lawn where Chloe and Luca waited. "And is that…"

Gabriel shifted his weight. "It's Luca."

Isaac proudly looked Gabriel up and down. "Who *are* you?"

"Just me," Gabriel said. "You're lucky you're wearing a suit. Mom and Dad might have thought you were a girl for a second."

"HA!" Isaac laughed genuinely. Gabriel found himself smiling. "Fuck, man, I should have worn a dress! I did that once to an after-party…it was incredible."

"Seriously?"

"No one cares in New York. It's great."

"I should visit sometime," Gabriel said. He meant it. He looked back toward the lawn and hefted the case of beer. "I'm going to drop these off."

"Alright, it's good to see you."

"You too," Gabriel said.

Gabriel plodded down the steps into the grass, finally reaching Luca, Chloe, and Mr. Ali. He peeled open the case of beer and set it at their feet. Mr. Ali was in the middle of relaying a story about a massive storm on the ocean a few years ago.

"…and *BOOM*, there was a lightning strike a hundred yards away," Mr. Ali said, left arm gesturing wildly, right hand keeping his drink steady. Luca's mouth hung half open, and his hands rested on his head. "I almost shit my pants."

Chloe nudged Gabriel, leaning close. "He's cute."

Gabriel nudged her back. "He's mine."

"Uh!" She smacked his arm. She opened a beer and took a sip, eyes warm and bright. "And he lets my dad tell stories, so dad already loves him."

Chloe's hand found his, and she gave him a reassuring squeeze.

Gabriel smiled.

She had no idea how much that meant to hear—how much *any* of this meant. To have all three of them here *right now*, holding nothing back…

It was as if his whole world lit up in gold.

EPILOGUE

TO BE GABRIEL MOORE

THIS IS THE end of a wedding, and these are the threads that make up a life:

People dance and laugh and share stories with friends they haven't seen in years. Couples sit close at abandoned tables while bartenders polish glasses and wipe down bottles. Music shakes the very foundations of the earth. Fireworks whistle and *BOOM* in your chest, showering the night with dazzling colors.

It is a wonderful thing to be a part of. It is even greater to have for yourself.

Take a minute, now, to imagine how it feels to give away your voice for nineteen years:

Don't speak up; let others speak for you. Make yourself small and unobtrusive, and avoid disagreement. Become everything to all people, moldable clay in their hands.

To be Gabriel Moore—in this moment—is to be a voiceless, solitary figure at a quiet table, wondering, *could this possibly happen for me?*

He wonders how many of these people will support his marriage to a man.

Some will make up reasons for why they skip the wedding. Some will paint on smiles, but there will be sorrow underneath. Some will leave their kids at home so they will not have to witness two men in love.

He wonders how long it will take to gain the acceptance of those around him. He wonders how long he must hold himself back…

But then there's a small, internal voice whispering his name.

Gabriel.

What?

They know.

They know what?

They know, *don't you get it?*

They already know, and there's nothing left to hide.

Wait…

Oh my god.

WAIT.

This is what happens when everything changes, and it is like the breaking of a dam:

Realization explodes through every cell of your body. You gasp for breath because you've never really breathed before. A lightness fills your spirit as you finally *get it.*

You are the only person standing in your way.

This is Gabriel Moore as he reclaims his voice:

He gets out of his seat. Smooths his blazer. Tells himself he will not be afraid.

For there is no fear in love.

His head bobs with the music as he approaches the dance floor.

Adrenaline floods his limbs as he sways with the beat, eyes locked on a single figure. And then he's grinning like an idiot because he's never been all that good at dancing, but Luca doesn't seem to mind. In just a few minutes, Gabriel is holding Luca's hand, then whispering in his ear, squeezing him tight, both arms wrapped around his waist.

If he cares to look, he will see a few people's dancing coming to a halt, and laughter turning into tight lips and squared jaws, and maybe parents brooding on the sideline.

But Gabriel doesn't look. There's no need to see their disapproval. It was all bullshit, anyway. And he *knows*—after all this time, regardless of what the future holds—he will never be so alone again.

THIS IS THE end of a wedding.

These are the threads that make up a life.

And *this* is what it means to be Gabriel Moore.

POSTSCRIPT

THIS IS A heavy story, but not without reason, and certainly not without hope.

It is meant to open eyes to what some queer people experience while growing up in religious settings. It is also meant to show that as long as you are breathing, there is always a way forward, and full acceptance of yourself *is* the path toward a happier life.

I understand how personal religion and sexuality are. As such, it would be impossible to capture every experience in one book. Gabriel's story is just one brushstroke in a much larger picture. Even so, I believe there is much for us to learn from his journey.

For those who relate, I hope this story puts words to things you've never been able to say aloud. For everyone else, I hope you have gained a deeper understanding of some of the things you might never experience.

To all, thank you for reading. It means so much that you're here.

A SPECIAL THANK you to my close friends and early readers: Annie, Cleo, Nick, Trent, Cooper, Sarah, Riley, and Mitch.

PLAYLIST

INTRO

SUN BLEACHED FLIES | ETHEL CAIN

MAIN

PEAS | BOYLIFE
LIVE FOR ME | OMAR APOLLO
DON'T WAIT FOR ME | JOSH GARRELS
SEEDS | YOKE LORE
FOREIGN HANDS | GEORGE OGILVIE
RUN | RYAN CARAVEO
DEMONS (ELDORADO) | KHAMARI
HOW TO FIND YOURSELF | DYLAN OWEN
FEEL GOOD | MATT MAESON
STAND BY ME | BOOTSTRAPS

END

THOROUGHFARE | ETHEL CAIN

AUTHOR RECOMMENDATIONS

NOVELS

BEARTOWN | FREDRIK BACKMAN
HOW IT FEELS TO FLOAT | HELENA FOX
THE MISEDUCATION OF CAMERON POST | EMILY M. DANFORTH
THE PERKS OF BEING A WALLFLOWER | STEPHEN CHOBSKY
THE SILENCE THAT BINDS US | JOANNA HO

NON-FICTION

BOY ERASED | GARRARD CONLEY
EDUCATED | TARA WESTOVER
HEAVEN AND HELL | BART D. EHRMAN
TO SHAKE THE SLEEPING SELF | JEDIDIAH JENKINS

MOVIES

A SINGLE MAN | 2009
CALVARY | 2014
GIANT LITTLE ONES | 2018
GOOD GRIEF | 2024
HANDSOME DEVIL | 2016
IN & OUT | 1997
THE PERKS OF BEING A WALLFLOWER | 2012
PRIDE | 2014
THE WAY HE LOOKS | 2014

TV

OUR FLAG MEANS DEATH | 2022
SEX EDUCATION | 2019
YOUNG ROYALS | 2021

ABOUT THE AUTHOR

DAVID SLOCUM IS A WRITER AND ARTIST FROM DENVER, COLORADO. SOME OF HIS FAVORITE THINGS INCLUDE: BOOKS, CATS, ICE HOCKEY, THRIFT STORES, AND THE SEASON OF SPRING.

TITLE FONT | ITC AVANT GARDE GOTHIC PRO
BODY FONT | ADOBE GARAMOND PRO

WORD COUNT | 95,893